TURNABOUT

Former cop Frankie O'Neil's best friend has just taken a high dive out of a plane—without a chute. He'd been working with a couple of cops, Hill and Fetterman, to figure out a complicated scheme involving a shady business at a financial services company. They'd been using a computer system to hide what's been going on, and the police need help to figure out their scheme. With O'Neil's friend gone, they turn to him as a replacement. The trouble is, O'Neil doesn't trust anybody except his young protégé, and they set out to find out who is really responsible for the strange death of Tim Clayton. Money's involved, and lots of it. When O'Neil's wife is suddenly taken, he has no choice but to unravel the tangled skein of corruption and missing money made possible by a mix of old-fashioned corruption and a new breed of criminal..

SHALLOW SECRETS

A captured killer implicates an impossible suspect. A cop's career is ruined. When James Robinson abruptly leaves the force, he walks away from law enforcement forever, disgraced publicly and privately, his life in complete shambles. Or so he thinks. Years later, another killer is caught, and when lovely reporter Sabrina Wells seeks his help, Robinson won't even listen. Until she shows him a note in his own handwriting, tying him to a victim he'd long since thought put to rest. Haunted by a promise from his past, Robinson and Sabrina travel north to Baker County, Florida, where they uncover a nest of seemingly unconnected murders. Or are they? Past and present come together in a sweltering mix of passion and murder. Can Robinson escape the sins of hi

killers—in the process? Or wi

stalker who knows more abou

TURNABOUT

SHALLOW SECRETS

by Rick Ollerman

STARK HOUSE

Stark House Press • Eureka California

TURNABOUT / SHALLOW SECRETS

Published by Stark House Press
1315 H Street
Eureka, CA 95501, USA
griffinskye3@sbcglobal.net
www.starkhousepress.com

ISBN: 1-933586-47-8
ISBN-13: 978-1-933586-47-2

Cover design and layout by Mark Shepard, www.SHEPGRAPHICS.COM

First Stark House Press Edition: September 2014

FIRST EDITION

CONTENTS

TIMEPIECES: THE NEW OLD WORLDS OF RICK OLLERMAN

by Cullen Gallagher

Conventional wisdom separates the critics from the authors. It's a literary prejudice akin to that school-age fallacy, "Those who can't do, teach." (It was memorably extrapolated by Woody Allen in *Annie Hall* to also include the coda, "And those who can't teach, teach gym.") In grade school, that is a perfectly acceptable philosophical outlook on life: a way to assert one's own sophomoric superiority over their teachers. As we grow older, however, we discover that such dichotomies are rarely so simple, and that conventional wisdom is often just misinformed malarkey.

Such is the case with the critic/author division, and this volume of Ollerman's novels is the proof.

□ □ □

I first got to know Rick Ollerman through his critical introductions to Stark House's books. The first one I read was in Peter Rabe's *The Silent Wall* and *The Return of Marvin Palaver*. It was immediately apparent that what I was reading more than just an "introduction"—it was the transcription of a deep conversation between reader and text.

> *"His sentences are often stark and at the same time rich with subtext; idiosyncratic, yet so deftly written their intent remains clear."*

And that was just the beginning. It was the sort of rigorous, perceptive critical analysis that fans of noir fiction long for yet rarely find. Ollerman took one of my favorite writers, explained to me in intimate details why I loved him, and then provided me with dozens of new insights and reasons to love him. A finer and more insightful essay on Rabe has yet to be written.

Ollerman was my new best friend, and I had never even met the man.

Future introductions were included in the books *Nothing in Her Way* and *River Girl* by Charles Williams; Jada M. Davis's never-before-published country noir masterpiece, *Midnight Road*; two West Coast countercultural novels by John Trinian, *North Beach Girl* and *Scandal on the Sand*; and several others. In his critical essays, Ollerman does more than just remember books that have unjustly fallen through the cracks, he reminds us why they deserve to be remembered, and of the rich legacy that was almost lost. Most importantly, he treats paperback originals not as some low-brow curiosity, but as literature, the way they should be. His is an invaluable insight and knowledge that should be treasured and revered for generations to come.

That is Rick Ollerman the critic.

Now, meet Rick Ollerman the author.

□ □ □

Ollerman writes the types of books that he would love to write about. High-octane noir. Mystery laced with action and doom. Thrillers with big black heart at the core. Gruesome crimes. Investigations that bring out the worst in people. Spiritually broken protagonists with nothing much to lose because they've already lost it all. Driving plots told with breakneck pacing, where each passing page brings the incessant timer that much closer to zero. His style is a fond homage to the pulpy élan of 1950s and 1960s paperback originals, but it's not imitation or pastiche. Ollerman's stories are of their moment, and the stories and characters thoroughly contemporary.

Imagine Lionel White and Charles Williams writing a computer caper and you have an inkling of what *Turnabout* is like. It is equal parts heist-, revenge-, buddy-, and techno-thriller, topped off by a killer chase through Florida swampland for the big finale. The story is about a cop, Frankie O'Neil, who decides it is time to retire after his marriage starts to fall apart and a fellow cop commits suicide. By chance, he falls into the then-new business of computer consultation. But after a tech colleague is found murdered floating in the ocean, O'Neil is pulled back into action by two cops who were working with the victim on a money laundering case.

As the title suggests, *Turnabout* is no straightforward mystery, the characters aren't simply good and bad, and the moral situations are never just right and wrong. After all, the book is about an ex-cop colluding with an obese pickpocket and a computer-obsessed custodian, and they're breaking into offices after hours to battle corrupt businessmen dealing in stolen money that is also wanted by equally corrupt cops.

The title also suggests an instruction to turn around and travel back in time. Even though it is set in the not-so-distant past of the early 1990s, to newer generations these primitive days of the computer boom will seem like science-fiction. As Ollerman explains in his preface, "These books were written back in the days when the technology most of us use every day was either not invented yet or still very uncommon. There was the Internet, but no world wide web." In this light, I don't think *Turnabout* could be written today, and I'm sure many publishers wouldn't have the guts to even publish it. The very qualities that make it such a timepiece, on the other hand, are also what make it such a valuable piece of literature. It offers us an insider's view into a world on the precipice of an enormous change, the magnitude of which even the characters are unaware of, despite what they say. *Turnabout* exists in a technologically naïve world to which we'll never be able to return. Ollerman, however, makes it possible to revisit that world, if only for a few pages.

> "You've got to remember what I said about computer security. There's no such thing. When personal computers were designed nobody dreamed of the kinds of things we'd be doing with them today. Nobody knew how clever we could be with them. … Anything someone can think of to secure the data, someone else can think of ways to un-secure that data. We can't outsmart ourselves."

The second novel here, *Shallow Secrets*, is the dark beast of the two, a grim and brooding blend of noir and backwoods horror that suggests a lost weekend shared between Robert Bloch, David Goodis and Harry Whittington.

Whereas in *Turnabout*, O'Neil left the police force just as the darkness began to touch him, in *Shallow Secrets*, the protagonist wasn't able to get out so clean. Ex-detective James Robinson is fully engulfed by darkness. He carries within him a shattered marriage, a girlfriend murdered by a serial killer who he'd let crash in his house, a crime that he himself was officially implicated in but never given the chance to redeem himself. He also told the girlfriend's bother he would get to the bottom of it, a promise he never fulfilled. So, he leaves the force and becomes a recluse, fixing motorcycles to pay the bills. Now, six years later, another serial killer has been caught, and he will only talk to Robinson, which pulls him into the case both as an unofficial investigator, and also as a suspect.

The vacuous blackness that is consuming Robinson is brilliantly manifested in his home—or, rather, in the sinkhole that has literally swallowed the rest of the housing development, leaving only Robinson's house on unstable ground that will surely give way in a matter of time. This is, without a doubt, high among the most noir homes ever, physically representing the spiritual crisis that is plaguing Robinson throughout the book.

> "You're like my life," he said to the sinkhole as he popped another can. "A goddamn black hole that swallows everything that comes near it."

This scenic trope also shows the literary quality of Ollerman's writing, an inspired touch that plunges the story into a surreal, symbolic world apart from the rest of the story. I'm not sure if it is intentional or not, but it reminds me of the beached whale in John Trinian's *Scandal on the Sand* that washes up in the first chapter and haunts the characters and landscape for the rest of the novel. Like the whale, the sinkhole is a moment of magical realism in an otherwise realist narrative, a metaphorical anchor for the book's overarching theme of life losses that are beyond our control.

□ □ □

In the 1950s, these two novels would have been published by one of the premier paperback houses such as Gold Medal, Lion, or perhaps Ace, who would have issued it as one of their signature "doubles" that could be flipped over for the second book. Sadly, Gold Medal and Lion are gone, and Ace no longer offers those literary double features. But thankfully, we do have Stark House Press, who honors their legacy not only by reprinting their classics from half a century ago, but by issuing new work that carries on in their tradition. Rick Ollerman, critic and novelist, represents the best of both worlds.

And now, without further ado, here's Rick Ollerman.

—JUNE 2014
BROOKLYN, NY

AUTHOR'S NOTE

These books were written back in the days when the technology most of us use every day was either not invented yet or still very uncommon. There was the Internet, but no world wide web. Instead of a browser, you would typically log in to a university system somewhere, one that allowed the public to create login IDs, and use line commands to do things like post questions to user groups; you could log back in after a day or so to see if someone's posted an answer.

Graphic user interfaces weren't in use, either, not on every day computers. After the PC revolution, the next step was creating local area networks. That was magic enough without even thinking about broadband networks covering multiple locations.

This was a world with cell phones, but they were rarities, big handheld things that looked like consumerized military walkie-talkies. Pay phones still roamed the earth. Answering machines used cassette tapes. Cameras took pictures on film that needed to be developed, not CCD devices that saved digital files on removable media.

No Al Qaeda or 9/11 attacks had yet led to the TSA and security checkpoints at airports; anyone could still go right to the gates without a ticket, to pick up or see off anyone they wanted. Gas and airplane fuel wasn't so expensive and private pilots weren't as uncommon as they've become.

In Florida, pythons had yet to take over the Everglades, Big Sugar had yet to agree to sell to the government, and there was still at least some border area between Miami development and actual swampland.

People haven't changed that much, though. There are still good guys and bad guys, cops and robbers, and occasionally, ordinary people who get caught up in things they wish they hadn't.

TURNABOUT
∎ ∎ ∎ ∎ ∎ ∎ ∎ ∎ ∎
by Rick Ollerman

To Melissa Sue,
the girl who wants everything

There was no moment of transition, no segue, no sense of anticipation. There was no feeling of standing atop a ladder and feeling your weight shift, realizing recovery wasn't going to happen, then gently falling away. There was no reaching behind you, no bracing for impact.

There was an abortive startle reflex: a wild grab, a mad rolling of the eyes, a massive clench of the abdomen. But it was too late; you were already gone.

One moment you were held up in the sky by an airplane. In another, you weren't.

The impossible surge of panic vanished, ousted by thoughts that were like pictures in your mind. You were no longer *thinking* your final thoughts, you were *seeing* them.

Marie....

Two seconds have passed. You're falling at forty four miles per hour.

You see/think the image in your mind of the tandem skydive you made a few years ago, and you spreadeagle like you did in that training those years ago on that beach in Mexico. You let the pressure of the air pushing your arms and legs back, molding your torso into a reverse arch.

Three seconds. Sixty six miles per hour.

You move only your eyes up to look for the plane, afraid to move your head and risk your tenuous stability. With nothing at that precise point above you, you move your eyes down quickly. You feel a false sensation of calm that's really intense concentration when suddenly the panic floods back and breaks over you like a hammer: *I'm falling! I'm going to die!*

Marie....

Four seconds. Seventy eight miles per hour.

The wind scrapes at your eyes and you see the water beneath you through heavily blurred streaks. You see flecks of white that may be whitecaps on the waves below. You see an irregular shape that could be a boat. For an instant you feel your muscles freeze, your body suddenly paralyzed, but it passes and nothing's changed. You're still falling and the sound of the wind ripping past your ears swallows your hearing the way the tears in your eyes have stolen your vision.

Five seconds. Ninety miles per hour.

Unable to focus, you see/think/feel your body slamming into water as solid as cement. There are so many tears, you're nearly blind. There's so much noise, you're virtually deaf. A vague field of emerald green is rushing up to meet you, accelerating from all corners of your remaining vision, racing toward a single, central point directly beneath you.

Six seconds. Ninety eight miles per hour.

Marie....

Extra moisture flies past your stinging eyes as your tear ducts surge with a final emotional release. You wish you could feel yourself cry one last time. You wish you could feel warm tears instead of this painful....

I'm going to die!

Can you really smell the ocean?

Seven seconds. One hundred and four miles per hour.

Hope. You see/think an image of cliff divers in Acapulco. The water's rock hard surface is below you, but what if you can hit it just right? Is there a 'just right'? What if?

Eight seconds. One hundred eight miles per hour.

Increasing wind resistance has slowed your acceleration but you can't notice. You're nearly at the point where wind resistance stalemates the force of gravity. You bend your knees the barest of fractions, feeling the drop of your legs.

Nine seconds. One hundred and ten miles per hour. Terminal velocity.

Your feet and knees meet the surface of the water at the same time, your body no longer belly to earth. You're torn nearly in two as your legs make contact with the water, which separates them at the surface a minuscule fraction of a second before your body drives down between them.

Marie.

CHAPTER ONE

It was a clear spring Sunday and the park was full of people walking along the asphalt trails after church. Mothers were arriving at the wading pool with their children and some kids were playing baseball on one of the diamonds at the north end. Two basketball games were running side by side on adjacent courts, separated from the tennis players by a chain link fence.

It was pure street ball, very little passing, few jump shots, just do it off the dribble and take it to the hole, baby. More than a game, it was a way of life for some of them. The park was a low cost country club for Tampa's under privileged.

From the parking lot fifty yards away, two men in rumpled cotton suits walked up and stood at the edge of one of the games. They watched patiently, waiting for a break in the game, not speaking to each other.

In the middle of a play, someone noticed them and called out, "Yo man, I've got to go." A number of the players looked around, saw what they didn't like and moved to a picnic table where they snatched a tee-shirt or a ball from the bench. Very quickly they filtered out of the park. The other game stopped and it too broke up.

The remaining players from both contests moved to one of the baskets away from the men in suits and began taking shots. One man stayed on the court where he had been playing, waiting for the invevitable. He was bent over with his hands on his knees, looking at the ground. "What are you doing here, Hill?"

"We need to talk to you, Frankie," said the bigger of the two men. The other one grinned at him.

Frankie O'Neil straightened up and looked behind him. There were barely enough people left for one game. "Leave me the fuck alone, Hill."

He began to walk away from the policemen toward the remaining players, wondering if he'd still be welcome. Behind him Hill called, "Come on, Detective."

O'Neil turned and marched back, stopping just short of the man's face. Hill was a few inches shorter than him but there was a hardness there, a discernible quality that had nothing to do with running miles in the park or lifting weights at the gym. He didn't flinch when O'Neil jabbed an index finger into his chest.

"Where the hell do you come off coming down here calling me out in front of these guys?" He kept his voice down but his anger was visible. "And what's this 'Detective' shit? I stopped being one of you guys a long time ago."

"We just want to talk."

"Well fuck you, Hill. And you, too, Fetterman." Neither of the men moved. "There's probably fifteen guys here now that will associate me with you two clowns and by next week that'll be everywhere. These guys don't like cops and they don't like assholes. I'm surprised they even let you park here."

"Now listen, O'Neil—"

"No, you listen," O'Neil said jabbing his finger again. "You just fixed it so I can't play here anymore. Or anywhere else in the fucking city. These guys think I have anything to do with cops and even if I get on the court they'll have to roll me off on a stretcher. I'll be playing with punk ass kids and wheezing old men at the goddamned Y." He turned and walked across the court to the picnic table. He picked up his tee-shirt and ball and started for the parking lot.

"We have to talk, Frankie," called Hill.

O'Neil didn't stop. "You want to talk to me, call me at the office."

The two men turned and watched him leave. Fetterman spoke up. "I can stop him."

"No," said Hill. "Let him go. We'll get to him later. Or he'll get to us."

He threw the basketball at a chair as he walked into the house. Katy heard him come in and walked out of the kitchen wearing an old fashioned apron over a pair of shorts and a cut off tee-shirt.

"What's wrong?" she asked as she stepped up to give him a kiss.

"Nothing," O'Neil told her, kissing her back. "I'm over it, anyway." He watched the basketball roll off the chair and come to a stop under a table. "What are you doing in the kitchen? I thought I was making lunch today."

Katy saw that he was fine and laughed at him. "Comedian. I thought I'd whip something up both of us could eat."

O'Neil spread his arms wide and said, "At least let me help."

"Frankie, if I asked you to separate an egg for me, what would you do?"

"Take it out of the box? Away from the other little eggies?"

"Uh huh." She turned to go back to the kitchen. "Go take a shower, stinky."

O'Neil peeled off his sweaty tee-shirt and said, "You know if you give me a few more guesses I bet I could figure that one out." He turned and headed up the stairs leading to their bedroom.

Halfway up, Katy called from the kitchen. "Honey?"

O'Neil stopped climbing. "Yeah, sweets?"

"John called earlier and left a message on the machine. He wants you to call him as soon as you get in."

"I'll do it up here." O'Neil made it to the bedroom and collapsed on one side of the bed. His body still allowed him to play ball with the hustlers every weekend but it had become a lot harder and needed a longer period of forgiveness after each episode. He scooped up the phone and speed dialed his business partner. "John, hi, it's me. What's up?"

"Frankie."

O'Neil pushed himself to a sitting position when he heard the way his friend said his name. "What's wrong, buddy?"

O'Neil heard the sound of a deep breath being drawn on the other end. "Where've you been?"

"Playing ball all morning. Are you okay?"

John didn't answer right away. O'Neil waited, giving him time. "I don't want to be the one telling you this."

A cloud of rising anxiety made O'Neil feel sick to his stomach. "Christ, John, telling me what?"

"Marie Clayton called me. She said she tried to reach you but you weren't there."

The cloud turned cold. "What happened?"

"I– Tim is dead."

O'Neil squeezed the phone in a white knuckled death grip and he clamped his eyes shut as John continued talking.

How could Tim be dead, he kept thinking. His best friend, closer than a brother. How could any of what John was saying be true?

"Wait a minute, man. You're saying someone threw him out of an airplane?"

"Marie said that Tim didn't come home Friday night. He had left her a note saying he might have to go out of town for a client and that he would call her, but he never did. He didn't even sign the note.

"Apparently, two guys were fishing in a skiff south of the Gandy Bridge yesterday morning. They were out there alone when they heard a sound like a shell exploding and saw a splash. They went over to check it out and they found him."

"Was he already dead?" Stupid question.

"He was bearly in one piece."

O'Neil heard Katy coming up the stairs but he didn't open his eyes. "They didn't see what happened?"

"They said they may have heard a small airplane a couple of minutes before but they're not sure. But when you're fishing in Tampa Bay a few miles from an airport that wouldn't make much of an impression."

"Were there any other boats around? Did anybody else see it happen?"

"You're thinking like a cop again, Frankie. No people, no boats, and the water was too damned shallow for a submarine."

"Christ," O'Neil said, scraping his fingers through his hair. "I don't believe this. There's no possibility they're wrong?"

"I guess the noise was pretty bad. Really big. Marie—" John paused, taking another breath. "Marie said she saw the body."

Neither man spoke for a minute. O'Neil blinked his eyes open and saw Katy framed in the bedroom doorway, wringing the kitchen apron in her hands. "Give me a while, I'll call you back."

He hung up the phone and turned to face his wife. Katy stopped moving and stared at a spot on the floor near O'Neil's feet. "Tim's dead," he said simply.

The words hung in the air between them, filling it with unspoken emotions.

Quietly she asked, "What are you going to do?"

O'Neil wanted to ask her, what are you so frightened of, but that was a different thing, he knew. "I don't know," he said. "Something. I have to do something."

"As a cop, Frankie?" She said the word with a surprising bitterness.

"As who I am."

O'Neil wanted to stop talking, to pay some attention to the war of emotions taking place in his head. "I love you, sweetheart."

"I know," she said. "But I'm going to have to leave again, aren't I?"

Katy looked up and there were tears streaking down her cheeks. Without any more talking, they were both aware of something that neither of them had words for.

O'Neil stood and moved into the bathroom. A minute later, steaming water hissed from the shower and did not stop until a long time later.

Katy never moved.

The shower was numbing, as if it were cold, but billowing sheets of steam rolled over the curtain bar and blanketed the bathroom walls with tiny beads of moisture. O'Neil almost lost his footing on the slick porcelain as he got out of the shower and grabbed a towel from the rack. His body was on auto-pilot as, still naked, he walked out of the bathroom and over to the bedroom phone.

"John, I need an airplane."

"Frankie? Is that you? Are you okay?"

"Yeah, it's me."

"Are you all right? What are you going to do?"

"I'm fine, John, and don't keep asking me questions. Please."

After a silence O'Neil didn't have the patience for, John said, "Martin, our database guy, he's a pilot. I think he flies with a club or something out of Lakeland but I don't think he's been doing it long."

"Doesn't matter, I just need him to do it a little longer. I'll call him. Do one thing for me, will you? Tell Marie you let me know what happened."

"You're not going to call her then?"

"No more questions, John. I can't come up with the answers. Goodbye."

O'Neil got dressed and left the house. Katy had left some food on the table but wasn't in the kitchen. He knew he should eat something, especially after playing ball, but his stomach was rolled up like a frightened caterpillar. He picked up a dry-erase marker from the counter and wrote a message to Katy on the magnetic board on the refrigerator and then left without looking for her or saying a word.

In the living room his wife sat on the sofa with an overstuffed pillow curled up into her legs. She heard the front door close and smeared the tears across her cheeks with her left hand. She stared at the saltiness glittering on the diamonds on her wedding band. "I'll put the eggs away, Frankie."

In the kitchen, on the refrigerator, a sign said, "I love you so very much."

CHAPTER TWO

The drive to the Lakeland airport took him almost 45 minutes. Sunday afternoon traffic should have been lighter but there was congestion at the interchange at 301 where the State Fair had opened a week earlier. O'Neil's mind was turning thoughts over and over in his mind, all of them slippery things, none of them grabbing hold. Everything kept cycling back to the single question, Why Tim?

The airport at Lakeland was a large regional operation approximately forty miles due east of Tampa International by air. Martin Cox walked out of a building as O'Neil pulled into a newly paved parking lot that smelled strongly of fresh tar. The building was a large aluminum hangar with a sign painted in red and blue on its side: New Aero Training Center.

Martin raised his hand when he saw O'Neil and called, "Over here, boss."

O'Neil nodded and pushed a pair of sunglasses high up on the bridge of his nose. He didn't want to meet anyone's eyes. He followed Martin through a gate onto the tarmac in front of the hangar. Martin stopped in front of a beige and blue low winged Piper, looking uncomfortable. "I'm sorry about your friend, Mr. O'Neil. It's a horrible thing. John said you were close."

O'Neil turned his head and studied Martin's face through gray tinted lenses. "You spoke with John?"

Martin nodded and broke away, quickly moving to drain the condensation from the Piper's fuel tanks. "I don't know where you want to go, sir, but this won't be bad for just two of us. It should do 85, 90 knots on a day like this."

"It won't work," O'Neil said. "The wings are low, I need to be able to see down. Straight down. We need a plane with high wings, like a Cessna. I should have mentioned it on the phone."

Martin's face took on a lost look, an expression that made him look much younger than he was. "Let me see about the club's 172. It's scheduled to be down for an annual but I'll see if they'll let us take it."

O'Neil nodded for him to go ahead.

Twenty minutes later the Cessna 172 was fueled and pre-flighted, and O'Neil and Martin lifted off into the dense and humid Florida air.

"I'm going to need to know where it is you want to go, Mr. O'Neil." O'Neil refused a headset and Martin was forced to shout over the noise of the propellor.

"West," O'Neil yelled back. "Head west. I want you to take me over the bay south of the Gandy Bridge but not as far as the Pier."

Martin nodded and almost said, "That should take about fifteen minutes from here," but didn't. Sitting together in the tiny cockpit they climbed to a thousand feet above the earth but stayed a million miles apart.

"How high do you want to go?" asked Martin.

"High enough," grunted O'Neil. High enough to die.

It wasn't long before they were over the gray-green Gulf of Mexico waters that O'Neil had described. They cleared land and O'Neil told Martin to keep going and not to circle. "Just stay over the water," he shouted.

Could you smell the ocean up here like I can, Tim? Did you know you were going to die?

The earth was laid out in front of them, flat, with the afternoon sun waning in their eyes. The perception of the horizon was lost to the moisture in the air, the range of vision stopped well short of the horizon. The air itself blocked the earth's edges. The airplane droned on, a repeating variance in pitch coming from the propeller, low to high, low to high. It sounded like kids in the park with those old motorized airplanes that flew at the end of guide ropes attached to a handle. The hypnotic sound would grow louder then fade as the toy plane was guided round and round in circles.

It wasn't an accident, was it? Your seat belt would have been on, the door would have been closed, but those things didn't help you. Why did somebody want to see you die?

O'Neil pressed his forehead to the clear plexiglass window on the door next to him and looked down at the water, away from the sun. He looked as straight down as he could, past the metal peg that served as a kind of step. It was welded to a strut that led down to the covered wheel. Beyond that, empty space filled the area between the plane and the ocean below. "Slow the plane down, Martin."

"Pardon me?"

"Slow the plane down."

Uncertainly, Martin reached forward and throttled back the engine to just above stall speed, staring at O'Neil, not sure he had heard correctly but not wanting to ask again. The altimeter read eleven hundred feet and they were flying west-southwest on a heading of 245 degrees, following a line that led directly out to the Gulf of Mexico.

This whole scene was getting weird and it didn't start out all that routine, either, thought Martin. Frankie O'Neil and John Sanders owned and ran the software consulting firm where he had been lucky, he thought, to begin working after college. When Sanders had called him and told him that O'Neil would be asking a favor, a man whose best friend had just been killed, Martin had dropped his plans for the afternoon and was only too happy to help. Actually, he felt proud just to be noticed. But right now he had no idea what was going on with the man sitting next to him. O'Neil's face was tightly set, the muscles at the corners of his jaw set rigid. This guy is losing it, Martin thought. Head out to the Gulf, fly 'high enough,' slow the plane down cold like a glacier slowly worked its way down from somewhere north and settled into the pit of his stomach.

O'Neil placed his hand on the door handle and turned it downward. The door didn't move, held closed by the pressure of the air flowing along the outside of the plane. "Slow it down more," he shouted over the noise.

Martin nearly swallowed the wad of gum in his mouth. "What– what are you going to do?"

"SLOW THE PLANE DOWN!"

For a long second, neither man moved, the droning pitch of the propellor noise drilling into the heads of both of them, the sense of hearing dominating all others. Slowly Martin reached forward again and throttled back the plane even more. The little Cessna shuddered as it began to stall and Martin quickly dropped the nose slightly then added a little more power to the engine. What did I get myself into, he thought furiously. There is a crazy man in this airplane and I don't want anything to happen to him. I don't want anything to happen to *me*. He concentrated very hard on the numerous gauges and dials in front of him, seeing them all but not aware of any of them.

O'Neil pushed the door open. It resisted but he could do it with one arm. A foil gum wrapper rose off the floor and zinged past his ear into space. He was oblivious to the pilot as he unclasped his seat belt with his right hand. Now he could lean his head out the door and see the turquoise water shimmering in the sea breeze below. *Is this what you saw, Tim? Was it green and pretty and peaceful? Did you remember all the time you spent fishing in the Gulf, the time spent here swimming and sailing and enjoying life? Is this what it looked like? Is this what you saw as you died?*

He turned his body and swung his legs over the side of the seat, dangling them eleven hundred feet above water as hard as concrete. Rushing air caught his sunglasses and ripped them from his face. O'Neil tried to watch them fall into the water but they blew backwards, toward the tail, and he lost sight of them almost immediately. *Surely it wasn't like that for you, my friend.*

O'Neil edged closer to the open door, extending one leg further into the airstream. There was constant pressure pushing him towards the tail and he had to keep the muscles of his arm flexed in order to hold it in place. He leaned forward, left arm extended and elbow locked, forcing the door open against the air pressure. His right arm held him inside the plane as he leaned his body far enough outside the plane so that he could see the water rolling out directly below the wheel.

Holy Mary, Mother of Christ, Martin swore and shut his eyes. If we run into a thermal or hit some turbulence....

Martin banked the plane to left slightly in a subtle attempt to gently angle his boss back into the airplane. O'Neil's head whipped around and he looked at Martin for the first time during the flight. "Don't."

Martin automatically leveled the Cessna's wings and glued his eyes to the artificial horizon indicator. Silently, he began to pray, his lips moving. He wouldn't look at O'Neil again.

O'Neil turned back to the door and studied his foot hanging from the tiny airplane, a universe of empty space between it and the rolling surface below. He tried to get his mind around the concept of freefall and what it would be like to fall for some part of your last minute alive. To be perfectly fine and healthy, but knowing with absolute certainty that you were going to die when your fragile body crashed into the water below, smashed to pieces inside as your 110 miles per hour blaze through the air was interrupted by a planet.

What did you think about, Tim? Were they the same things I would think about? Were you panicked? Were you accepting? God damn it, what was it like to be the target of such a slow bullet?

For long minutes they flew into the sun, neither man moving an inch, each held captive by their inner thoughts. I've never seen a man die, Martin thought, his eyes still glued to the panel before him. If he wants to jump, I can't stop him, not without crashing the plane. I won't watch him die. Oh God, why did he have to call on me?

O'Neil sat stock still, legs hanging out of the airplane door, his body perched literally on the edge of his seat, left arm propping the door open, his right hooking him to the plane itself. *I can't do any more, Tim. I can't know what you felt, what you thought. But I know it shouldn't have happened, damn it, not to you. Probably not to anybody.*

He closed his eyes then very slowly pulled his legs back into the airplane. He let the door close itself against the fuselage as he swung forward in the seat and turned the handle upwards to lock it. "Martin," he said as softly as he could and still be heard over the airplane noise. The young pilot didn't move. "Martin," O'Neil reached over and put his hand on the other man's shoulder. "Let's go home."

Moisture salty as the ocean below glistened on Martin's face as he banked the plane around and left the open Gulf behind. Next to him, O'Neil fastened his seat belt around his lap. It would be a hell of a thing to fall out now.

CHAPTER THREE

The sunset turned the sky into an arrangement of surrealistic fluorescence, bright pinks and blues, reds and oranges, purples and yellows. It looks fake somehow, O'Neil thought, like a cheap painting in a plastic frame. He squinted into the disappearing sun as the sky painted itself with the colors of its odd spectrum and slowly turned to dark. The gentle waves slapping the sides of the bowrider turned from silver to gray to black as the eyes gave up the ability to see the colors of the night.

O'Neil lay on the bottom of the boat, fingers clasped behind his head as he stared into the sky, propped up by a wedge of life vests. The smell of the sea was strong and as he breathed deeply it gently stung the inside of his nose. Glare from the nearby city took over the edges of the night sky and the sounds of rushing traffic carried from the distance across the water.

Lost in his grief, his mind drifted back to a summer from his college years, a few months spent exploring the myths of the Southern California coastal lifestyle. It was in Hollywood, supposed home of the stars, that he and Tim Clayton had met.

Traffic along Hollywood Boulevard had been brisk and the sidewalks were full of tourists and homeless people, sharing the glamour and the misfortune of the city. The lines of shops were mostly dirty, rundown dives offering sleazy tee-shirts at three for ten dollars and electronics stores, the kind where you make a purchase and they keep the box for the next customer.

O'Neil was walking the sidewalk, reading the names in the stars embedded in the concrete sidewalk, fascinated by the history yet appalled by what the reality had become. It's not what they show on TV, he thought. O'Neil stopped at a star stained with something that had crept out from a recessed doorway and rubbed at it with his foot. As he cleared the mess, the name on the star said 'Charles Chaplin.' There was no one to look after him here.

It was in a little diner advertising vegetarian chili and fruit smoothies that he had met Tim Clayton. O'Neil had stopped in to try a Malibu Sunrise with mango slices and then perhaps a bowl of the chili. The diner was old, sheets of dull chrome hammered over the tops and sides of the counter and tables. It looked and felt like a restaurant from a Hemingway story.

After O'Neil ordered, he stood up from the counter and went to use the rest room. Two urinals, one vacant and one being used, were mounted on the wall across from the door. The one in use was mounted in a normal position two feet off the floor. The empty one looked like something you might find in a circus. It was full-sized but it was positioned near the floor, set barely an inch off the ground. Separating the two was a metal section of wall bolted to the tiles.

As O'Neil stepped up to the open urinal, the man using the normal one looked over his shoulder and said, "Hey, how's it going?"

O'Neil replied without thinking. "Not too bad," he said. He looked down at the urinal and unzipped his fly. Considering the unusual plumbing fixture, he said, "Looks like I've got the small one."

The guy gave him an odd sort of look, nodded, and left the restroom after a quick stop at the sink. It took O'Neil a minute to realize what had just happened. When two men are standing side by side relieving themselves, even with a wall blocking each other from the elbows down, the last thing you say is, "Looks like I've got the small one."

He washed up and left the bathroom shaking his head and feeling stupid. At least he was from out of town and far from home.

The dining counter was shaped like a horseshoe with two ends extending out from the kitchen and meeting to form a generous "U" shape. Along one edge was the food O'Neil had ordered. Directly across was the guy from the bathroom. It was the middle of the afternoon and there wasn't anybody else in the place.

Well, isn't this awkward, thought O'Neil as he sat down and unfurled a napkin across his lap. Maybe we can compare sandwich sizes next.

The waitress, an unnatural blonde with hair of a shade not normally found in nature, stepped between them and asked, "You want anything else with that, honey?" O'Neil said no thank you and dropped a spoon into his chili. When the waitress moved away, the guy across from him was smiling. "I won't say anything about it if you won't," he said cheerfully.

O'Neil spread his hands open and smiled back, embarrassed. "I was talking about the urinal, you now, how it was hung so far down on the wall." O'Neil felt his face begin to turn red. "I didn't think about what I was saying."

The other man laughed out loud, an out of place sound compared to the atmosphere on the street outside the door. "I know it. I've been sitting here holding my breath trying not to laugh."

They both laughed then, draining O'Neil's embarrassment and putting him at ease. They introduced themselves and had an enjoyable conversation while they ate their lunch across from each other. The new guy's name was Tim Clayton, an engineering major from Pasadena, and about a year older than O'Neil. When they were through eating, they took a walk down to Graumann's Chinese Theater and Tim showed him where concrete impressions of Marilyn Monroe's and Jane Russell's hands were embedded in adjacent sidewalk panels in front of the theater. One of the actresses had written "Gentlemen Prefer Blondes" starting in one panel and crossing over to the other.

They talked about old movies, famous actresses, famous dead actresses, California, college, and careers. Both shared an optimism about the future, Tim because of the bleeding edge engineering work he looked forward to being a part of, and O'Neil, who wanted a career in law enforcement because of the contribution he thought he could make to society. And they became friends. They spent the last weeks of summer exploring Southern California together, Tim as enthusiastic tour guide. When it was over, O'Neil had had enough "cools" and "groovys" and was ready to head back to his relatively laid back home town of Tampa, Florida.

Tim drove O'Neil to the airport and saw him all the way through to his gate. "Who knows," he said. "Maybe I'll end up in Florida one day myself." Which he did, three years later, when he transferred to Orlando in the employ of a major theme park corporation. They renewed their friendship and took frequent trips across Interstate 4, with it being O'Neil's turn to show Tim life on the "other" coast. O'Neil had graduated from the University of Southern Florida and had joined the Tampa police force. Both men had thought their lives were on track, headed in the directions they wanted.

That may have been true for Tim, who had a habit of sometimes drinking too much beer and proclaiming how life was being so good to him. His career had taken off, leading him into computers and information systems and new career paths that hadn't even existed ten years earlier. Things were a little different for O'Neil.

He had gotten married to a nurse he had met while delivering a pair of shot up pre-teen gang members to Tampa General one night. They fell in love and bought a house. But being a cop was hard, and he found he didn't like seeing only the worst parts of the city he grew up in and thought he loved. Bad feelings started to manifest themselves and the longer he kept at it the more he ended up hating the job. The city itself was becoming something different to him. The stronger these feelings became, the harder he worked, as if the job was rotten because he wasn't trying hard enough.

His relationship with his new wife suffered and she left him when he didn't show up for a counseling appointment; he had fallen asleep in his car after working an extra night shift. When one of the lieutenants in his squad retired after 22 years of sterling dedication to the job, drove home after a celebratory dinner in his honor, and 'ate his gun' as they say, O'Neil finally walked away.

He took his wife, Katherine, on a cruise and they worked at patching up their young marriage. She forced him to learn how to relax and together they worked to restore his over-stressed mind. A few months later, he proclaimed himself healthy, optimistic, and out of a job.

That's when Tim called and suggested he get out of Tampa for a while. "Come on up to O-town," he said. "The only thing up here big enough to take seriously is DisneyWorld and how hard can that be?" Tim had set up shop as an independent consultant and had offered to teach O'Neil his field.

For three years O'Neil worked with Tim learning the business until Tim had developed a sort of pre-mid-life crisis of his own. He bought a 30 foot sail boat and took off, declaring that he wanted to discover the "rest of the things" Florida and the world had to offer. O'Neil moved back to Tampa and started his own business with a man he had met while working with Tim.

They kept in touch when they could, which meant O'Neil would get an odd post card here and there from some exotic port or island he had never heard of. One day an envelope arrived from Antigua with a wedding picture clipped behind a letter. On the back of the photo was scrawled the words, "By the way, you're going to love Marie." Six weeks later the couple had moved to a house in Sarasota, about forty miles south of Tampa and the two friends were reunited.

For O'Neil, business was doing well and growing. He and Katy were happy, and they had started talking about raising a family. He and Tim didn't see each other as often as they'd like, but each of them had been involved with some large projects at work and spoke often enough on the phone.

And now this. A large single engine plane flew low overhead and O'Neil sat up in his boat. Suddenly, things had become very different.

He had no idea what Tim had been doing or who might have wanted to kill him. He hadn't even spoken with him for about a month. But O'Neil knew he couldn't just put on a suit and tie and go to work in the morning, try to cope with the loss of his friend. He wasn't sure what he could do, but he knew he could do more than that.

He drifted along the surface of the water for hours, ignoring the passage of time but unable to keep from feeling its weight. He wouldn't mourn his friend any more; he had done that earlier today in a small airplane at eleven hundred feet above the waters of the Gulf of Mexico. He would miss him though, for a very long time, and probably forever. O'Neil owed his memory at least that much.

When dawn finally cracked the edges of the long night, O'Neil slapped a couple of handfuls of the bay onto his face and started the engine. It was time to move. He wasn't sure to where, but he knew it always hurt more to just stand still and take it.

CHAPTER FOUR

Monday turned out to be even warmer than Sunday, about 10 degrees hotter than the norm for that time of year. O'Neil had returned home after taking the bowrider back to its slip and taking a shower at the marina. He was trying to stay away from home as long as he could. Familiar things were feeling out of place and he wanted to keep moving, avoid his daily routine.

Katy was gone when he got there, like he knew she would be. There was a note on the refrigerator board saying she went to stay at her sister's for a while. It was signed, "I love you – Katy." He picked up a paper towel and wiped the board clean without reading the rest of it. Some things would have to wait.

O'Neil called the police department and asked to be connected to Detective Hill's desk. He was told the detective wasn't in and O'Neil left a voice mail asking Hill to meet him at the same park with the basketball courts from the day before.

Thirty minutes later, standing ten feet from a basket, O'Neil was mindlessly shooting free throws, barely aware of when the ball actually went through the net. It was close to two hours before Hill showed up, his partner Fetterman inevitably in tow. Both men walked up and stood behind O'Neil, not saying anything until he turned around.

"I was sorry to hear about your friend Clayton," said Hill in a professional tone, the only sincerity certain kinds of cops use when it suits them. "I'm sure he was a good man."

Like you would know, O'Neil thought. You're a badge with the emotional range of a reptile. He nodded and led them to a playground-scarred picnic table with attached benches. They took seats around the table and looked at each other, Hill with the same half smirking expression O'Neil suddenly remembered from his previous life. He wanted to find out what the police knew about Tim's death and he didn't think Hill would make it easy. Still, they had sought O'Neil out yesterday here at the park, on a Sunday, and that didn't make sense unless there was something they wanted from him. Fetterman took a pocket knife from out of his trousers and began to carve his initials into the table.

"So, Frankie, after you quit the force, you never came around any more. We thought we might have done something, you know, to offend you or something." It wasn't his words that made him come off like an asshole, O'Neil thought, it was the way he said them. As if there was a hidden meaning behind every sentence that only he knew. Some long-time cops did that, said things to get under your skin, like the more uncomfortable they made you feel the more at ease and in control they felt themselves. Not all cops were like that, but too many were the same as Hill.

"When I left I was done with it all. I wouldn't have known what to say to any of you."

"Well, that's all right," Hill said like he was doing O'Neil a favor by understanding. "Usually when a guy just up and quits something like that it shows they probably didn't have as much in common with the other guys as they might have thought." In other words, don't feel bad because you didn't belong; you weren't one of us to begin with.

Hill was wrong. The only part about being a cop that still meant something to O'Neil was how close he had been to the other guys. They were all players on a team that had forced them to depend on each other, sometimes for their lives. O'Neil had been as much a part of it, as much a part of the group, as anybody. At least for a while.

You're a real sweetheart, Hill. Take the good and make it bad as long as it keeps you feeling good. You small bastard. "I want to know about Tim."

Hill chuckled and hit his partner's biceps with the back of his hand. Fetterman's knife skipped out of the letter "B" and carved a new groove across the table. Looking at the initial, O'Neil realized he couldn't remember Fetterman's first name. He wasn't sure now if he ever knew it. "So now you want to be a cop again, eh, Frankie, is that it?"

"I'm just trying to find out what happened to my friend." Otherwise I wouldn't be sitting here listening to your shit and watching your little puppy play with his toy knife. A pause and then, "Look, you guys are the only cops here. We both know I didn't stick it out."

Hill settled back, like O'Neil had surrendered something and he had just won a prize. The truth was, Hill had never known why O'Neil had left the force. He hadn't had any problems with the other guys and he had risen through the ranks like a natural. Maybe he was soft in his head or pussy-whipped at home or something. Hill couldn't understand why anybody in their right mind would give up a job where nobody could tell you what to do. Except other cops of course, but that was different. Rank would always have its privileges. O'Neil must be some kind of underachieving misfit or something.

"All right, Frankie, we'll talk about it. But we don't know much." Next to Hill, Fetterman was scratching away on a new section of tabletop. He had finished with his initials and now he was working on a more complicated figure of some sort. O'Neil couldn't identify it but whatever it was, it was gradually spreading across the surface. Jesus, he thought, this guy is hard on picnic tables.

"What we do know is yesterday morning, at approximately 7:45 a.m., two brothers from Gulfport were in a fishing boat in the waters south of the Gandy Boulevard bridge. They claim they heard a noise and a loud splash. They didn't know what it was, said it sounded like a gun shot only louder. They may have heard a small airplane fly above a few minutes before, but they're not sure."

"I didn't know people fished in that part of the bay," O'Neil said.

"Yeah, we're checking out that part of their story. They may just be a couple of morons in a boat, like half the dickheads in Florida on a weekend. They said they didn't see anybody else out there, maybe a few boats passing by, so maybe it was a good place full of fish nobody knew about." Hill scratched his forehead with dirty fingernails. "Or maybe it didn't occur to them that they never saw anybody fish there because there wasn't anything worth catching. Probably they just don't know what they're doing. Anyway, it looks like they'll probably check out okay. The boat was full of tackle and fishing gear and they haven't been in any trouble before except for matching sets of DWIs. Those they take turns renewing every year like library cards."

That's cute, thought O'Neil.

"They pulled in their lines and pointed the boat in the direction of the noise. About fifty or sixty yards away they saw something floating in the water. Evidently your buddy was wearing a windbreaker that had filled with air and was keeping him afloat." An ugly expression formed briefly on his face, then passed. "Weren't for that, he would've sunk like a stone, been down there a few days at least. Anyway they got to him and pulled him into the boat but he was already dead. The legs were torn from the body but still attached. The other unusual thing were some pieces of fried egg in his hair but we think one of the brothers probably puked on him and didn't want to cop to it in front of the other one. I haven't seen the autopsy report yet, but cause of death appears to be consistent with a fall from a substantial height into the water. Or I guess at the speed he would have been going, it would have been 'onto' the water."

Good one, Hill. "What about this airplane they heard?"

"Well, they're not sure they heard one, but hey, the body had to come from somewhere, right? That's our assumption at this point although any plane would have had to fly relatively low to stay out of the TARSA." He looked at O'Neil who did his best to not show a reaction. "That's the restricted airspace controlled by the tower at an airport. If they did fly into the TARSA, or if they had their transponder on, somebody may have picked up an ID on them."

O'Neil stood and walked in a circle, turning his back to the table so he could relax the expression on his face without showing Hill his distaste. Listening to him talk and looking at that smirk brought back a taste of all the stress and ill feelings O'Neil had walked away from years before.

"But why did all this happen? Why would somebody want to take Tim Clayton for a ride in an airplane over Tampa Bay and throw him out? I appreciate what you're telling me, but do you guys have any idea what kind of motive there might have been?"

Hill detached himself from the bench and stood up, stretching. He never liked talking to someone who was standing while he wasn't. For that matter, he generally disliked people who were taller than him. "Well Frankie, we may, but then again we may not."

"And that's supposed to mean what?"

"You see, we came out here yesterday morning to have a friendly talk, like we're having now actually, but you were a bit rude. More than a little, and you didn't even know why we wanted to see you. Now I could tell you some things that you probably want to know but they are of a somewhat confidential nature. Details of a pending investigation, you know. But I need a little help in return, Frankie. We didn't come out here yesterday or even today just to give you a show and tell session."

And I yelled at you in public and in front of your partner and now you need to show me who's boss. Games, games, games. "All right. I apologize for yesterday. Okay? I didn't mean to make things hard on you guys. I'm asking you now, please just tell me, do you have any idea who killed Tim or why?"

"Geez, O'Neil, slow down a little, will you? He just got himself killed yesterday. This isn't the only issue on the agenda here. There are other factors at play you don't even know about." Hill looked back at Fetterman who seemed oblivious to the conversation. His work on the table had continued to grow in scope and was now swallowing some of the older carvings on the table. O'Neil still couldn't make out what it was.

"Okay. What did you want yesterday? When you came out here?"

"Well, that's a whole other thing, Frankie." Back to his first name. "And it does have something to do with Clayton, although possibly not his murder."

"But it could, whatever it is?"

"Who can tell? But I don't know, Frankie. Your best friend's been killed, you look like you haven't slept all night, you got to feel like shit warmed over. With your grieving and all, maybe we should wait to talk about it until you get some rest, feel a little better. It can keep for a few days, can't it, Fetterman?" Fetterman gave a slow nod, hardly acknowledging the question and not breaking his rhythm with the knife.

O'Neil was too worn out to play any more. He sat down at the table again and said, "Look, Hill. You can keep filling my card but I'm not going to dance with you. If you've got something to talk to me about, do it now. Especially if it might shed some light on what happened to Tim. Just knock off the crap, okay? You're right, I feel like hell and I'm really not in the mood."

"Well Hell's Bells, Frankie, you really do have some balls tucked away in those panties, don't you? Okay, let's not draw this out any more. Here's the skinny. But I need your word, before I tell you anything more, that you repeat this to no one."

"Repeat what, Hill?"

"No shit, O'Neil. I'm working an investigation and your buddy was helping me out. He's gone so now I've got to find some way to get out of the hole he left me in. That's what we came out here yesterday to talk to you about. But I can't let you, ex-cop or no, screw this up with any side investigations of your own. No loose talking with anything I might tell you about our little project."

"And this investigation of yours that Tim was helping you with, you think that might have something to do with why he was killed?"

"I need your word, O'Neil."

"All right, Hill, you've got it. I'll play by your rules." *Now tell me what the fuck you got my friend involved with.*

Hill nodded and motioned for him to have a seat while he remained standing so he could look down at O'Neil as he spoke. "Have you ever heard of a business called the Walter Lankford Company?"

"Off West Shore Boulevard on Cypress?"

Hill nodded. "That's the place."

"All I know about them is that Tim put in a network over there a few months back." O'Neil thought about it for a moment. "I believe they had around a hundred or so computers they needed to connect as well as some wide area routers and internet connectivity."

"Very good, Mr. O'Neil. How come you're able to remember it so well?"

"Nothing spectacular, Hill. Tim stayed with my wife and I whenever he did a job in Tampa. It didn't happen that often so it's not terribly difficult."

"Okay, I can buy that. Anyway, you've got it right. It turns out these guys are big into their computer system, their networks. In fact, their whole business, from what we can tell, couldn't be run without it."

"That's not so unusual these days."

"Well, it depends on the type of business that they're actually in, though."

"What does that mean?"

"Money laundering. They take in dirty money, invest it legitimately in hard to trace places, and return net worth to the original 'investor.' Keeping a little something off the top, of course."

"Hill, that's about as unsurprising as their dependence on their networks. Uncovering drug money in Florida is like finding sunscreen on the beach."

"But there is something unusual about this case, O'Neil. It's all mine."

"What about the feds?"

"There are no feds, not at this point. The problem is, I've got information but I don't have hard proof. If I give up what I've got now, I'm pulled out of the whole thing and this enchilada gets served up nice and warm to the FBI." He held up his hand before O'Neil could say anything. "Before you give me the rules and regs crap, I'm well within protocol to investigate my source, see if he's yanking my chain or what. Officially speaking, there's no evidence that the Lankford Company is anything other than what they say they are, a financial services and investment company."

O'Neil thought this out for a minute. "So you don't really have any proof they're doing anything criminal?"

Hill said, "That's right."

"So what the hell are you doing using a civilian to help you investigate a possible felony? Your investigation may have gotten him killed and you don't even know if they're breaking the fucking law?"

"Jesus Christ, O'Neil," Hill shouted back. "If somebody farts on an elevator, you can tell something's wrong by the way everybody scrambles out of the fricking box when the doors open. You don't have to be plugging your nostrils with your necktie to believe it. You think I'm jerking you off or something? What the fuck do you think I'm doing here talking to you, you son of a bitch?"

O'Neil didn't know what to think at this point. He was feeling angry at everything and everybody. "Settle down, Hill. I'm just trying to see how this all fits in with Tim." He took a deep breath to calm himself down. He didn't want to completely alienate Hill just when he had gotten him talking. "How did he actually get involved?"

"I'll get to that if you just shut up and listen. I'm trying to paint a picture for you here, before we get to the details. May I continue?"

"Please."

"Thank you very much. Anyway, it seems that the Walter A. Lankford Company *may* be involved with laundering money for a group of South American businessmen, possibly out of Venezuela, we're not sure yet. If the information we have is true, we can't just search their offices, tap their phones, and read through their garbage. We can't do all the normal crap we do. Care to guess why?"

"You tell me," O'Neil said.

"Because they don't talk on the phone, they don't throw shit in the garbage, and the only thing they do by mail is order fancy underwear for their girlfriends through Victoria's Secret catalogues."

Fetterman spoke for the first time, as if Hill had set him up and it was time to deliver the punch line. "They do it all by computer," he said, then bent back to his work.

"That's right," agreed Hill. "So now you see what keeps this whole party going. But if they were just storing illegal data on their computers, that's no big deal. We could grab them and get that shit off, decode it or do whatever the hell our guys would do, and we'd be good to go."

"And the problem with that is..." O'Neil prompted.

"The problem, Mr. Ex-cop computer nerd, is that what if there isn't anything stored on their computers or floppy disks? What if there's absolutely nothing on the premises physically linking them to any crimes?"

O'Neil began to see what Hill was getting at. "What you're trying to tell me is that they run everything through their computer networks."

"Everything. That's how they communicate with each other, how they move the money, how they track it, the whole deal. And none of it exists until Lankford links their computers to someone else's. They can start it up or shut it down as easy as turning on and off a light switch."

"Can't you go after the individual employees? Look at who's making more money than they should and focus on them?"

"They've got over two hundred people working there and most of them are normal working stiffs. They do a legitimate business. And even if there were some way I could get approval to go after each one of them, if one wrong person finds out, the whole case is blown."

"What about wire taps?"

"I don't know what the hell to tap. But you're the expert, you tell me. How would you track it down?"

O'Neil thought about ways to hide your real business on a computer network. The Internet is named for the word 'internetwork,' which is exactly what it is. An enormous number of government, university, medical, and private computers all electronically linked together to form a single, easily accessible network. A user in Baltimore can log on and swap electronic mail or files with a user in Switzerland as easily as he can with somebody two doors down in the same office building. There would be countless ways to arrange something like this using the internet, O'Neil thought.

Someone could access a remote database somewhere that was programmed to access another one somewhere else, and so on and so on, and that data could be sent to your network just like any other data. There would be no limit to how deep you could take an arrangement like that. Performance could be an issue, how long it would take to actually see a particular piece of information on your screen, but clever programmers could minimize that. The data could also be encrypted so that an electronic eavesdropper wouldn't be able to understand what he was looking at.

A computer could also be connected to the Internet wirelessly using radio or a microwave dish making it extremely difficult to trace.

"I see the problem," O'Neil said.

"I thought you might."

"What about the person who tipped you off to the whole thing? Can you get at it by going through the inside? That may be the only way you're going to find out what's going on with those computers."

Fetterman spoke again, this time without looking up from the table. His design had stopped growing and instead was taking on more detail. "Can't do that. Informant's not talking anymore."

"Lean on him, then. I know you, Hill. At least I used to. There's not a lot you won't do to get a make a break for yourself."

Hill looked back at O'Neil and didn't move. "Problem is," Fetterman went on. "The informant is not talking to anyone at all. At least not since yesterday."

What they were trying to tell O'Neil exploded across his brain. "You sons of bitches!" he said, rising to his feet. "You motherfucking sons of bitches!"

"Hey, calm down, O'Neil," said Hill. "What exactly do you want us to do, huh? We didn't get his ass killed, he got that done by himself. We're trying to find out how it happened."

"How it happened is he was working for you and you fucked up and left him hanging. Tim wasn't a hero, he wouldn't have done anything like this on his own." At least not without talking to me first. *God damn it, Tim, why didn't you come to me with any of this?*

"Like it or not, O'Neil, we didn't leave him anywhere. He left us. Isn't that right, Fetterman?"

"Yup. Yesterday was the second time."

O'Neil found it hard to believe what they were saying. "So why the hell didn't he come to me with any of this? That would have been more like Tim than to go to you guys, people he didn't even know."

"Christ, O'Neil, figure it out. You guys were like best friends, right? Two peas in a pod. He was best man or something at your wedding, wasn't he?"

O'Neil nodded.

"By the way, I never got my invitation. Anyway, you're his best pal who used to be a cop but you went a little nutso and walked away from the job."

O'Neil looked at him sharply.

"Or whatever, but you lost your wife for a while, didn't you? Took a little trip to La La Land, someone said." Hill had a 'don't blame me' expression on his face. "So here's your buddy, he knows about a crime, he isn't sure how you'd react and he doesn't want to cause you any stress or heartache, so he takes it right to the cops. Which is what he should do anyway, according to the law. So tell me, Frankie, just where exactly did he go wrong?"

At the point somebody decided to kill him, you asshole. *Was that how it happened, Tim? Did you really think you were saving me from something by not coming to me first? Was it my fault this happened to you?*

"So now what?"

Hill put his foot on the bench across from O'Neil and leaned his elbows forward on his knee. "Well, now it gets interesting, I hope. Really interesting."

As Hill spoke, O'Neil's eyes focused on the surface of the table where Fetterman was doing his carving. Without taking his eyes off it, he stood up and turned around so he could see it from the right side up. Under the scrapings and gouging of Fetterman's Swiss army pocket knife, the envy of any Boy Scout, was the image of a large morning sun appearing over a horizon made up of the sea. A small airplane was flying between two clouds and below it the surface of the water was disturbed by an incredibly detailed splash pattern that blossomed high above the waves. In the lower right corner were the initials 'FB.'

You are one sick son of a bitch, thought O'Neil.

CHAPTER FIVE

Katy's sister answered the phone on the second ring. "Hello," she said.

"Rachel, it's Frankie. I need to speak to my wife."

"Your wife, Frankie?" She didn't bother to hide her disapproval. She waited a beat, then said, "Hold on, I'll get her."

When Katy spoke into the phone, O'Neil felt a banging start in his chest. "How are you doing?" he asked her.

"I'm doing fine, honey. I'm thinking about you a lot."

He was afraid to ask, but he did anyway. "Good or bad?"

"Oh, Frankie, you know I love you so much. It's just that I can't go through that again. You know."

"Yeah. I do."

"Really, honey? You get that puppy with a bone thing and you keep gnawing away, all in some parallel universe where nobody else exists. Even me. You don't drop that bone until it's gone. It's bad for you and it's bad for me."

O'Neil swallowed. "I'm sorry, Katy, I–"

"No, don't apologize. It's the way that you are and I– I don't love it, but in a way there's something to admire. You just have to let things go sometimes and you never do. It hurts us. It hurts me."

"I love you." It was all he could think to say.

"Tell me what you're going to do."

"I met with a couple of the cops I used to work with. They think they know what happened to Tim. Or at least who was behind it. They want me to help go after them."

"And you're going to do it?"

"Honey, I don't know how not to. If these people out there killed Tim and there is something I could do to make them pay for it, how could I just walk away? I don't know what I would do tomorrow or the day after or any other day but I don't know how I could just leave it. I have to do it, Katy."

"You don't have to explain it, honey. We've been there before. Just remember this is why you quit the police. You just take care of you, huh? If somebody killed Tim.…"

"Don't worry, nothing's going to happen to me." That's easy enough to say, thought O'Neil.

"Do one thing for me, okay Frankie?"

"What's that?"

"After all this is over, whatever it is, you put me in one of those little parallel universes and focus yourself on me for a while, okay?"

"You've got yourself a deal," he said.

After the phone call with his wife, O'Neil went upstairs and collapsed into sleep. He dreamt of computer networks and airplanes but when he awoke, all he could recall were bits and pieces of scattered images. Nothing concrete, but he knew this case had been at the center of all of them.

As he took a shower and got dressed, he thought about what he needed to do. He hadn't wanted to discuss it with Hill, told him he had to think about it first, but he did have a few thoughts already. Obviously, there were two ways to go about getting at Lankford: go after the people or go after the computers.

Going after somebody actually involved with the company would be time consuming and risky. One word from them or one mistake and they would reveal the whole thing to the wrong people. If Hill had considered that a viable option, he would be pursuing it himself and he wouldn't need O'Neil. They couldn't consider going after whoever it was Lankford was communicating with because they had no idea who they were or even where to look. Even if they did, there was nothing to make them cooperate.

So it made the most sense to go after the operation from the computer end. The network at Lankford was the one place they knew of where the information they were seeking actually went *to*, regardless of where it came *from*. Also, it was the only place they knew of where the actual information must be unencrypted and readable by human eyes. Somehow, O'Neil had to find a way to get access to that office. He had to get time on their system.

He left the house and started driving toward his office. From home, it was about a twenty minute drive but he did it on automatic pilot, his thoughts still focused on the Lankford Company. It was near midnight and the sky was a moonless black when he pulled into the parking lot outside of his building. There was a faint hint of salt water in the air as he stepped out of the car and walked to the building. The bay was only a half mile or so to the west.

The building itself was a one story pre-fabricated concrete affair that was typical of west coast Florida office space. O'Neil-Sanders Inc. leased thirty five hundred square feet at the northeast corner of the building. This included a warehouse area in the back and two bathrooms, both of which were badly in need of redecoration. The previous tenant had marketed party supplies to private corporations and their taste had run to something that could have been called "early Carnival." One of the toilets was green and the other was yellow. Of the two, most people chose the green, probably because the yellow one always looked like it had recently been used.

O'Neil unlocked the door and walked over to the console that controlled the burglar alarm. He did this out of habit, ready to key in his four digit security code within the allotted 45 seconds, but for some reason the alarm had already been turned off. Last person out forgot again, he thought, irritated. They had been robbed once before which had prompted the installation of the alarm system. He would leave a note on John Sanders' desk asking him to remind everybody to pay attention when they left.

He walked past the reception area and down the short hallway to his office. Halfway down the twenty foot passage he stopped when he saw a small light coming from his office. The lamp on his desk was turned on. He listened carefully but he couldn't hear anything other than the soft sounds of his own measured breathing. The alarm was turned off and somebody had been in his office. Or was still there. His mind jumped to Hill and Fetterman and he felt uneasy but wasn't sure why.

Take it easy, he thought. There was no sound coming from the open door and no moving shadows in the light. Chances are John or one of the programmers had gone into his office for something and had simply left the light on.

Quietly, he moved forward and leaned the top part of his body around the door frame. The movement caused the person sitting behind O'Neil's desk to start, jumping literally inches out of his chair. His feet had been propped on the edge of the oak desk and a magazine had been in his lap.

"A little jumpy, aren't we?" said O'Neil. "No, no, don't get up," he added as the man started to rise. Instead the man bent down and picked the magazine he had been reading off the floor. He was young, in his early twenties, and he smiled up at O'Neil as he sat back in the chair, startled but not at all bothered by the situation.

"You scared the hell out of me, man," he said.

"How about that," said O'Neil. "Who are you?"

"Cleaning crew. I'm new though, just been doing your building for about three weeks or so. Do you work here or were you sent by Mr. Farley?"

"Mr. Farley?"

"The manager of the cleaning company. They told me he sends people out sometimes to check on the new guys." There was a question in his voice.

"No, right the first time, I just work here." O'Neil sat down in one of the two visitor's chairs he kept just inside the door. "What's your name?"

The kid looked more comfortable and said, "Reed Larson. I didn't mean to do anything wrong. I finished the cleaning and I was looking at some of the computer magazines on the desk." He held up the cover of the current *PC Magazine*.

"That's all right," said O'Neil. "Take them home with you if you want. I don't think I'll be getting to them any time soon." Larson was thin, slightly unkempt with a few days growth of beard, and O'Neil saw no reason not to believe him. "What do you know about computers?"

Reed flashed him a smile of naturally white teeth. "Not much, but I'd like to. Cleaning offices is cool 'cause people leave you alone and you've got your days free. It's not my life's ambition or anything. Something like this looks like a lot more fun."

"Something like what?"

"Computers, programming, all of it."

"But the cleaning is all you do?"

"This is it. At least right now. This your office?"

O'Neil apologized for not introducing himself and he stood up and shook the other man's hand. An idea had been forming in his mind. "Tell you what," he offered. "I'll tell you what I can about cracking the computer business if you'll help me out with the cleaning industry."

"This crap? Are you serious?" O'Neil nodded. "That's a little weird, isn't it?" O'Neil shrugged. "That'll be a short conversation on my end. What do you want to know?"

They talked for almost two hours, mostly as Reed had guessed, about the computer business. He didn't run out of questions but he was scheduled to clean one more office suite by morning. O'Neil asked for his phone number before he left and wondered if it would be all right if he called him in a day or two. He might have a few more questions for him.

"Sure thing," Reed said. "You thinking of branching out or something?"

"Something like that."

A kind of friendship had taken root between them during their talk and Reed was grateful for the sort of information O'Neil had given him. It also didn't hurt, he thought, to make a contact in the business. They shook hands again and he left.

O'Neil sat behind his desk in the chair Reed had occupied. He wanted to take some time to think about the most important thing he had realized about the cleaning business: that with little or no supervision, workers were given a set of keys and passwords to the security systems of the places they cleaned. Without those, they couldn't do their jobs. Who were these people, really?

CHAPTER SIX

O'Neil spent the hours between eight and ten at home making phone calls. He deliberately kept himself from dialing Marie Clayton's number, knowing from somewhere deep inside that he would not be able to talk to her. The more that he thought about what he could say the more numbing this inability became. The worst part, he thought, was that he didn't know whether or not he should be feeling ashamed of himself. There was no question he was feeling guilty.

Eventually he dragged himself upstairs and collapsed onto the bed, bothering only to kick off his shoes. He had been pushing his body, depriving himself of rest, wanting to get used to sleeping during the daylight. If things worked out as he was planning, he would need to be more alert come night time.

At 3:00 p.m. he awoke, momentarily disoriented by an early morning time and a bright afternoon sun. He rolled off the bed and exposed himself to a cold shower before ambling down the stairs to the coffee maker in the kitchen.

Hill had called and left a message on the machine around lunchtime. O'Neil thought about calling him back but decided against it. He didn't want to talk to him unless he actually found something out or needed some help. He was pretty sure he was going to need to break a law or two in order to penetrate Lankford's electronic maze and he didn't want Hill to know anything that could come back at him later if he could help it. He was willing to work with Hill but not *for* him.

O'Neil checked his watch and picked up the phone to dial Reed Larson. He had no idea if he would be waking him up or what his daily schedule was like but O'Neil had thought about how he wanted to proceed and was anxious to begin as soon as possible.

The phone rang just twice and Reed picked it up sounding as awake as he had been the night before. The fruits of youth, thought O'Neil. They exchanged small talk and O'Neil asked him if he had a name for breakfast at five in the afternoon.

"McDonald's is pretty much McDonald's anytime," said Reed.

O'Neil chuckled and asked if he would care to join him at a place more familiar to O'Neil's own culinary disposition, a small café near the University of Southern Florida on Fowler Avenue. "There's something I'd like to talk to you about along the lines of our conversation last night."

"Sure," Reed told him. They had gotten along well when they had met.

Reed appreciated the opportunity to meet someone who could conceivably give him a job one day. "Name the time."

They hung up after another minute or so of talking and O'Neil poured some water into the coffee maker as he thought about what he would need to tell Reed. He needed the man's help but he didn't want to lure him into something potentially dangerous just because it was convenient for him. He found what was left of the fresh coffee and spooned it into a filter. How bad could things get as long as they had the cops on their side, he wondered.

Sitting on the edge of the counter waiting for the warm aroma of the coffee to find its way across the kitchen he wondered why that last thought didn't make him feel any better than it did.

James Rooker didn't particularly care for computers, any more than he felt any great connection to large kitchen appliances or digital stereo components. But he knew a money making opportunity when he saw one and in the early eighties he jumped into the personal computer revolution with both feet. In those days, anyone hanging a sign on their front door that said "Computers for Sale" had to be either a buffoon or a total idiot not to make at least some money. James Rooker was neither. He made out quite well.

In fact, James Rooker was a shrewd if somewhat less than totally honest businessman who took full advantage of his customers' lack of technical sophistication. They were coming to him for expert advice and that's exactly what he would give them. It didn't bother him that at all that his recommendations were carefully designed to keep his customers one step behind the industry's leading edge. If they bought for tomorrow as well as today, where would his market for upgrades go?

Now, unfortunately, the market was maturing and people were no longer buying the hardware at the breakneck pace of even a few years ago. And when they were, as often as not they were buying through the mail or at these electronic superstore monstrosities that had sprung up like weeds after a Texas rainstorm. Smaller companies like Rooker's just couldn't compete with the lower prices these stores could offer through their "volume purchasing." Also, the average user had gotten much smarter and it became harder and harder to talk even the dumber ones into buying something they did not need or want.

But, as he had heard somewhere, within every crisis there lies an opportunity. One just had to be smart enough to find it. Rooker recognized that once all these companies had purchased their computers, they would be searching for ways to network them all together. The profit niche for the smaller operations like Rooker's would be the consulting fees he could charge to peddle the expertise that would make this possible. But first, of course, he needed to acquire some.

He found that to be fairly easy. He could take these young kids and their diplomas fresh from the local technical colleges and use them for the grunt work. They didn't have to be paid much since the competition for jobs was fierce and they had no real-world experience. The opportunity to be a professional and to gain that experience kept Rooker in a good supply of recruits. His turnover was inconvenient but that was a fairly easy price to pay.

The only remaining problem was one of attracting new customers. A sign on the door was no longer the most effective way of drawing in the desired clientele. And for some reason, word of mouth didn't seem to work for him the way it did for his competition. Questions concerning the quality of his work never entered his mind.

On the morning following the death of Tim Clayton, one of James Rooker's more prosperous rivals, he read the article written about the possible crime with a keen interest. Could it really have been an accident? Clayton had been something of a one man shop, he knew, providing the consulting services himself and contracting out any labor or installation work. It would seem, if viewed with the shrewd business-like mind of a James Edward Rooker, that a spate of potential customers had abruptly been made available. Deprived of their main source of data processing resources, Rooker figured that he was ideally suited to pick up where the unfortunate Mr. Clayton had left off. All he had to do was come up with an angle for making Clayton's customers see that, too.

What a way to start your day. He felt a little sorry for Clayton but on the other hand, he hadn't known him all that well. They had come in contact mostly when Rooker was trying to sell to one of Clayton's clients. It had usually been unsuccessful. Actually, it had always been unsuccessful but he could change all that now, he thought, if he could work quickly. He needed to come up with enough of a list of the orphaned businesses to give him a head start before they began looking elsewhere. If he did that, he could easily double the number of his own clients, he was sure. Opportunities like this didn't present themselves to James Rooker very often and this was certainly one he wouldn't dream of letting pass.

CHAPTER SEVEN

"No shit, you used to be a cop?"

O'Neil took a sip of coffee and nodded. "Yup. And now I'm a computer nerd. If you don't believe me I can show you my pocket protector."

Reed laughed. "No, I'll take your word for it." He pushed his plate aside to make room for his elbows. "So how'd you get out of being a cop? And into working with computers? Or shouldn't I ask?"

"No, that's all right," O'Neil said, signaling the waitress for more coffee before he started. "I was rather hoping you would, actually." He waited a moment while the woman filled his cup. He thanked her before she walked away.

"I think most cops could probably tell you a story like this one. This is only unique because it's mine. There are a lot of cases that come out the way they're supposed to, where you solve the crime, catch the crooks, and whatever passes for justice gets done. But in the end, when it's finished, nothing seems to have been fixed or made right. A lot of things turn out looking a lot worse than they had been before.

"There was a couple from Michigan, the Bickfords there name was, that packed their two little girls into the family station wagon and drove down here for two weeks of vacation. They were going to do the beaches, theme parks and all the usual Florida tourist things. On their way down, they drove through an ice storm in Kentucky and almost slid into the side of a tanker truck filled with liquid petroleum. They were a little freaked out over how their trip had almost ended and they decided to lay over for a day and give the ice a chance to melt. Recover their nerves a bit. They arrived in Tampa a day late and since they had missed their check-in date, their hotel had given away their room."

"They never called the hotel, said they'd be late?"

"Harold Bickford told me later that they had been so flustered after their near accident that they never thought of it. At least not until they were almost there. Anyway, the hotel was full and the Bickfords hadn't confirmed their reservation with a credit card so they were forced to look for another room. It took several hours and since they were well into losing the second day of their vacation, they took practically the first thing they could find. It was two weeks after Christmas, prime tourist season and there wasn't a whole lot available." He paused, looking through the plate glass window into the front parking lot. "It would have been better for the Bickfords if the whole damned city had been sold out."

"What happened?"

"Ramon Cruz and Bobby Padilla, two shitheels from Ybor City, decided to have a big night out. They scored a few rocks of crack cocaine, boosted a car, and for some unknown reason became fixated on Margot Bickford when they saw her sitting in the station wagon at a convenience store. Harold was inside paying for gas. They pulled up next to her and began propositioning her as if she were a hooker. When she told them she wasn't interested, Padilla told her that what she needed was a pimp and he dropped his pants and hung himself out the window so she could see his qualifications. The two little girls were asleep in the back seat but Margot was terrified they would wake up. Harold finished paying for the gas, came out of the store, and Cruz and Padilla took off. The Bickfords drove to yet another motel, this time one with an open room due to a last minute cancellation. They didn't know that Cruz and Padilla had followed them.

"The two of them sat in their stolen car, watching while Harold unloaded the station wagon he had parked in front of a ground level room. Margot put both girls to bed and began to undress so that she could take a hot shower before retiring for the night. You can probably guess where this is going."

"Not really. I'm trying not to think ahead."

"Are you okay hearing this stuff?"

"Beats me. I'm not usually squeamish or prone to nightmares if that's what you mean."

O'Neil nodded and picked at the cuticle of his left thumb with his other hand. "Cruz and Padilla, each holding a pistol and one of them with an eight inch hunting knife, kicked in the motel room door a short time later. They bound Harold and the children with nylon rope Padilla cut from the window blinds. Over the course of the next several hours they repeatedly raped Margot on one of the double beds and forced her to perform a variety of sexual acts while her family, bound and positioned on the other bed, were made to watch. Whenever Margot tried to fight them, one of the men would take the hunting knife over to the children and comb through their hair with the serrated edge of the knife.

"After Cruz and Padilla had had their fun, they each took their pistols and shot Margot once in the head. One of them then shot Harold twice in the chest and the other one shot him in the groin. The little girls, although spattered with blood and pieces of their mother, were never physically harmed."

O'Neil stopped talking. Reed had slumped back into the booth and was slowly shaking his head.

And the children? He looked at O'Neil.

"The girls were six and seven," he said, reading the young man's mind. "You want to take a minute? Wash your face or something?"

Reed nodded and made his way off to the men's room to find a sink and some cold water.

I've put him into shock, thought O'Neil as he drank more coffee. The waitress appeared on her own with a refill. "Thanks," he told her.

A few minutes later Reed came back to the table, dabbing moisture from his face with a paper towel.

"Doing all right?" O'Neil asked him.

"I'm okay," said Reed. "You know, it's one thing seeing stuff like that in movies or even on the news but you were actually there. You can feel it more somehow, listening to you talk about it." He reached for his own cup and took a long sip. "If that were me in that motel room, and two guys were doing that to my wife, and my kids...."

"You would have had to sit there and take it, just like Harold Bickford did."

"Man." Reed shook his head slowly and looked up at O'Neil. "I can't even imagine it. Not how I would feel. How did you deal with things like that?"

"That's the point of the story. I'm sorry, I should have thought more about it before I told it to you like that."

"No, it's okay."

"Then I may as well finish it. You deal with it by turning off part of you. You deaden inside. You stop feeling certain kinds of things."

"Like what?"

"Compassion, for one. You want to help the victims, but you really can't. You want to kill the asshole scumbags that do these things, but you can't do that either. So you find yourself having to accept that this is the way it is, the way it has been, and the way it always will be. Sometimes all we can be are the cleaning crew ourselves."

"But you're not like that anymore?"

"I try not to be, not since I quit being a cop. I noticed that ordinary people, people who weren't cops, could still go to sleep at night not overly troubled by what kind of stink hole we've turned this world into. And I didn't think I could make that change. I couldn't make it better and still do my job. My wife wanted to leave me. I decided I wanted to be like everybody else. Right about this time, something else happened.

"There was a detective that had been around forever. Eddie Rossenburg. We all liked him, looked up to him, really. He hit retirement, went home, and two weeks later killed himself with his own gun. He'd been shot at lord knows how many times but never once in all those years had he ever been hit or wounded. Until he did it himself.

"All those years on the job, you think he makes it and just like that, he pulls his own curtain. Game over. Shocked everybody. We talked about it for weeks, wondered why he did it, went through the whole nine yards. But nobody seemed to catch on. Except me. At least I thought I did. I told myself I knew exactly why he did it. And I knew that even at my relatively young age, I had already had enough."

"Are you okay with that now? Or are there parts of it you miss?"

"I don't like quitting. I didn't get into it on a lark, I got into it because I believed in the job. I respected it, like most of the other guys. The going got a little tough for me and I left, but everybody else stayed. They took it. I don't know how to explain it, but quitting was both the hardest thing I've ever done as well as the most necessary, for lack of a better word."

"How did it work out? How are you today?"

"I'm happy, I live a reasonably normal life. Katy came back. There's still a chunk missing, I think, something I'll never get back. And every couple of days I need to spend a little time pushing some of the old things back into their little holes. I know I'll never read a newspaper again."

They sat in silence for a few minutes, O'Neil sipping his coffee, Reed gazing through the window at the small clouds of fog forming over the water-filled ditch along the highway.

"So tell me what happened to Cruz and Padilla."

"Plea bargained down to avoid the chair. They're in for life. 'No possibility of parole.'"

"It shouldn't be that easy for them. How about the family?"

"That's harder." O'Neil thought a moment before he answered. "This sounds cold but I don't know and at this point especially I don't want to know. I can tell you the facts of the case, I can tell you how it happened, but there's no way I can make you understand how it felt to be part of it. The anger, the impotence, all of it just gets so big, makes you feel so ineffectual...."

"The pressure is enormous. You can't sleep, your health goes to hell, and you go on a diet of straight booze and Rolaids. But always, deep down at the very heart of it, you know that no matter how lousy, how ugly, how bad you feel about all of it, it's nothing but a small pimple on a fly's ass compared to what Harold Bickford and his daughters had to go through on that night."

O'Neil turned to look out the window. "If that had been me, if that had been my wife, the last thing in the world that I would have wanted was to have lived through it."

O'Neil slowly took another sip from his cup. He was drinking the coffee out of blind habit rather than thirst. The act of picking up the cup and putting it back down was a thin tether to the present. When he spoke again Reed could barely hear the words. "I can never think about the daughters. I push them off into a dark place and I don't think about them. They were never there, they couldn't have existed."

Reed wouldn't have spoken then, but O'Neil looked at him, gray eyes staring as if asking, is that so terrible? "Maybe that's just sane," he offered.

O'Neil let his focus sink downward into the table somewhere beyond. As Reed looked dumbly at the top of his head, he heard, "Maybe it is."

They sat that way for a much shorter time than it seemed, just a minute really, before O'Neil straightened his back and raised his hand to signal the waitress. Reed could see new lines on his face that he hadn't noticed were there before. "You still live this stuff, don't you?"

"First half of show and tell is over. I'll buy you a piece of Key Lime pie and tell you the other part of the story."

"I hope it has a happier ending."

O'Neil spoke to the waitress for a moment, than she was gone. "Actually, Reed, it doesn't. This is what I really wanted to talk to you about. My best friend was killed last weekend."

Reed stared at O'Neil, waiting for some kind of punch line. After a minute he said, "You're serious?"

"Yes, I am."

"Holy shit."

"I'd like to tell you about what happened to me after I quit being a cop, how I got into the computer business. At the end of it I'm going to ask you two things, neither one dependent on the other."

"What's that?"

"I'm going to ask for your help about what happened to my friend, and I'm going to offer you a job."

"A job? But I don't know anything."

"I'll teach you. You can come work for me and we'll see how you do."

"I don't know what to say. I'd love it. And of course I'll help you with– what happened. Just tell me what you want me to do."

Two slices of fruitless pie and plastic whipped cream arrived at the table as O'Neil told Reed all about Tim Clayton and what he had meant to him. He told him about the murder and his later conversation with Hill and Fetterman. At the end of it, pie untouched, Reed said, "I'm hooked. I don't know why you picked me or what I can really accomplish, but I'll do anything you think that I can."

O'Neil reached across the table and slapped Reed in the shoulder. The gesture was in some way both a thank you and an acknowledgment. "Wait until you hear what I have planned first."

"How bad can it be? Just tell me I don't have to dress up as a woman. I'd really hate that."

O'Neil smiled back. "That's Plan B. Let's just hope that Plan A is the one that works."

CHAPTER EIGHT

The air temperature was in the low seventies, barely warm enough for na-
tives to take their shirts off. On the beach, where the heat reflecting off the
sand made it hotter, bright red and white islands of tourists burned slowly
throughout the morning. A group of frolicking Canadians were the only
ones enjoying the water as the Gulf of Mexico was still cool, just beginning
its springtime climb. In a few weeks it would become nearly eighty degrees.

"Oh my God."

"What is it?" O'Neil asked. "You got something?"

"We're gonna need wider angle lenses on these things."

"What are you talking about?" He reached over and took the binoculars
from Reed's eyes. "Let me look."

"Do you see her?"

O'Neil worked the focus knob with his finger. "Oh my God."

In the binoculars was a very large woman wearing green pants and a short-
sleeved shirt. She was pointing with one arm and seemed to be giving directions to the person she was speaking with.

"She has the enormous biceps of the truly fat."

O'Neil studied her carefully through the binoculars. "You don't see many
people of that size in Florida."

"That's because animals that big generally became extinct about 250 million years ago," said Reed. "Hell, you need to put down the binoculars and
back up a ways if you want to see all of her at once."

O'Neil started walking toward the beach. "Not if we want to talk to her.
Try to be nice. Or I'll tell her you don't have a girlfriend."

Reed jogged a little in the sand to catch up. "Wait a minute, you mean that's
who we're looking for?"

"It's a little hard to tell, but I think so. If it is, she's put on a lot of weight.
But I think it's her."

They made their way across the sand from the wooden hut that served as
refreshment stand, gift shop, and changing room for the south end of
Clearwater Beach. Both men were wearing shorts and carrying their shoes
in their hands while black-headed laughing gulls swooped and glided at eye
level all around them. "I'm always worried those things will fly into my
head," Reed said. "That's why I never buy food here."

The woman was spreading a double-sized bed sheet across the sand,
weighing the corners down with items taken from a large canvas beach tote,
as they approached. When she saw Reed and O'Neil, she immediately

dropped her massive body into a sitting position on the center of the sheet and clenched a meaty forearm around her bag.

O'Neil slowed his pace as he approached the edge of the sheet. "That's you, isn't it, Lu?"

She looked up at him and shook her head slowly. "Last time they took me out of here when I didn't want to go it took twelve of them and a flatbed truck. You two don't look like you got that much firepower."

Reed looked away to keep from showing her his grin. Now that she was sitting down, he thought, how could she possibly get up without that much help?

O'Neil dropped down to his knees so the woman wouldn't have to squint into the sun. "Relax, Lu, we don't want to take you anywhere. We just want to talk to you for a minute."

"Yeah, I've heard that one before." She made a snorting sound through her nose. A sea gull landed on the beach next to O'Neil and began to walk along the edge of the sheet. "I know this game. Just what is it you want?"

"Well, the first thing is I want to know if you remember who I am."

She wrinkled her forehead in mock surprise and waved the back of her hand at him. "Remember you? You're some cop, aren't you? Or isn't that right? What's your name?"

"Frankie—"

"O'Neil," she said, raising her voice and nodding her head. "I do remember you. It's going back a few years but yeah, you're the same guy. I heard you quit being a cop, though. What's the deal?"

"I'm not a cop any more, that's true. My friend isn't one, either. We really do just want to talk to you."

Reed nodded to her in what he hoped was a reassuring way. He couldn't get over the size of the woman's neck; it was as big around as one of his thighs.

"Well, hell, as long as you're not going to bust me for anything, have a seat." She waved O'Neil down. "But you," she said to Reed. "Sit over here a little closer." She patted a spot on the sheet next to her and smiled sweetly, her suspicion melting away.

Reed wasn't sure what he should do. Was she serious? The woman didn't even know him. He looked at O'Neil who nodded at him, then moved to take the offered seat.

Uncomfortable, he sat down next to the large woman, carefully avoiding any contact with the spread of her body. Maybe this won't be so bad, he thought. I just don't want to have to touch her.

Without warning, Lu unwrapped her left arm from around her bag and swung it out and backwards toward Reed's head. He ducked as fast as he

could but the meaty hand caught him squarely above the right ear. If he had-
n't seen her swing and start to move, the blow would have taken his head
off. As it was, his movement plus the contact sent him rolling off the sheet
and into the sand. His ears were ringing as he sat up holding his head.

"Tell your boyfriend, O'Neil, that it's not a good idea to laugh at people
where they can see them. I'm fat, I know, but I'm not blind. Or stupid. Now
tell me what it is you wanted to talk to me about or leave me alone."

O'Neil looked over at Reed who was sitting slumped forward, a look of
painful surprise still on his face. "He's sorry, Lu, he just doesn't know any
better. Do you, Reed?"

"Obviously not," he heard himself say through the background noise in
his head. "I apologize, ma'am, for my lack of sensitivity as well as for my poor
manners."

"Nice comeback," she told him. "Go ahead and relax, I'm not going to hit
you again." Reed told her thank you and sat back in the sand, careful to be
at least an arm's length away. He was going to have to be gentle for the next
week whenever he used a comb.

"I need to find someone with the particular skill set you used to employ
in your work," O'Neil said to the woman. He was trying to be tactful; he
needed Lu to put aside her natural distrust if he had any hopes of her helping him.

"Uh huh," said Lu. When they had met, Mary Lu Bates, now known mostly
as "MamaLu" Bates, had been scraping out a living for herself picking the
pockets of the tourists that annually peppered the sands of the beaches. It
hadn't been something that she'd get rich at. In this kind of setting, there
sometimes just weren't that many actual pockets to pick. Still, she had skill
and she could afford to be a regular at most of the restaurants near the beach
where the tourists went to spend their money.

She hadn't been all that ambitious, and that's not something that helps in
any line of work. She liked the beach and if she became too prolific she'd attract too much attention, something a lone pickpocket needed to avoid. She
merely worked enough to support her relatively modest lifestyle: A single
bedroom efficiency apartment one block off the beach and freedom from the
stress of deciding what she would do if she had to choose to make an honest living.

All that had changed one day when she met Carl Pantucket and fell in love.
Carl was a visionary, she thought, a self-styled entrepreneur with small
dreams and a big mouth. To his credit, the fact that he hadn't been able to
cut it in the professional world did no damage whatsoever to his self-image,
which consistently buoyed his ego with pictures of a misunderstood man
who's time was simply yet to come. Carl's belief was such that when he in-

herited $150,000.00 of his mother's estate, he merely considered it as part of that time coming due. Justification for a life of meaningless failures. So he graciously accepted the money and did what he thought a great man like himself should be doing. He bought an imitation Italian suit and opened a donut shop on the beach.

The shop was on the same block as MamaLu's little apartment and one day, when she stopped to buy an éclair, they struck up a conversation and eventually, after many more pastries, fell in love. He was the only man she had ever told about what she did for a living. This intrigued Carl because lately the donut shop hadn't been doing too well. Business decreased dramatically in the winter months which unfortunately coincided with the operation of Tampa Bay Downs in Oldsmar. With his newfound money and lifestyle, he had quickly developed a love for fast horses. It was his misfortune that he only bet on the slow ones.

After an intense period of romance, which included all the free donuts either of them cared to eat, Carl one day was forced to declare himself bankrupt. A donut shop without customers and a bookie with a mean streak forced Carl to realize that, while it had looked promising for a while, his time had not yet actually come. He approached Lu with the idea of her picking pockets again, maybe bankrolling a franchising venture for a string of "Carl's Deluxe Donut Shoppes" up and down both sides of the peninsula. Lu finally admitted she knew a loser when she saw one. It just took her longer sometimes with people she cared about.

She threw him out. It hurt, but she knew it was for the best. Carl accepted it stoically, as if he'd been through something like it before, kissed her on the nose and announced that he would be moving to Minneapolis. She asked, why Minneapolis, and he said he'd heard they had good welfare and unemployment programs up there and it was important for him to make a positive start.

Months of depression followed. Lu had never been in love before and she had no idea that the fallout could sometimes be more intense than the passion. Like a lot of people, she turned to the solace she found in the refrigerator. Already blossoming after spending months hanging out in a donut shop, things for Lu went from bad to worse. It became evident that a person of her newly acquired stature simply didn't fare well in an illegal occupation that depended on one's ability to be quick and sure with one's movements. She had sized herself out of the market and now she needed a career change.

The beach itself provided the answer, as MamaLu had come to believe it did for most things. She became what she liked to call a professional beachcomber. Rather than scavenge the sands for interesting shells or misplaced

pocket change, she developed a talent for observing beachgoers and the vehicles they arrived in. She would wait for them to put their money and keys
in their shoes and then go swimming or walking down the beach. She would
switch the keys with a dummy set and then raid the car. It required the development of a new set of skills but she was proud that she could teach herself some new tricks at this particular stage in her life.

She was doing well, actually, a lot better than when she had picked pockets. People tended to leave more in their cars than they brought with them
down to the beach, especially in the way of ladies' purses. She didn't have
to pull as many jobs as she used to in order to make her quota.

Life was getting better in these post-Carl days, she thought. Until now anyway, when an ex-cop turns up on her figurative door step asking her questions. He had busted her once when she worked a Buccaneer game at the
stadium in Tampa during one of her rare forays inland. He had been decent
enough about it at the time, she remembered. But a cop was still a cop. And
what, she wondered, did he know about her current activities?

"Why are you coming to me?" she asked O'Neil.

"I need some help with a problem I have. You were, or even are for all I
know, a professional pickpocket. I need to find someone with that kind of
talent."

"Is there money in it?"

"Of course."

"How much?"

"Well, that depends," O'Neil told her, "if you're interested in the job yourself or if you've got somebody you're going to recommend."

"Just what is this 'job' you're talking about?"

Reed looked at O'Neil and wondered if it was a good idea to tell this
woman anything. Although he had faith in her ability to beat the hell out
of anybody foolish enough to get within arm's reach, he just couldn't imagine her being subtle enough to take somebody's wallet out of their pocket
without them being aware of it. It's O'Neil's call, he thought. He edged another few inches away, just in case she decided she knew what he was thinking again.

"I need someone to lift a set of keys off someone who cleans buildings,"
said O'Neil.

The truth be told, MamaLu had serious doubts about her own ability to
perform like she had in the past. But a set of keys? Hell, that's how she'd been
making her living the past six months.

"Then they've got to be put back," O'Neil added.

That's a little different, she thought, but still she should be able to figure
out something that wouldn't be too difficult. "So this is like some janitor,

huh? Where does he keep the keys, in his pocket, on his belt, or where?"

"We don't know yet, but we'll find out and tell you before you actually have to do the work."

"What happens to the keys before they get put back?"

"We make copies of a few of them."

MamaLu laughed and shook her head. "I never thought I'd see the day," she said. "Did you figure out a way to beat the system, or what? Why does an ex-cop want to take off a building with the help of a professional thief? What's the big score here, O'Neil?"

"Uh uh," he told her. "There's no score other than the keys, and the 'why' is not part of the deal. If you're interested, tell me how much it will take."

No score. Yeah, right. This guy's boosting keys for the fun of it. He must be on to some seriously big shit, being an ex-cop and all. "Five grand," she said.

Reed almost gagged and laughed despite himself. Five thousand dollars? Maybe she could do the job but for that kind of money they ought to be able to figure out something cheaper. He watched O'Neil, who hadn't flinched. He must know what he's doing, Reed thought.

For the next five minutes, MamaLu and O'Neil dickered over a price. They finally agreed on a sum of two thousand dollars for one night's work. MamaLu also agreed to make the copies herself. It had become a recent hobby of hers, she told them; she'd be glad to do it for an extra ten percent.

She held her hand out to O'Neil, who reached forward and shook it. Reed stood up and began walking away. There was no way he was going to let her grab hold of his hand. She blew a kiss at the back of his head and called, "See you around, sweetie."

O'Neil told her they'd be in touch in a week or so and hurried to catch up to his friend. "That's done," he said.

"You trust that over-inflated Rocky wannabe to do this thing right? You think she's capable?"

"I think so. That should be good money for her and I haven't been able to figure out a better way to get at those keys. Back when I knew her, she could do some amazing things with those hands. By the way, how's your head?"

On the beach, MamaLu peeled off her shirt to reveal a massive yellow halter top. She laid back on her sheet and thought about taking the day off. These guys had to be after something big. They had to. Ex-cops wouldn't just turn into felons without looking at a huge payoff. And who better to get away with a crime than a criminal who used to be a policeman? Yes, sir, today was definitely going to be a vacation day. In fact, it would probably be best to be extra careful for the time being. She wouldn't want to get pinched now and spoil things.

She lay back in the sun. There was some serious planning to be done.

An hour later, O'Neil and Reed were sitting in O'Neil's kitchen sipping fresh squeezed orange juice from a container in the refrigerator. "So the next thing we've got to do is get me inside Lankford's office," Reed said.

"Right. And I'm hoping that won't prove to be too difficult. The more legitimate we can make it appear, the better off we'll be if something goes wrong. I have no idea how many times we're going to need to be in there."

"But if they don't store any data in the office, what is there to go after?"

"Even if we assumed they did store their actual data onsite, we probably wouldn't want it. They probably use an encryption scheme that we couldn't break and we'd just be wasting our time."

"The cops can't bug the phone lines that connect them to the Internet?"

"They could probably tap into those, but you've got to remember that they have a couple of hundred computers in the place, all doing the things normal computers in brokerage houses do. All that traffic across a network cable is broken up into many, many tiny little pieces. We'd have to locate the ones we're interested in, find a way to string them together, and even then I assume the data they'd contain would be encrypted."

Reed pulled a chair out from the small kitchen table and sat down. "So what do we do?"

"Well, think about it. Where is the one place on the computer that whatever you're working on is displayed for you, completely undisguised, in plain English?"

Reed arched his eyebrows. "The screen?"

"Usually referred to as the monitor, but yes, the screen. You've got to remember, the computer itself provides the security measures, human beings aren't that smart. And if I'm going to tell the computer to do something, how do I do it?"

"You type it in at the keyboard."

"Exactly. *After* you type it in, the computer can encrypt it or translate it or do whatever you want. But I'm willing to bet that they type their information in the way the see it—in plain English."

"So how do we get at it?"

"In a way, we're going to bug the monitor and keyboard. People always move to safeguard their computers, they rarely if ever think of the peripherals. At least that's what I hope."

"Do you know how to do that?"

O'Neil nodded. "The keyboard, yes, the monitor, not yet but it shouldn't be too difficult to figure out. What we've got to do in the meantime is get you in at Lankford's so we've got the physical access we need."

Reed tried to stifle a yawn. It was barely one in the afternoon but his internal clock said he should still be sleeping. "So I quit my job and then what? Apply at, what is it, 'Bay Area Cleaning Service'?"

"That's it. That part of it is all up to you."

"Well, like I told you, it shouldn't be hard to catch on with them doing something. Cleaning services are almost always shorthanded, people just up and quit all the time. It's not that easy being a vampire when everyone else you know lives their lives during the day. But there's no way of knowing how much work they'll give me, or where it'll be."

"That's all right," said O'Neil. "Just beg off Wednesdays and Fridays if you can. That's when Lankford's offices get their weekly cleaning."

"How'd you find that out?" Reed asked.

"That was easy," O'Neil told him. "I went to their office and saw the decal on the door for their security monitoring company. I called them up, told them I was a cop investigating phony cleaning service break-ins, and they told me. If you know how to make people think you're a cop, they'll tell you almost anything."

"Phony cleaning service break-ins?"

"Get out of here so I can take a nap. I want to do some work tonight and Tim's funeral is tomorrow in Sarasota."

Technical expertise had never been one of James Rooker's strong points in business. That honor would have to go to his silver tongue and his willingness to manufacture the truth whenever he needed it. With these skills, he felt he was ideally suited for the consulting business.

He had been able to compile a list of eight companies he knew had been clients of the late Tim Clayton. This morning he had begun visiting some of them in person. He found that it was much easier to feign sincerity when you were actually face to face with people. Rooker considered that a lesson to be learned by careful watching of interminable hours of political election coverage on television.

So far, it had been a good day. He had been to two of the companies on the list and both, after expressing disappointment and sorrow at the news of Tim Clayton's death, had promised to call Rooker the next time they needed something done. He had no reason to doubt their veracity but he figured he would find out if they meant it when the virus he had left behind on their systems kicked in.

The third place on his list was called The Walter Lankford Company. They were into financial services or stock brokering or something, he didn't care what it was. He presented himself to the receptionist and asked if it would be possible to speak to the network or computer administrator. Before she had a chance to discourage him with their 'No Soliciting' policy, he added that he was with the company that had installed their computer network. She thought it was odd that she hadn't seen him before and that Rooker didn't know Mr. Darwin by name, but she'd let Darwin deal with that. She wasn't paid to be anyone's bouncer.

Ronald Darwin appeared from around a corner made by an arrangement of those modular walls that were used to create small cubicles for the lower level employees. He was smartly dressed and he came straight to Rooker and held out his hand. Rooker shook it while introducing himself.

"What can I do for you, Mr. Rooker?" asked Darwin.

"I wonder if we could go somewhere and sit down. I have some news that concerns your computer networks that I'd like to share with you."

Darwin gave him a curious stare and motioned him to two chairs set along the wall next to a cherry coffee table with a gray marble top. Rooker estimated that the chairs couldn't have cost less than five hundred dollars apiece. He wouldn't even guess at the table. "Does this have something to do with the death of Tim Clayton?"

So they were already aware of it, Rooker thought. That should be all right, as long as they hadn't already found someone to replace him. Rooker nodded and began to explain how shortly before his death Tim had approached Rooker about the possibility of combining their two companies for the sole purpose of offering a stronger, more competitive service. He had felt that the two of them each brought different things to the table and thought that it would be beneficial to the existing customers of both companies if the merger actually took place.

"Tim never mentioned anything about this to us," said Darwin.

No, he wouldn't have. They had both been waiting until they had worked out all of the details. Unfortunately, their conversations had been interrupted by the unwelcome and untimely event of Tim's death. A terrible, terrible tragedy.

"Do you have any idea why this would have happened to Tim?"

"Me?" said Rooker. "I have no idea whatsoever. This whole thing comes as quite the shock. He was a good man. One of the absolute best." At least as far as Rooker knew. He'd only met the man a couple of times in passing. Darwin seemed satisfied with the story he had told him.

"What can I do for you today, Mr. Rooker?"

Here we go, thought Rooker. He explained why he was there this morning, at no charge of course, to take an informal survey of the computer networks and systems that had been installed by Tim's company. Then, in the future, should The Walter Lankford Company require additional services, Rooker would be in the best possible position to efficiently accommodate their needs and requests. It would just take a few minutes and all he would need was a password to get on the network and an open terminal.

In these early days of networked computers, actual experts were few and far between, with very few less than giant-sized companies having their own in-house specialists. This was a golden age for independent consultants. Because there were so few internal staff, businesses were quite used to allowing outside people full access so they could do what they needed. The end users were barely proficient in their applications; the behind the scenes stuff was so much science fiction.

Darwin agreed to let Rooker take a look. He wasn't sure he completely believed the man's story, he seemed too showy where Tim had been very down to earth, but he wanted to watch him closely and see exactly what he did. He led Rooker past the receptionist to his own cubicle, a tidy arrangement of technical manuals and trade magazines. He indicated that Rooker should use his own chair and parked it in front of the computer monitor on his desk.

From his briefcase, Rooker removed a form he had generated last night on his laser printer and proceeded to fill in the appropriate blanks. He entered several commands into the computer and was disappointed to find a very effective anti-virus program. The little trick he had played on his first two stops this morning wouldn't work here.

The man Darwin was standing over his shoulder and watching him like a hawk. If Rooker had any chance of winning their business, he would have to appear competent at the keyboard. He began to move to different areas of the network file server's hard disk and call up lists of the individual files. "I'm checking out the directory structure," he said to Darwin. "That tells me a number of things, like if your storage has been set up logically, if you have enough space allocated for your users, things like that. I found thirty-seven installations of Doom on one drive at a client's last week."

"Doom?"

"A computer game. Takes up a lot of hard disk space and bogs down the network when people start playing it. On company time, even."

Darwin grunted. "Can you check for it here?"

"Sure," Rooker said, and he typed in a "dir" command that would search all the subdirectories on the network drive for the program. After a minute, three instances were listed.

"Want me to get rid of them?" Rooker asked.

"No," Darwin said, making notes. "I'll take care of it."

Rooker was about out of things to do when he noticed something strange. There was a directory entry that appeared empty yet at the same time the computer was showing it as occupying some space, as if it contained some files. Ah, now this is clever, he thought as it dawned on him what someone had done. This entry that appears as a directory with no files is really a file by itself. It wasn't actually a directory at all.

Darwin was still in the cubicle but had stepped back to have a conversation with someone who had come looking for him. Rooker quickly slipped the blank floppy disk he usually carried in his shirt pocket into the drive on the computer. Within twenty seconds he had made a copy of the file and returned the disk to its home in his shirt. Rooker just couldn't resist anything this clever. Something worth hiding was too often worth money.

He glanced over his shoulder. Darwin was still speaking with the other person and had been joined by another. Rooker deftly typed in a command that displayed the contents of the mystery file on the screen. It was a short list of four names followed by a twelve digit hyphenated number, something he hadn't seen before.

"Are you almost through here, Mr. Rooker? I'm afraid I have to get back to work."

Rooker cleared the screen and swivelled around in the chair. If Darwin suspected anything untoward, he gave no sign. "Of course. I've got what I need, Mr. Darwin." He stood and handed the man another business card. "If anything comes up in the future, I look forward to the opportunity of doing business with you." They shook hands and Darwin showed him to the door.

Outside, in his car, Rooker sat and adjusted the air conditioning so it blew across his face. For some reason he tended to perspire when he got excited. He had only had a quick look at the names in the computer file, but something about one or two of them had struck him as familiar. He touched the plastic disk in his pocket to reassure himself it was still there.

Obviously, someone had tried to disguise the existence of this file. If he hadn't been so familiar with how some viruses make files appear after they had been infected, he never would have noticed it. Had it been Clayton? And if so, why? Rooker put the car in gear and slowly began to drive. Somehow he had to find a way to identify those four names.

CHAPTER NINE

The church parking lot was full but not overflowing. O'Neil sat in his car and watched the people entering through a set of iron-bound doors with inlays of stained glass. He recognized a lot of them as people he knew, although most not well. It was amazing how many friends a good man has when he dies, he thought. He wondered how many would show up at his funeral.

He wasn't ready to go inside yet. Funerals were for the living, not the dead, and whatever catharsis they provided he had gone though during the flight of a small airplane and a night spent on his little boat. Still, he wasn't ready to say goodbye, not while whoever had killed his friend went unaccountable. You don't just walk away from something like this, smooth the hurt over with a funeral service and a wreath and get on with your life. At least O'Neil couldn't, not in a situation like this.

He thought about Tim's wife, Marie. He still hadn't spoken with her since the murder but he knew he would have to today. God, what she must be going through. O'Neil felt a little guilty for not spending some time with her, but he knew she was being well taken care of. And although he hadn't spoken with Katy since that night when he called at her sister's, he knew that his wife would have taken the time to get down here and see Marie.

"Fuck it," he said angrily and reached forward to start the car. He drove slowly out of the parking lot. It's Tim I want to see, not his family and a bunch of his goddamned friends.

His mood, not good to begin with, turned bitter and dark as he drove toward the cemetery where Tim's body would be buried. Alone with the demons in his mind and the ghosts in the ground, he would wait until everyone else showed up.

The cemetery itself was an old one, but it was nice. O'Neil wondered if there was such a thing as a new cemetery; he had never heard of someone buying land and starting one.

Large oak trees provided a measure of relief at sporadic intervals from the Florida sunshine. The plot awaiting Tim Clayton touched a small patch of the shade offered by an ancient scarlet oak. Not mindful of his black cotton suit, O'Neil sat with his back against the trunk of the great tree, careful to check for ants. Surprisingly, there didn't seem to be any.

He sat that way for two hours, his mind drifting over mostly nothing as he contemplated the hole in the ground that would accept the body of his friend. Absurdly, he wondered what they did with the soil that would be displaced by the presence of the casket.

Eventually the long train of cars arrived and quiet mourners began to make the slow twenty yard walk along a gravel path toward the plot. Pallbearers carried the casket from the hearse and placed it on the belts that would lower it into the ground, to be buried beneath sandy dirt and bittersweet memories. O'Neil stood and brushed pieces of dried grass from his trousers. Without removing his Carerra sunglasses, he moved to the rear of the gathering crowd and tried to disappear.

It didn't work. A gentle pull at his elbow and he turned to find the veiled face of Marie Clayton looking up at his. "Frankie," she said.

Around them, the other mourners eased away slowly, allowing the two of them the grace of some privacy. "Hello, Marie." He reached for her and she came into his arms for a brief embrace. They held each other for several breaths until Marie backed away and took hold of O'Neil's wrists.

"I was going to call you," he said.

"I know you were. I talked to Katy. She said you were taking it hard."

"All of us are, Marie." O'Neil couldn't help scanning the crowd.

"She's not here. She said she didn't want to get in your way. Are things okay with you two?"

Good God, O'Neil thought. With all her problems she's worried about my marriage. "We're doing fine, Marie. Really, we are."

She nodded and looked down. "I watched for you at the service but I didn't see you. It was beautiful."

"I'm afraid I only made it as far as the parking lot."

"Oh, God, Frankie," she said and moved herself closer again. Her hair smelled like salty tears and lilacs. "What happened?"

What could he tell her? Instead of talking, he concentrated on holding her tightly.

"I know you want to ask," she said into his shoulder. "And I want to tell you. But if he was in any trouble, he never mentioned anything to me about it. Nothing at all. I have no idea why anybody would have wanted to do this to him."

O'Neil shushed her, told her she didn't have to say anything. "I'll be all right," she said. She let O'Neil go and stepped backwards, dabbing her eyes with a balled up handkerchief. "He loved you, you know. He said you and he should have been brothers."

Emotion welled up in O'Neil's eyes and he struggled to contain it behind the lenses of his glasses. We were brothers. Marie reached forward and held one of his hands. "I have to go," she said. "Promise me you'll come down to dinner soon."

O'Neil tried his best to manage a nod.

"Promise," she repeated.

"Yes, I will," he half croaked. Marie nodded and turned to make her way to the side of the casket which hung, poised for eternity, above its grave.

Somewhere in front of him, a priest from the church began a prayer. Without listening to the words, he let his mind slip into the cadence of the speech as the rest of the group joined in.

His peace only lasted a few minutes. A gruff whisper erupted in his left ear. "Something wrong with your phone you don't return your calls, O'Neil?"

"Hill." O'Neil turned his head and looked at the detective. There were breakfast stains on his tie but at least he had managed a black suit. Fetterman stood behind him, an indecipherable grin plastered across his lips.

"I'm not too happy about this lack of communication. I thought we had an understanding going, that we're working on the same team."

"Take it easy, Hill." He stepped away from the funeral so as not to disturb the ritual with their conversation. "Things have been a little hard lately. It hasn't been all that easy to concentrate on things."

"And in the meantime you want us to sit back and wait for you to feel all better before we move ahead on this thing."

"Give me a fucking break, Hill. This is the goddamn funeral of my best friend and you're here busting my balls. If you were a little more human and not so much of a baboon, you might understand what the hell I've been going through."

That had the effect on Hill that O'Neil had been trying for. The detective looked at his partner then brought both hands up to his throat to fix an imaginary problem with his tie.

"All right, O'Neil." He backed off. "But better sooner than later, you know what I'm saying?"

Yes, I know what you're saying, O'Neil told him. "I've been working on a few things but I need some more time to put them together. When I do I'll call you so we can talk about how to use them to get at Lankford."

"You sound just like your dead buddy. Just be sure to call soon. We've got some other avenues we're looking into."

"Do you have more to go on?"

Hill sent a thin stream of saliva squirting through the space between his two front teeth into the soft grass between his own feet. "Not really. We cleared the brothers who found the body and we haven't been able to track the plane. Might have been a smuggling plane on its way out of the country. Who knows?" He motioned to Fetterman with his head and they started to walk off toward the lines of parked cars. "Clayton had valium in his blood, too. A lot of it. We're checking his medical records. We'll be waiting for your phone call. See you at the reception."

The burial ceremony broke up a few minutes later, most of the words had already been spoken at the church. Several people found their way to O'Neil and they shared their condolences and asked if he would be going to the reception after the service. It was being held at someone's house in Bradenton and was on O'Neil's way back to Tampa. "No," he told them. He wouldn't be going to any reception. He had work to get to. He didn't speak again to Marie.

On the ninety minute drive back to Tampa, he found himself thinking about Hill and Fetterman. If you don't have any new clues, he thought, just what 'other avenues' are you pursuing?

There was a message from Reed on the answering machine when O'Neil got home. He had gotten the job with Bay Area Cleaning but he wouldn't find out what they wanted his schedule to be for another day or two. He'd check back later to see what O'Neil wanted him to do next.

O'Neil pressed the button to reset the tape and walked into the room he used for an office when he worked at home. So far, so good, he thought. But the next step is up to me.

He hung his jacket over the back of his chair and removed his tie as he waited for his computer to boot up. He had a lot of programming to do before they were ready for Lankford and even then it would be a crap shoot. He had no illusions about what they were doing. Whether they were successful or not he knew what the consequences would be if they were caught. He wondered if Tim Clayton had known, too.

Writing a computer program can be a grueling, demanding task that often requires long periods of solitude and intense concentration. It is an uncommon mix of technical skill and artistic creativity that turns long hours into brief minutes, drawing the programmer deep into a place far separated from the world around him.

Alone in his home office, O'Neil had tapped into this electronic Nirvana and for the first time in days had not been consciously aware of the terrible events that had recently affected his life. The afternoon had raced by at light speed, blurred but productive, and he had made good progress on the program he needed for Lankford's.

The phone on his desk rang just after seven o'clock. O'Neil's mind jerked back to real time as he reached for a pencil and wildly jotted a note to himself so he wouldn't lose his current thought. He picked up the phone on the fourth ring and said hello.

"Hey, bud, it's me." Reed. "What's up, were you sleeping?"

O'Neil rubbed his eyes as if he had been. "No, I'm just here coding away."

"Good, I'm glad to hear I'm not the only one getting things done. How was the funeral?"

"Fine," he said. He told him he hadn't seen much of the ceremony, but he had put in an appearance and spoken to Tim's widow. That was enough. "Hill and Fetterman were there, too."

"Your two cop friends?"

"Yeah. They were leaning on me pretty heavily to tell them what I was doing for them. They don't know about you and they certainly don't know about Lu, and that's the way I want to keep it. I didn't tell them much."

"How come? They're going to get at you sooner or later, aren't they?"

"You've got to think about what we're doing here. Not only are we talking about breaking a couple of dozen state and federal laws, Lu Bates is likely violating parole and I'm paying her to do it. If somebody at Bay Area Cleaning or, heaven forbid, Lankford's, came across what we we're trying to do, we'd be so far up Shit Creek we wouldn't need paddles because there wouldn't be anywhere to go. Hill and Fetterman may be cops, but that doesn't automatically qualify them for the Good Guy Hall of Fame. My gut tells me that the less they know, the better this thing will be. For all of us."

"What about if something goes wrong and we need their help?"

"Ask me that again if something goes wrong and we need their help."

"I get your point." O'Neil couldn't tell if Reed was bothered by his opinion of Hill and Fetterman but there wasn't anything he could do about it. Reed would just have to trust him. "Did you get the message I left earlier? I got the job with the cleaning company."

"Yes, I did," said O'Neil. "Congratulations."

"Thank you very much. They are a little short-handed, which means the owner and his wife are having to go out and clean the buildings themselves, so they loved me. They'll come up with a schedule for me tomorrow, probably."

"How about not working Wednesdays and Fridays?"

"I asked, but they said they couldn't promise. I didn't want to push it too hard. I'm the new low guy on the totem pole, remember. We should talk about what you want me to do next."

O'Neil's stomach had begun to let him know what it wanted him to do next. "I want you to pick up a couple of large pizzas and a six pack and get over here. We can talk more about it then," he said.

It took Reed an hour to get the food and appear at O'Neil's house. O'Neil had taken a shower and changed clothes, having somewhat reluctantly powered off his computer. It was hard to walk away from a program once you were heavily into it. Leaving it behind became easier when you were nearly finished and most of what was left was filling in the cracks and tweaking the small details that were necessary to present a finished product. That was the grunt work of computer programming and O'Neil had never met anyone who enjoyed it. Most of them just skipped doing as much of it as possible.

They watched the Orlando Magic play the Chicago Bulls on television while they ate. "I'm not much of a fan," Reed said.

"Hell, without basketball, there'd be no reason for cable TV," O'Neil told him.

"Not counting the Playboy Channel, you mean."

O'Neil smiled. "Of course." Reed had a knack for keeping a conversation light, a talent O'Neil admired. The more he got to know the young man, the more he liked him. That led him to think about the situation at Lankford's and what they had ahead of them. "We need to talk about where we go from here."

Reed knew instantly what O'Neil was referring to and washed down the last of the pizza with a mouthful of light beer. "Okay, let's hear it," he said.

O'Neil used the remote to lower the volume of the TV. "There are a number of things that we could try to break into Lankford's computer system and look for evidence we could use to bring them down, maybe find out what happened to Tim. But what you have to understand is that where computers are concerned, no matter what we do, we're going to leave traces of ourselves behind. That's just the nature of the beast. So the trick is to try something they probably haven't thought of, something outside normal security precautions that they might not notice."

"How could they overlook something that could cause them so much damage?"

"Good question. Remember they're supposedly doing everything illegal over their wide area network, or WAN. This is what you call it when you link one computer network to another over a phone line or some other kind of connection. From their point of view, security mostly means protecting how that connection is made and to whom the connection is with. Since they don't store any of this information on their own computers, they already feel very secure every time they simply turn off their computers. It's the equivalent of hanging up the phone. Whatever they were doing just goes away."

"And we're going to ignore all that, for the reasons we talked about before?"

"Exactly. Even if I could think of a good way to do it, we'd be dealing with all kinds of legitimate as well as illegitimate data, cable taps, and last but not in any way least, encrypted data that would probably be impossible for us to read. So we'll be taking a different approach."

"Through the monitor and the keyboard."

"And that's why I need you at Lankford's. No matter what we do, we're going to need physical access to the computers. We need a door key, we need the pass code for their security system, and we need to establish a semi-plausible excuse for one of us to be in there after hours."

"You would be referring to me. And my mother thought I wasn't going anywhere when I became a cleaning person. How exactly are we going to do all this?"

"We need to find an excuse for you to go to Lankford's while the regular cleaning guy is there. Somehow, you need to find a way to get the security system pass code from him. I also need to know the exact brand and model of the keyboard in Walter Lankford's office."

Reed reached for another beer as he thought about this. He wanted to make a joke of some kind but he knew that O'Neil was being very serious now. "I'm sure I could find a reason to stop in. I could show him I'm from the same company, tell him I'm new and my girlfriend moved out and took all my garbage bags, something stupid like that. I'm on my way to do my buildings and could I grab a few bags from him so I don't have to stop at a 7-11 and spend my own money."

"How did you know to stop there, at the building he was at?"

"You mean how did I know he was from Bay Area, too?" O'Neil nodded. "I saw a list of clients when I was hired and the name of that one stuck in my mind?" This was a question.

"You saw the list and you remembered that one because your aunt married a man named Lankford back home in Baltimore, or wherever your back home is. That should sound like a strange-but-true coincidence and he won't think past it. Hopefully."

"Okay. That gets us some free garbage bags, but then what?"

"How strange would it be for you to show up the next time he was there and show your gratitude by helping him do the cleaning?"

"I don't know," Reed said. "He'd probably appreciate it. He'd be able to get out of there in half the time."

"That's what I was thinking. And then while you're there, you'll need to find Lankford's office and flip his keyboard over. There should be a label with the information I need. Write it down and get it back to me."

"What about the pass code?"

"That's a little harder. The only thing I can come up with is if you can manage to be watching him while he punches it in. What do you think?"

"Beats me, I've never tried it before. I guess that would work unless he's some kind of anal retentive and won't let me stand behind him. When do we put this glorious plan into action?"

"I want you to go over there Friday night, if you can. We need to get this moving so we can get something to Hill and Fetterman before they come looking for us. If you can borrow the bags Friday and be grateful next Wednesday, then I think that's about the best we can do."

On the TV, the Bulls had taken a two point lead with just over a minute left in the game. O'Neil turned the sound up and motioned for Reed to watch as a slow motion replay of a slam dunk was shown. He wanted to relax the mood. "Hugh Heffner could never do this," he said.

Reed laughed. "But how much do you know about Miss September?"

O'Neil made good progress on his programming task. He had figured out a way to capture the signals being sent to the monitor from the computer and store them in an electronic file. There were still significant things to be worked out, but the next thing he planned to do was create a routine that would take that file and create an image on another monitor. He would then have the two main components of his monitor bugging program and would have to find a practical way to implement it at Lankford's. Which in this case meant being as undetectable as possible.

Saturday morning Reed called with news of his stop at Lankford's the night before. "It went great," he told O'Neil. "The guy's name is Ray Alvarado and he gave me half a box of fifteen gallon two-ply poly garbage bags. Said he was glad to help. Real nice guy. He looks like he's about thirty five or thirty six years old, he's married and has three kids. He works days at the dog track in St. Petersburg."

"Great going. So you spent some time with him, got to know him a little bit?"

"Yeah, we shot the shit for about a half hour before I left. I didn't want to hold him up so when I go back Wednesday he wouldn't have a bad association with my face. Most cleaning people want to get done and get the hell out as soon as possible."

"We'll make a spy out of you yet. Anything else happen?"

"I got the keyboard for you."

"Get out of here. How'd you manage that?"

"It was almost Ray's idea, the way it worked out. Turns out the man likes to fish and he asked me if I did, too. I told him not really, and he said I didn't know what I was missing, especially living here in Florida. So he takes me into this plush office and shows me a stuffed tarpon or something that's hanging on the wall. Very few people catch these fish from shore, he says. He hasn't done it yet, but he got close twice last year." O'Neil heard Reed yawn on the other end of the line. "I'm sorry, I still need a few more hours. I'm losing my train of thought."

"About the keyboard."

"Yeah, the keyboard. I admired the fish, whatever the hell it was, and I put my hand on the desk behind the keyboard next to the cable. I tried to point at some part of the damn fish and would you believe, I somehow managed to accidentally pull the keyboard off the desk. Of course when I picked it up, I couldn't help but turn it over and look at the label."

"Of course you couldn't. What did it say?"

"It said 'Keymatic' for a brand name, and after where it said model number it had the numbers '5251.' I didn't have time to get the serial number."

"No need. What you got was perfect."

"Well I'm going back to bed, then. What's up next?"

"Sleep until noon. I'll pick you up and we'll go shopping at the computer store. We'll come back to my place and we can play Humpty Dumpty with a keyboard."

In the middle of another yawn Reed said, "I can't wait." O'Neil smiled and hung up the phone. The kid was coming through. They just might have a shot at pulling this off.

They went to the computer superstore that was in Tampa, near the stadium, and found the exact keyboard they were looking for. "It's extremely popular as a replacement model," said the salesman. He looked too young to remember a time when there weren't personal computers. They agreed and paid forty-five dollars for it and brought it back to O'Neil's house.

"So what exactly are we going to do with this thing?" Reed asked O'Neil. "I assume we're going to bug it somehow and pull a switch with the one in Lankford's office. Am I right?"

O'Neil had the keyboard upside down on his desktop as he pawed through the drawers looking for tools. "Close, but not quite. Switching the keyboards themselves is too risky. It would be too easy to notice the difference. Not only would the new one be cleaner and look different, it would probably have a different feel to it when you typed on it, even though it's an exact replacement. We're just going to use this one to practice on." He found a zippered vinyl pouch and opened it to reveal an assortment of tools. O'Neil extracted a small Philip's head screwdriver and began to remove the tiny screws from the bottom of the keyboard.

"Practice on it how?"

"Every time you press a key a code is sent to a buffer in the computer. The computer knows what you've typed by reading the buffer. The buffer only holds so much information and then it begins to override itself. When you turn the computer off, the contents of the buffer go away."

"How does that help us?"

O'Neil held up a small computer chip and a round silver disc. Reed stepped closer and looked at the objects in O'Neil's hand. "Is that a camera battery?" asked Reed, pointing to the disc.

"Exactly. And this is a memory chip." O'Neil extracted a small collection of tiny wires from another desk drawer. "We're going to connect them both with this thing and wire it into our new keyboard here. Every brand is a little different but once we know how to do this one right we'll install it at Lankford's. Then, whatever gets typed into the keyboard will be stored in the memory chip as it's passed on to the buffer and the electricity from the battery will keep it from discharging when the power is turned off. We pull the chip and the battery, read the codes, and we should have all the user ID's and passwords that we'll need to access the network."

Reed sat down in a chair across from the desk. "I'm impressed," he said.

"No matter how hidden your password, how difficult you make it to get into the system, you still have to type the secrets into the keyboard to make it work. So that's what we're going after. This whole concept was originally an idea of Tim's that he developed when he was hired by a bank to analyze their security. He always thought that one day logins and passwords would go away and we'll connect to our computers with our fingerprints or something."

"It's only right for him to be helping us out with all this." Reed thought about what he had just said and jerked his head up abruptly. "I'm sorry, boss. I didn't mean to make a joke about your friend. I–"

O'Neil looked into Reed's face. "Don't worry about it," he told him. "You didn't offend me. Believe me, it would take a lot more than that from you. Helping me go after these bastards means more to me than I can tell you." He waved for Reed to move closer to the desk. "Now come here and I'll show you how this is done. You need to practice."

CHAPTER TEN

MamaLu Bates lay back on her sheet and closed her eyes against the afternoon sun. She felt the heat on her skin that let her know it was past time
for an application of sunscreen. She preferred the spray on kind best because
she could cover her entire body in about a third the time it took her with a
cream or lotion. Also, she didn't have to get her hands all greasy, which was
an important consideration for someone in her line of work.

She'd get up in a minute and make her way down to the beach stand on
the other side of the food grill to see what they had. Right now, she just
wanted to take a second to relax. It had been a good afternoon for her. She
pulled one job on a German couple that showed up in a rented mini-van and
scored big. Big enough to stop for the day. She had even managed to return
the keys after she had finished in the parking lot.

The guy had put the keys in his shirt pocket and then stripped down to
nothing but those disgusting bikini briefs that these Europeans all seem to
wear. I swear, they're like Madonna they think they look good no matter
what they wear, she thought. Belly fat rolling down almost covering the little pouch that held them in. Didn't they know what they looked like?

It was such a double standard, she thought, and she was as guilty of it as
anyone. People with a weight problem just weren't treated the same as other
people, especially on the beach among all the 'beautiful people.' But that
would change for her, she knew. With the five hundred bucks she just took
out of Mr. Bikini Brief's wife's purse, she would pick up the key cutting machine from the CashAmerica pawn shop and be ready for the job with that
cop, O'Neil.

That would be the big score, she thought. It had to be. An ex-cop would-
n't risk getting busted and getting his cop ass sent to prison without a very,
very good reason. A reason MamaLu could cash in on if she was smart
enough to do it.

She pictured herself with a swollen bank account and lots of time on her
hands. First thing she'd do, she'd fly out to California, find one of those fat
farm places that took people like her and worked and massaged her down
to what she still considered to be her 'normal' size. Then maybe she'd dress
up like Madonna herself and take a trip to Europe, show those foreigners
what a good looking body really did for a bikini bottom.

Maybe she could even find someone who wasn't as much of a loser as her
Carl had been. Maybe settle down, start up a family. Life had finally smiled
on her for a change when that cop showed up. All she had to do now was

take advantage of it.

Rooker wasn't having much luck with the names in the computer file he got from the Lankford Company up in Tampa. It was frustrating because he was sure that one of the names was familiar to him but he couldn't figure out how. He didn't even know if the names were important, and he had no idea what those funky numbers were for. Or if they represented anything meaningful.

He sighed and tossed his reading glasses onto the paper printout of the names. Maybe he was hallucinating, making it all up. These four guys in the file could just be four guys in a file. But somebody went to some trouble to hide the thing, not just protect it with a password or something that you could do with a word processor. Somebody wanted those names hidden and they didn't want anyone else to find them.

But Rooker did find them. And whether or not he could parlay that into some form of profit or not, he didn't know. How could he, until he found out what the names in the file meant? All in all, it was a very frustrating situation.

After he had driven back to his office from his visit at Lankford's, he printed out a copy of the file and asked his secretary if she knew anything about a Ricardo Rivera. Maybe he had even been a client or something. But she just shrugged. Only thing the name reminded her of was some drug guy that got busted in Tampa a few months back. Wasn't that his name, she had asked. That rich guy, was supposed to have a bunch of money nobody could find?

Rooker didn't know. He always thought his secretary was a little wacky anyway. Besides, in Florida what drug dealer didn't have a pile of money stashed somewhere? They wallpaper with the stuff down in Miami.

Still, though, the more he thought about it the more the notion stuck in his mind. Maybe he had seen this guy Rivera's name on TV or something a while ago. He could almost picture the connection but wasn't quite sure of himself. Every time he tried to concentrate on it, his mind would conjure up an image of his secretary with her 1950's brunette bee hive hair-do saying, 'I don't know, wasn't that the name of the drug guy in Tampa?'

What the hell's a 'drug guy'?

Let's say Rivera was this person. Who did the other three names in the file belong to? Were the four of them connected? He tried to think of them as missing persons, people he knew but that had disappeared. What did one do to find a missing person? You call the cops.

Something turned over in his mind. The cops. Didn't he just meet two cops at the reception after Clayton's funeral? Of course he had, the one guy who looked like he used his tie for a napkin and his partner, the one who didn't say much. Maybe they could help him out, give him a few ideas. If they worked it right they wouldn't have to know where the file had come from.

First thing, though, he had to remember who the cops were. He hadn't paid much attention to their names; he never did unless someone was a potential client. The one with the tie, he was drawing a total blank. But the other name, there was something it reminded him of, something he'd seen on TV.

Fetterman. He didn't remember a first name but he was sure the last was Fetterman. The same name of some dumbshit army officer in the mid 1800's that thought he could whip all the plains Indians by himself. He went after a small group of warriors one day and against orders followed them too far from the fort, right into a full-scale ambush. His entire party had been massacred and then mutilated. Rooker smiled and reached for a Tampa phone book. Public television had actually done him some good.

He dialed the number for the Tampa police department and asked how he could get in touch with Detective Fetterman. The woman put him on hold and a minute later a man's voice come on the line. "This is Hill," the voice said.

Hill. That had been the other cop's name, the one that did all the talking. Rooker put on his best salesman's voice and told him who he was.

"You're who?"

Rooker told him again. "James Rooker. We met briefly at the reception following Tim Clayton's funeral. Terrible thing, that was." Rooker caught himself and quickly added, "Clayton's death, I mean. Not the reception. That was lovely."

'Lovely'? Hill didn't like to have conversations with grown men that used the word lovely, especially when he didn't remember who the hell they were. He wrote the name 'Rooker' on a sheet of paper and turned it towards his partner who was seated at the desk across from him. Fetterman, who was in the middle of sharpening a pencil with one of the tools from his pocket knife, read the name and shook his head. He didn't recognize it, either. Hill didn't try hard to mask his annoyance.

"What can I do for you, Mr. Rooker?" he asked with an edge to his voice.

Rooker picked up on the detective's mood and tried not to let it sway him. He made up what he hoped was a somewhat realistic story of coming across a list of unidentified names at one of Tim Clayton's old clients. Their computer had apparently been affected by a power surge or a lightning strike or some damned thing and the names had been part of a file that had become corrupt. Of course, since Tim was gone, they had called in Rooker as their new consultant.

It was very important that his client identify these names so that certain accounts and records could be restored to order. Rooker was just wondering if maybe Hill and Fetterman, in honor of the late Tim Clayton, might be able to offer some suggestions as to how he might go about finding out who these men were.

When he was finished, Hill couldn't help but laugh. "You're kidding me, right? We solve murders here, Mr. Rooker, not run errands for local businessmen. Call a private detective if you want to find somebody."

Rooker didn't want to give up yet. Private detectives cost money. "Maybe you'd just let me read you the names, okay? I have reason to believe one or all of them could be from Tampa. You just might be familiar with them." Without waiting for an answer Rooker read the four names into the telephone.

There was a long moment of silence on the other end. Rooker wasn't sure if he had angered the policeman or if something maybe had gone wrong with the telephone connection. Finally, Hill spoke again, but this time the edge was gone and there was something new there.

"Mr. Rooker? Maybe we can help you out after all. Why don't you tell me where we can find you. I think we need to get together in person."

Rooker smiled. Something in his story must have worked, or maybe the detective did recognize some of the names. Whatever the case, he was pleased he was able to make something happen.

CHAPTER ELEVEN

Wednesday night at Lankford's went smoothly. Ray Alvarado happily accepted Reed Larson's offer of help, though he assured him it wasn't necessary, he'd been happy to help the new guy out. But if Reed really wanted to help clean tonight, Ray would be grateful for the company. Some guys actually brought their wives or girlfriends along to help them work but Ray wouldn't even consider that. Trini took care of the kids all day and kept up their own house. Let her relax a little when the sun goes down, Ray thought. It's my job to bring home the paycheck.

They worked fairly quickly, Reed going from office to office removing the half-full garbage bags and replacing them with empty ones, Ray pushing a vacuum cleaner across the carpet in each room. There used to be two of them assigned to clean this place, Ray had said. Now it was just himself but that was okay since this was the only building he had to do two days of the week.

After Reed had hauled all of the garbage outside to the dumpster, he washed the dishes stacked at the sink in the little kitchen and scrubbed the insides of the microwave oven. It was amazing the messes people were willing to create at work that they wouldn't tolerate for a minute inside their own homes. After he was through there, he joined Ray and together they dusted the table and television in the conference room, as well as the computer monitors on each desk.

"That's about it," Ray announced after the last screen was clear. "We can go home."

Maybe you can, Reed thought, but I still have three of my own to clean downtown.

They made their way through the building turning off the lights and meeting again at the front door. "Don't move," Ray told him and pointed at the motion detector mounted on the wall. Ray was standing at the security system keypad and Reed was slipping on his windbreaker by the front door. The receptionist's desk and twenty feet separated the two of them.

Shit, Reed thought, I fucked up. There was no way he could see the keys that Ray was about to push from where he was. Damn it! O'Neil was counting on him and here he was, sleeping at the wheel. He should have been paying more attention to what Ray was doing. Without hesitating he started walking toward him. It was all he could do.

"Hold it there," Ray said, holding up his palm. "I can't turn this thing on if you're moving."

Reed had to stop at Ray's gesture. If he pushed it any more Ray would be suspicious. He wondered how pissed O'Neil was going to be.

Ray entered five numbers into the keypad and motioned Reed toward the door. "Sixty seconds." He motioned Reed to follow him out.

Ray took a set of keys out of the back pocket of his jeans and locked the front door. What the hell am I supposed to do now, Reed thought. At least I see where he keeps his keys. Got that one right.

They walked down the short sidewalk to their two cars. Reed had parked his beat up Toyota next to Ray's pickup and as they got there Ray stopped and offered Reed his hand. "I want to thank you very much for your help," he said as they shook. "You didn't need to do it but I am very grateful that tonight I can go home early."

Reed gave him a genuine smile. "You helped me out last week, remember? I'm just glad you let me repay the favor. It was good to meet you, Ray."

"I enjoyed meeting you, too," he smiled back. "You'll have to stop in again and we'll talk some baseball. The season's almost here. Maybe one day I'll even get you out fishing."

Better that than baseball, Reed thought. Or maybe not. Reed didn't think a lot happened in either sport. In any case, Alvarado was being polite more than anything else. "Sure thing, Ray. See you around," and he turned and walked to the driver's side of the Toyota, deeply disappointed with himself.

The point of being there tonight was to get the security passcode but he had-n't even come close. He had let Ray catch him off guard and he had failed.

He opened the door and climbed into his car. Next to him, the gray pickup truck started with a rumble and slowly backed away from the curb. Angry at himself, Reed reached into his pocket and dug for his car keys.

Somewhere behind him, Ray changed gears and began to move forward out of the parking lot. Reed jumped out of his car and ran after the pickup. "Ray!" he shouted, waving his arms. "Hold up a second! Ray!"

Alvarado heard him and halted the truck. He rolled down his window as Reed caught up to him. "What's wrong?" Ray asked. Concern showed at the corners of his eyes.

Reed shook his head, mocking himself. "Like an idiot, I left my car keys in-side. I took them out of my pocket when I was doing the kitchen and I never picked them up again. I need to get back in. Just for a second."

"Okay, I'll park the truck."

"Hell, Ray, that's okay. Just give me the key and I'll run in. I know right where I left them."

Ray sat forward and extracted his key ring from his back pocket. It would be all right; they both worked for the same company. "It's this one," he said, holding the ring out by a single key. Reed took it and said he'd be right back.

When he was several yards away, Ray called out. "You will need the pass-word for the burglar alarm."

"Oh, yeah," said Reed turning back toward the truck. "Almost forgot."

"No problem. It is '84841' to get in, '84842' when you leave."

"Got it," Reed said and turned to jog back to the front door. He got it all right, and he wasn't going to lose it. Inside his left pants pocket, his car keys made chinging sounds as he ran. He slowed down to a fast walk so that Ray wouldn't hear the noise.

"Are you sure we need the fat chick? I mean, I had the keys in my hands. If I could do that again, maybe switch them—"

"Hold on," O'Neil interrupted. "It's not your job to get the keys. If some-thing went wrong, not only would we not have the keys, at the very least you'd be out of the game. I need you too much to risk that. If Lu blows it, all we lose is a little time and we can always try something else."

"You'd still be out your two grand."

"Believe me, the last thing in the world I'm worrying about right now is money." O'Neil moved the phone to his other ear and said, "You just don't like that woman."

"Anybody hits me upside the head like she did generally doesn't leave a very good impression. No pun intended."

"You deserved it and you know it. Anyway, you've got the passcodes so I'll head out to Clearwater and find Lu. Do you see any problem with her going to work Friday night?"

"You mean as far as with Ray? No, I think one day's as good as another as far as he's concerned. But I'm supposed to work four buildings tomorrow."

"That's fine, I don't want you anywhere near Lankford's when this goes down. We'll leave this all up to Lu."

"Oh. Okay." He sounded disappointed. "Just tell her that there are two keys she'll need to get. One for the front door that says 'Schlage' on it, and one for the president's office. That one says 'Uniface.' There are two or three other Unifaces on the key ring, though. You'll have to handle that somehow."

"I was going to have her copy all of the keys, just to be sure. Go back to sleep and I'll get back to work. Thanks again, Reed. I don't know how I'd do this without you."

"Sure." Reed said it sarcastically but O'Neil was being serious and he felt complimented. "Give my love to your beach buddy and I'll talk to you later."

O'Neil said goodbye and hung up the phone with a guilty tear at the corner of his conscience. He walked into his office and set his keyboard in his lap. Reed had really come through for him. Just don't screw this up, he told himself. You've lost one good friend already, you don't need to lose any more.

There he is, MamaLu thought as she watched a pair of headlights turn into the parking lot in front of the Walter A. Lankford Company. From where she was, a hundred yards away and across the street, she couldn't be sure it was the right vehicle, but the timing was about right.

She walked around the corner of the building she was using for cover and worked her way behind the wheel of her extended cab pickup truck. She'd give him a minute then cruise the street and make sure it was really him. Then she'd get the truck ready and go into her act.

Lord, please help me to not blow this thing, she prayed as she pushed the power button for the stereo. She spent a few minutes fidgeting with the controls, picking up one country music station after another until she forced herself to sit still. The twangings of a slide guitar ground through the air around her but she didn't pay attention. This was a very important job and she hadn't done this kind of work in a very long time. That made her nervous and that was a bad thing. Nervous in her profession meant mistakes and there weren't too many ways to explain the presence of your hand in someone else's pocket.

Damn it! Stop shaking, she told herself. This could be her ticket to a new life, away from the petty crime and beach cops in short pants and bicycles. A turning point, that's what this was. A way to go back to being pretty Mary Lu Bates from Alabama, not MamaLu or Mama anything, just a sweet little Southern girl from the panhandle who liked the beach. A girl who used to have a weight problem and maybe a questionable past, but was now blossoming into a strong, independent woman of means. She was a butterfly ready to leave behind her cocoon.

But only if she worked this right. She took deep breaths as she started the truck and slipped it into gear. She didn't really have to figure out everything the cop was doing, just enough so she could hold it over his head. If she got in there, worked it out, and walked away with whatever prize O'Neil was after, great. She'd be in control. But other than that, she planned on making herself a new partner in his enterprise. The threat of blackmail or exposure should be enough to bring them to a satisfactory middle ground. An arrangement that would get her off the beach and into a new life. First stop, the Malibu Health and Weight Loss Retreat in sunny Southern California. First stop to a new Lu, she thought. She liked that.

She drove her truck slowly down the street and got a good view of the vehicle parked in front of the Lankford Company. The magnetic sign on the driver's door said, "Bay Area Cleaning Service." That's the one, she thought and pressed down on the accelerator. She forced herself to keep taking deep, slow breaths. It wasn't time yet. First, she had to get back to the interstate, get the truck going good and hot, and then she'd be back. She had a schedule to keep and the night was young.

Ray Alvarado had just finished emptying the last of the executive garbage cans when he heard the front door open and close. He had never been in the habit of locking the door once he began cleaning; he went out to his truck too much. But his heart always skipped a little if someone walked in during the night. It was usually just some employee picking up something he had forgotten, something like that, or occasionally even someone stopping to ask directions to a night club somewhere. He put down the garbage can he was holding and walked toward the front.

"Hello?" he heard someone call softly. It sounded like a woman's voice, unusual out here at this time of night. He walked around the partition into the receptionist's area and there she was. A woman, yes, and what a woman. Ray wasn't a big man himself, maybe a hundred and forty five pounds after a large meal, but she looked to him like she could easily go double that. There was a worried look on her face, almost as though she were about to cry, Ray thought, and he asked her if she needed some help.

"Something's wrong with my truck," she said. "I was driving down the street and all of the sudden a bunch of smoke came pouring out from under the hood. And there was some kind of funny smell. I didn't know what to do. I saw your lights on and pulled in."

Ray gave her a reassuring smile and stepped up to the front door. "Is that it there?" he asked her. Parked next to his own was a purple and black pickup truck with an extended cab and tinted windows.

"Yes," she told him. "That's it. I don't know what to do. I don't really have anyone I can call."

"Would you like me to take a look?" Ray offered.

"Oh, would you mind? I would really appreciate it. All I know about cars and trucks is how to fill them up with gas and drive them away. I have some money, though. I can pay you."

Ray extended his arm and held open the door for her. "Don't be ridiculous," he said. "Let's go out and take a look." They walked down to the end of the short sidewalk, Ray in front of the woman. There wasn't enough room for them to walk side by side and not step in the grass. "This is a nice truck," he told her. From up close, the custom paint job and windows gave the vehicle a sleek, menacing look.

"Thank you," she told him.

Ray knelt down and poked his finger into a greenish puddle that was still collecting under the truck. "This is your engine coolant," he told her, sniffing at the glycol. "Why don't you get in there and pop the hood for me?"

MamaLu did as he asked. Alvarado lifted the hood and held it while a last steamy cloud found freedom and escaped. He propped the hood open with a metal rod and peered at the engine for a moment, then went to the rear of his own truck and plucked a disposable flashlight from a utility box.

MamaLu climbed out of the driver's seat and stood on the curb behind Ray as he inspected the engine. "Here's your problem," he told her. "The hose for the antifreeze has come loose from the reservoir." He held the loose end in his fingers so she could see. MamaLu placed a hand on his lower back and bent forward to look but slipped off the curb. She had to grab Ray with both of her arms around his middle to keep from falling into the truck. He tried to support her weight as they performed an awkward dance in a slow circle around each other. "Are you okay, miss?" Ray asked as MamaLu regained her equilibrium.

I'm perfect, she thought. You've got a dummy set of keys in your back pocket and I've got the real ones clutched in my left hand. That wasn't so hard. Like riding a bicycle, she still had the touch. "I'm okay, thank you. I didn't mean to be so clumsy. I didn't hurt you, did I?"

Ray smiled because the lady so easily could have. "No, no, I am fine. Let's get your truck back together and you can go on your way."

"You can fix it?"

"Yes, of course. Just let me get some water and I'll fill the reservoir until you can replace it with real antifreeze and then you'll be fine."

Ray was even more surprised when the woman walked into the building the second time. He had been finishing up the vacuuming when he felt someone tap him on the shoulder. He hadn't heard the door and he must have jumped a foot off the ground when she touched him.

"Mother of Christ," he breathed as he turned around to face her. She took a step back, a worried look on her face, but he held out a hand. "No, no, it's okay. You startled me a little is all." He felt his heart thumping in his chest. "Is everything all right with your truck?"

MamaLu returned his smile and produced a fruit basket she had been holding behind her back. "The truck's fine. I just brought this for you for being so nice to me." She jiggled it once in the air. "Here, take it."

"That's not necessary. I am only happy that I was here and was able to help you."

"No no no. I'm not going to argue about it. It's just a silly basket of fruit and I absolutely insist that you take it." She thrust it at him again. "Go on. It doesn't mean we have to get married or anything."

Embarrassed, Ray ran his fingers through his thinning hair and reached for the basket. No sooner did he take it then MamaLu stepped forward and crushed him in a mammoth bear hug.

"Thank you again," she said. She embraced him warmly and lifted him several inches off the ground. Ray was powerless to do anything about it. Both of his arms were pinned to his sides and he couldn't have hugged her back if he had wanted.

"Uh, you're welcome again. My wife and I will enjoy your gift very much, I'm sure." It was all he could think of to say. He put extra emphasis on the word "wife."

"You do that," she told him and with both hands grabbed hold of his butt and squeezed. Oh my God, he thought, swearing again. He felt his keys pressing into his right cheek as she released him. I am helpless in the path of this woman.

Lu backed away and said with a different voice, "I'd give you a kiss but you probably couldn't stand it, sweetie. See you around." She turned and ambled out of the building. It had taken her more than an hour to copy the keys back at the motel room she'd taken, but it was done and now she had returned the originals.

The night had gone very well, she thought. Yup, she told herself, I've still got it.

As she drove her truck to the 24 hour restaurant where O'Neil was supposed to be waiting, Ray went to the front door and locked it with his key. He had been happy to help but he just wanted to finish his cleaning and go home. The big woman had turned so aggressive. He hoped that she was done with him now and would not come back. He set the basket on the edge of the receptionist's desk and looked at the assortment of apples, oranges, bananas, and kiwis wrapped in translucent cellophane. Where had she gotten a fruit basket this time of night?

Rooker was feeling decidedly uncomfortable. These two cops, Hill and Fetterman, weren't treating him as he'd hoped and he was now beginning to feel as if maybe he had stumbled into something by mistake. Something the Tampa police didn't like and by extension, something he would rather have left alone.

The tail lights of the brown sedan he was following flared and veered to his left, off the pavement and onto a gravel road. The moon was barely half full and Rooker had to strain to see enough of the road to stay on it. Fortunately, the two cops weren't in a hurry and were making it easy for Rooker to follow. A mosquito buzzed in his ear as too late he rolled his window up against the insects and the tangy smell of the swamp after dark. Spanish moss hanging from the branches above the road swept over his car as he crept along the winding trail.

They had driven east out of Sarasota, turned north at Myakka City and out of the county altogether. Where the hell were they taking him? Maybe they were going to show him something that would answer some of his questions, instead of just asking their own, like they did back at his townhouse where they had met. He wasn't sure he cared any more. At this point, he was wishing he'd never found the file with those names in it at that client's office. Or at least that he hadn't had the bright idea of asking the police for their help. What the hell could they show him out here, anyway?

The road seemed to have ended but they picked their way through the trees without it. Fifty yards or so ahead of him, the brown sedan stopped at the entrance to a slight clearing, big enough for three or four cars to park side by side. Rooker pulled up behind the sedan and shut off his car. This better be good, he thought as he opened the door and stepped out into the soft sand.

He could hear water sounds coming from somewhere in front of the sedan. A narrow river cut its way through the land just ahead. He stood impatiently, trying to control his annoyance as Hill and Fetterman took their time getting out of their car. This whole night has been bullshit, he thought. Somewhere downriver a night bird or frog made a reptilian croaking sound that had him jumping. Wild Florida. Bug and creature capital of the world.

"What the hell are we doing out here?" Rooker demanded. The damp, heavy air muted his voice and he didn't sound nearly as authoritative as he wanted. Being this far removed from civilization made him nervous.

Detective Hill answered him with a crooked smile. "Why Mr. Rooker," he said. "We just came out here to continue our little exchange of information. That's what you wanted, wasn't it? I mean, that's why you originally called us, right?"

Fetterman scrounged a fallen stick from the brush next to where they had parked and brought out his pocket knife. He moved to a position a step behind Rooker and began to slowly whittle the dead branch. Rooker felt little shavings bounce off the backs of his legs as something different bit him on the ankle. He danced a little as he rubbed at the spot with his other foot but didn't say anything. Something definitely was not right with this situation. His annoyance evaporated and became something much more disturbing. He began to realize that he was afraid.

"Now I don't want any more crap, I don't want any more stories. I want to know why you have those four names and I want to know how you got them. And I want you to tell me all this now." Hill stuck his face half a foot in front of Rooker's. "All of it. Right now."

Rooker said nothing for a moment as he considered what was happening to him. Would these men actually hurt him, cause him pain? They were policemen, officers of the law, for Christ's sake. As a taxpayer and a citizen they worked for him, didn't they? He may have been unethical, certainly unprofessional, he knew that, but James Rooker was no threat to society. That ought to count for something. "I told you already, back at my home. I don't know why you have to hear it again." A small warm spot of artificial courage settled into his stomach. Rooker slapped at a mosquito on his cheek. The bugs were eating him alive.

Hill looked over Rooker's shoulder at Fetterman. It seemed to Rooker that he was the only one moving as he waved at the unseen cloud of insects swirling around his head. Something else bit him on the same ankle as before.

After a long minute, Hill said to Fetterman, "Do you believe him?"

Fetterman's knife made a slow rasping sound as it cut through another layer of stick, then stopped. "Not with that face, no."

"Let's try another one, then." Hill brought up a meaty fist and stepped forward as he drove it into the center of Rooker's face. Blood exploded from a fractured nose as Rooker's world went dark and light at the same time and he sagged backwards into Fetterman's arms.

Hill wiped at his knuckles with a handkerchief taken from his back pocket. "How about now?" he asked his partner.

"Yeah, I think he's starting to look more sincere." He took a step back and let Rooker fall the rest of the way to the ground.

Hill bent down and peered into Rooker's damaged face. "How about it, Rooker? Do you have anything else to say?"

Rooker's mind was in shock and all he could manage was a kind of groan that formed bubbles of blood on his lips. His eyes gazed feebly back at Hill, who straightened up and said to Fetterman, "Bring him over here."

Dragging Rooker by walking backwards with his hands hooked in Rooker's arm pits, Fetterman followed Hill a few yards on a short trek toward the river. Hill stopped in front of a mound of white sand that rose like a miniature volcano about a foot out of the ground. Similar mounds, separated by at least twenty feet from each other, punctuated the landscape made dully visible by the soft reflected light from the half-full moon.

"I hate these damn things," said Hill. "How about you, Rooker? Do you hate these little guys? Why don't you say something to them about it." With the bottom of his foot, he swept away the top half of the mound revealing a dark, writhing stain. "You know what a quail is, don't you Rooker? You know, the bird." He knelt down to where Fetterman still held Rooker's upper body off the ground and gave him a light slap across both cheeks. Rooker squirmed and made groaning noises while blood continued to flow downward onto his chest. Hill took Rooker's chin in his hand and turned it so the wounded man's eyes were looking into his own.

"Quail lay their eggs in little holes they dig in the ground, not in a nest up a goddamned tree somewhere. Problem is, these little guys over here," he motioned toward the half-mound with his hand. "They moved up here from South America and just like that, there went the neighborhood. At least for the quail. A colony of these critters move through a quail nest for breakfast. Leave behind nothing but pieces of dried up shells and tiny little bird bones. What do you think about that, Rooker? How do you think it would feel to be picked apart and eaten by a couple hundred thousand hungry little bugs? Find yourself a new spot on the local food chain, what do you think?"

Rooker's eyes fluttered several times and three nasally syllables escaped through lips thick with crusting blood. "Arr ess mee."

Hill released Rooker's chin and stood up. "Arrest you? Mr. Rooker, we can't arrest you. You haven't broken any laws that we know of. Besides, we're only two counties away from our legal jurisdiction." He looked up at Fetterman. "Hey, how're your arms holding out? You been holding him up a few minutes now."

"He's starting to get a little heavy."

"Set the man down and get yourself a little rest. You're working too hard." Hill reached down and took one of Rooker's arms while Fetterman shifted over to the other. They flipped Rooker over so his stomach was on the ground and held him just above the mound.

Thick drops of blood, black in the moonlight, spattered the sand below him as Rooker shook his head feverishly from side to side. "Remember the quail," he heard Hill say. Then they dropped him on his face.

Bright lights illuminated the inside of his skull as the impact on his damaged nose drove a shock wave of pain backwards into his brain. He tried to lift his head off the ground but for some reason he couldn't. His mouth was full of sand and other things as he spit and struggled to breathe through the dirt. As the pain from his nose subsided he became aware of a tickling sensation on the rest of his face, his neck, and even the inside of his mouth as he maintained his struggle for ragged breaths of air. Burning pricks of fire followed, first a couple, then a few, then hundreds and even thousands more as the angry colony began to attack and feed on the body of the intruder.

Rooker flailed his arms and legs wildly, trying desperately to push away from the fire ants and protect his face at the same time. Hill waited for a full two minutes before lifting his foot from the back of Rooker's head. He rolled away and scrambled wildly, clawing at his face as his momentum brought him dangerously close to another mound. He spit with every breath, trying to clear his mouth and throat. In one motion he pulled his shirt off and over his head and flung it into the brush.

The two police detectives stood side by side, watching impassively. "Would you look at that," Hill said. Rooker was using the little fingers of both hands to dig the tiny red ants out of his bloody nostrils. He couldn't see as his eyes swelled shut with pain, tears, and the effects of formic acid.

"That's gotta hurt," said Fetterman.

O'Neil stood as MamaLu entered the restaurant and approached his booth. "A gentleman," she said and worked her way into the seat across from him.

"Coffee?" O'Neil asked as he seated himself and picked up the pot he had been nursing.

"No thanks, don't drink the stuff." She pushed aside her cup and plopped an oversized purse on the table between them. "Let's get this over with."

"How did it go?"

"Beautifully. He never had a clue. Nice butt, though."

O'Neil let that one go. "So you got the keys?"

Lu took her hand out of her bag and slid a ring of keys across the table to him. "Hot off the press. That'll be two thousand dollars, please. Plus two hundred for the cutting."

He deposited the keys in his jacket pocket and took a plain white envelope from his briefcase and handed it to her. He waited while she held it in her lap and counted the bills. Looking up she said, "I'll need fifty bucks more for expenses."

"Expenses? What are you talking about?"

"A motel room. I had to have some place to cut the keys, didn't I? Here, I brought you a receipt." She handed him a piece of paper from a place called the All American Motel on Kennedy Boulevard. He had never heard of it. O'Neil took his wallet out of his pocket and took out the money. He wasn't about to argue over fifty dollars.

"Thank you very much," she told him and started to ease sideways off the bench. "It was a pleasure doing business with you." And it was. She was still high from the buzz she got after she had put the original keys back into Alvarado's pocket without being caught. She had her touch back and it made her happy to know that. If she thought about it, this had probably been her happiest night since she dumped Carl Pantucket.

She stood and said goodbye to O'Neil. He got to his feet and said, "Thanks for the work." MamaLu gave him a smile and then turned to leave. You'll be seeing me again, she thought. Don't think you won't.

When he could speak again, Rooker pushed some sounds upward through his burning throat. "They were eating my face." He worked his eyelids and tried to see the two cops standing somewhere in front of him. "They were eating my face," he repeated.

"I know," said Hill.

"We saw," said Fetterman.

Rooker wailed, "Oh my God," and collapsed backwards onto the ground in a sitting position.

"I don't think I'd sit there if I were you. You're a little close." Hill poked a finger in the direction behind Rooker. "You're on another mound."

Rooker rocked wildly forward and swiped manically at the seat of his pants with both hands. In the dim light, his bare chest was the same pale shade of gray as the ant mounds around him. His face looked ruined, a grotesque image of what it had been. The man was broken and all three of them knew it.

Hill stepped forward. "Okay, Rooker. I'm tired of feeding the animals but you need to know I've got all night if I need it. So do you, incidentally. But as soon as you tell me the truth about those names, this thing can be over. Now what do you say?"

Rooker reached forward and tried to feel where the man was standing. Hill didn't move as Rooker's hands found his face and then his shoulders. "I'll talk to you. I'll do anything you want."

"I know you will," Hill told him.

Later, when it was over, Hill asked Fetterman what he thought about Rooker's information. "Do those numbers he gave us help?"

Hill shrugged. "They're something, I guess. But they're just account numbers. Without passwords…." Hill didn't bother to finish.

Fetterman nodded. "We've still got O'Neil."

The two men climbed into their sedan and carefully backed up and turned around in the clearing. As they drove out toward the gravel road, the reddish glow from their tail lights cast an eerie pallor on the naked body of James Edward Rooker. His broken form lay spreadeagled face down across an angry nest of swarming fire ants, still lips parted slightly as if offering a silent and unheeded apology to the creatures whose nest he unknowingly disturbed.

CHAPTER TWELVE

Saturday morning dawned brightly across the Florida sky, improbable colors gradually turning to more common shades of blue. A light veil of fog hung over the ground, hinting at a heavier blanketing outside of the city. O'Neil stood on the balcony adjacent to the kitchen and thought of his wife. She's still at her sister's, safe and away from all this. Whatever this is. At least her life can stay close to normal.

So far they hadn't accomplished much by way of finding out who had killed Tim Clayton. All they really had was Hill's and Fetterman's view of what had happened and some of the tools to allow them access to the Lankford Company.

He kept thinking in terms of "us" or "we," counting more than himself, and that was a concern. How much should he allow Reed Larson to get involved? He knew as he asked himself what his answer was. He was going to find out who killed Tim and why, whatever it took.

The phone rang around ten in the morning. As expected, it was Reed checking in, calling to see how it had gone the night before.

"Lu Bates came through," O'Neil told him. "We're in."

"That's good," said Reed. "I feel better with her out of the picture. She is, isn't she?"

"You're just afraid she'll hit you again."

"Wouldn't you be?"

O'Neil laughed. "That's beside the point. But yes, she's out of the picture."

"Good. What do we do next?"

"I want you to take me in to Lankford's tonight. We'll make sure that the keys work and I want to check out a few things on their computer system. We'll bring Lankford's keyboard back here and install our memory chip, then we'll switch them back."

"You don't want to install the memory thing there, at his office? Wouldn't that save us a trip?"

"I'd rather risk getting caught twice doing nothing obvious with a legitimate employee of their cleaning service than getting caught once with a dissected computer and a soldering iron. That's a bit harder to explain."

"That's why you make the plans, boss."

O'Neil told him to come by that evening. They'd have some dinner and go over to Lankford's later. By the day after tomorrow, Monday night, if everything worked as it should, not only would they have access to the building itself, they'd have the password to Lankford's computer network as well. And if they've got any hidden skeletons in their electronic closet, O'Neil thought, we're going to find them.

The night was long but uneventful. They went in at midnight and checked the keys made by MamaLu Bates. They worked perfectly. O'Neil verified that the physical layout of the computer network was what he expected, based on his familiarity with Tim's work as well as on his conversation with Hill. In Walter Lankford's office, he powered on the computer and watched as it booted up and eventually paused, prompting for a network user name.

"Are you going to type anything in?" Reed asked.

"No. This just tells us that the first thing he enters when he boots up is his log in name. The next thing the computer will ask for is his password."

"Are you sure? Can you test it?"

"Yes, I'm sure, and yes I can test it, but we don't want to. The system could be logging failed attempts to access the network and somebody might check it out. We don't need to risk it." O'Neil turned the computer off and bent down to unplug the keyboard from the back of the machine.

"Monday night, after the computer has been used for a day, I'm going to ask you to come back here and remove the memory chip. Then we'll dump

what it's got into a file on my computer. I've got a program that will translate the digital data in the file into the proper alpha-numeric characters and
all we'll have to do is read the first thing that was typed before the code for
the 'Enter' key. That will be the login name."

"And the second thing will be the password." Reed looked down at the
computer on the floor as O'Neil put the keyboard into a gym bag. "I know
we've gone through a lot to get here, but somehow all this seems too easy."

"You've got to remember what I said about computer security. There's no
such thing. When personal computers were designed nobody dreamed of
the kinds of things we'd be doing with them today. Nobody knew how clever
we could be with them. As far as the machine itself goes, the key is having
physical access. Anything someone can think of to secure the data, someone else can think of ways to un-secure that data. We can't outsmart ourselves."

O'Neil took the keyboard they had brought from home and set it on the
desk where the original had been. "Let's get out of here and get this over
with. The night is not so young."

"And neither are you," Reed joked.

O'Neil socked him in the upper arm. "I don't need that from you. Let's go."

Hill called O'Neil at eight o'clock on Monday morning, getting him out
of bed. Staying on his late night schedule, O'Neil worked on the software
program that would record the signals sent to Lankford's computer monitor until early in the morning. There was one part of it that needed to be
completed and he hoped to finish it in a few more hours. After he spoke to
Hill, he knew he would get it done that day no matter what.

"So what you're telling me," Hill had said, "is that in a week you haven't
done shit on this thing. Is that right?"

O'Neil swallowed his response as it started to rise from his throat. Whatever he got out of Lankford's, he wanted to have it for some time before he
gave it to Hill. He needed to give him a reason for the delay without telling
him what he was really doing. "No, that's not right. I think I may have found
a way into their network but it's going to take a little time to set up."

"Oh, yeah? Tell me about it."

"They're connecting their network to others through the Internet, right?
Most businesses aren't connected directly to the Internet unless they're providing a service on it. What Lankford does is use a service provider for their
connection."

"And what does that mean?"

"Just that rather than have special systems set up just for the Internet,

Lankford uses their own equipment to dial into the service provider, who offers the actual connection. I think I have a way to penetrate the connection from the provider itself."

"So you'll be able to follow what they're doing on the network?"

"If I get in." He didn't want to sound like he had anything substantive yet. "It looks good, but I won't know until next week."

"What the hell, O'Neil. If you can break into this provider's network next week, why can't you do it this week?"

"Because I'm not breaking in at all. A year ago, I worked a contract with the same company that provides Lankford's service. I tried to break into their network from the outside, to show them how it could be done so they could plug the security holes. I think I can convince them I'm doing some kind of follow up work so they'll let me do some more poking around. That's how I can get at Lankford."

As a lie it may not have been great, but he just needed to convince Hill to hold off for another week or so. By then, O'Neil hoped, he'd at least have something from Lankford's system tying them to Tim's murder. He wanted to deflect Hill's attention so he asked, "Once I get on, is there some kind of specific information you think I should look for?"

Hill grunted into the phone. "Yeah, there are a few things I can give you. You just get hold of me when you get your access."

So he did have something else, O'Neil thought. Apparently Hill had his own secrets to keep.

"Tell me this, O'Neil. You working with anyone else on the this, someone we should know about?"

Shit. Could he have found out about Reed or MamaLu? "Who do you mean, Hill?"

"I'm talking about another computer consultant, a person who knows networks, someone like that. If you are, O'Neil, I've got to know about it."

If they knew about Lu Bates, she'd probably be back in jail. He could check that out. And if they knew about Reed, they'd know he wasn't a computer pro, that he was more or less just some kid O'Neil had come across. Was Hill just fishing or did he have a specific reason for asking?

"What are you talking about, Hill? My own company doesn't even know what I'm doing. As far as they're concerned I'm just taking time off. No one else knows what I'm doing."

"All right, O'Neil." He seemed satisfied. "Keep it that way. But you let me know as soon as you get into that network. Then we're going to have a little meeting."

O'Neil told him of course he would. He couldn't wait.

Monday night was their busiest yet. O'Neil went with Reed on his cleaning assignments to get them done and out of the way as early as possible. It was just after ten o'clock when they were ready for Lankford's.

"All you want me to do is remove the memory chip you installed in the keyboard and bring it back?" Reed asked O'Neil. "You don't want me to do anything else while I'm there?"

"No, that's it. Just be very careful not to break the connection with the battery. If you do, whatever is stored in the memory will go away and we'll have to put it back in for another day. The whole operation shouldn't take you more than fifteen minutes."

"No problem. I'll be back at your house in an hour."

O'Neil waited until Reed had driven out of the parking lot in his old Toyota, with mop handles, broom handles and a vacuum cleaner all visible through the windows from their positions in the back seat. If Hill and Fetterman knew about Reed, they most likely had seen him at Lankford's or had seen him with O'Neil. Which would mean they were either watching Lankford's building or watching him. There hadn't been any sign of them doing either. O'Neil started his own car and pulled out after Reed. It wouldn't hurt to make sure.

He picked up Reed's tail lights before he hit the interstate and followed him to the West Shore Boulevard exit. Reed went south a quarter of a mile then turned off at Cypress. O'Neil kept going for a few blocks before circling back and slowly driving down the street containing Lankford's building. Reed's was the only car in any of the parking lots that he could see. Satisfied, at least for now, he turned around and headed home.

Half an hour after he got there, Reed pulled into the driveway, a characteristic grin stuck across his face. "How's this, boss?" he said as he held out the memory chip wrapped in a paper towel.

"Perfect," O'Neil told him as he carefully picked it out of Reed's hand. "Let's go see what this baby has to tell us."

He led the way into his office where his computer sat on top of the desk, its cover removed and on the floor. Two thin wires, extending from somewhere inside the computer, were draped over the side of the case. Carefully, O'Neil connected these to the memory device Reed had brought him and powered on the computer. When it was finished booting up, O'Neil typed in the name of a program and a second or two later, numbers and letters began to scroll across the screen. "Looks like it's working."

The scrolling stopped and the prompt reappeared as the last set of characters dissolved into nothingness. "Cross your fingers," O'Neil said as he typed something else into the keyboard. The screen turned blue and an orderly set of words and sentences, as well as groups of numbers, were displayed in small white letters.

"Did we get it?"

"Right here." O'Neil pointed to the upper left hand corner of the screen where the letters 'WAL' were displayed followed by the word 'ENTER' in square brackets. "This file shows everything Lankford typed into the keyboard, followed by the enter key, which shows up like this." He moved his finger to the word in the brackets. "Any time you see something in these brackets, that's where he pressed a non-alphabetic key like enter, backspace, or an up or a down arrow."

"Something that doesn't represent a letter or number."

"Or punctuation. Exactly. Now look up here." O'Neil pointed back to the letters 'WAL.' "Remember that the first thing he needs to enter is his login name. After that he enters his password." O'Neil dropped his finger down to the next line where the characters 'LIBRA*NOIR' appeared.

"Does that make sense?" Reed asked.

"It sure does. It's what's called a strong password. It's two words, one of which is not found in an English dictionary, and an asterisk."

"I get it." Reed moved in closer and examined the figures on the screen. He could imagine Walter Lankford sitting at his mahogany desk entering all of his secrets into his computer, taking it for granted that he was the only one who would be able to see them. "I feel like I'm reading my sister's diary," he said.

"Your sister didn't murder anybody, I hope."

"If she had, it probably would have been me." Reed turned and faced O'Neil. "When do we go back to Lankford's?"

O'Neil picked a diskette up from the desk and waved it at Reed. "How about now? We've got the password and there's no reason to wait." He didn't want to tell him about the pressure from Hill. "You drive, cleaner man."

Twenty minutes later they pulled into the parking lot at Lankford's. O'Neil told Reed that he should park around the corner of the building, out of sight from the street. Reed did this and they walked along the sidewalk back to the front door. As they entered the building, O'Neil told him how the monitor bugging program worked.

"There are three parts to it," O'Neil began. "One part captures the information sent to the monitor, the second part is a file that holds that information, and the third part is the program that reads the data file and recreates what Lankford's screens looked like. The program we're going to install here will load itself every time he turns on his computer."

"Won't he be able to tell that it's running?"

"Not unless the program itself does something to make him notice. Although if somebody calls up a list of everything that's in memory, or if they look at the configuration file that loads all of the device drivers, they'll see it on the list. We just have to hope they won't do that. Or, if they do, that they won't have any reason to check out what it's doing."

"How likely is that?"

"It's a pretty good bet. Your typical computer today will automatically load several program that are built like this. Once they're installed there isn't any need to do anything more with them. Just let them be. Your average user has never even heard of them."

"Good. Then I don't feel so dumb."

They had turned off the alarm system, re-locked the front door, and had now just entered Walter Lankford's office. Before they turned on the lights O'Neil crossed the room and rotated the rod that closed the Venetian blinds. "Make sure we remember to open these back up when we leave."

"Got it."

O'Neil moved to Lankford's desk and turned the computer on. When it asked for the login name and password, O'Neil entered the initials and the words they had read from the keyboard file. He was rewarded with the familiar operating system prompt, a letter followed by a colon and a greater than symbol. "We have access," he told Reed, who was smiling.

Sitting down in the chair behind the desk with Reed watching over his shoulder, O'Neil copied the file from the diskette in his pocket to the computer's hard disk drive. He removed the floppy when it was finished and began typing commands into the keyboard. "As far as being discovered is concerned, I'm more worried about the file that will hold the information that we capture."

"Why's that?"

"Mainly because it can get fairly large. See, the video card in the computer is continually sending signals to the monitor and if we tried to capture everything it sent, we'd fill up the hard disk in a matter of minutes. I wrote the driver program to capture data every few seconds, and then only to save the data that has changed since the last capture. That way we don't save multiple copies of the same image. But still, even though I'm compressing the data to save space, I'm limiting the size of the file that gets created. I'm afraid if we let it get too big, Lankford will run out of disk space and get somebody in here to investigate."

"But doesn't that mean we won't be getting everything?"

"To a certain point. But we don't have any idea how much data we need to get. We may get everything we need, or we may get nothing. We don't know. We'll just have to hope what we do will be enough."

After a few more minutes, O'Neil was finished installing the program. He spent another fifteen showing Reed how to move the holding file off the hard disk and onto a series of three and a half inch diskettes. When Reed declared his confidence, O'Neil switched off the computer and the lights. Reed moved to the windows and opened the blinds. When the office was physically as they had found it, the two men left the building.

During the short ride home, Reed said to O'Neil, "I want you to know that I'm taking all this very seriously."

"What do you mean?" O'Neil turned to face him.

"Well, you know, sometimes I make jokes about things when I probably shouldn't. In case you haven't noticed, I have a habit of usually saying whatever pops into my mind without questioning it. I just don't want to give you the wrong impression. This is the first thing I've ever done in my whole life that means anything to anybody. If these guys are involved with drugs and killing people, I want to see them go down, just like you do. I want to help. It makes me feel like I'm doing something worthwhile, something more than emptying other people's garbage cans. I just want you to know I'm glad you feel that you can trust me like this."

O'Neil turned back and stared through the windshield at the white lines painted between the lanes on the highway. He thought about Tim Clayton's being drugged and thrown out of an airplane, Tim's wife Marie at her husband's funeral, his own feelings of guilt for not even having been aware that his friend, his brother, had been in danger. After a few long minutes, he said to Reed, "Just be careful." He didn't look at him.

The atmosphere in the car changed with the shift in O'Neil's mood. "Just be what?" Reed asked, trying to loosen it up.

"Shut up and drive."

Marie Clayton called Tuesday afternoon shortly after O'Neil had finished eating breakfast/lunch. Damn it, I'm an idiot, he thought as he heard who it was. He hadn't forgotten about their conversation at the funeral, but he hadn't made the time to call her, either. Not yet. And now here she was having to track him down. "I'm sorry, Marie," he told her. "I should have called you by now."

"That's okay, Frankie. Really. How are things going for you?"

What stupid questions we all have to ask each other at times like these, he thought. We have to ask them to show that we care and that we're concerned, but how are we really supposed to answer them? I'm fine. I'm okay. I'll survive. I've changed. I'm bitter. I'll never be the same. I'm still pissed. I'm going after the guys that did this and I'll see them pay.

"Going okay," he told her. Stock answer.

"Good," she said. "I'm glad to hear that. I really am."

There was an awkward pause as O'Neil refused to give in to the urge to ask her the same question. It wouldn't matter how she answered, they both knew how she was feeling. There weren't any good words for that.

Finally Marie said, "I was wondering when we could get together for the dinner we talked about. There are a few things I'd like to ask you about. If it's okay."

"Of course it is, Marie, you know that. Anything you want to talk about over the phone?"

"No, no. Just a couple of things I want to go over with you. I don't think it's anything to worry about."

O'Neil didn't have any idea about what she could be talking about. "Any time you want, Marie. Just pick the night."

"Thanks, Frankie. I was thinking maybe you could come down Friday night? There are still some other issues I have to deal with."

"Friday night's fine. I'll pick you up and we'll go some place quiet."

"You can bring Katy if you'd like."

O'Neil sucked a long, deep breath through his teeth. "I don't know, Marie. Katy's staying at her sister's right now. She's giving me some space I need, and it's hard on both of us. I don't think it's quite the time yet."

"You know, Frankie, during things like this, most people need somebody they can be with."

"Marie—"

"That's okay, Frankie. I already talked to Katy, she said you had some things to work through. I just don't want to see anything bad happen to you two. Tim used to tell me you carried a lot of baggage from your past and some things were hard for you. I just want you to know that I love you both."

"We love you too, Marie." That was safe, and he said it quickly so he didn't have to think about receiving comforting words from a woman who had just lost everything. What gave him the right to feel so bad compared to her?

They held on for a minute in a silence that was more comfortable than the one before. Marie said she'd see O'Neil on Friday then quickly said goodbye and hung up.

O'Neil put down the phone and thought about his wife as he looked up at the battery powered clock hanging on the kitchen wall. She'd still be at the hospital working the day shift in the emergency room. He missed talking to her, hearing her voice, telling her he loved her. Marie was right. He did need somebody, only now was not the time. Not for him.

CHAPTER THIRTEEN

That night, O'Neil went with Reed to clean more buildings. There were three of them and they started early, impatient for the time when Reed would go to Lankford's and retrieve the file produced by O'Neil's bugging program, which was how they thought of it. An electronic snoop on Lankford's digital dealings.

When it was finally time, O'Neil told Reed to be careful, that if someone at Lankford's had in fact noticed something wrong with their system, it was conceivable somebody might be there waiting. They agreed that O'Neil would take his car and drive past Lankford's building while Reed waited in his Toyota a few blocks away. O'Neil would meet him there and tell him if everything was clear.

Reed halfheartedly balked when O'Neil suggested he unload his cleaning supplies and carry them into the building to keep things looking as routine as possible. If he were to get caught, he would just be the cleaning guy. If whoever caught him knew Reed was there on an off day, he could claim a scheduling problem or something had caused him to come a day early. "That's just a lot of extra work for nothing," he complained.

"Think of it as a favor to me," O'Neil told him. The two men left O'Neil's house shortly after eleven thirty. Forty five minutes later O'Neil told Reed it was okay to go in. He would stay there, on the corner where Reed had been waiting while he did his drive-bys.

An hour passed until Reed pulled his Toyota up next to O'Neil's car, facing the opposite direction and aligning the driver's side windows so they could talk. "Got it," he told O'Neil. "It was quiet as a tomb in there."

O'Neil had been fiddling with the radio, advancing the tuning dial click by click, momentarily listening to each station as it grew from static to music or speech, and then back to static. He had found it difficult to concentrate while Reed had been gone. Now all he felt was relief. "You can't come up with a better simile than that?"

Reed shot him a grin through the open windows. "Let's head back to my house," O'Neil told him. He began to relax as he pulled out of the parking lot and turned toward the highway. He hadn't been aware that he had been so tense.

When they arrived, O'Neil announced that he had decided to get some sleep. He'd start with the file first thing in the morning. If Reed wanted, he could sleep on the couch rather than drive home.

"How can you just go to bed without looking at what we've got?" Reed asked him. "I thought you were going to devour this thing. Bloat yourself on coffee and pull an all nighter."

"I thought about it, but I'm already tired. That file is huge and it's going to take hours to go through it and I don't want to risk overlooking something important. We're going to get a file like that every night and there's going to be a lot of material to go through."

"Do you mind if I look? I'm still kind of jazzed after going in there tonight."

"Not at all," O'Neil said. He led the way into his office and restored the file Reed had backed up onto six diskettes. Then he entered a command and a new image appeared on the monitor. He stood up and Reed took his place at the desk. "Every time you press enter, the computer will show you the next screen image that was captured. Press the escape key when you've had enough."

"And what exactly is it I'm looking for?"

O'Neil gave him a shrug and a yawn. "We probably won't know it until we see it. All we really have to go on is that somewhere buried in that file may be a reason to kill someone."

With characteristic humor, Reed asked, "Doesn't it give you nightmares to talk like that right before you go to bed?"

"You have no idea how many things give me nightmares, pal. I'll see you in the morning."

Reed was asleep on the living room couch when O'Neil came downstairs after his morning shower. It was a little after ten and O'Neil decided to hold off on breakfast so he wouldn't disturb Reed. Instead, he headed for the office and Lankford's computer file.

The bugging program he had written captured the equivalent of an image of the screen every few seconds as long as there was some activity on the computer. O'Neil found that extrapolating what had occurred during the brief intervals between the screen captures became mildly addicting. The jumps between screens were sometimes confusing, but on the whole he believed he could follow most of what was going on. After an hour or two of viewing screen after screen after screen, he felt that he would in fact be able to reconstruct the activities of Walter A. Lankford on his computer.

When Reed walked in with a tray full of peanut butter and jelly sandwiches, O'Neil had totally lost track of the time. "It's past noon, man. This was all I could find in the kitchen."

O'Neil forced his mind to break free of the rhythm of the flickering monitor and rubbed at the back of his neck. "Mine was starting to hurt last night when I turned that thing off," Reed said. "Have you come up with anything yet?"

"Not yet," O'Neil said as he bit into a sandwich. There was more peanut butter than jelly and he scraped at the roof of his mouth with his tongue. Reed laughed at him and said he liked the sandwiches that way.

"So does my wife," O'Neil managed through the stickiness. "She thinks peanut butter should be fun."

"Don't you?"

"Maybe not on a sandwich. How long did you stay up last night?"

"Too late. Even after I wanted to quit, I kept pressing that damned enter key, looking at just one more screen. It was like being hooked on some incredibly boring video game. I kept thinking, 'Just one more and I'll go to sleep.' I didn't have any clue what I was looking at but it was hard to make myself stop."

"You didn't see anything that looked interesting?"

"Not to my untrained eye."

They finished the sandwiches and O'Neil focused his attention back on the computer. There was nothing suspicious that he could see. He worked through the entire file once, broke for a trip for some fried chicken with Reed, then went through it all again. The day had long since been over when he turned off the computer and rubbed his tired eyes.

Reed put down the magazine he was reading and rotated into a sitting position on the leather couch. "Anything?"

"No. It's like you said. It doesn't look like there's anything wrong there, but I'm not sure I'd be able to recognize it if there were."

"Maybe they only break the law on Wednesdays."

"You're a real help, aren't you? I guess we'll find out if you're right. We should probably give your buddy Ray a couple more hours before we send you to get today's file."

Reed studied his watch for a moment then said, "We could probably check it in an hour or so. He should be out of there by then."

"Sounds good," O'Neil said as he stood and stretched. "I'm going to drop some Visine in my eyes and lie down on the other couch. Are you going to stay awake?"

"I've napped on and off all afternoon."

"Then wake me if I doze when it's time to go. We'll work it like we did last night."

Thursday and Friday were virtual repeats of Wednesday with Reed going into Lankford's and copying the file and O'Neil spending the next day studying it. He had been keeping a list of items he thought might be questionable, things he wanted to go back and look more closely at, but so far nothing had come remotely close to looking like an illegal activity. During another fast food lunch on Friday afternoon, Reed asked him what he thought this meant.

"I'm not sure," O'Neil told him. "It could be a number of things. Possibly Lankford himself is clean and somebody else in the firm is doing the dirty stuff. Or maybe it's just been an off week for money laundering, I don't know. Maybe every transaction we're looking at is bad and we're simply too ignorant to see it."

"But you believe that Lankford has to be in on the action."

"It makes the most sense. In a firm that size, with the president and sole stockholder actively running the business himself, if he isn't doing it he knows it's going on. I can't believe an employee could pull off a scam like this and remain invisible. Lankford has to know where the money's coming from and where it's going."

"But if it's not him, say he's given this department to someone else, how do we find that person? We can't bug all the computers, can we?"

"We probably could, at least for a while, but we wouldn't have a prayer of being able to read every file we get. That's not the answer."

"So what is?"

"I'm not sure. Hill said that he had something that would help us. I was hoping to come up with something first, before we went to him, but it may be time to give him a call."

"I get the feeling that you really don't trust this Hill guy."

"No," O'Neil said. "That's not it, exactly. Saying that I really don't like him would probably be more accurate. I just don't want to put ourselves in a position where we *have* to trust him. We're better off if we can stay a little bit in front."

"You're being a control freak, huh?"

The telephone rang and Reed reached behind him and picked up the cordless phone from the kitchen counter and tossed it to O'Neil. He caught it with one hand, extended the antenna and pushed the talk button. "Hello," he said.

"O'Neil," came the single word.

O'Neil moved the phone away from the lower part of his face and mouthed, *Speak of the devil.* "I was just thinking about you," he said.

"Don't even tell me," said Hill. "My knees go weak. I need to know where we are with this thing."

O'Neil swore to himself. Reed could see that he wasn't happy. O'Neil had wanted more time to figure out exactly what he was going to tell Hill and now he had to wing it. He started with, "I'm making some progress."

Hill jumped all over that. "What the hell does that mean? How much progress?"

O'Neil had a sinking feeling that told him he wouldn't be able to control this conversation. He felt like a child about to be caught in a lie to his parents. He tried to change the direction they were going. "It means that I would like to know what I need to look for on Lankford's network. You said you had something that would help."

"What we've got won't do you a bit of good until you can actually get on that damned network." Hill paused for a moment. "Son of a bitch, O'Neil, is that what 'making some progress' is? Did you get access to their network without letting me know? Tell me, goddamn it, and tell me now."

Boom. Just like that Hill had laid it open. "I was able to get on for a while today," O'Neil surrendered, trying to remain consistent with his earlier story. "Just for a short time. I need to know from you what to look for the next time I get on."

"Why the hell didn't you call me, O'Neil?" Hill exploded into the telephone. "I've been sitting on my ass all damned week waiting to hear from you. What the hell are you trying to pull? I've got a goddamned investigation I'm trying to run here."

"Give it a rest, Hill. I'm not trying to pull anything. I told you, I was just about to call you when the phone rang. I can get on the network and watch what's going on. Now it's time to tell me what it is you've got so I can check it out."

O'Neil stopped talking. He knew that Hill wasn't used to having someone stand up to him. Hill was a boss and a bully; he told people what to do and he beat down any resistance as hard and as fast as he could. That was how he got things done as a cop, and that was a fundamental reason why O'Neil had never gotten along with him. There was no room for other people, be they innocent or guilty, victim or bystander, help or hindrance. There was only Detective Hill, who always did what he needed to take what he wanted. When it happened to coincide with the job, he could be an effective policeman.

"I need to know exactly how you get on that network," he said after a minute, with an edge to his voice.

"No way, Hill. I have access, and that's all I'm going to tell you about it. I don't want this going back against anybody." He wanted it to sound like he was protecting a friend.

This time, he got an unexpected laugh. "Frankie old buddy, I sometimes get the feeling you don't have a lot of faith in me."

Imagine that. O'Neil said nothing.

"Got a pen handy?"

O'Neil stood and walked to the dry-erase board on the refrigerator. Uncapping a black marker from the counter, he told Hill he was ready.

"I'm going to give you four names. I need to know every scrap of information you can come up with connected with any of them. And I mean everything, even if you find something that doesn't seem to make sense to you. It might to us."

"Because you've got the bigger picture?"

"Always."

Hill dictated the names of four men while O'Neil wrote them on the board, then told O'Neil to call him after the weekend on Monday. He said they would need to keep in closer contact from now on.

O'Neil pushed the talk button a second time to end the conversation. Reed was sitting at the tiny kitchen table, looking at the names O'Neil had written but not sure of everything that had just happened. "So how're we doing, boss?"

"You never know with that guy," O'Neil told him. "I'll fill you in later. I've got to get ready for tonight. I'm driving down to Sarasota to have dinner with Marie Clayton."

"That's right. I forgot that was tonight. What about today's file from Lankford's?"

"You don't need me. Just be a little extra careful and do a drive-by before you go in. You know what's up."

Hill hung up with O'Neil and related their conversation to Fetterman who was sitting at his usual place across from Hill at his own desk. "Uh huh," Fetterman said when Hill had finished.

"I think we may have been a little too loose with our Mr. O'Neil," Hill added, his voice low. "I think maybe we need to start checking out some things, make sure nothing's going on that we should know about. What do you think?"

Fetterman looked back at Hill with the same unchanging expression he had worn as long as the two of them had known each other. "No time like the present," he said.

CHAPTER FOURTEEN

MamaLu Bates sat in her truck and watched car after car slowly leave the parking lot of the Walter A. Lankford Company. She'd been watching every night this week and by far this had been the most rapid exodus. She glanced at the dime store clock stuck to her dashboard with an adhesive strip. 6:05 p.m. Thank god it's Friday, she thought. Yuppie go home.

She waited another fifteen minutes until there were only three cars left in the lot. Two of them she recognized as having stayed late every night, usually leaving close to six thirty. She dropped the truck into gear and glided across the street and parked next to the one closest to the front door. As she worked her way out of the truck, she could see some activity inside at the reception area. Better hurry, she thought. Can't let them leave too soon.

From the bed of her truck she plucked an ancient Hoover vacuum cleaner, easily lifting it with one arm. With the other she scooped up a box of garbage bags and a collection of spray bottles she had scrounged from the maintenance closet of her apartment building. Thus armed, she made her way up the short sidewalk and kicked at the front door three times. Inside, one of the men who had been standing in the lobby moved to open the door.

"Hold that for me, will you, sport? Thanks." MamaLu waited for him to walk all the way out of the building and hold the door from there before she went inside. The lights had been turned off and three people, two men and a woman, looked to be in the final stages of wishing each other well for the weekend. Got here just in time, MamaLu thought. All three watched her enter the building and drop her supplies at their feet.

"Are you here to clean this place?" one of the men asked, trying and failing to suppress a grin.

That's not obvious? "I didn't come here to have you guys invest my vacuum cleaner," she told him. "Bay Area Cleaning Services." She had gotten that from the magnetic sign on Ray Alvarado's truck. "I've got a scheduling conflict tonight so I have to start a little early."

"Where's the regular guy?" asked the woman.

"Ray? He'll be here in a while, help me finish up." He'd be there in a while all right, but she planned on being long gone by then. She picked up her stack of garbage bags and started to move around the receptionist's desk away from the front of the building. If they were suspicious they'd come after her, ask her more questions. If not, they would probably just leave.

She saw a room in the back with a small kitchen that she thought must have served as the company break room. Since she didn't know the first thing about cleaning buildings, let alone a fancy office suite, she thought she could go in there and bang some dishes around until the people up front left. As far as she was concerned, they had served their purpose. She had gotten into the building without having to know the password for the security system.

After five minutes, when nobody had followed her to the back, MamaLu returned to the front door area. Her vacuum cleaner and spray bottles were as she had left them but the building itself was otherwise clear of people. They had even been so helpful as to have locked the front door, trusting that she had her own set of keys.

She dropped the garbage bags on the floor next to her other things and fished in her pocket for her new key ring. O'Neil had said that the two most important keys for her to copy were the one for the building and the one for the president's office. She'd locate that and start there.

It should be three or four hours before Alvarado showed up, based on when he had arrived last Friday as well as this past Wednesday. Still, she didn't want to cut it that close. Even though she had no idea what she was looking for, whether she found it or not she'd still be talking to O'Neil in the morning. She looked around at the framed artwork on the walls, the expensive wooden furniture. This place was obviously doing well and that suited her.

That's the magic word she thought as she tried a key in the locked door: Prosperous. Whether she figured out what O'Neil and that kid were after or if she had to resort to blackmail to get some of it, that's where she was headed. MamaLu Bates had a date with prosperity.

It took O'Neil nearly an hour and a half to drive the seventy miles to the Clayton home in Sarasota. Save for the long bridge over the bay the drive was long and flat, scrubby swamp lands lining each side of the highway. So far, at least, this part of Florida had been mostly spared from the ravages of the developers' bulldozers. It wouldn't stay that way.

Images of captured computer screens flickered through his mind as he drove, a montage of meaningless names and numbers. After studying a four day supply of information from Walter Lankford's computer, he had yet to find anything suggesting money laundering. He was primarily looking for the transfer of large amounts of money out of the country.

For a foreign drug cartel operating in the U.S. it is very difficult to move their huge profits safely across international borders. The ideal method is to find a way to get it into the banking system where it can easily be converted to other currencies and transferred somewhere else.

A number of things make this difficult. With a million dollars in twenty dollar bills weighing a hundred and twenty five pounds, physically moving the money poses its own challenges. To get that much money into a bank in any form would require the filling out of a Cash Transaction Record, or CTR, paperwork the government requires for deposits greater than ten thousand dollars. The system is designed to leave a trail.

So far though, O'Neil hadn't seen any signs of it, which was not to say they weren't there. There was always the possibility of smurfs, people used by the drug lords to open accounts with smaller, less noticeable sums of money. Even in that case, he should be able to see traces of it leaving the country after it was in the system.

Then there were the four names Hill had given him. He'd have to go through all that data again to look for their presence. That might lead to something.

O'Neil found himself aware of the fact that he had entered the subdivision where Tim had bought a house upon his return from the islands. With a dock behind it on the Gulf of Mexico, he and his bride had never been far from the sea that had brought them together. Until now.

He pulled the car into the driveway and parked. He had many memories, many associations with this place, and he could feel the anger and frustration inside him kindle themselves into the start of a rage. God damn it, Tim. Why didn't you tell me any of this had been going on? I could have helped.

Things could have been different.

A light came on over the front door and O'Neil quickly stepped out of his car, taking deep breaths. He was here for Marie and he refused to let her see the pain he was feeling. She had enough of her own.

He met her at the door where she appeared wearing a pair of simple slacks and a white blouse with large padded buttons. They embraced for half a minute before Marie broke away, pulling the door all the way closed and leading O'Neil back toward the driveway. "I was going to invite you in," she told him. "But I just want to get the hell away from here for a while."

They were quiet as they drove to the restaurant. The dinner rush was over and the dining room was mostly empty as they were seated at a table in the corner, over the water. Half of the room was built on a wooden platform that extended over the slow current and brown waters of an estuary leading to the Gulf. A fine screen mesh made up the walls and chirping insect sounds passed unfiltered into the restaurant. Enclosed candles were the only source of light, one per table. An intimate atmosphere for lovers and secrets, O'Neil thought.

"I want to thank you for coming to see me, Frankie. You don't know how much I appreciate it."

O'Neil made an awkward gesture in the air above the table with his hand.

"Don't thank me, Marie. It wasn't a favor. I came because I wanted to see you."

"You're sweet, Frankie."

A waiter appeared at the table and O'Neil ordered a carafe of red wine for the two of them. He returned a minute later and O'Neil dismissed him by telling him he would pour. He filled two glasses and placed one in front of Marie. When he was done, he stared at the reflection of candles on the outside of her glass and wondered how far the light reached into the wine.

"I wanted to ask you about some business things that have come up since Tim's death."

O'Neil kept staring at the wine glass until a delicate hand lifted it from the table, paused, then gracefully put it back. He realized they were about to talk about Tim's death and that made him sad. "What are you going to do, Marie?"

"There are some things that need to be settled. Then I think I'll leave for a while, get out of Florida. If I sit in that house and do nothing I'll lose my mind in two days. I need to move around, see things go past me. Remind me how to live life."

He sat listening to the wife of his murdered best friend and knew that he had nothing to offer. He sipped his own wine and said nothing.

"My mother lives in Vermont, did you know that?"

O'Neil shook his head.

"I've never been there before. I miss seeing mountains. You almost forget they exist, living here. Everything is so flat."

She slid her cloth napkin out of its plastic ring and twisted it around her fingers. "There are a few things that need to be taken care of, though. I want to ask you what you think I should do with the business."

The waiter reappeared and quietly stood beside the table. O'Neil noticed him and the man began to recite the evening's specials, all of which featured a seafood entrée. Marie tried to say she wasn't hungry but O'Neil told the waiter to bring them two of the broiled grouper specials. "You have to eat, Marie," suspecting she hadn't been.

She nodded as she continued to play with her napkin, not wanting to lose her train of thought. "I didn't know if–" She stopped herself then began again. "I don't know if you have any desire to take over the business. I need to ask you that first."

This was a surprise. "Is that what you want? Do you want me to take it over?" He hadn't given any thought at all to what would happen to Tim's business. Mentally he kicked himself. The business hadn't ended with Tim, it had passed to Marie and she would need to deal with it.

"Well, no, I'm not asking like that. Ron Pauley made me an offer to buy the company. He says that there's a lot of value in the maintenance agreements Tim had as well as in the work in progress. I don't really have any idea what he's talking about. I just want to do what's best."

Pauley was a local Sarasotan who had often worked for Tim on a contract basis. O'Neil knew him and respected his work. "Sell the company, Marie. Tim would have approved and it is probably the best thing for the customers. If that's what you want to do."

"I think so. The accountants say the offer is fair but I just thought I should check with you to see if, you were maybe interested before I answered. I didn't know if this was something you had thought about."

"I have a business in Tampa. Tim's clients would be happier with someone closer to home, I'm sure." O'Neil reached across the table and squeezed her hand, the one without the napkin. "Take the money, Marie. It's okay."

"Thanks, Frankie. Tim had insurance, and I'm going to sell the boat, but the money will help."

They sat alone in the near dark, breathing the humid air and listening to the night's sounds. The water beneath them made almost no noise as it slowly passed beneath their feet. In a little while, their food arrived and they began to eat.

During the meal they spoke lightly of Katy, Marie respecting the unspoken situation between her two friends. O'Neil answered her questions but didn't offer more, himself not comfortable talking about it. When the waiter returned for their empty dishes and dessert orders, they both said no to more food and asked for coffee instead.

"Thank you for the dinner, Frankie. The food was wonderful. I didn't realize how hungry I really was."

"I'm glad you enjoyed it."

"You know," she said, wrinkling her forehead. "There's something else I can ask you about, if it's all right. Of course, if I sell to Ron this would become his problem but I'm not sure there's anything to worry about."

"What is it?"

As the coffee arrived, Marie asked, "Have you ever heard of a man named James Rooker?"

O'Neil thought about it for a moment, then said, "No, I don't think so. Who is he?"

"He was a consultant like you and Tim, I guess. From Sarasota. A couple of days after the funeral, several of Tim's customers called the business number. They were very nice and very sweet, but they all wanted to know about this man James Rooker. It seems he was going around to some of our clients representing himself as Tim's partner, someone who was taking over the company. They wanted to know if it was true, if he was who he said he was."

"Do you know him?"

"I met him at the funeral otherwise I never would have known who they were talking about."

"What did you tell the customers?"

"The truth. That I had no idea why this man would be telling them this and that it wasn't true as far as I knew. I don't know that Tim ever met him."

O'Neil sipped at his own coffee, then slowly shook his head. The things some people will do to make a buck, he thought. Let the body grow cold, for Christ's sake. "I'll talk to him, Marie. I can put on my cop act and tell him to back the hell off. I'm just sorry you have to put up with this kind of thing."

Marie shook her head. "That's just it, Frankie. I don't. He's dead. It was in the paper this morning."

"He's dead? What happened?"

"The paper said he was murdered. They said he had been badly beaten but they didn't know the exact cause of death yet."

"No, they'd have to wait for an autopsy. Did they say who did it?"

"They don't know."

O'Neil listened carefully as Marie recounted as much of the story as she could remember. When she was through, O'Neil sank into the back of his chair. The mortality rate for computer consultants in Tampa Bay was going through the roof, he thought. He poured another half glass of wine for himself and Marie.

If this guy had been low enough to try to steal a dead man's business from his widow, he had probably had other enemies as well. Provided this wasn't some random killing, the police should be able to find whoever did it. Usually if the victim provoked enough rage in his antagonist to get himself beaten to death, the path back to the killers was reasonably clear. "What was he like at the funeral?"

"Oh, I don't know. He didn't make much of an impression on me although I wasn't exactly in the best state of mind. I saw him with the two policemen from Tampa that are investigating Tim's death so I wondered if you knew him."

O'Neil straightened in his chair. "Say that again."

"I saw him with the two detectives from Tampa that are investigating Tim's death." Concern wrinkled her features. "Frankie, what's wrong?"

"Something, maybe. I don't know." It had struck him when he heard her make the statement about the Tampa police. Something at the edge of his thoughts, flitting like a firefly, visible during the occasional spark. Marie stayed silent as she watched O'Neil. His forehead was creased and he was staring at a spot on the table between them.

What had Hill and Fetterman been doing with another computer consultant? Had they had someone else working on the Lankford case? Their knowing each other seemed to be a pretty big coincidence.

"Marie, was one of the companies that called you about this guy the Walter A. Lankford Company?"

Marie's face took on a nervous look in the candle's light. "No," she said. "One of them was from Tampa but they were an office supply wholesaler or something. The others were all in either Sarasota or Bradenton. I kept a list but it's back home if you want to see it."

"No, that's all right." He reached forward and squeezed her hand again. "Don't worry. I just think too much, sometimes." Still, something was tugging at him and he didn't like it. "Would you excuse me for just a minute? I need to find the bathroom."

She gave him a nod and an uneasy smile as he stood and walked out of the dining room to the front of the restaurant.

There were pay phones located just outside the doors leading to the bathrooms and O'Neil stepped up to the first one, lifting the handset to his ear. He punched in his credit card number followed by his home phone number and waited until his machine answered the call. His own voice asked him to leave a message and after the tone he said, "Reed, if you're there pick up the phone." A pause. "Reed."

Nothing happened.

He repeated the statement and hung on for a minute longer, willing the phone to answer him with Reed's voice. Then he hung up and dialed again, this time trying Reed's number. There was no answer there, either.

He stood by the phones, unsure of what he should do. As far as he knew, there was no connection between this Rooker guy and the Lankford Company, no real reason to grow alarmed. On the other hand, there was a definite link between Tim, Rooker, and Hill and Fetterman. What did it mean that the two cops were the only ones still breathing?

Fuck it, he swore to himself and went back to the table. He had to do something.

Marie hadn't moved. She was still sitting in her chair, staring patiently into the flickering fire dance of the candle, imagining herself as a stick of wax, half of which lay in molten pebbles piled around its base. "I'm ready to go home," she said to O'Neil without looking up, as if sensing his urgency.

Wordlessly, O'Neil left enough money on the table to cover the check and led Marie by the elbow out to the car. As he opened the door for her she broke the uncomfortable silence by saying, "I just can't get away, can I?" Without waiting for an answer, she lowered herself gently into the car seat. O'Neil didn't know what to tell her.

He was tense during the long drive back to Tampa. When O'Neil thought of Marie he felt guilty, upset with himself that he had been unable to provide a quiet, relaxing evening for her. There was just too much going on, it seemed. Too much at stake.

He checked his watch for perhaps the twentieth time, then looked at the speedometer. Tampa was a lot closer at ninety miles per hour but it would still take him over an hour to get there. Traffic was almost nonexistent and he knew that if he came across a cop he'd be pulled over and ticketed in a heartbeat. He didn't want to lose that time.

Hill and Fetterman hadn't told him everything; he knew that. But he also knew that he hadn't told them everything, either. The question is, had what they kept from him caused the deaths of two men? He remembered Hill asking him if he was working with somebody else who knew computers. The thought chilled him as he considered if that was what Hill had meant.

He needed to find Reed, that much he was sure of. Find him and regroup before moving ahead any further, possibly walking into a situation they couldn't walk out of. He wondered if that had been what happened to Tim Clayton and this James Rooker.

He looked at the time again but it didn't help. He had no idea if Reed had already gone to Lankford's, if he was on his way, or even if he was there right now. There was just too damned much he didn't know and he gripped the steering wheel tighter and watched the speedometer needle as it edged further to the right, his knuckles throbbing with tension and frustration. If something happened to Reed because of Hill and Fetterman....

He let that thought trail off in his mind. It was not a possibility he was prepared to allow to happen. If Hill and Fetterman were setting him up, if they had had something to do with the death of his friend, he would find a way to make them accountable. It may be melodramatic, he thought, but he would find a way to make them pay.

Somewhere to the south of him, a lonely woman sat on the deck of a sail boat tied to a dock behind her home, and cried.

CHAPTER FIFTEEN

Once he hit Tampa, O'Neil had to force himself to slow down as he turned off the freeway. He had been speeding for so long that traveling at the speed limit felt as though he were hardly moving.

The moon was a mere sliver and spray from overnight sprinkler systems peppered the windshield making the night seem darker than it was. O'Neil rolled down his window and felt the warm humid air cover his face like a mask. He wanted to have a clearer view as he drove by Lankford's.

He turned right onto Cypress and kept the car moving at a steady speed five miles an hour slower than it had been. Lankford's was dark, the parking lot empty. There was no sign of Reed or anyone else.

He drove further to where the street ended at the bay and slowly turned the car around. If anyone were to see him, he was just another out of state transplant who had turned down the wrong road. As he drove past Lankford's building again, from the west this time, he had a brief view of the lot where he had told Reed to park. It was also empty.

Okay, he told himself. He's not here but there's no sign anything's wrong, either. He headed back for the highway and accelerated toward his house.

The driveway was empty and no lights were on. Same story as Lankford's. Still, he left the car in front of the garage and went inside, hoping to find a message or some kind of sign.

The light on the answering machine was blinking once. He pushed the play button and walked into the kitchen as he heard his own voice speak to him from the tape. He flicked the light switch and as the fluorescent lights flicked on overhead, he saw that the dry-erase board on the refrigerator was blank. He turned to walk out of the room then froze. Hadn't he left the four names from Hill on the board?

O'Neil took a step toward the refrigerator then stopped. No, he had erased the board after he had copied the names onto a legal pad from his office. Calm down, damn it, he told himself as he turned off the light and left the kitchen. It doesn't help to be so damned jumpy.

He passed back through the living room on the way to his office, the only other place in the house that Reed might have been. It too was empty and there was no sign of anything wrong.

Picking up the telephone, he dialed Reed's number again. After the fifteenth ring he hung up. Where the hell could he be? Without a clear plan, O'Neil took a felt tip pen out of a drawer and wrote, "Reed– If you get here, stay here!" on a sheet of paper and tore it from the pad.

He found some tape in another drawer and took a piece from the dispenser, attaching one end to the paper. He went back to the living room and slid a chair to a position across from the front door and posted his note so it wouldn't be missed by anyone coming in. The he left, jogging out to his car in the driveway.

The only thing he could think to do at this point was drive to Reed's apartment, make sure things looked all right there. The problem is, he thought, I don't know where the hell it is. All Reed had told him was that he lived somewhere in Town and Country. That wasn't a great help.

O'Neil slipped the car in gear and backed out of the driveway. He was going to make another run past Lankford's when something occurred to him. He had given Reed his duplicate key ring, a set of spares he kept in case something happened to his own. That meant that Reed would have access to O'Neil's office as well as his house.

It was an easy twenty minute drive that O'Neil made in twelve. As he turned into the familiar lot of O'Neil-Sanders Inc., he could see Reed's Toyota parked lazily across two spaces in front of the building. Son of a bitch, O'Neil thought as he parked and hurried to the front door.

It was locked and the lights were out. O'Neil unlocked the door and strode directly down the short hallway to his office. The green shaded lamp on his desk was on, much like it had been the night he had first met Reed.

This time he wasn't in the chair behind the desk. He was lying in a curl halfway to a fetal position on the couch that O'Neil used when he entertained customers. O'Neil slapped hard at the bottom of Reed's feet then stood back near his desk. Reed jerked awake, startled, until he saw O'Neil and standing in the light. "Don't do that, man. You'll give me a heart attack or something."

"Better you than me. I've been trying like hell to find you."

"How was dinner?" Reed rubbed his eyes and yawned.

"Terrible. I'll tell you about that later. Did you get to Lankford's?"

Reed looked at his watch. "Oh, man. Not yet. I mean, I went there once but I didn't stay. I came here to wait for a while and I guess I fell asleep. Did you go?"

"Just to look for you. Why didn't you stay?"

"There was a car in the parking lot and some of the lights were on inside. I didn't see anybody but I didn't know the car, so I backed off. It wasn't Ray's. What's up?"

O'Neil related what Marie had told him about James Rooker, Rooker's connection to Hill and Fetterman, and what he feared it all might mean. When he was finished, the two men sat quietly for a moment, considering.

"So you raced all the way back here to see if I was okay?"

"Amazing, isn't it?"

"Well, thanks anyway." He shook his head like a wet dog coming out of a bath. "So what are we going to do next?"

"You're going home. I want you far away from this until I know more about what's going on. I'm going to make one more trip to Lankford's and disable the bugging program for the time being. Beyond that, I don't know yet."

"I don't want to run out on you like this."

"You're not running out on me. I'm asking you to walk away from it."

"Same difference." Reed strafed through his hair with his fingers. "I'm not trying to argue something with you, I just want to let you know that I don't want to do it. I don't want to run or walk away like I'm scared because I'm not. It doesn't feel right."

O'Neil stood up and held the chain that would turn off the desk lamp between two of his fingers. "Tell you what. For now let's get ourselves over to Lankford's and finish up there. We can talk about this later." Reed stood up and O'Neil pulled down on the chain. There was enough brightness from the lights in the parking lot coming through the windows to allow them to see their way out.

On the ride over to Lankford's, together in O'Neil's car, neither man had much to say.

O'Neil unlocked the door and Reed walked in ahead of him and turned off the alarm. Without switching on the lights, O'Neil waited and followed Reed to Walter Lankford's office, which he also opened. Once in, Reed moved to close the blinds and O'Neil went behind the desk to the computer.

He seated himself in the brown leather chair and reached for the power switch on the computer, housed on the vertical case beneath the desk. He pushed the button until it clicked then pulled his hand halfway back. "This is odd," he said.

"What is?" Reed asked. He walked around the desk next to O'Neil and looked at the computer monitor.

"Not there," O'Neil told him. "Down here." He motioned toward the space under the desk with a nod of his head.

"What? That's a garbage can."

O'Neil pulled the small plastic container out from under the desk and looked closely at the contents. Then he picked it up and held it out to Reed. "What's that?"

"The obvious answer would be 'garbage,'" Reed said. "And since it is lying in a garbage bag in somebody's garbage can, I'd pretty much have to go with that." He reached into the container and withdrew his hand, a brown

Snickers wrapper pinched between two fingers. "Or am I missing something?"

"The whole point," said O'Neil. "What happens here on Friday nights? On Wednesday and Friday nights?"

Reed cocked an eyebrow. "Oh."

"If Ray Alvarado cleaned the office, which would have included emptying the garbage cans, who–"

"–threw away the candy wrapper," Reed finished. He handed the garbage can back to O'Neil who returned it to its place under the desk. Then he placed a diskette in the drive and began the process of removing the file containing the screen information that had been captured that day. After a minute, he removed the diskette and replaced it with another. He hit a key on the keyboard to continue the process. Reed hadn't moved.

"When did you see that car tonight?" O'Neil asked him. "Was it before Ray would have been here, or after?"

Reed didn't hesitate. "It was after. Definitely after."

O'Neil thought on that for a moment, again switching diskettes when the current one became full.

"What do you think it means?" Reed asked.

O'Neil shook his head slowly. "I don't know. Maybe nothing. Maybe Walter Lankford stopped by before we got here. Maybe Ray got hungry while he was cleaning and popped a candy bar."

"But these things wouldn't worry you."

"No, they wouldn't. What does is that there are too many things going on here that we don't understand. The more things we find, the more nervous I get." He swapped another diskette out of the drive. "On the other hand, it could be I'm just being paranoid. What do you think?"

Reed moved around the desk and sat in one of the two chairs that were facing it. "I don't know, boss. You're in charge here."

O'Neil shook his head again and another few minutes went by as he continued the removal of the computer file from Lankford's machine. When he was through, he sat up in front of the monitor and rapidly typed in a new command. He told Reed he was disabling the bugging program. He wanted to figure more of this out before they exposed themselves in Lankford's office again.

"Sounds like a good idea."

O'Neil turned off the computer and the monitor and Reed moved to reopen the blinds. As they were leaving the building, O'Neil stopped him. "What kind of car was it that you saw earlier?"

"It wasn't really a car," Reed said. "It was a pickup."

Oh no, thought O'Neil.

"I didn't see the make or model or anything, but it was one of those extended cab jobs."

"What color was it?"

"Purple and black. Really slick looking. I think the windows were tinted but I'm not sure, it was hard to tell in the dark. Why?"

O'Neil didn't answer the question. Instead, he swore softly, almost to himself.

They were outside the building walking through the parking lot to O'Neil's car. Reed tugged on O'Neil's upper arm, making him stop. "What is it?" he asked. "What's wrong?"

"I know that truck."

They drove to Clearwater, to the beach where they had first found MamaLu Bates. They had no idea where she lived and no clear idea where to begin looking.

"It's almost 2:30 in the morning, boss. How are we going to find her?"

"I don't know," O'Neil said as he pulled over and parked at a meter on the side of the street. "But we've got to try."

They walked along the sidewalk fronting the public beach, stopping at the pay phone kiosks as they went. There was plenty of artificial light shining down from the street lamps and the motels across the street. A mole cricket scurried across the sidewalk under their feet and made a sound like a flash bulb popping when Reed stepped on it. "Whoops," he said.

The first kiosk had a short length of frayed cable swinging back and forth carelessly in the ocean breeze. No phone books. The second one had a copy of just the yellow pages, and the third one had the white ones, too. O'Neil snatched them up and balanced the hard plastic cover on his knee as he looked up the name 'Bates.'

After a minute, he let the books drop and resume their dangle at the end of the cable. "Nothing," he said and turned toward the ocean. They couldn't see it from the sidewalk, a rolling mound of sand was between them, but the white noise of the waves washing onto the shore filled the air like the mist from a dense fog.

O'Neil led Reed back to the car. They drove through the streets near the beach until fatigue was mixing with futility and O'Neil turned the car toward home. It was an absurd hope, he thought, trying to find her truck.

They decided to leave Reed's car at O'Neil's office for the night and drive directly to O'Neil's house. As they pulled into the driveway, not long before the appearance of the sun, Reed asked, "Do you have any idea what's going on?"

O'Neil shook his head no. "I wish I did." Those were the first words he had spoken since they had left the beach.

CHAPTER SIXTEEN

They were back in Clearwater a short time later after managing just a few hours of sleep. The senior citizens were out walking the beach and the laughing gulls were gathering in the sand in front of the snack bar, waiting for breakfast scraps or the arrival of the careless tourists.

O'Neil went to the employees working the counter and then to the cooks preparing the food, describing MamaLu and asking them if they had any idea where she lived or how he could find her. Several of them recognized her and said she was a regular but didn't know anything more about her.

They moved across the street to the restaurants and shops that were open, catering to the early morning trade. O'Neil asked the questions while Reed as often as not waited outside, fighting down his lack of sleep.

A little over an hour into their search, O'Neil walked out of a corner diner that looked like it had been serving greasy breakfasts since before any of the chain hotels had been built across the street on the beach. "We've got something," O'Neil said as Reed fell into step beside him. "Guy inside says he knows her well, she's eaten breakfast there for years. Said she lives in the apartment building a block up this way. He said he would be surprised if she didn't show up for breakfast in an hour or two." Reed didn't answer, he wasn't sure what to say.

They walked up to the apartment building, what looked like a large two story gray house with painted white shutters and window trim. Outside the front door were eight rusty black mail boxes hanging in two rows on nails driven directly into the wood siding. A black plastic label said 'L. Bates' on the mail box third in on the bottom row. "This is it," O'Neil said.

There were eight worn and weathered doorbell buttons mounted vertically along the right side of the door frame. Standing behind O'Neil, Reed could see no way to match the proper buttons to the names on the mail boxes.

The door itself was a steel screen mesh with broken supports welded laterally a third of the way up from the bottom and a third of the way down from the top. The middle section was pushed in, partially broken off from the frame. It looked as if it had been kicked in a number of times. On the other side was a hallway leading back to the rear of the building.

"Push this in a little more, will you?" O'Neil indicated the broken mesh. Reed stepped up and applied pressure with both hands until O'Neil could reach in and turn the handle from the inside. As the door started to open, O'Neil said, "Hold it until I get my arm out."

Once inside, they walked down the hallway reading the little cards tacked to the front of the four apartment doors on the ground floor. At the last door on the left hand side, Reed stopped and said, "Here it is." The faded white paper had the name 'Bates' typed crookedly across its front.

Reed stepped to the side as O'Neil joined him. "Now what?" he whispered. "Do we knock?"

"Not if we don't have to. I don't want anybody else to hear." O'Neil grabbed the door knob and turned it lightly until it stopped. There was a dull click as the latch cleared the catch in the door frame. It was unlocked.

O'Neil let go of the knob and they stood in the hallway and watched as the door swung slowly open, carried inside to the wall by the force of its own weight. They had a view of half the apartment, neatly decorated but without much style. Across from the door, on the other side of the living room, was the small kitchen. O'Neil could see something large on the floor. "Get inside," he told Reed. "Quickly."

They entered the apartment and O'Neil gently pushed the door closed with the top of his foot. "Don't touch anything."

"No problem," Reed said. He put his hands in his pockets and swiveled his head as he scanned the room. His eyes followed O'Neil as his friend moved toward the kitchen. Then he saw it, too.

"Oh, shit," he said, whispering again.

MamaLu's immense body lay in a grotesque sprawl across the kitchen linoleum. Her eyes were wide open but there was no life there. Her throat was an ugly series of black and purple blotches.

"She's dead, isn't she?" Reed asked.

"Yes, she is."

O'Neil knelt down beside Lu Bates, careful to avoid the sticky puddle of partially evaporated waste that framed the lower half of her body. He examined the marks he saw on her wrists and then studied the fingers on her left hand. Reed watched, simultaneously repulsed and fascinated, unable to turn away and unsure of why.

"She was handcuffed," O'Neil said. "And some of her fingers are broken, you can see by the knuckles."

Reed didn't comment.

Her shirt had been cut open from the collar all the way down and one half lay across each breast, not meeting in the middle, leaving a gap of several inches. She looked as if she were wearing a vest. O'Neil gingerly lifted the edges of the fabric and slowly pulled them up and back. MamaLu's bra had been cut as well and it lay across the top of her breasts, one of which was now exposed to the still air of the tiny kitchen.

O'Neil counted twelve small but deep puncture wounds surrounding the nipple. He looked around the kitchen for the sort of small utensil he thought might be there. He didn't find one. O'Neil thought of the carving Fetterman had left on the picnic table in the park that Monday several weeks before, of the Swiss army knife he had used and how many implements it contained: different sized blades, a bottle opener. He looked again at MamaLu's wounds.

A corkscrew. A scratch awl.

He stood up and turned away from the body. Reed's face was ashen as O'Neil took him by the elbow and steered him toward the door. "You going to be all right?" he asked.

After a moment, Reed nodded his head. "I just need a minute."

"No time, buddy. We have to go now." He opened the front door and motioned for Reed to pass through, thankful that so far, at least, Reed hadn't bent over and emptied his stomach.

The hall was as quiet now as it had been when they had arrived. Without rushing, the two men walked out of the building and headed down the block the way they had come. When they were back at the car, O'Neil asked Reed how he was feeling. "A little better. The air helps."

"If you're going to lose it, now's the time."

"No, I'm all right. Just be thankful we didn't stop for an Egg McMuffin on the way over."

They got into the car and O'Neil pulled out onto the street. "Something I didn't tell you about Hill and Fetterman," O'Neil said. "The quiet one likes his pocket knife."

As they came to a stop in front of O'Neil's garage, another car pulled in behind them, blocking the mouth of the driveway. O'Neil recognized it in the rear view mirror while Reed swiveled in his seat. "What's going on?" he asked.

"Turn around and don't say anything."

They heard one of the doors open and slam shut. O'Neil opened his own door, said, "Stay here," and stepped out onto the concrete.

Through his window Reed heard him say, "'Morning, Hill. Nice of you to turn up."

The other man's footsteps stopped and a gruff voice said, "Is that so?"

"I've got something for you."

It was occurring to Reed that if these cops were doing the things O'Neil thought they were doing, both of their lives could be in danger. For the first time, the reality of what they were involved with hit home. It was suddenly easier to sit in the car and stare at the glove compartment. He started questioning the series of choices that had brought him here.

He heard O'Neil say to Hill, "What's wrong with Fetterman?"

"He's good where he is."

O'Neil considered that for a moment. "Okay," he said and began to walk toward the house.

Hill followed him for a few steps then stopped, turned, and bent forward. With his hands on his knees, he peered through the windshield at Reed. "What about him?"

Reed felt his insides tighten as, still staring at the glove box, he heard O'Neil say, "This has nothing to do with him. This is just us."

Hill stayed where he was for a moment, studying Reed's face before straightening and turning away. "If you say so," he said.

O'Neil hadn't stopped moving and was already at the front door. As the two men disappeared inside, Reed tried to force himself to relax. Images of MamaLu's pale white body lying gracelessly in a puddle of filth made him keenly aware of the second policeman sitting in the car behind him, not fifteen yards away.

He had a wild thought about getting out of the car and running madly down the street. Fight or flee. He didn't know what O'Neil was planning, if anything, and he had no idea what was going to happen inside that house.

"I haven't been completely honest with you," O'Neil said.

"You're kidding."

O'Neil ignored him. "I've been able to get information off of Lankford's computer system for the past week. I haven't seen any sign of illegal activity but I haven't had a chance to look for anything regarding those names you gave me. I want to give you all the information, see what you can do with it."

O'Neil moved to his computer and turned it on. Hill didn't say anything. He just stood where he was, hands in his pockets, watching O'Neil.

"I'm going to show you how to use a program I wrote that will let you look at what was happening on Lankford's computer. It's not hard but you should take some notes." He looked to Hill in the center of the room. Move, you bastard prick, O'Neil thought. Do something.

"Why all the bullshit, Frankie? Why not let me know you were in there? I gotta tell you, I'm bothered by this attitude. This whole dishonesty thing."

Was he serious? This murdering son of a bitch? Cool it, O'Neil told himself. He had to sell his story right now or both he and Reed might not make it past this afternoon. "You know why I'm doing this. I want to find who killed Tim Clayton, and why. If I got you in there, at Lankford's, you wouldn't need me any more and you could cut me out. I didn't want that to happen."

From his spot in the center of the room, Hill stared at O'Neil, who was fighting to keep his pulse from accelerating, keep from showing signs of the stress and nervousness he was feeling. He was tight beneath the skin, but he couldn't allow any of it to show. Not yet.

Slowly Hill said, "So why change your mind now?"

Forcing himself to speak at the same pace, O'Neil told him, "I don't know. I guess I'm older and wiser, something like that. I don't want to put myself through it any more. I thought I did but I changed my mind. I'll do what I can to help you get them, but you get paid for the dirty work so you do it. I won't my own life back. It's not worth it to me."

Hill grinned and looked at the floor, casually shaking his head back and forth. O'Neil knew this expression, the 'you never could make it as a cop' look he had seen from Hill before. "Okay." Hill reached inside his jacket pocket and pulled out a notebook and pen. He joined O'Neil behind the desk and said, "Show me how this thing of yours works."

It didn't take long. Hill knew how to use a computer and O'Neil walked him through the steps of restoring the program and captured files to the computer. He showed him how to start and use the reader program as well as how to exit it once he'd finished.

Hill took two pages of notes while O'Neil began to back up the appropriate files to a set of diskettes. "So you've got, what, a week's worth of info off Lankford's system? You can see everything that guy did for the past week?"

"Yes."

"And you can get more." Meant as a question.

"Let me know when you're done with what I've given you and I'll get more."

Hill held out his hand and O'Neil gave him the box of diskettes. Without another word, they left the house and walked out to the cars parked in the driveway. The single occupants of each vehicle were just as they were when O'Neil and Hill had gone inside. O'Neil stopped next to his car. Hill didn't seem to notice. "Let me know what you find," he called.

"Of course," Hill said as he opened his door and slid into the seat. He pulled the door shut and stuck his head through the window. "Just be sure you're somewhere I can find you."

O'Neil gave him a nod and watched as Hill started the car and backed it away. Don't worry, he thought.

After the two cops had disappeared down the block O'Neil turned and motioned for Reed to get out of the car. "How you doing?"

"Oh man oh man oh man."

"You okay?"

Reed looked down the block to make sure that the car was really gone. "I feel like I've been sitting in front of snake, waiting for it to strike. Cripes."

"Did he do anything?"

"You kidding? He didn't have to." He combed his hair back with his fingers. "How'd it go in there?"

O'Neil told him. "Now we have to hurry."

"Why?" Reed asked. "It sounds like he bought it."

"He did. That's why he left. But he'll be back."

"How come?"

"Because I didn't give him Lankford's data. I gave him the junk I used for testing while I was writing the program."

"Oh boy." Reed followed O'Neil into the house, who led him back to the room with the computer. "So tell me this," he said. "Which is the one with the knife? The one that was with you, or the one that stayed with me?"

"The cobra."

"It figures."

O'Neil picked up the phone and dialed the number for his partner, John Sanders. He recognized the voice that answered and said, "John, this is Frankie."

"Frankie! I was just thinking about you. How are you doing?"

"Not too bad." His partner's voice reminded him there was another world out there, the one he tried so hard to find when he quit being a cop. No dead bodies, no lost friends, no dirty policemen. Katy.

"Seriously? I know you, buddy, and that's your stock answer."

"Things are kind of complicated right now, John. Look, I need you to do a couple of things."

"Sure, Frankie. Tell me what you need."

"You've got to get to the office and make sure we have backups of everything and get them off site. Don't leave anything we can't afford to lose."

John said, "Okay," somewhat hesitantly, like somebody was speaking to him in a foreign language and he wasn't getting the meaning. "That's mostly done anyway. Are we expecting a hurricane I haven't heard about?"

"Something like that."

"All right, then. I'll do it first thing Monday morning."

"No, John, you've got to do it now. As soon as we get off the phone. And I want you to make sure that nobody, even you, is alone in the office after hours. Especially you."

There was an uncomfortable silence on the line. Then, "What's going on?"

"Probably nothing, John. These are just precautions."

"Against what? Is something going on we should know about, Frankie?" O'Neil wasn't sure what he meant with that 'we.' "I don't think so."

"Are you all right?"

"John, I've got to go. Get over to the office, get the backups, then get out of there. If any police show up, don't tell them you've spoken to me."

"Oh, Jesus, Frankie, the police?"

But he had hung up.

"What was all that about?" Reed asked.

"I don't want Hill trashing my office looking for the real data from Lankford's computer." O'Neil opened a desk drawer and withdrew a blank tape for the backup unit attached to the computer. "And we have to do the same thing I told John to do. We need to get this stuff off this computer and get the hell out of Dodge." O'Neil inserted the tape into the drive and typed a command into the computer while a high speed whirring sound seeped out of the backup unit.

"Could you please just talk to me for a minute? I mean, I know we're in a hurry, but I don't like having this feeling that I don't understand what's going on. You can tell me to go to hell if you want but I would really like to know what's happening here, especially if we're in more danger now than before."

O'Neil forced himself to slow down and sit back in the chair. He was tense, like a sprinter in the blocks, but he didn't want to overlook Reed.

"I'm sorry," he told him. "I wasn't expecting anything like this to happen to you. Or to Lu Bates, either." He held his palms to his eyes and applied pressure. Tiny explosions of light rebounded from somewhere in his skull to the insides of his eyelids. Reed lowered himself into one of the chairs and waited.

"As of now, we know of three people killed because of this thing, whatever it is. Tim Clayton, my friend, someone named James Rooker whom I don't even know, and Lu Bates." O'Neil looked somewhere deep into the computer monitor. "I should have handled her differently. It's my fault she's dead."

Reed wanted to argue but didn't know what to say. After a minute he asked, "What was she doing at Lankford's?"

"I think she made a set of keys for herself and I think she was trying to get her hands on whatever it was she thought we were after. Something like that. It doesn't really matter. Whatever she was doing, it crossed her with Hill and Fetterman and she didn't deserve that. She didn't know anything worth getting killed for."

The same ugly images filled Reed's mind and imagination and he fought down another wave of nausea. He wondered how long it would take for him to be able to forget the details of what he had seen in the apartment.

"And now, we have to assume that Hill and Fetterman know everything she did, which means we have to assume they know about you." He caught and held Reed's eyes. Although Reed couldn't see it, he could hear the emotion behind his friend's words. "We have to be very careful about everything we do from here on."

"And what are we going to do?"

"Something's broken and we're going to fix it. The first thing we do, we get our stuff together and get the hell out of here. I don't think we want to be here when Hill and Fetterman come back." Reed nodded emphatically. "Then we get your car out of the lot at my office and back to your apartment. From there we'll find a hotel in St. Pete or somewhere and set up shop."

"Which means what?"

"We find out who those four names belong to and why they're so important."

They wound up at an unlikely place called the Tropicana Resort on St. Pete Beach, southeast of Tampa on the Gulf of Mexico. Nestled between two hotels belonging to two different national chains, the Tropicana catered mostly to senior citizens and college students, guests with enough money to stay at the beach but not enough to complain about the quality of the facilities.

O'Neil took a first floor single room with a set of double beds and he and Reed unpacked their suitcases and the notebook-sized portable computer O'Neil had brought. "We need to find a phone," he told Reed when they had finished.

"What's wrong with this one?" Reed asked, pointing to the telephone that came with the room.

"It's not a pay phone," O'Neil said. "If anything else goes wrong, I don't want to leave a record pointing to someone else who could be hurt."

"You're getting awfully serious on me, boss."

"It should have happened sooner."

Reed followed him out of the door and they walked two blocks up Gulf Boulevard to a phone booth where O'Neil paid in a quarter and dialed a number from a piece of paper he had tucked in his pocket. He let it ring until it was answered by a machine and then he hung up.

"No go?" Reed asked.

"We'll have to keep trying. In the meantime, let's go back and take another look at the data from Lankford's. Now that we have some specific names to look for, hopefully we can learn something about what's been going on."

CHAPTER SEVENTEEN

O'Neil finally reached Jody Ebberts just after eight o'clock that evening. Jody was a research consultant that O'Neil had worked with professionally. She told him that she was surprised to hear from him and was on her way out to dinner.

"Surprised?" O'Neil asked. "Why?"

"Just because it's been a while since I've talked to you. How're things at good old O'Neil-Sanders, Inc.?"

"Same as always," O'Neil answered carefully.

"So what are you doing calling me on a Saturday night when I'm about to go out on a date? What's so critical?"

O'Neil told her that he had a job for her that he didn't think would be anything unusual. But it was very important and he needed it done as soon as possible.

"You're not going to ask me to cancel my plans for tonight, are you? I've really been looking forward to this."

She offered her services on the following day, but she would have to charge him her weekend rates plus a rush fee.

O'Neil agreed easily. "That's fine, Jody," he told her. "Let me tell you what I need."

"Hang on one sec while I grab a pen." O'Neil heard a hollow clunk as she dropped the phone onto a table or counter. A few seconds later she picked it up again. "Go ahead."

O'Neil read her the four names that he had gotten from Hill from a piece of paper in his pocket, being careful to spell each one so there wouldn't be a mistake.

"Geez," she said. "A couple of these guys are familiar, I think. Who are they supposed to be?"

"I don't have any idea. I need anything and everything you can get me on these guys. I assume they have something to do with the Tampa Bay area or Florida but I could be wrong. Other than that, I don't know a thing about them."

"Okay," Jody said, considering. "Are there any particular places you want me to check?" Jody performed her research by using her computer to query enormous collections of magazines, newspapers, databases, encyclopedias, and a number of other on-line sources.

"I don't want to tell you to look for anything in particular," O'Neil said. "I'd just be guessing and I wouldn't want to steer you in a wrong direction. I just need everything you can find for me."

"That's pretty wide open, It could take me more time than you think."

"Time is critical, Jody. I won't tell you why, but it goes beyond business and I need your help."

O'Neil heard the sound of a sigh come over the phone. "All right, Frankie, you got me. But not until tomorrow, okay? Then I'll hit it hard until I get what you want. Deal?"

"Deal."

"Good," she said. "Now I've got to get moving or I'll be late. Give me your phone number so I don't have to look it up."

"You can't call me, Jody. I'll have to check in with you."

"Are you out of town or something?"

"Something like that. I'm staying away from the office for a bit and I'm a little hard to reach."

They said a quick good night and O'Neil returned the phone to its cradle.

At least I hope I'm a little hard to reach, he thought. He walked back to Reed and the hotel, looking up at the darkening sky, trying to remember when was the last time he had taken Katy out on a date on a Saturday night.

"You are one pale skinned white boy."

Reed looked at his reflection in the hotel room mirror. "You forgot to mention my bathing suit's ugly, too."

"I didn't want to come on too strong."

"I see." Reed puffed out his chest and turned sideways. "Nobody's going to believe I'm not tan because I spend all my time in the gym, are they?"

"'Fraid not." The lights were out in the hotel room and O'Neil was standing at the window, looking out between the edge of the curtain and the door. It was nine o'clock on Sunday morning and already the sun was hot and the sky a rich blue. "You know what the problem with Florida is?" he asked Reed.

"What's that?"

"You look out at a day like this, the sunshine, blue skies, gentle breezes, waves beaching themselves at your feet, and it's just too damned hard to believe in all of the crime, violence, and drugs we live with after dark. We should just give it all back, the whole state, to the old people and the cattle. Rip out the air conditioning and go back to pre-tourism days. Better yet, give it back to the Seminoles. Let them handle it."

"What about the cow pies on the shuffleboard courts?"

"It's better than tortured bodies on the kitchen floor. Or broken ones pounding into the ocean."

Reed stepped away from the sink and sat on the edge of one of the beds.

"Boss, I'm sorry about what happened to MamaLu."

"It's okay, Reed."

"I feel so disrespectful, like I need to apologize to somebody but I don't know to."

O'Neil turned around and cleared off the top of the lone table in the room. He took the portable computer out of its case and set it on the tabletop, along with a legal pad and pen. He didn't answer Reed.

"Boss, I've got to ask you something."

O'Neil had powered on the computer and was waiting to begin the process of loading in the captured data from Lankford's. He looked up at Reed and waited.

"You're going to look for the presence of those four names in the data that we've got, I'm going to burn like a lobster killing time on the beach, and in the meantime we wait for your friend to do her work."

"Yeah?"

"Well, what then? What exactly are we going to do once we get to that point?"

O'Neil typed a command into the computer and fed it a disk. He pressed the return key and the sound of the spinning three and a half inch platter resonated through the dim silence of the room.

"We're going to stop this thing." Again he met Reed's eyes. "Whatever it is, we're going to see it end."

After a moment Reed nodded his head and mouthed the word, 'Okay.' Then he plucked a towel from the wire rack on the wall above the sink and left for the beach, momentarily flooding the room with morning brightness as he softly opened then closed the door.

O'Neil had been serious. He had seen it in his face despite the dimness of the room. He trudged through the warming sand towards the salt water of the Gulf of Mexico and thought about what O'Neil told him. *We're going to end this thing.* Reed hadn't known what to answer. All he could think of were two questions that seemed stuck, spinning unanswered in his mind: what would they be able to do to stop Hill and Fetterman, and what would have happened to him if they had found him at Lankford's instead of MamaLu.

"I've got all four of them. It wasn't that hard, either. Actually, you'll probably recognize these guys yourself from reading the morning paper."

"I don't think so. I don't do that anymore."

Jody Ebberts laughed. "You're probably better off that way. I'm kind of a news junkie myself, though. Comes in handy in this line of work."

"What kind of stuff did you get on these guys?"

"Let's see, mostly what I have are Florida newspaper accounts, along with some magazine things, a few of them national. It fills in who they are, where they're from, and what they got arrested for. I need to ask you how far back you want me to go."

"What did they get busted for?"

"The drug trade, Frankie. You really don't know anything about these guys, do you?"

O'Neil told her no, that's why he called her. She laughed again.

"Well, here's a synopsis of what I've got."

He listened without interrupting for fifteen minutes until Jody stopped and asked, "Now do you need more than that? I mean, I can keep going, try to find out what their sixth grade teachers wrote on their report cards, stuff like that, and that's assuming they have those things back in old Mexico. Or do you have what you need?"

What she had was probably perfect, he told her. "But I have one more favor to ask you," he said.

"Oh oh. And you've already used most of my Sunday. What is it now?"

O'Neil glanced at his watch. It was nearly six o'clock and he hadn't seen Reed since mid-afternoon. "Could I talk you into meeting me somewhere with everything that you've found? You can stay on the clock and I'll buy you dinner. I would really appreciate it, Jody. This is important."

She hesitated just a moment before answering. "You've got something going on here that involves more than just your business, don't you?"

"Yes," O'Neil answered. "It's something of a personal situation."

"All right, Frankie," she said with no more questions. "Tell me when and where."

He suggested a time and a restaurant in the area called Rocky Point, near the Tampa airport. Jody said she'd meet him there and they hung up. O'Neil stood for a moment, leaning against the pay phone kiosk, wondering if he had all the pieces now. And if he could make them fit.

He left the sidewalk and walked across the sand, angling toward the water in the direction of the hotel, looking for Reed. That was another piece that had to be figured out. He had to find something to do with Reed.

They met Jody at the restaurant and spent an hour going through most of the material she had brought. While O'Neil read the printouts of the newspaper and magazine accounts, Jody spoke with Reed, whom she claimed looked like a raccoon because of the white image of sunglasses that seemed tattooed on the red skin of his sunburnt face.

After the dinner, Jody left for home with her fee and a generous bonus, and O'Neil and Reed drove into Tampa, contemplating what they had learned.

"Where are we going?" Reed asked.

"I want to check something."

The two men rode in silence, O'Neil driving while Reed watched the lights of the city flash and sparkle as they traveled by.

They left the highway at the exit they would take if they were going to O'Neil's house, but drove on past the normal street and turned two blocks further down. Before Reed could ask him if he had done that on purpose, they turned again and Reed decided to keep silent. O'Neil drove for another quarter mile before pulling the car over and parking at the curb.

He reached up and slid the lever for the car's dome light to the 'off' position so that it wouldn't come on when the doors were opened. "I know this sounds cloak-and-daggerish, but I want you to sit here in the driver's seat and keep the keys in the ignition. If anybody comes up to you or if I'm not back in twenty minutes, I want you to get out of here and get your ass back to the hotel."

"And do what?"

"I don't know, get a good night's sleep then work on your tan." He opened the door and got out of the car. Reed slid across the seat and took his place.

"What are you going to do?"

"I told you. I'm going to check on something." And then he was gone, heading across the street and away from the car.

Crickets filled the air with night sounds and the sulfurous smell of reclaimed water erupting from underground sprinklers assaulted his sense of smell. He walked quickly to the corner, and rather than turn and continue down the sidewalk, he moved into the front yard of the house that was there. He walked down the block this way, along the fronts of the houses, until he reached the next corner. There he paused, observing.

Nothing seemed out of place or looked any different than it should. Intellectually he knew that this didn't mean much, that if somebody were watching for him, they would have placed themselves in a position far harder for him to spot. Satisfied there was no obvious surveillance, O'Neil turned and ran past the first three houses to his left, away from the street he had been following.

Here he stopped again, hesitating just long enough to see that nothing save himself had moved. He sprinted silently across the lawn in front of him, crossing the street and pulling up in a crouch between two sleeping houses. His chest was heaving as he fought to control his breath and subdue the effects of the adrenaline rushing through his body. Past the back yard of the house on his right, his own was visible in the ambient light.

He had no idea what Hill's next move would be. He was only just now beginning to figure out what had been going on. But he was reasonably sure that they would be coming after him. How desperately or how hard he had no idea. If they were as motivated as he suspected, they almost certainly would have made a stop at his house.

His breathing slowly caught up to him and he studied the back of the structure. The yard in front of him ended at a low cinder block wall that separated the two properties, the one he was on and his own. He crept across the St. Augustine grass to the row of cinder blocks where he stopped again, crouching behind it. His house looked normal. A layer of sweat, drawn out by the humid night air, blanketed his body as thick as a second skin.

Staying low, he slid over the two foot wall and used his hands to help him in an almost crab-like walk that took him to the back of the house. He stopped again, the only signs of movement his own. A cricket silenced its chirping as he leaned against the outside wall, apparently not comfortable with O'Neil's presence.

He had positioned himself beneath the windows that looked into the room that was his home office. From the back pocket of his black denim jeans he pulled out a slender miniature flashlight.

In one motion, O'Neil stood, turned, and clicked on the flashlight as he directed the beam through the glass and into the house. Immediately, it was clear that the room had been wrecked. Papers from his file cabinet were everywhere, his desk had been overturned and the chairs were on their sides against the far wall. His computer lay smashed and broken on the floor.

The violence of the sacking was apparent as the beam of the tiny light tracked across the numerous gaps and holes that cratered the interior walls. Violence that had been directed, O'Neil knew, at himself.

These bastards are for real, he thought. Were they really the ones that killed Tim?

He moved his thumb over the switch of the flashlight and swung the beam across the room once more, terminating its arc at the office entrance. O'Neil had seen what he had come to see and now it was time to go.

As he cut the power to the light, the office door exploded inward, freeing itself from the top hinge and slamming hard into the wall. Without hesitating, O'Neil pushed away from the house and took off in a sprint, across the yard and angling away from the line of sight of the window.

He gave in to the adrenaline as he felt it drive his legs in a pounding rhythm, pushing him farther and faster than he thought he could go. Behind him lights appeared in the window he had just left as he rounded the corner of a neighbor's house. He didn't like the idea of running away but he knew that at this point he had no choice.

They had wrecked his house, he thought, and they were still there, waiting for him to come home.

CHAPTER EIGHTEEN

Early Monday morning, two men riding in a brown four door sedan pulled into a parking space just outside of the Gulf Coast Memorial Hospital in northeast Tampa. In front of the space was a painted metal sign that read, 'EMERGENCY ROOM PARKING ONLY.'

The two men got out of their car and looked at the entrance to the building. One of them said to the other, "What time you got?"

The second checked his watch. "'Bout eight thirty."

"When I called this morning, they said she'd be here by eight, eight fifteen. Jump in the back seat and wait for us." He started walking toward the entrance. Without turning his head or raising his voice he said, "This shouldn't take too long."

Inside the hospital, there was no sign of the frenetic energy and activities that would have taken place during the weekend. Instead there was a sterile quiet, made up of an empty pastel waiting room and a woman in a white sweater reading a newspaper behind the receptionist's window. "May I help you?" she asked as he approached.

"Yes, ma'am, I believe you could," he said, flashing his best southern gentleman smile. "I'm looking for a Ms. Katherine O'Neil. I was told I could find her here this morning."

"Katy's in one of the doctor's offices," the woman said, returning the smile and reaching for her phone. "Who can I say is calling?"

"Just tell her a friend of her husband's is here to see her, if you would."

"I'd be happy to."

He waited at the window while she dialed an extension and spoke a few words into the phone. When she replaced the handset in its cradle, the man said, "Thank you very much," and wandered back toward the waiting room, out of easy hearing of the courteous woman.

A minute later, a tall woman in a nurse's uniform came out of a door further up the hall and stopped briefly at the window, exchanging some words. Then she turned and walked up to the man in the waiting room.

"I'm Katy O'Neil," she said. She kept her hands in the pockets of her smock, unsure of how to take her early morning visitor. "You asked to see me?"

Dark hair, dark skin, nice figure. Old Frankie's done all right for himself. "I'm Detective Randolph Hill of the Tampa P.D., Ms. O'Neil. I'm here at your husband's request." As he spoke, he offered one of his business cards. She took it with trembling fingers.

"Frankie? Is he all right?"

This is good, Hill thought, relaxing. She doesn't know anything's wrong. "Ma'am, I'd like you to step outside for just a moment, if you would. There's a gentleman in my car and I'd like you to take a look at him."

"A gentleman?" Concern wrinkled her forehead. "Should I get a doctor?"

Hill shook his head no. "That's not necessary, ma'am. Your husband told us where to find you and suggested we come here."

With a quick glance back at the receptionist's window, Katy nodded and said, "After you."

Instead of turning and leading her out the door, Hill reached forward and took her elbow, intending to guide her to the car. After a moment's stiffness, she allowed it and they walked side by side down the short hallway, through the glass electric sliding doors and out of the building. The bright morning sunshine was already promising a hot and humid day, making itself felt as they walked away from the hospital air conditioning.

"He's in here," Hill said, bringing her to the sedan and opening one of the rear doors. The door he chose was the one across from where Fetterman sat, picking at the dirt under his fingernails with one of the small tools from his pocket knife. Katy climbed in and Hill quickly closed the door behind her.

"What do you want me to do?" she asked as Hill got into the front seat on the driver's side.

"Look at him," he told her indicating Fetterman, who turned his face past her toward the rear window so that she could see the red and purple bruise on the left side of his face.

Katy brought her hand up and gently felt the bones in his cheek and jaw, and then looked into both eyes one at a time. Then she did it again. "Well, this doesn't look like it's anything serious. Did you get in a fight?"

Hill made a snorting sound from the front seat. "Somebody hit him, all right. Didn't she, Fetterman?"

"Yeah, but you should see the other gal."

Katy sat back against the seat, away from Fetterman. "Where's my husband?" she asked.

"Actually, we were hoping you could tell us."

Katy looked at Hill for a moment, and then at Fetterman. Feeling uneasy, she turned and grabbed the door handle, pulling it toward her with both hands. The door was locked. Before she could do anything more, Fetterman grabbed her by the shoulder and pulled her into the back of the seat.

In a voice loud enough to make her stop squirming, Hill said, "We want to know where we can find you husband."

Katy, still pinned to the seat by Fetterman, said almost proudly, "I don't know. We've been living apart for a couple of weeks."

They looked at each other for a long moment, each taking the other's measure. Hill was impressed by the control in this woman's attitude. Finally he said, "Okay," and turned to start the car.

"Wait a minute," she said to his back, struggling to sit up. "You can't just take me away from here!"

"Sure we can." Hill backed the car out of the parking space and then put the car in drive and headed toward the street.

Behind him, Fetterman was attempting to lock a set of handcuffs to Katy's wrists. "No!" she screamed as loud as she could. "Somebody help me!"

Hill stomped on the brakes and inertia carried both Fetterman and Katy to the edge of the rear seat. "Somebody help me!" she screamed again as she lurched back. The windows were rolled up and there was little chance that anybody outside the car could hear her. There was nobody in sight.

"Silly girl," Hill said. "Don't you know you have the right to remain silent?" He brought his left hand up and over the edge of the front seat, already clenched into a fist, and sharply drove it into her chin. Katy slumped sideways into Fetterman.

"That's better," he said. "I'd rather listen to the radio."

"Good morning," Reed managed through a yawn, contorting his body into a crooked stretch. He pinched the sleep from the inside corners of his eyes and pushed himself up into a sitting position. O'Neil was in the chair in front of their little round table, his face illuminated by the dull glow of the computer screen. Like the morning before, the heavy drawn curtains kept the hotel room dim, depriving them of the mid-morning sunshine.

"You haven't been sitting there all night, have you?"

O'Neil answered first with a yawn of his own, then, "No. I went to sleep a little after you did. I just got up about a half hour ago."

Reed looked doubtfully at the other double bed. It did look as though it had been slept in. He threw the covers off his own bed and yawned again. "Well, I'm no good without my morning shower. I'll be out in a minute."

It was more like thirty. Reed eventually emerged from the bathroom wrapped in one towel and scrubbing the wetness out of his hair with another. He dug a set of clean clothes out of his gym bag, dressed quickly, then moved to look over O'Neil's shoulder. "So where we at?"

O'Neil was slow to answer. He still had to decide what he was going to do with Reed. On the screen was an image from Lankford's captured data. It was a complex form and one of the four names Hill had given them was at the top. In the bottom right hand corner was a number with a dollar sign in front of it, something over fifteen million dollars.

"Whoah," Reed said. "That's some serious bucks." He watched as O'Neil picked up a pen and copied the amount to a sheet of paper. He wrote it below another number, one that was even greater.

"Follow the money," O'Neil said, laying his pen down on the pad.

"What do you mean?"

"It always leads back to the center of whatever is happening."

"Are we there? Do we know what the center is yet?"

"Not quite, no." O'Neil hit the escape key to exit the program then reached to the side of the computer and powered it off. "I have a good idea but I have to do some more digging before I can be sure."

Reed grew excited and stepped around the table into the center of the room. "Then that means we're almost through, doesn't it? It's almost over." O'Neil didn't say anything.

"We can take what we know, turn it over to the D.A., who hopefully won't try to kill us, watch the bad guys go to jail, and check the hell out of this vacation paradise." Reed felt the pressure they had been under ebb out of his body as he paced a circle on the floor. He was on the moon, disregarding the effects of gravity. He hadn't been aware of just how much tension he had been holding.

"Not quite."

"What's that?" Reed asked, a blanket falling over his euphoria.

"We don't have any hard evidence."

Reed looked at O'Neil with wide eyes, incredulous. "Boy, there's one in every crowd, isn't there? What do you call all this?" He gestured toward the computer. "And MamaLu, your friend, this Rooker guy. What about them?"

"We know they're behind all this, Reed. We know what they're doing. But they can come right out and tell us to our face and unless we can physically demonstrate it in a court of law it won't mean anything to anybody."

"Well, that's just great. That's fucking great. What about us then, goddamn it? Are we supposed to just slink around like rats or cockroaches digging for scraps while they go off killing anybody they choose? While they come after us?"

Reed's characteristic humor was gone. O'Neil sat up in his chair slowly. Damn it, he thought. He should have seen this coming. Now he had to see if this thing would blow itself out or if his friend was truly going to lose it.

Reed spun in another circle in the center of the room, then stopped, facing his unmade bed. He raised his arms high above his head, hands clenched into fists, and pounded his upper body hard into the mattress, bending at the waist, folding his knees and letting himself sink to the floor. He lay there for a moment, his face in the sheets, while O'Neil remained in his chair, poised to stand. Half ready to help, half ready to thump the bed himself.

After a minute, Reed rolled over with his back propped against the bed, and pulled a sheet down over his head. "That really sucks, boss, you know that?"

"Yes, it does."

"No, I mean this sheet stinks." He pulled it off his face and cast it back on the bed. "What the hell are we paying for, anyway? No HBO and smelly sheets. I knew we should have packed our own linens." He pushed himself to his feet and smoothed his hair back with his fingers, then managed a shy grin. "Sorry for venting there."

"That's all right," O'Neil said, relaxing himself. "I would have done the same thing last night but I didn't want to wake you."

Reed bent down and shoveled the remainder of the sheets and bed spread back onto the mattress. "So take a shower and let's go get breakfast or lunch or whatever's appropriate. I don't even know what time it is."

He moved to the sink and picked his watch up off the counter top. It read half past eleven in the morning. "Then you can tell me about all this circumstantial evidence we've got and what it means."

O'Neil pushed back from the table and got to his feet. He's better now, he thought. At least for a while.

The car stopped again. It had stopped before, but she couldn't remember how many times. Two, she thought, but it may have been more.

Katy lifted her chin and watched the clouds of dust roll and swirl outside the car windows as it settled. She tried to sit up but her back ached from the bumping and jarring of the last part of the drive. They had turned off the highway a while ago; she couldn't remember when. She hoped it wasn't important.

The two men who were with her were talking but it was hard to listen. They weren't looking at her anyway.

Dusty heat pushed its way into the car as two of the doors were opened and the men got out. She watched through the windows as they walked away into a small stand of trees and disappeared. She was alone. This should be significant somehow, she knew. She should get away.

Using her hands, she grabbed hold of the back of the front seat and pulled herself into a sitting position. That was better, but she didn't like having to move both hands at once. Why were they chained together? Her head was throbbing.

It was hard, forcing her body to move sideways across the car seat toward the open door. It was difficult to move at all, with the dull pain in her jaw and the murky cloudiness in her brain. The fog was telling her to lay back, to close her eyes, give in to the dull sleep she had been fighting.

She wouldn't do it, though. She knew what was wrong with herself, the word for it was in her mind somewhere though she couldn't come up with it, couldn't separate it and pull it down from the clouds. You've got to move, you've got to get away from these men, she told herself.

She swung her feet out of the car and tried to lean forward, to move her weight over her legs so she could stand. Instead she had to half turn and use both her hands to push off the metal frame, eventually getting to an upright position, surprising herself with how steady her legs felt.

Go, she commanded herself. Start walking. Don't be here when they come back.

Dust was in her eyes and nostrils and she was squinting against the mid-day glare. She had no idea where she was and no idea how far they'd come from Tampa. Tall grasses, clumps of trees, and a pair of worn tire ruts that disappeared off to her right were all she could see.

She focused on the trees where the two men had gone. What were they doing? They didn't abandon her here, did they? But that would be good, she thought, suppressing a momentary panic. Then she could go and find her husband. Frankie. He'd help her get home. He'd deal with these two men.

Something about the tire ruts called out in her mind, something about a road, and she began to think that she should walk that way. That makes sense, doesn't it? Follow the road around the trees. Roads lead to places. Places away from here.

She was going to move, going to start, when they walked out from the trees. She felt another rise of panic as they dropped the boat they were dragging and began to walk towards her.

"No!" she yelled and took two steps backward, away from the men. There was a new feeling, a falling sensation, and somewhere inside she tensed for the impact she knew would come. Instead, there was a scratching and scraping as her body dropped backwards into a young mangrove tree. Twigs and branches pulled at her hair and clothes and a feeling of helplessness rose out of her stomach as she watched her feet rise higher than her head and she sank past the ground.

And then she was through, splashing backwards head first into brown, shallow water she hadn't known was there.

"Leave her in the car, she's not going anywhere. She's still loopy from when I hit her."

Fetterman shrugged okay and both men opened their car doors and stepped out of the air conditioning and into the heat of Florida's spring sun. They had left their jackets in the car and Hill undid the buttons at his wrists and rolled his sleeves up to his elbows as the disturbed dust from the road settled around them. A last look into the car showed the woman still slumped in a corner of the back seat.

"You think it's serious?" Fetterman asked.

"No. Mild concussion, at most. I tagged her pretty good, though." Hill began walking toward a stand of low trees. "Let's get the boat."

They walked a few yards to the trees and disappeared into the clinging branches, both men protecting their eyes from little branches and twigs. They stopped at a regularly shaped mound covered by a camouflage net. "Let's drag it out first and then get the motor."

They pulled the net off the flats boat and left it to one side. There was enough room here to flip the shallow water boat onto its bottom so they could drag it to the river. Hill took hold of it by the bow on one side, and Fetterman took the stern. They cleared the trees with the boat between them and angled towards the car.

"Look who's up," Hill said. He motioned forward with his head and dropped his side.

Fetterman looked ahead and saw the woman watching them over the roof of their car. He lowered his side of the boat to the ground and began to walk toward the rear of the car while Hill walked toward the front. They weren't too worried about her at this point. There really wasn't anywhere for her to go. Besides that, she was half out of it and still handcuffed.

Before they had taken half a dozen steps toward her, she screamed the word "No!" then disappeared suddenly behind the car.

"Shit," Hill swore and broke into a run, quickly covering the remaining twenty yards between them and the woman. His partner was just behind him as they came around the car in time to see a pair of white clad feet disappear through the branches of a mangrove tree.

"The crazy bitch fell in the river," Hill said. They stood for half a minute trying to see signs of Katy through the leaves and branches but the foliage was too thick. Hill moved off to his right about forty feet where they had planned to put the boat in the water. There was a break in the mangroves and the land sloped gently into the water. Standing at the edge of the mud on the river bank, Hill leaned forward but all he could see was part of a single white smocked arm.

"I don't know what she's doing," he called to Fetterman. He began to draw his gun out of the holster on his belt but turned and scrambled up the bank instead. "She looks like she's just sitting there. Let's hurry and get the damned boat. Mating season for gators should be over but I don't want her in the water with those dinosaur sons of bitches."

"Did you see one?"

"No, but there could be a gator hole anywhere in here."

Both men jogged back to the boat and quickly slid it down to the bank of the narrow river, where they left it with the bow just touching the water. The white arm was no longer visible but they could hear Katy moving around in the water. Hill thought about wading in after her but knew that with the soft mud on the river's bottom he wouldn't get there faster than the boat.

They turned and ran back to the trees and their camo netting. A five horse-power motor had been wrapped in a piece of tarp and stored underneath the boat itself. Leaving the blue plastic behind, they carried the motor to the river and hung it off the boat's transom. Hill climbed aboard and Fetterman pushed off, jumping into the back as they glided away from the shore. He began to work at starting the motor.

As they floated into the middle of the river they could see Katy as she stood bent over in the water, swinging her arms below the surface. "What the hell's she doing now?" Hill asked of no one. After a minute or two the motor caught and sputtered into a steady purr. Fetterman guided the boat upriver, then idled. Hill climbed over the side and dropped into the river muck, and scooped the woman into his arms.

She tried to struggle but his hold on her was too tight. "Bring it in closer," he said to Fetterman. "I can't walk with her in this crap." Fetterman eased the craft in front of his partner who dropped the exhausted woman onto the bottom of the boat.

"My shoe," she moaned. "I lost my shoe."

"I know the feeling," Hill said, easing his way over the bow. "But don't worry. You're not going to need it."

Katy never heard him. She stopped trying to sit up and let her eyes close against the sun. In a moment, she was passed out where she lay.

"Let's get back to the car and load the supplies, then get the hell out of here."

She woke up later to a gentle rocking and constant vibration, something different than the car had been. She had no idea how long she'd been out but the thoughts in her head seemed clearer.

Her body was stiff and sore and the longer she was awake the more aware she grew of how uncomfortable she was and how much she needed to move. She struggled to get into a sitting position and as the small boat rocked back and forth from her movements she remembered what had happened to her.

The realization froze her body and she turned her head to look at the men who were with her.

"Don't worry, little darlin'," the one in front said. "We're almost there."

She sat still for a moment, her shackled hands grasping the edge of the boat. She turned to her right to look at the other man, the one who had been in the back seat of the car with her, but he just looked back with a blank expression on his face.

Gradually, she settled into a seat on the floor of the boat, oblivious to the thin layer of water there. She noticed she was only wearing one shoe. She tried to swallow but her tongue was thick and her throat was dry, making her gag.

"Here, drink some of this." The man in the front held out a clear plastic water bottle and she took it from him. Hill, she thought. His name was Hill.

She coughed up the first swallow but then was able to keep some down. She cleared her throat and knew she could speak if she wanted, but she had nothing to say. Instead she looked out at the acres of empty scenery as they drifted steadily by.

The river was much wider here than it had been by the car. On all sides, except for the path of the river stretching out in front of them and the trail of it behind, the landscape looked the same. Bushy red mangroves lined the shore, sawgrass and clumps of pine and cypress trees punctuated the land behind. Except for the sounds of the motor and the boat moving through the water, the air was still and quiet. Long, tall American egrets, white ibises, brown pelicans and other birds were the only other visible life.

She thought about jumping off the boat, maybe trying to capsize it and swim for shore, but she had nowhere to go. Her hands were still chained together, she had only one shoe, and she had no earthly idea where she was. In a swamp somewhere in a small boat with two armed men, who said they were policemen, who were kidnapping her.

The man in the front of the boat pointed a little ahead and to his left. The other one said, "Got it," and turned the boat in that direction. Katy moved her head to see where they were aiming.

At first she couldn't make out anything more than just unbroken shore, but as they moved closer she could see a break, an opening into another branch of the slow moving river. It was partially obscured by a clump of mangroves which made the opening visible only from a particular angle but there was enough room for them to go through it easily.

The new part of the river wasn't as wide across, maybe thirty or forty feet, and the water appeared slightly darker, a deeper shade of brown. A horsefly buzzed around her head, lighting several times as she tried to shoo it away. She saw bright spots if she moved her head too quickly.

Why were they doing this to her? They had mentioned her husband and she wondered if something could have happened to Frankie. She looked at Hill sitting in the bow of the boat and decided not to say anything. They weren't likely to tell her what was really happening.

They followed the river around another bend and stayed closer to the shore. They moved along the inner bank to a small break in the vegetation where there was a low wooden dock that was little more than some boards laid in the mud and dirt at the water's edge.

Hill clambered out over the bow and tied the boat to a mangrove branch as the other man silenced the motor. The rear of the boat drifted lazily back toward the direction they had come.

"Come on out, missy. The ride's over." Hill stood with one foot on the planks and the other in the boat where he had been sitting. He held his right hand out toward Katy where she would have to stand to be able to reach it. She sat there, staring at it, unable to decide what to do.

"Come on, let's go. You know the line, lady. There's two ways we can do this. Hard or easy, but we're doing it now."

Katy remembered this same man offering one of these hands to her as a fist in her face earlier in the day. Slowly, she brought her stiff legs underneath her and with her hands on the seat ahead for balance she forced herself to stand. Hill reached forward and grabbed the chain linking her wrists and pulled her all the way up and out of the boat.

Her legs didn't work quite like they were supposed to and she couldn't make them keep up with the strength and speed of Hill's pull. She scraped one of her shins along the side of the boat and would have collapsed on the shore if Hill hadn't grabbed her around the waist. He started half walking, half dragging her along the wooden dock toward a weathered shack, an ancient hunting cabin made of wood.

There was a hasp and a padlock on the door which Hill opened with a key from his pocket. The one room cabin was dark, the only light coming from the opened doorway.

"Get in," said Hill.

Numbly, Katy stood her ground on the muddy sheet of plywood that terminated this end of the makeshift dock. She didn't want to go in there. In desperation, she looked around her and saw Fetterman walking up the dock with his arms full of grocery bags. To her left and to her right were fields of sharp edged sawgrass, capable of tearing at her thin cotton clothing and slicing into unprotected skin. She knew she was in a swamp, probably far south of Tampa, though she couldn't be sure. And she knew she had no place to go.

Roughly, Hill grabbed her hair and drew it tight around his fingers as he clenched it in his fist. He pulled her face close to his and said in a low voice, "Don't make me tell you twice."

A beat. Then he released her hair, surprisingly gentle, as if to give her a real choice about whether or not she actually wanted to go inside.

Fetterman came up behind them and stopped. Hill moved back from the doorway, leaving her room to pass. Slowly, her eyes down, Katy walked inside and stood, waiting, while the men came in behind her and closed the door.

CHAPTER NINETEEN

"I think we need to send you on a little vacation."

"What?" Reed lifted his arms, palms up, and turned a slow 360 in the center of the hotel room. "Away from all this?"

O'Neil ignored him. "Do you have a passport?"

"Sure, back at my apartment. I spent a few weeks in Europe right after in high school. Where do you want me to go?"

O'Neil took the local yellow pages off the top of the dresser and brought it to the table next to the computer. He opened it and found the listings for travel agents, then copied several numbers onto his legal pad. "The Cayman Islands. I think it's the best way to short circuit Hill's and Fetterman's plans without anyone else getting hurt." Including you, he thought.

Reed plopped down on the corner of the bed nearest O'Neil and the table. He was excited at the sudden prospect of going somewhere, doing something positive. "I've always wanted to go to a place like that. What do you want me to do there?"

O'Neil closed the book and folded the sheet of paper. "Find a really big piggy bank." He put the paper in his shirt pocket and sat back in his chair. His watch showed a time a few minutes past five o'clock in the afternoon. Too late to call an agent today.

"We don't have any hard evidence against Hill and Fetterman, at least not yet, and without it we can't make them stop playing at whatever game this is. But I think we can take away their little prize. With no carrot at the end of their stick, maybe they won't follow it so far."

"Okay," said Reed. "So what exactly do I do in the Cayman Islands?"

The air conditioner kicked to life and O'Neil had to raise his voice. "You're going to become a very rich man. I need you to get down there and find the biggest bank you can and open an account. Call me with the details and get a good night's sleep in a nice hotel. If everything goes all right, a day or so later and you can walk in there and collect the object of Hill's and Fetterman's wet dreams."

Reed gave a low whistle through the space between his two front teeth. "You can do that from here? You can make that happen?"

O'Neil nodded at his friend. "I think so. We have the passwords for the four accounts they're interested in from our original keyboard bugging program. Lankford actually accessed all of them on the day we had that thing installed. And after watching a week's worth of business replayed on our own computer, I think I can arrange to transfer most of the money."

Reed lay back on the bed, staring at the mold-accented relief of the textured ceiling paint. It looked like a giant piece of white bread that had been left in the refrigerator too long. "Then what?"

"I don't know yet," O'Neil said after a minute. "I call Hill, tell him the game's over, we've got the prize. Then find a way to pin what they've done on them somehow. This thing won't really be over until they've answered for what they've done. I won't let it."

Reed thought about it, then said, "You know they're going to be royally pissed." Still staring at the ceiling.

"Good," said O'Neil. "We'll have that in common."

They drove to Tampa to Reed's apartment building. They had no idea whether or not Hill and Fetterman knew enough about Reed to find out where the young man lived, but O'Neil wanted to be sure. From a pay phone on the same block he dialed the number for the Tampa police headquarters on Florida Avenue and asked for Detective Hill.

"Just a moment," the voice on the other end said.

"Whoa, hold on there a second," O'Neil said before she could put him on hold. "I don't want to leave a message on that damn voice mail thing of his, I want to speak to him directly. This is important." He pronounced the word 'important' as three long syllables without the letter 'r.'

In the same practiced monotone, the voice answered with, "You won't have to, sir. He came in a few minutes ago. Please hold and I'll put you through."

"Damn!" O'Neil said loudly into the phone, holding the voice again. "I can't speak to him now. My pen ran out of ink."

"Sir?"

"I'll have to call back," O'Neil said and hung up. In his normal voice he told Reed, "Let's go inside. We should be okay."

O'Neil waited near the front door of Reed's second floor apartment after checking for signs of a possible visit from Hill and Fetterman. The apartment was a mess although not in the same way as O'Neil's house had been. "It always looks this way," Reed offered.

"You need a cleaning service."

Reed dug through some drawers in a bureau until he found his passport, which he dropped into a plastic grocery bag along with some extra clothes. He filled another and said, "All set."

They drove back to St. Petersburg, admiring the silver blue color of the rolling water as they drove over the long bridge that crossed the bay. It had been a long time since either of them felt like they could notice things like that. The color of the water, the shape of the clouds, the beauty of Florida apart from the man-made things.

They weren't going to hide, they weren't going to run, they were about to mount an attack. It felt good, a measure of control restored to O'Neil's life. He let his mind wander with the pleasant feelings, drifting to a place where this was all over and he could go back to the life he knew. Back to the life he shared with his beautiful wife. Back to Katy.

God, how he missed her.

The euphoric feeling from the evening before carried over into the next morning. Reed whistled and sang as he showered and went through his daily ritual, and O'Neil could see that the earlier tension had all but evaporated. The stress of being sought by men like Hill and Fetterman had given way to a mild sense of adventure, courted by the anticipation of an unexpected trip to an exotic island.

The only problem with that, O'Neil knew, was that the feeling wasn't deep. A light in a child's room to give comfort in the dark. But in this case there were real monsters under the bed.

After a sit down breakfast at a local diner, they drove to the offices of one of the travel agencies on O'Neil's list. There, they reserved a seat on a flight from Miami to Owen Roberts International Airport in George Town on Grand Cayman island. Though the travel agent assured them in her best promotional manner that the tourist season lasted all year round, there was no problem buying a ticket on the 4:30 p.m. flight. There was also space at all of the hotels and they ended up selecting a place called the Clarion.

From there they went to a branch of O'Neil's bank where he made a withdrawal and gave the cash to Reed for spending money. The final stop was at the Tampa airport where they waited for a shuttle flight to carry Reed to Miami.

"They do speak English there, don't they?" Reed asked O'Neil as they sat in one of the airport bars. A waitress appeared at their table and they both ordered a coke.

"Yes, they speak English but they drive on the wrong side of the road."

"That's okay. I'll look both ways before I cross the street."

"Look the other way first."

There were no windows in the bar, no distractions except for a pair of big screen TV's that were both tuned to the same daytime talk show. The waitress came back with their drinks and Reed paid her with money that had come from O'Neil. "Thanks," O'Neil told him.

Reed smiled back. "It's the least I can do for the man who's going to make me a millionaire." He tipped his drink to O'Neil in a mock toast. "Seriously," Reed said after draining half of his drink. "I arrive in George Town this evening and take a cab or a shuttle to the hotel. Tomorrow morning, I choose a bank, open an account, and get instructions for wiring money to it. Then I call you in St. Pete, give you the info, go back to my hotel and slurp strawberry daiquiris with the tourists."

"That's all there is to it," O'Neil told him. And there won't be anybody there trying to hunt you down. "Tomorrow night I'll go into Lankford's and arrange to convert as much of the four accounts' holdings as I can and have it all wired to the new bank. If everything works out, in a few days you'll be loaded."

"But then what? I buy a yacht and skip out on you with the cash?"

O'Neil finished his coke and shrugged. "There are worse ways for this to turn out." On the television screens a skinny man and an overweight woman dressed in leather biker clothing were performing a strip tease. Even with the sound turned down they could hear the hooting and cat-calling from the studio audience. The more leather the wannabe bikers peeled, the more tattoos became visible. I'd pay not to see this, O'Neil thought.

"Seriously," Reed said. "What do you want me to do after I get the money?"

"Seriously, I don't know yet. After we get the money, I need to talk to Hill. And then we'll have to see."

"But he still knows you know about the people they've killed. You don't think he'll come after you?"

From the TV's came a burst of applause as the people on the talk show were down to exactly three pieces of clothing between them. Together they made up approximately one half yard of fabric. Their tattoos did a more thorough job of covering their pale bodies.

"Like I said, we'll have to see."

With Reed on his way to the Caribbean, O'Neil returned to the hotel on St. Pete Beach. He spent the following day reviewing Lankford's data and adding to the notes he had been taking. A large percentage of the four accounts' holdings were in cash and they would be easy to transfer. He would simply do his best with the rest of it.

Reed had called that morning at close to ten o'clock. There hadn't been any problems with the bank and everything was ready to go on that end.

The last concern was that Hill or Fetterman could be watching Lankford's, although O'Neil thought that unlikely. There was no longer the ruse of uncovering murderous money launderers to entice O'Neil to ferret out information from Lankford's system. Since they didn't know O'Neil was aware of what was really going on, they would have no reason to expect him to go back there.

"Frankie!" Hill boomed into the phone. "How the hell are you? Is this a social call or are you calling to report a crime?"

O'Neil didn't answer for a minute. After his long night at Lankford's, he had come back to the hotel and taken a long, steamy shower before passing out on top of one of the room's stiff double beds. When he had finally awakened, he had gone down to the beach and plunged into the warm Gulf water for a slow, easy, methodical swim. After an hour or so, he left the relaxing sea, took another shower, then slowly drove in to Tampa and yet another anonymous pay phone. The detective had been at his desk when O'Neil finally placed the call. "It's not social, Hill," he said.

The other man chuckled. "So you have knowledge of a crime, do you?"

O'Neil was feeling at ease, no longer harried and desperate like he had been a few days ago. He was actually looking forward to tearing apart Hill's bravado and listening to the man as his cocky composure fell away. "Just yours, you cheap bastard."

"Really."

"Yes, really. Four convicts, pushers and smugglers, all investigated by you and your partner. They went to jail, their money went to the Walter A. Lankford Company. While they do their time, Lankford manages their portfolios. Presumably they get out of prison one day and their fortunes are there, intact and waiting for them. The Feds missed the money but it didn't get by you."

"Not much does."

"Save it, Hill. You don't have to act tough anymore. You got Tim Clayton involved to help you get the money out of Lankford's. When he found out what you were after, you doped him and pitched him out of an airplane. What did James Rooker do, Hill? Who was he? Was he part of your master plan or did you just pick him up along the way?"

For the first time, there was a change in Hill's voice, but it wasn't a softening. Although he lowered his volume, it wasn't a break in the macho façade. "Him and that fat friend of yours, the pig from the beach. She died poorly, that one. She was a fighter, though. She got her licks in on poor Fetterman. Of course," Hill said quietly, unashamedly, "she paid for it in the end."

O'Neil would have hit him if he could. "It's over, Hill."

"Is it, O'Neil? You know about Rooker. I'm surprised. And I'm curious to know just how quickly you found our Ms. Bates. I wasn't sure how much I trusted you that morning at your house but you must have known about her by then, I think. Obviously you knew about me and Fetterman." He paused for a moment, trying to prompt a response from O'Neil. "Can you prove any of it?"

I'm going to enjoy this, Hill. "Not yet. Soon, though. That's not the important thing right now."

"No, I'm sure it's not. You're absolutely right." Unflappable.

"Listen to me, you pompous asshole. You have no idea how happy I am to give you this piece of news. As of now, the game is over. There is no more money. There may be a little real estate left over, your standard pot to piss in, but the rest of it is gone, pal. You played this game, you son of a bitch, and you lost."

"What are you trying to say, O'Neil?"

O'Neil thought there was a slight edge to his voice. If there was, good. Fall hard, you prick. "I transferred the money, Hill. I took away the pot at the end of your sick, twisted rainbow."

Hill didn't say anything.

"You've done all this for nothing."

Still silence. Have a heart attack, you bastard. Save me some work.

In the same jaunty voice, Hill said, "Well, I think that just may be your problem, old son. You're going to have to get the money back."

O'Neil didn't believe what he was hearing. "I don't think so, Hill. What I think is you're going down."

Again, Hill chuckled into the phone. "Before you get back up on that high horse of yours, Frankie boy, let me ask you one question. Listen well."

"What is it?" O'Neil was losing patience.

"Have you talked to your wife lately?"

An icy fist grabbed O'Neil's heart and squeezed. The world in front of him shattered like a pane of glass, shards filling the air around him, closing up his nose, his mouth. Choking him. Oh my God....

In a painful movement, he forced air into his lungs, back up through his throat, then out through his lips. A slow, hoarse whisper cracked his awareness. "What did you do?"

Hill's maddening laugh again. "Go home, Frankie. Check your mail box. There's a little piece of something in there. A piece of her soul."

Before O'Neil could produce another sound, the phone went dead in his hand.

CHAPTER TWENTY

Gene McFarlane was a Florida cracker, so called because of the place where he was born, the family he was born to, and the way he lived his life.

Gene's older brother Roger had a lot to do with that life, given that he assumed responsibility for raising Gene after their parents had been killed in a boating accident. Roger McFarlane spent his time growing up as both a mother and a father, trying his best to be something he wasn't. Gene spent his time growing up trying his best to be like Roger. Again, someone he wasn't.

It was hard for Roger, as it would be for any boy. Barely eighteen and taking care of his ten year old brother, he had to be creative in order to survive. There wasn't a whole lot of industry coming out of the tiny man-made piece of ground known as Everglades City, but he worked at what there was, usually scraping just enough work to get by.

He built docks and cleaned boats on the Barron River for the rich Northerners that snowbirded and lived in the quarter million dollar homes in the otherwise poor city. Maybe six hundred people lived here year round and most now lived off what they made during the winter, in tourist season when the Yankees came down.

Other times of the year, when money was harder to come by, Roger would pack supplies and his little brother into their small shallow water boat and head into the Ten Thousand Islands to do a little gator poaching. From his father, Roger had learned that country well, better than most of the rangers that worked the Everglades National Park. Roger had never been caught.

It was hard work though, and there was no way they could ever kill enough gators to really get ahead. They just took what they needed to hold them over until the next building or boat cleaning job came through. The odds of staying out of prison were better that way.

As the years went on and Gene grew bigger and more able to take care of himself, Roger began to disappear overnight. He told Gene he had some special work that he and some of his local buddies had to do, and that the late hours meant it paid better.

Uh huh. Gene knew what that meant. He may not have been book smart like most of the tourists he met but he knew what was going on. And life did get better over the next couple of years. The two men moved into a newer double-wide trailer closer to the water and burned the old one, the single that had belonged to their parents. Gene regretted it a little after it was done but he had been too drunk to really remember the circumstances. "The evils of the drink," Roger told him as he drained the last of another six pack. "I don't recall it much, neither."

It was a little ironic when Gene got himself a job giving boat tours out of the Everglades Ranger Station into the park itself. He thought it was funny that he was making money off his knowledge of the area, same as his brother but in an entirely different line of work.

Roger was spending a lot more time away from the trailer than he had in the past. Gene suspected that he was out of the country a lot having graduated from the job of running shallow water boats through the maze of mangrove islands and sand flats between the mainland and the Gulf. There seemed to be a lot more money, too. Boxes of it, sometimes, that Roger couldn't always hide.

"One day soon," Roger would tell him. "Maybe next year, we're gonna move ourselves outta here, get us a nice house like those Yankee tourists got. Some place away from here."

Gene didn't feel too comfortable with the idea of moving away, leaving behind the only place he had ever really known. Sure, he'd gone into Miami a few times, and Naples, but he couldn't imagine actually living in places like that. Too many people moving somewhere way too fast. "Why don't we buy us one of these houses here, on the river? We can stay home and have some Yankee build us a dock."

"Can't get us one of these big houses down here," he said. "Wouldn't look good." That was as close to talking about Roger's line of business as they ever got.

Things changed for Gene when his brother failed to come home one day. It had happened before, Roger staying away later than he said he would, but he had never been gone this long before. The days stretched to weeks and Gene finally began to realize that after all these years of feeling lonely, ever since their parents had died, for the first time he would be facing life by himself. All alone.

The local men, all the swamp rats and smugglers that had known Roger, weren't any help. None of them would admit to knowing anything about the affairs of the man, their one time confederate. "The trouble with this business," one of them told Gene, "is that everybody you deal with is a criminal. You cain't trust nobody."

There was some money in a shoe box under Roger's old bed but not enough to last more than a few months. Gene had no idea what Roger had done with all the money he had made. Gene tried the one bank in town but they wouldn't talk to him either. For all Gene knew, the money could have been buried in the swamp somewhere, or stored in a locker on some boat. Wherever it was, Gene knew, it wouldn't help him now. He'd have to help himself.

Doing what, he had no idea. The boat tours were seasonal and barely cleared minimum wage.

Gene began to realize that all his life he had been taken care of. The money in his pocket came from the tips and wages he made giving the tours but it had been Roger who paid all the bills each month. It had been Roger who put the food on the table and the beer in the fridge. Now there was no more Roger and Gene had to decide what to do.

There really wasn't much of a choice. He could move to Miami, compete with all the Cubans and Haitians for some low paying unskilled laborer's job, but being a cracker he knew he couldn't exist in the city. Wouldn't matter if he could get a job. He knew the city would get him somehow. Suck away his mind, who he was.

He wasn't much of a carpenter, like his brother had been, and he didn't really care for the idea of scraping the hulls of rich men's boats. Poaching might be something if it paid more but there were too many gator farms out there now, raising the animals in concrete block houses and butchering them when they got to be eighteen inches across the belly.

Gene came to the conclusion that if he was going to have to provide for himself he was going to try to do it like his brother. Who knows, he thought, maybe a knack or something ran in the family.

Gene himself had no connections and no real idea of how to get any. He didn't even have a boat big enough to haul anything worthwhile. It wasn't as though business was likely to find him. He decided to have another talk with his brother's friends.

The first time he tried, he got lucky. There was a man they called Midge, Gene never knew why, that used to go off with Roger on some of his earlier overnight trips. Midge clapped Gene on the back with a powerful hand and said he could probably help him out.

Midge was an enormous bearded man who wore a string around his neck with dozens of shark, bear, and alligator teeth hanging down, making clattering noises in his long, tangled chest hair as he walked. His 'Glade pearls,' he liked to call them. He led Gene out to the back of the bar and asked him if he knew what a mule was. Gene shook his head, thinking of course he did. Some kind of donkey, wasn't it?

When Midge told him what it really was, Gene smiled. He'd heard of people doing that, he just hadn't known it by that name. He said he thought he could do it. Swallow and shit. He'd been doing that all his life. Shouldn't be a problem.

Midge took the string from around his neck and held it draped over a massive palm. With his other hand he unsheathed a highly polished Bowie knife and used it to separate some of his bony charms. After a few seconds of work, four small yellowish objects were centered in his hand. Midge pointed at them with the tip of the knife and said, "Don't fail on me, boy. I won't be happy."

Gene assured him he wouldn't and Midge closed his fingers over the human canines then put his knife away. The next night he handed Gene a plane ticket and a list of instructions as he again advised Gene against the circumstances of failure. Gene told him he'd handle it and took the ticket.

A week later, after obtaining a passport over in Naples, he left for Colombia. It was the first time Gene had been on an airplane and the first time he had been to another country. Both were unsettling to him.

He began to wonder about what it was he was planning on doing. The plan was to meet a man in a hotel room who would hand him up to eight sealed condoms filled with cocaine. He would take them back to his own room, roll them in some oil, and swallow them whole, one at a time. After that, it was board the plane for home, induce vomiting or diarrhea, whatever it took, and get the damned things out of his system. Once he delivered them to Midge, he would collect his money and appreciate the retention of his dental work.

But what if they broke? He couldn't help worrying about it. All it would take was one, the latex condom rupturing in his stomach or his intestine, releasing who knew how many ounces or grams of that snow white shit directly into his body. He'd die, he knew. He'd never taken drugs before in his life, but he knew he'd burn up fast, overdosing in the heat as his body temperature approached 110 degrees. He'd heard all about it and he didn't want to die like that. When the man in the hotel had given him the condoms, he had slapped him on the shoulder and said in heavily accented English, "Get home quick." Gene could still hear his wicked little chuckle.

The plane ride back to Miami had been sheer hell. Before they had even taken off from the airport in Bogota they had been delayed on the tarmac for almost three and a half hours. Mechanical failure. Before they left the ground, Gene's shirt was soaked through with perspiration. He could almost feel the acids in his stomach dissolving the thin latex tubes he had swallowed.

Once in the air, he wondered if the change in air pressure at altitude would make his digestive system work harder, faster.

This was a mistake, he thought, mopping his forehead repeatedly, trying consciously to slow his breathing. Ferrying drugs aboard a boat, eluding authorities in the islands where he had grown up, that was something he could do. But this, this was something else entirely. He was smuggling the drugs inside his own body, for Christ's sake. This wasn't normal.

Aside from the vision of his veins and arteries choking themselves on the sudden influx of narcotic powder, his heart bursting and exploding inside his chest, Gene vividly recalled the polished knife lovingly caressing the human teeth on Midge's pearl necklace. He had no doubt that Midge had shown him the knife for a reason, and the least Gene had to fear was the loss of his teeth. In a constant state of near panic, Gene kept himself rooted to his seat for the entire length of the three hour flight. He was afraid to move, afraid to add any ingredient to the possible disaster he carried inside himself.

When they touched down in Miami, Gene could have passed out in relief. In a superhuman test of will, he forced himself through the cattle call of customs without drawing attention to himself. From there he almost ran to the nearest rest room and claimed the first open toilet as his own. He had pains in his gut now, his lower abdomen, and he swallowed two Ex-Lax tablets as he lowered himself onto the toilet.

It was a very unpleasant feeling when the first one came out, goose bumps breaking out across his thighs and arms, but Gene almost cried he was so thankful. He counted carefully, not wanting to get up until every last one of those damned things was pushed through his body, never relaxing, always afraid that any one of them might rupture, get caught on something on the way out, just before it cleared his asshole. Never again, he thought. His days as a mule were over.

Finally, the last condom exited his spent body and Gene slumped forward, exhausted. He had to spend some more time waiting for the effects of the laxatives to subside, but he didn't mind. It was over and he had made it. He was tired and stinking of dried sweat and public bathroom, but he had brought the drugs in. All he had to do now was pick those little white torpedoes out of the toilet and boogie on back to Everglades City. To Midge and his knife and that damned spooky necklace.

Gene finally stood up and looked over his shoulder. It was hard to imagine how much money that ugly mess was worth. He took a half step forward and bent over to pull up his pants then stumbled and fell into the door of the tiny cubicle. The whoosh of water from the flushing toilet sent a bolt of electrified panic down his spine.

On his knees he turned and dove towards the toilet bowl in time to see the last wad of crumpled tissue get sucked into the hole at the bottom. In a futile gesture he grabbed for it, grabbed for anything, jamming his hand up to the wrist into the small opening.

Oh my fucking lord, Gene thought as he looked up at the piping coming out of the wall. What the fuck happened? There was no way to flush the damned thing, no goddamned lever to pull. Christ! he swore again. He hadn't done anything!

He pulled his hand out of the toilet and wiped it in his shirt as he got to his feet. Staring in disbelief, he finished fastening his pants as he took a step back toward the door. Again the toilet flushed itself.

The damned thing was like the automatic doors to the terminal! It flushed itself when he moved away from it! How the hell was he supposed to know, God damn it? Nobody ever told him anything about fucking automatic toilets.

Now the coke was gone because Gene didn't know how to take a shit in the city. What the fuck was he supposed to do?

He stood in the stall for another half hour, trying to comprehend what had just happened to his life. Things had looked so good just a few minutes ago, and now....

Numbly, Gene made his way out of the airport and bailed his rusted out truck out of the long term parking lot. He tried to guess at what exactly Midge's reaction would be when Gene told him that his entire shipment was gone, lost to the sewers in automatic toilet land somewhere south of Miami. Gene's thoughts weren't pleasant.

He decided he couldn't go home, at least not to stay. To go at all would be a risk since Midge knew when he was due back but Gene couldn't think of anything else to do. He began the long drive north and west down highway 41 toward home.

Hours later, he arrived at his trailer, packed some more clothes into his bag, and jogged down to the beach. No sign of Midge.

The bass boat with the 9.9 horse was tied to the dock, exactly like it should have been. Gene untied her and climbed aboard, never looking back at Everglades City, his home, afraid of what he might see.

He headed north, away from the national park, eventually arriving at the mouth of a river almost at the very top of the Ten Thousand Islands. The river had been straightened by the Army Corps of Engineers and it looked more like a man made channel or canal than anything that was created by nature. Gene followed it upstream for several miles, heading inland, before turning into one of the many small tributaries that took him even deeper into the swamp.

He knew this area almost as well as he knew the flats and islands near Everglades City. His father and older brother had built a primitive cabin deep in the swamp, a secret place to store their gator skins after a hunt. Gene didn't think anybody else knew it existed. He could hole up there until he figured out what to do about Midge. There should be spare fuel and canned goods he could live off for days. And there was always fishing tackle.

It was remote country, similar in that regard to the Everglades. It was a few feet higher above sea level so the collection of plants and animals was quite different, but there were no roads back here, no tourists, and no federal park rangers. This made it all the more shocking for Gene when a screaming woman in dirty white clothes burst through the brush and plunged into the water alongside his boat, crying desperately for help. Could this day get any weirder, he thought.

O'Neil drove past the edge of recklessness as he wove through the four lane traffic across the Howard Frankland Bridge into Tampa. Traffic was thick, there was probably a concert or something at the stadium, and O'Neil pounded his steering wheel with an open hand.

Cursing, he pulled onto the right shoulder and drove past the long line of cars to the next exit. He didn't care what was causing the traffic. He'd make it home on the back streets even if it took slightly longer than sticking it out on the freeway. He needed to be moving, going forward. He couldn't take sitting still.

Long minutes later he whipped onto his driveway, no longer wary of anybody watching or waiting for him. Why should they be, he thought. They had him in their back pockets now. Slamming the transmission into park, O'Neil was out the door before the car stopped rocking. Then he was at the front door, pulling handfuls of junk mail out of the box, throwing them onto the cement around him.

O'Neil feared to inhale, not wanting to validate the passage of time with his own breathing, afraid with all his soul to acknowledge what Hill had done. What O'Neil had allowed to happen. Now he had to discover what Hill had meant by "a little piece" of Katy.

At the bottom of the box was an object, very flat and wrapped in a man's handkerchief.

O'Neil, moving in slow motion, was puzzled as he gingerly reached in and picked it out of the box. It was a photograph, he could tell that before he pulled away the edges of the fabric. An instant Polaroid of Katy, a close up of her face, an ugly purple bruise around her chin. Her eyes were open and the whites were showing as she strained to look to her right. A man's hand was holding the top of her head immobile against a wall or a floor, and a pair of pursed lips were making contact with her cheek. Fetterman's lips.

O'Neil let out a vicious wail as he slumped to his knees and pounded the side of his hand into the sturdy oak of the front door. The sudden rage gave way to frustration and for an instant he stopped breathing. He tried to keep his heart from beating, to alter reality, change the world with the force of his will. God, I am so sorry, he shrieked inside his mind. What have I done?

He held the photograph at arms length, tears blurring the image of his wife as he struggled to blink them away.

I am going to kill you, you son of a bitch. I'll see you and your bastard partner choke on each other's fumes as you fry in Hell.

The anger cut through the grief and O'Neil stood, trying to focus on his plans, on what he had to do to get his wife back. In a trance, he unlocked the front door and went inside.

The place had been casually searched, the brunt of it having occurred in his office. There were no holes in the walls and nothing was broken out here. O'Neil moved to the answering machine and pushed the play button.

After the third consecutive message from Rachel that opened with a string of profanities demanding to know what O'Neil had done to her sister, he stabbed the rewind button and silenced the machine. He'd call her in a while, after he figured out what he could tell her that would keep her out of the way.

He had to think of this whole situation as dispassionately as he could. He had to be logical, in control of himself as if he were still a cop and this was just a routine investigation. It was somebody else's wife that had been kidnapped. If he responded to Hill with his emotions, he knew he'd lose everything.

Hill has Katy but what he really wants is the fifty-eight million dollars O'Neil transferred to the Cayman Islands. Katy wouldn't be hurt as long as Hill thought he could get the money. The important thing was to not let him get his hands on both Katy and the money at the same time.

O'Neil walked across the room and began trudging up the stairs, shedding his clothes as he climbed. He needed a shower; a hot, steaming, cleansing waterfall coursing over his body as he tried to wrestle his mass of guilt into a different corner of his mind. Perhaps in the shower his tears wouldn't burn as badly. He didn't think so but he had to try.

CHAPTER TWENTY ONE

Later, a much more controlled O'Neil picked up the phone and dialed Hill's office. He knew the man would still be there and he was.

"What's next, Hill? You seem to be calling the shots now."

"I take it then you found the picture. Sorry about her face but the girl didn't want to behave. That reminds me, you know the one about what fifty thousand abused women have in common?"

"I'm not playing your games, Hill."

"Sure you are, Frankie. You just haven't admitted it yet. Come on, what do all those women have in common?"

"I don't know."

"They just wouldn't listen. Get it?" Hill barked a short laugh across the line. "I love that one. Used to tell my wife that joke all the time."

"Right up until she left you."

Hill hooted with laughter. "See, Frankie? I knew you could play." The humor drained out of his voice. "Now I want my money."

"I want my wife."

"And thus we have the basis for our new relationship."

"You can have it, Hill. Just give my wife back. Now."

"Not so fast, Frankie boy. It's not quite that easy."

O'Neil's stomach felt like it had been squeezed and compressed into a small brick, settling into the bottom of his gut. The longer they talked, the harder it was to stay calm.

"Why the hell not, you bastard?"

"Mind your temper, O'Neil. Strong emotions can get in the way of accomplishing your goals. Remember that."

The dictum of the lizard. O'Neil didn't reply.

"Once my partner and I receive the money, we will be requiring new identities to go along with our new fortunes. Needless to say we'll be moving out of the neighborhood, as well. This takes time to set up, Frankie, you know that. I didn't expect you to find out the truth let alone do what you did, and I need a few more days to complete the arrangements."

Days? For an instant O'Neil's vision went black. He squeezed his eyes shut.

"If I give her back to you now I'm still vulnerable, aren't I? That wouldn't be a smart thing to do."

"How much time?" O'Neil stammered.

"I believe I can get everything done in four days."

"Four days? No fucking way. Damn it, Hill, you've won. Take your goddamned money and give her back!"

"Touching, Frankie, but—" he drew out the words as if he were actually considering it, putting on a show. "I think not."

All right, O'Neil told himself. Take a breath. Sit on your emotions. The goal is to get Katy back. Take some control. "Four days, Hill. Concourse G at the airport in Miami, four o'clock in the afternoon. There's a deli kiosk with a lunch counter about a third of the way down, in the north end. I want the three of you sitting there, including Fetterman. When I see my wife, unharmed and healthy, I'll bring you the money."

"Miami, Frankie? For Christ's sake—"

"That's where it has to be, Hill."

There was silence on the other end as Hill considered it. There were some definite advantages for him there. "You know that once I have the money my interest in the O'Neil family simply ceases to be?"

"As long as you don't have both at the same time."

Hill chuckled. "All right, O'Neil. We'll do it your way. Miami actually works out well. Will there be any trouble from Lankford? I don't like loose ends."

"Is that what Tim Clayton was? And James Rooker and Lu Bates? Were they loose ends?"

"Don't push too hard, Frankie. We made the mistake of offering your boyfriend a cut of the proceeds in return for his help. In the end, I didn't trust him. Rooker was just a sleazebag shakedown artist and the fat lady was your fault. Let it alone, it's all history."

O'Neil slammed his palm into the table holding the phone. "Tim was never working for you! He wouldn't have done that!"

"You may be right, Frankie. I don't know what his real intentions were. I'd say we could ask him about it, but you know..." Hill trailed off.

In a cold voice, O'Neil said, "You are a true son of a bitch."

"Shut up. Now what about Lankford?"

O'Neil forced an answer. "He has his own problems, I think. He doesn't know about me and now the money is gone. Who's he going to complain to? He'll probably be standing right behind you in the line for a fake moustache and dark glasses."

"That's funny, Frankie. But let me tell you one more thing. I can see why you picked the airport at Miami. It makes sense. But don't you fuck with me on this. There are other things we can do to your wife, you know, things that won't kill her. Do you understand me?"

O'Neil felt the brick in his stomach convulse. "You keep that sick motherfucking partner of yours away from her."

Hill was laughing softly as he hung up the phone.

Gene's first thought was to gun the engine and get the hell away from this woman. Out here in the swamps there was no sense of community, no love thy neighbor sentiment among the few misanthropic individuals that occasionally crossed each other's paths. Out here it was strictly mind your own business and don't look too hard at anybody who might pass by. Law in the swamp was something you made up as you went along.

But this woman moved quickly, and she was a looker, he could tell that even through the mess of her hair and the wild look on her face. Before he could decide what to do she had reached the side of the boat and was pulling herself in. Gene had to throw his weight to the opposite side to keep her from capsizing the boat.

He studied the place on the shore where the woman had come from. There wasn't a lot of solid ground around here but there was a good-sized piece back in that direction. He couldn't see or hear anyone coming after the woman and there weren't any other boats on the river, so that was something. Still, her presence made him nervous and he had enough to worry about. "Woman, get the hell out of my boat," he said.

She looked at him, wild eyed and exhausted, and Gene could see the shape of the bruise along her jaw line. No sir, he didn't want no piece of this.

The woman pushed against the side, forcing herself into a sitting position, again threatening to tip the boat. For the first time, Gene noticed the handcuffs connecting the woman's wrists. Jee-zus Christ, he thought. This one's in trouble. "Go on," he said. "Get out of my boat."

"No," the woman croaked at him, gasping for breath. "You've got to help me!"

She tried to pull herself towards the stern and the engine, but Gene reached across the boat and put a hand on her shoulder, holding her back. "We've got to get out of here," she shrieked. "Before they come back!"

Gene let her go as she ran out of energy and stopped trying to get past him. Nervously, Gene scanned the bank behind her. Still no sign of anybody else. From somewhere above came the whine of a small airplane.

The woman reached out and grabbed one of Gene's hands, who instinctively tried to pull it away. He wasn't comfortable with intimate gestures from anybody, let alone a stranger, but she was desperate and she held on. "I'm going to put you off my boat," he told her.

"No, you can't. You don't understand," she pleaded. "Two men forced me down here. They left me chained up in a shack but I got loose. You have to help me get away!"

"Lady, I got my own troubles and I don't have to do nothing you say." Gene snapped his wrist suddenly and his hand popped out of her grasp. He shifted closer to the throttle and said, "Soon's I find a break in them mangroves, you're getting out."

"How can you just say that? I was kidnapped! They hit me!" She moved toward him again but he half rose and put a hand on the top of her head, pushing her back down. "Please, you've got to get me to a town or some people. A phone, anything!"

"No, I don't. Now sit still and stop moving." Gene guided the boat closer to the shore line, looking for a place to unload this woman. He couldn't see where she had come out, but there wasn't any place big enough to beach the boat. He'd throw her overboard right now if she didn't look like such a fighter. He didn't want to risk capsizing, sending everything he had left in the world to the bottom of the river.

"Don't you want anything?" Katy asked him. She was trying to think of a way to get through to this man. She couldn't let him just leave her. She had to reach him somehow.

Gene tried to ignore her. He knew what he had to do.

"Money? Do you need money? A new boat, a truck, anything?"

For a minute she didn't think he was even going to answer her. But then, in his low guarded monotone he said, "How much money?"

Katy felt herself flush with relief. "Whatever you need. My husband and I aren't rich but we make a good living. We can get money against our house, we have our savings."

"Half a million dollars?" Gene had no idea how much it would cost to replace the cocaine he had lost but that sounded like a big enough number. If this woman could get him out of trouble with Midge, he had a reason to help her out. He heard the whine of the small airplane again, this time louder, but when he glanced up he couldn't see it.

Katy was thinking, how in the hell can we come up with half a million dollars? She and Frankie couldn't possibly raise that much. Maybe half to three quarters of it if they sold everything and borrowed from all of their friends. It didn't matter whether they could or not, though. She had to stay away from that shack. "Yes," she said. "Half a million dollars."

Gene throttled the boat back, keeping just enough power to keep from drifting downriver with the current. "What I will do is this," he told her. "I can put you off at a spot up ahead a ways, then head back down till I get to a phone. If somebody brings me the money, I'll come and take you out of there. Otherwise, I'll leave you there. That's the deal."

Katy wasn't sure what to say. She couldn't bear the thought of being left out in the swamp for a minute longer than she had to be, but she was afraid that if she tried to dicker with him he'd just dump her out now and be gone. Her mind flashed back to a picture of the inside of the shack where she had spent the previous night chained to a metal ring mounted in the ceiling. She was ready to agree to anything.

"All right," she said. "Give me something to write with."

Gene slid his small tackle box out from under his seat and opened the topmost section. He dug his fingers through a compartment in the upper tray until he came up with the small stub of a wax pencil and handed it to Katy. She looked around her for something to write on then felt her own pockets when she didn't see anything. From her smock she pulled out the business card Detective Hill had given her back at the hospital. She felt sick when she recognized it for what it was.

She turned the card over on her knee and very carefully, so she wouldn't destroy the damp paper, wrote Frankie's name and their phone number on the back. Satisfied that it was legible, she handed the card and the pencil to Gene. "Maybe it would be better if you took me with you," Katy tried, gently.

There wasn't any way in hell Gene was going to risk being seen anywhere along the river carrying this woman. "That ain't gonna happen," he said.

Somewhere upriver the airplane noise had been replaced by the sound of an air boat.

"Shit," Gene swore as he took the card and the pencil and put them away in his shirt pocket. He scanned both banks of the river but there wasn't any place to hide. "Who was it that took you, anyway? That's not them, is it?"

Katy turned her head toward the approaching sound, whose source was hidden behind a bend in the river.

"I don't think so," she said. "They had a boat like this one, and when they brought me I think it was against the current."

Gene didn't answer. He knew they weren't fast enough to outrun an airboat on the open river. Reluctantly, he kept them where they were, waiting for the craft to appear. He didn't know what kind of trouble this woman represented but he knew he didn't want any part of it. Except for that half a million dollars.

It was an airplane, not an airboat, that emerged from around the point, a blue and white high winged Cessna on floats. Gene and Katy were close enough to the shore so they wouldn't have to move to be out of its way. Unable to do much else, they watched the plane slowly make its way downriver toward them.

They could see the outlines of two men behind the windshield, both wearing sunglasses and green headsets that bulged over their ears.

Katy made a decision. She raised her arms above her head and waved them at the pilot. "Put your arms down, woman!" Gene hissed, but the plane was already angling towards them.

Twenty yards in front of them the noise grew louder as the pilot applied more power and swung the plane around 180 degrees, then quickly dropped to nothing as he killed the engine and the propeller stopped spinning. Gene was reaching for the throttle of the boat when the man in the co-pilot's seat opened the door. In his hand was an automatic pistol and he was pointing it at Gene's face.

"I don't know you, mister," Gene said, raising his hands slowly.

The man reached up and peeled the large green headset away from his head and face and replied, "But she does. Why don't you bring her over here. Now."

Katy let out a short, involuntary scream. She would have jumped overboard if Gene hadn't reached forward and locked his forearm around her throat from behind, pulling her close to him as he settled back into his seat. With his free arm he guided the boat to a spot underneath the wing of the plane, his eyes never moving off the gun.

"Hand her over," Fetterman said when they were close enough to bump against the step of the plane. Katy tried to struggle but she could barely breathe from the grip on her throat. Somebody she couldn't see grabbed the chain between her wrists and began to drag her body up and into the plane, back first. Gene let her go and held onto the wing strut, keeping the boat close. As the pilot reached across his partner and pulled the woman into the plane. The man with the gun turned and stood completely on the step to make enough room for her to get by.

Gene had had guns pointed at him before but he realized perversely that those had all been held by people he knew. This was different. He could die in the swamp at the hand of a stranger.

He pushed off from the strut and reached for the throttle lever. The gun followed him around and was aimed into his face. Again Gene was about to vomit as he slammed the throttle all the way forward, anticipating the bullet that would end his life.

A shrill "No!" came from the woman inside the plane and both of her legs shot out the door, catching the gunman in the back and toppling him face first into the water. Gene stayed low and ran the little boat for all it was worth. He barely heard the single gunshot that sent a bullet ripping into the water behind him.

When he finally turned around to look, there was no sign of pursuit. The strut for the high wing and the propeller made it difficult for the stranger to get a good shot off and Gene rounded the bend the plane had come from feeling relieved. He had survived.

He knew where they were going. He'd seen that damn plane before, tied up outside an old hunting shack about a half mile from where they were now, well hidden up a branch of the river going east. Those assholes.

He eased back on the throttle a little to conserve his fuel. What a bitch of a day this had been. Two things he'd be reminding himself every day for the rest of his life: Stay out of the goddamned city, and, especially in the swamp, it don't pay to mix in other people's business.

CHAPTER TWENTY TWO

Some time later, after dark, O'Neil dialed the number for Reed Larson's hotel in the Cayman Islands. In an unexpected way, Reed's voice helped to soften the acid darkness that had slowly been eroding the edges of O'Neil's stomach.

"Hey, man, what's up? You know what, being a millionaire isn't anywhere near as hard as you may have thought. Are you coming down here? How's it going back home?"

"They took my wife, Reed," O'Neil said in a low voice. "Those bastards kidnapped Katy."

A cold silence clamped onto the line, Reed feeling like all the breath had just been sucked out of him. Oh my God, he thought but didn't say. He saw MamaLu Bates on her kitchen floor.

"I hate to keep asking you to put yourself in these situations, but I could really use some more of your help." O'Neil's voice cracked and he sounded tired. Tired and worn.

"Don't even ask, boss. Just tell me what you need and I'm there."

O'Neil inhaled deeply and told Reed about his recent conversations with Hill, including the arrangements they had made for the meeting in Miami. When he was through, he said, "I need you to book a flight from George Town to Miami in time for the meeting. Keep a couple of grand for spending money but withdraw the rest of the money as two cashier's checks."

"Two?"

"I think that way we have a better chance of getting Katy away from Hill and then working some distance between us. I want to be able to control the situation as much as I can."

"Do you think you can trust him to do what he says?"

"Hell no. But his main motivation is greed and that's what we have to use against him." O'Neil explained what he wanted Reed to do with the two checks. Reed repeated the steps and when he was done there was another pause, an awkward period of electronic silence. It was broken when Reed said, "We'll get her back, man. You know we will."

A moment later, O'Neil said, "We have to."

"What will you do between now and the meeting?"

"I don't know. Tomorrow I'm going to visit the state prison up in Starke, try something else. After that, I just don't know."

They talked about the money for a few more minutes before O'Neil finally ended the call. After they hung up, O'Neil lowered himself gently to a sitting position on the floor and stared at the faint shadowy patterns of the furniture in the living room. He and Katy had bought it together after he quit the police department and they had bought this house. As much as anything, this house and the things in it had been symbols of their new life together, an exorcizing of the demons that had pulled them apart when he was serving on the force.

He closed his eyes and held them shut until the next day's sun chased the dark away and the morning birds began singing in the front yard. The new life wouldn't help them now, he thought. But the old one might.

"Will you relax, God damn it!" Hill snapped at Katy. For the second time in two days he was half dragging her struggling body along the planks that made up the makeshift dock leading to the shack. Fetterman was behind them at the plane, extracting the additional supplies they had brought.

"Your husband isn't going to like seeing you looking like a porcupine from the splinters you're going to get if I have to drag you on your goddamned face. Now cut it out!"

Katy stopped struggling. There wasn't much of a point to it, anyway. There was no place she could go and the unpleasant emotional aftereffects of having almost gotten away, having come so close, were weighing her down like a suit of lead. It was a deeper despair than she had felt yesterday, before she had had the time to fully comprehend her situation. Now she just wanted to close her eyes, squeeze them shut until everything changed back to how it should be, the smells and the sounds, the people around her. It was time to wake up and go home.

"That's better," said Hill. With a mild shove in her lower back, he started her moving again. She continued walking under her own power.

The inside of the cabin was as she had left it. A single room containing a small wooden table that was almost as worn and weathered as the planks that lined the uneven floor. Two old, crooked seats were nearly touching under the tabletop. A metal bucket hung on a hook in one corner and a grime covered air conditioner lay on the floor next to an old Honda generator.

The walls were simply the rough unfinished insides of the twelve inch boards nailed to the cabin's frame. A few pages of yellowed newspaper were scattered here and there across the floor.

A fine place for pigs like these, Katy thought.

The air inside the cabin was hot, humid, and carried a musty stink that came from years of rot and uncirculating air. There was plywood covering the structure's two windows.

Sixty seconds after entering the cabin Katy's shirt was soaked through with sweat. Flies buzzed their way through the door and danced around her upper body.

There was a burning oil lamp propped on a shelf that jutted out of the wall to her left. Most of its light was lost in the glare of mid-morning that washed through the open doorway.

"Shame on you, girl, you left the lights on last night. I'd tell you to be more careful in the future but I don't think you'll have to worry about it." He turned a brass knob at the side of the lamp, lowering the burning wick and smothering it.

"Why?" Katy asked. "Don't I have one?"

Hill looked at her. "A future?"

Katy stood mute.

"Honey, we've all got one. For some of us it includes breathing, for others it involves funeral plots and maggots." Hill laughed explosively, a short, unbecoming bark. "You got a few good days left, don't fret it. You're just forcing me to leave you a babysitter this time. I can't trust you enough to leave you home by yourself, can I?"

Hill moved to the corner where they had left Katy the day before and picked up the slender length of chain that lay heaped on the floor. He passed it through his hands, examining each link until he got to the broken one. "Now how in the hell did you manage this?"

Katy didn't answer and Hill reached up and hooked two of his fingers through the iron ring that was bolted into a rafter in the ceiling. He bent his knees, allowing the ring to hold most of his weight. There was no give at all.

Fetterman entered the shack and dropped two grocery bags onto the table. Katy started as he walked in. She hadn't heard him come up the dock. She looked back at Hill, half hanging on the ring, who hadn't moved his eyes from her.

"You know what, partner?" Hill asked, staring at Katy, perspiration beading on his forehead and upper lip. "She won't tell me how she did this." He held the broken link out toward Fetterman with his free hand. "And I think that's something that I would like to know."

Fetterman grinned in response but Katy didn't see it. Her eyes were locked on Hill's and she shivered involuntarily. The temperature in the little building seemed to drop fifty degrees.

She took a step backwards, toward the door, but a body was there, making her stop.

"We're good partners, he and I," said Hill referring to Fetterman. "We both know what the other wants, what the other needs. Generally speaking, we do a good job of helping each other get it."

Fetterman put both hands on her shoulders and spun her around. He held her in front of him for a moment, digging his fingertips into the muscles of her upper arms. Katy looked up and saw a dead look in his eyes, tiny panes of shatterproof glass on top of his lenses. The man wasn't sweating, either. He was dry as a soda cracker.

He threw his hands forward, lifting her off her feet, driving her backwards into the wall. The air left her lungs and wouldn't come back. She lay against the wall, gasping through her mouth as Fetterman stepped toward her.

No, goddamn it! she thought, forcing herself to her feet. I will not let you do this to me, you bastard.

Katy swung toward Fetterman's face with both of her hands but the man sidestepped her blow. Still with no expression, he whipped a backhanded slap across her face, spinning her around and down to the floor.

She lay there, the dull ache seeping slowly into her skull, not wanting to move. Barely able to keep her eyes open. Words, noises, lights.

You win, you creep. I can't fight you.

When she turned her head to look at the man, prepared for another attack, there was a dark trickle of blood running down her chin from the corner of her mouth.

Hill saw her face and stood up straight, releasing the ring. "She's bleeding," he said. "You know I like that." He looked at Fetterman.

Even in Katy's painful condition she could sense that the atmosphere in the room had changed again. An electric energy had formed between the two men and she found it hard to look away from either one. Fetterman never took his eyes off her face.

Hill moved behind him and put his hand on his partner's shoulder. Together they walked slowly to the door.

"The best thing you can do right now, little lady, is lay right there and not make any noise."

Fetterman went outside and Hill stopped at the threshold, one hand on the door handle. "I'm serious as a heart attack, girlie. We'll be just outside."

He turned and was gone, pulling the door closed after him. Katy let her body slump all the way onto the floor. She tried not to listen to the sounds that came from outside the cabin a few minutes later, but in the dark and all alone, they were all she had.

CHAPTER TWENTY THREE

Gene McFarlane ran his little boat as hard as he could all the way up to the family hunting shack. Those motherfuckers had been set to shoot him, he knew, and if that woman hadn't kicked out they would have. "Shit!" he swore aloud to the swamp. Gene admitted to himself that without someone to look after him, he was failing in life. With his luck, the next new thing he tried would probably kill him for sure.

He tied the boat to a bush and waded ashore through half a foot of muck. The cabin door was unlocked and Gene kicked it open wide, hearing the sharp crack of splintering wood as the door rebounded off the interior wall. Gene stopped it with his muddy boot and stood in the doorway looking in.

This is a pathetic mess, he thought. A wooden table, faced by two home-made chairs on one side and a faded, cloth-covered couch on the other, stood in the middle of the single room. A few tin dishes dotted its surface, blanketed by heavy layers of dust and dirt. There were two windows, both broken, with pieces of screen mesh duct taped over most of the holes. Mismatching remnants of shag and pile carpeting, laced with mildew, covered most of the floor.

It's about as filthy and repulsive as the rest of my life, he thought.

He kicked over the table and smashed one of the chairs into the wall before slumping onto the damp and reeking couch. Loose springs jabbed sharply into his back but he didn't move. After a minute, he began to itch all over but he didn't get up.

Damned couch, he thought. I'd burn you now, you old pig, but I can't spare the gasoline.

Instead he scratched dirty patches of dead skin into the oily spaces behind his fingernails and felt the perspiration slide across his body, under and through his clothes.

This was as low a time as he had ever gone through in his life. It's not that there had been a lot of high times, either, living the life he had, but there hadn't been anybody trying to kill him before. Makes a difference, he thought. Makes a big difference.

He had to decide now what he was going to do about things. So far he'd been running but how long could he keep it up? Gene didn't hold a lot of lofty goals or ambitions but he couldn't see living the rest of his life out here, away from the only town he had ever known. Away from the Gulf of Mexico, the ocean. Even if he could survive in the swamp on a long term basis, the prospect didn't excite him.

Maybe he could try to kill Midge, or wait for him to disappear the way Roger had. That could happen.

Sure it could. And alligators will one day fly to Georgia.

Gene scratched at his neck, etching a trail of thin red streaks along the surface of his skin. He thought about the woman that had jumped into his boat. Earlier that day there had been a moment, just before the plane had shown up, he had thought he might have found an answer to his problems.

A gun in his face changed all that. But maybe there was still something there. Maybe the woman had been telling the truth and Gene could score some cash from this lady's old man.

He found the worn business card in his breast pocket and read the name and number the woman had meticulously printed on its back. What could it hurt, he thought. He already had people trying to kill him but at least in this situation he could still maybe get something out of it.

He stood up, walked outside, and slogged his way out to the boat. When this was all over, he told himself, there were three things that he promised himself he would never do again. He would never get involved with drugs, he would steer very clear of all strangers in the swamp, and never, ever would he take a shit on a goddamned toilet that knew how to flush itself.

The drive down from the small north Florida town of Starke was long and boring. More than three hours on interminably straight and flat roads coming out of the rural north part of the state. There weren't many people around to complain so it was probably as good a place for a maximum security prison as any other.

O'Neil had been there twice before, when he had been a cop, and it had never occurred to him that he would ever have a reason to go back. As he thought about Katy and thumbed the button that lowered his window and stuck his head into the onrushing heat and humidity of the airstream. There was an acid burning at the edges of his stomach.

He tried to imagine how she was, what she would have been feeling and going through, what she could be thinking at this exact moment. He had no idea and it made him ashamed. I've made you a victim, he thought, and I don't even know what that means.

It was long past dark when he finally turned into his Tampa driveway. He had checked out of the hotel in St. Petersburg earlier that morning since there was no reason to hide anymore. Hill wouldn't care where O'Neil was or what he was doing as long as he made it to the meeting in Miami in three more days. And as long as he brought with him a very large amount of money.

The light on the answering machine was blinking when he walked into the living room. There was a single message.

He didn't want to acknowledge it, didn't want to listen to Rachel or a salesman or a business colleague or a friend. What he wanted to do was slip into a coma until Saturday night when he could magically awake with Katy at his side, safe and healthy. Hill and Fetterman could be on a fast train to a festering hell, money and justice be damned for all he would care. Revenge was best suited for people who didn't care what it cost and who had nothing to lose.

He pushed the appropriate button and waited while the small cassette tape in the machine rewound to the beginning, then reversed itself and began to play. At first there was nothing, then the sound of recorded silence, and finally a slow, heavy drawl. It was the thick, almost slurred cracker speech of a native of the deep south. The message was simple and to the point.

"I met a woman today who said she was your wife. I'll call back tonight."

O'Neil sat down on the floor in front of the phone and hugged his knees to his chest. He did not move until the phone rang again, three hours later.

"Is this O'Neil?"

"Yes. Where is my wife?"

There was silence on the other end. O'Neil bit the inside of his lower lip, not wanting to spook the man at the other end of the line. He needed to find out who this person was and what he knew about Katy. Let him talk.

"Take it easy, man."

O'Neil inhaled slowly and evenly. "Okay," he said. "What do you want to tell me?"

There was another pause but it was shorter than the first. "Can you find where I am from this call?"

"No," O'Neil told him. "I can't trace you."

"That's good. Though I guess it wouldn't make much difference." There was another period of silence while the man came to a decision. "I know where your wife is."

O'Neil let out the breath he hadn't known he'd been holding. He squeezed the phone in his hand and said, "Go on."

"Pretty lady, beat up a bit. Someone had handcuffs on her, too. It was two guys in a float plane."

Was she at an airport? A private strip?

"When was this? What happened?"

Gene didn't know how much talking he should be doing. It sounded like the woman had steered him right, though. He just didn't want to screw things up before they talked about the money.

"Happened today. Woman jumped in my boat 'fore I could get her off. Wanted me to get her out of–" he stopped himself. "Where she was. She gave me this number and said you'd pay me."

She was somewhere near water. In the state of Florida that didn't narrow things down too much. "What happened? Why did you let her go?"

"They took her back. Nothing I could do about it except get killed and that wouldn't have helped you any. Your wife helped me get away."

"How do I get to her?"

"Bring me some money and I'll make you a map."

"How much money?"

"Your wife said half a million dollars." Gene waited to see if he would balk at the amount.

"That's a lot of money," O'Neil said drawing out the words and sounding as if he had difficulty with the concept. He waited for some kind of response from the caller.

There wasn't one.

The man was in no hurry to negotiate a lower amount, which was good. It meant that he could be telling the truth.

"If I can raise that much money," O'Neil said, "a map is no good. I need you to take me to her in person." O'Neil wiped his perspiring palms against his thighs.

"Who are you, man?"

"I used to be a cop. These men you're talking about killed my best friend and they're trying to get to me. I'll pay you the money, in fact I can pay you half again what you want, but you have to take me to her. We both go get her, then you get the money. That's the deal. I can't afford to screw around with my wife's life."

Gene didn't know if he should just hang up the phone and get away from all this or what. Now this guy was telling him what to do. It wasn't supposed to work that way. "Man, what are you trying to pull on me?"

"Not a thing," O'Neil told him. "But they've got her and they want the money, too. We have a meet set for Saturday but if you know where she is, and we move now, the money is yours. Seven hundred and fifty thousand dollars."

Jesus Christ. This was supposed to be a simple deal. Give me money, here's a map, go get your damned wife. But now Gene was supposed to go back there and maybe face those two guys if he was going to get anything out of this at all.

Shit. After this, he'd pay off Midge and get a job sweeping fucking sidewalks or something. These past few days had been too much for him. How had his brother dealt with people like this?

"You got a gun?" Gene asked O'Neil. "'Cause I think we're going to need it."

When O'Neil and the mysterious caller had finished making their arrangements, he immediately hung up and dialed Reed's hotel room on Grand Cayman. "We've got to make a new plan," O'Neil told him. "I'm going to get my wife."

"Slow down, boss." Both men could hear the excitement powering O'Neil's speech. "Slow down and tell me what's up."

O'Neil told him.

"Can you trust this guy?" Reed asked.

"I'm not sure."

"But you're going with him."

"There's no motive for him to do this other than the money he asked for. If he was working with or for Hill, you'd have to figure he'd know the stakes and be asking for a lot more. He described Katy, what her work uniform looks like. At the very least, I think he's seen her."

"Okay," Reed said. "What can I do?"

"Get to the bank and FedEx a cashier's check for seven hundred and fifty thousand dollars to me. I need it first thing in the morning. I'm going to meet this guy as soon as it comes."

"I'll go as soon as we hang up. What else?"

"I want you to set things up for the meeting on Saturday in case I don't get to Katy. Did you get a ticket to Miami yet?"

"Yesterday."

"Good. After the seven hundred and fifty thousand, get another cashier's check for half of what's left."

"Twenty eight million bucks, give or take."

"That's fine," O'Neil said, not caring about the actual amount. With Katy kidnapped it was so much Monopoly money anyway. "Get the rest in smaller checks, say two million dollars each. You need to get to Miami early enough to get a locker in a particular place. Write this down somewhere."

"Hang on, there's a pad by the phone here," Reed said. "Okay, shoot."

"Across from concourse G there's a bank of silver lockers next to an elevator. You have to get one of those. There are some green lockers across the hall, but those are the wrong ones."

"Silver lockers, next to elevator, across from concourse G. Not the green ones." Reed read the words back. "What do I want with a locker there?"

When O'Neil told him, Reed blew a long, tuneless whistle into the phone. "Man," he said. "You don't fool around, do you? I hope you know what you're doing."

CHAPTER TWENTY FOUR

O'Neil had compared the directions he had been given to a map of Florida but it didn't tell him anything he didn't already know. He was headed toward swampland, either part of or quite near the Everglades.

He followed I-75 south past Ft. Myers to the last exit before the toll stretch known as Alligator Alley, then went south to highway 41 heading east. It was close to a three hour drive from his home in Tampa and he had to stop once for gas and a cup of coffee.

The two lane highway cut a path through the swamp out of Naples then continued eastward away from one expanding Florida population toward another. For a time, garish billboards advertised gator wrestling and air boat rides, Indian souvenirs and boat tours; tourist related activities that a few long time local families had turned to for economic survival.

As he passed by the last manufactured home communities and into the Collier-Seminole State Park, the signs and billboards disappeared, giving up on the people who had found a way to resist the temptations and make it that far.

Man-made canals paralleled each side of the road, an additional buffer between the traffic and the swamp. Without mountains or deserts, Florida has only its beaches and its swamps, flat land barely above sea level, to fill its space on the map. Numerous stands of cypress trees obscured his view to the south, but through the breaks, as well as to the north, O'Neil could see acres and acres of sawgrass and palmetto expanding outward toward the line where the land stopped and the sky began.

Eventually, he made it through the park territory and into the Grand Cypress area. There was traffic on the road, cars and trucks on their way to and from Miami, bypassing the tolls of Alligator Alley. O'Neil wondered how many of them had any idea what they were driving through, the unspoiled land and wildlife they were passing by.

Somewhere my wife is out there, he thought.

He drove through the intersection with highway 29 and slowed down to a speed ten miles below the posted limit. He was looking for the landmarks he had been told about, and the dirt road that was supposed to take him from the highway down to the banks of a creek. The canoe he had tied to the roof of his car slid suddenly to the right as a large eighteen wheeler passed him in the other lane, speeding.

"Asshole," O'Neil swore, then forced himself to relax. Not the time, he thought. Don't lose it now.

He drove past a group of one-piece picnic tables on his right then slowed down even more. If he hadn't made a mistake and already missed it, on the other side of those trees up ahead should be a small break and the road he was seeking.

He saw the gap and put on his turn signal but there was no sign of a road. He thought about what it would mean if he couldn't find it, if he missed his rendezvous and lost this chance to find Katy. Fuck it, he thought and turned toward the break anyway. As he brought the car around from the opposite side O'Neil could see the faint but definite tracks that must have constituted what his mystery man had described as a road.

Slowly, with low branches scraping the sides of the fiberglass canoe, O'Neil rumbled across the uneven ground, giving silent thanks for the recent lack of wet weather. As things were, the car bottomed out repeatedly in the soft dirt/sand mixture as he slowly picked his way along the path.

The tracks did indeed stop at the shallow bank of a small creek, a current of slow brown water flowing past. The afternoon sun was oppressively bright and a butterfly danced around O'Neil's face as he stepped out of the car.

A gap in the vegetation along the creek bank somewhat explained the presence of the dirt road. It was a natural place to put a small boat into the water. O'Neil wondered how useful it could have been to legitimate hunters on protected land but in any case, the man on the phone had known about it and it had brought O'Neil here.

But where was the man?

O'Neil turned and looked back in the direction of the highway. He had driven maybe five or six hundred yards once he had found the tracks and now the only sounds he could hear were the buzzing of the flies around him and the soft gurgle of the moving water. No sight, sound, or sign of another living person, O'Neil thought. Total isolation.

He turned and walked down the soft slope at the bank of the creek, stopping just short of the edge of the water. To his right the creek continued southward until it bent sharply away and was hidden from sight.

To his left was a leafy mangrove tree and as O'Neil bent froward at his hips, trying to see upstream past it, a low voice with a pronounced southern drawl said, "Don't get too nosy."

O'Neil straightened and took a step back, away from the water, staring at the tree. A few seconds later, the faded green bow of a shallow water bass boat eased noiselessly around the overhanging branches. Inside the boat sat a man, red faced not from alcohol or poor health but from overexposure to the intense semi-tropical sun. He was wearing a pair of well-worn blue jeans, a plaid collared shirt, and hiking boots. On his head was a filthy baseball cap with a patch sewn to its front that was too dirty to read.

"You O'Neil?" the man asked.

O'Neil nodded.

"You got my money?"

"It's in the car."

The man reached down and started the boat's small motor. He turned it around against the current and gently grounded on the shore at O'Neil's feet. O'Neil reached ahead to pull it further in but the man said, "Don't worry about it. It's not going anywhere."

O'Neil stood back as the man stepped warily out of the boat into almost knee deep water and slogged his way onto the bank next to O'Neil.

"Let's see it," he said.

O'Neil went to his car and removed an envelope from the glove compartment. He also took a semi-automatic .45 caliber handgun and jammed it into the waistband under the front of his untucked shirt. He got out of the car and handed the envelope to the man.

"Aw, shit," the man swore. "You're giving me a damn check?" He didn't open the envelope.

"That check is a cashier's check. It's guaranteed. Write your name on it and you can deposit it in any bank you'd like and the money's yours, no questions asked."

"Shit," was all the man said. He was staring at the ground in front of his boots, feeling jacked around again.

"Look," O'Neil told him. "The money was out of the country. This was the only way I could get it here in time. When this is over, after we get my wife, I'll help you convert it to cash, traveler's checks, gift certificates, whatever the hell you want. But for right now, please, take the damned check."

The man looked up, studying O'Neil. He didn't have much of a choice. "How do I know it's really good?"

"How do I know you're really going to take my to my wife? You could be working for the men who took her. Something could happen to me out here and nobody would ever know it." They both knew the kind of something he meant.

The man turned his head to his left and spit a brown stream of tobacco and saliva into the ground. "I ain't working for nobody, 'specially those two sons a bitches." He nodded his head upward at O'Neil. "That your gun?"

O'Neil looked down at his stomach. The slight bulge was shapeless and barely noticeable under his shirt but this man had known it for what it was. "Yes."

The man opened the envelope and looked inside without removing its contents. "I guess we got to trust each other somewhat," he said and handed it back to O'Neil. "But when this is over I want this in cash. Don't want to deal with no banks." He looked at the canoe. "What's that for?"

"So we can get closer without them hearing us."

"Shit. What makes you think I want to get that close?" But he wasn't looking at O'Neil and he walked to the rear of the car and began to untie the canoe from the rack. O'Neil moved to the front and undid the rope there and together they lifted the canoe and carried it to the water, placing it next to the bass boat.

"What should I call you?" O'Neil asked.

The man spit again, this time into the water. "Call me Gene, I guess," he said. He didn't offer his hand.

He tied a line from the canoe to the back of the boat while O'Neil removed two paddles from the trunk and handed them to Gene, who tossed them into the canoe. "You 'bout ready?" he asked.

"Yeah, let's go."

"Let's get this done," Gene said and pushed the boat off the shore into the water. "Get in."

O'Neil walked into the water, thick soft mud sucking at his shoes, and carefully climbed into the bow of the boat. Gene pulled himself into the stern, not nearly so smoothly, forcing O'Neil to grab hold of the seat in order not to fall off. Gene started the motor and slowly turned the boat upstream.

There were no other people anywhere on the water. The swamps weren't like the oceans or the rivers in the cities where hordes of pleasure boaters, fishermen, and jet skiers clogged the surface. This land had so far been spared that. Instead, much of the fresh water itself was simply diverted for farmers and ranchers, slowly choking off the supply as the swamps and Everglades flowed gently south.

Toxic mercury levels were found in fish and the remaining wildlife was just a small fraction of what it was a hundred years ago. Not only were there posted warnings against eating the fish, other than gators most of the game had been killed off a long time ago.

O'Neil knew that somewhere around them there were other people like Gene, people who spent a lot of time in the swamps, hunting and trapping, maintaining the style of life of their grandfathers or even their fathers. O'Neil had no particular wish to know who they were or what exactly they were doing out here.

All of which made this a perfect place to hide someone.

A part of his brain was on autopilot, guiding his body but refusing to think of Katy, of how close they might be to finding her. The present would end when they got to the place where Hill and Fetterman were holding her and it would start up again depending on what happened after that.

Gene guided them onto a larger river with banks thirty or forty yards apart. There was a place where hundreds of birds, mostly white ibises and American egrets, stood along the sandy shore and inches into the water, ignoring each other as they searched and probed for food. As the boat approached, the birds gracefully lifted off and flew away, disappearing somewhere over the endless acres of sawgrass and palmetto.

Several times they saw alligators swimming in the water, like bony logs propelling themselves quietly against the current.

Eventually Gene brought the boat into the shelter of a natural depression in the shore line and grabbed onto the branch of a small tree. He tied off the boat and killed the motor. From his tackle box he removed a plastic bottle of insect repellent and applied it generously to his body.

"Swamp angels starting to come out," he said to O'Neil, indicating the declining sun with a nod of his head. "Want some?"

"Thanks," O'Neil said and reached toward Gene to take the bottle. As he rubbed a palm full of the white lotion into his face he asked, "What do we do now?"

Gene looked at O'Neil impassively, deciding whether or not to enter into a conversation with his passenger. Then, "We wait until it's dark. If they're where I think they are, it's not far from here."

"And if they're not?"

Gene shrugged.

O'Neil tossed the lotion back to Gene and studied the man's face. He decided not to say anything as he slouched back against his seat and tried to get comfortable.

To the west, the sun looked like a big orange ball, sliced horizontally into sections and pasted onto pieces of gray felt. They were stacked one on top of the other and dropped slowly in minute increments into the horizon.

Gene untied the canoe and refastened it to the bass boat as O'Neil watched from the bow, then put his head back and closed his eyes. O'Neil didn't move, gradually becoming aware of a low humming sound, as if someone were blowing across the end of an empty tube, listening to it grow in the air around them.

"Song of the swamp angels," came Gene's voice, as if he were reading O'Neil's mind. "Enough mosquitoes to pick your ass up and carry it to Cuba." O'Neil didn't reply.

An hour crawled by, Gene apparently napping in the bow and O'Neil not able to relax or concentrate on what would happen next. It was hard being so close to Katy and not knowing if she was all right, not knowing what had happened to her during the past two days. What could be happening to her now.

O'Neil turned his head to where the sun was just visible above the western edge of the swamp. Drop, you motherfucker, he swore silently, suppressing a rage that threatened to erupt out of the calm of the evening. He felt the grip of the pistol through his shirt. He thought of the feel of it in his hand and the expression on the two policemen's faces seen past the sight on the end of the barrel.

The boat rocked gently as Gene sat up, his eyes on O'Neil's. "There'll be time enough for that gun later," he said. O'Neil left the gun where it was and stared back into the western sky. Gene did not lay down again.

Something plopped in the water about fifteen feet behind them, something big sounding, and both men started, though Gene only in his eyes. O'Neil turned his head around, straining to see the ripple pattern as it pulsed in all directions through the now black water. He turned back to Gene, who said simply, "It's the swamp."

They sat that way for another half hour, each man with his private thoughts, thinking about their reasons for being there. Clouds of mosquitoes buzzed constantly around their bodies despite the repellent, and Gene finally pulled the canoe alongside the bass boat and said, "It's dark enough. We might as well get going."

O'Neil stretched his stiff legs in front of him and held the canoe in place as Gene gracefully moved from one craft to the other. O'Neil waited until Gene said, "Come on," then crossed over to the front of the canoe and sat down, reaching for one of the paddles they had placed on the bottom.

"Keep that gun of yours handy," Gene said as he released his hold on the bass boat and bent to pick up the other paddle. "They weren't too shy with theirs."

Both men put their paddles in the water and began to work their way against the current toward the middle of the river. "A lot of submerged tree trunks next to the shore," Gene said in a low voice. "We need to stay out here a bit."

There was enough light from the half moon to be able to see the individual trees pass by as they stroked past the shore. The persistent humming of the mass of mosquitoes gave way to the steady trickling and light splashing noises made with the paddles. Other sounds, louder and intermittent, punctuated the darkness as they passed, reptilian croaks tearing the quiet fabric of the night. Under the best of circumstances, the scene would have been unsettling, spooky and eerie in a place not belonging to man, for someone not used to it.

After ten minutes that seemed like ten hours to O'Neil, Gene whispered, "To the right. We go in there."

They paddled toward an opening in the shore line, a wide crack through trees that even in the dim light O'Neil could see would have been hard to spot had they been coming from upriver. As they passed through the mouth of this branch, O'Neil stared ahead, looking for any odd or irregular shape that could turn out to be an airplane. He skipped his paddle off the water and simultaneously felt and heard the whump of his paddle as it glanced off the water and smacked the side of the boat. He sensed Gene stop paddling and turned his head around to look.

"Be careful, God damn it!" Gene hissed. O'Neil nodded in the dark, feeling stupid, though he wasn't sure the other man could see it. Concentrate, you dumb son of a bitch. You'll get your own wife killed.

They drifted with the current for a few minutes, back the way they had come, slowly rotating in the water until O'Neil felt Gene begin to paddle again. O'Neil followed suit and they resumed their slow but steady progress up the river.

Perhaps fifteen minutes later, O'Neil felt a sprinkle of warm water drops fall across the back of his head. He turned to look at Gene who held his arm out, pointing to a spot ahead of them on the left bank. O'Neil tried hard but he couldn't make out anything other than the miscellaneous shapes of the trees and bushes.

Gene began paddling again and guided them gently to that same shore, planting the blade of his paddle into the river muck to keep them from losing ground to the current. O'Neil turned to face him and Gene motioned him closer with his free hand.

O'Neil turned around in the canoe and moved into the middle of the craft. He kept his hands on either side of the boat, not allowing it to tip too far one way or the other. "I don't see anything," he whispered as he settled into a crouch in the place where a middle seat would have been.

Gene put both hands on his paddle and leaned into it with his upper body, slowly forcing the canoe sideways. When they had stopped turning, he pointed again to a spot ahead.

"That big tree there," Gene whispered. O'Neil followed the man's outstretched arm to a tree that was taller than the others around it. "Follow it down." Gene slowly lowered his arm.

O'Neil finally saw it. There was a slightly irregular block shaped object beneath the tree's canopy that appeared to be man-made. Once he had spotted it, he felt his pulse quicken. Katy could be in there.

"Got it," he whispered back.

Gene began to paddle ahead slowly, and O'Neil turned and quietly took his paddle from the bottom of the canoe. He sat on his knees and paddled from that position, carefully matching Gene's strokes. A few cautious minutes later they were in front of the shack at a makeshift landing. There was no sign of any airplane.

Still whispering, Gene said, "Looks like this is the only place to land." There were no breaks in the trees and bushes that were close enough to allow direct access to the cabin other than the one leading to the front door.

O'Neil was about to ask Gene what he planned to do when a sudden noise and a broad shaft of light erupted from the cabin's front door. Both men instinctively ducked their heads below ground level as the door banged shut and the figure of a man moved toward the side of the cabin. When they regained their focus, the man was gone.

O'Neil grabbed Gene behind his neck and pulled his head to within inches of his own. "You coming or staying?" he demanded.

Gene pulled away, shaking his head. O'Neil turned and presented his ear. "Staying," Gene whispered. "I told you I'd take you here. If you're going to do something, go do it. I'll be right here."

Fair enough, thought O'Neil. This wasn't his fight. He put his paddle down and moved as fast as he dared to the front of the canoe. With some paddling by Gene, he was able to step from the canoe onto a warped section of plywood. He crouched low, hoping his silhouette would be swallowed by the mangroves and pulled the gun out of his waistband, quietly flicking off the safety.

The cabin was about sixty feet in front of him and the man who had come out had moved off to O'Neil's right. From the brief glance that he had gotten from the open door, he thought that it may have been Fetterman.

O'Neil took long, quiet strides toward the cabin, listening and watching for any signs of movement. Gene made no noise behind him.

At the door, O'Neil placed his ear as close to it as he could without making contact. There was no sound from inside.

Wanting to move quickly, O'Neil pushed the door open just wide enough for his body to fit through and slid in sideways, dropping to a crouch on the other side while using his hand to keep the door from slamming closed. He squinted fiercely against the new brightness, holding the gun in front of him.

Katy was on a chair in the corner, handcuffed with a length of light chain looped around the thicker one that connected the bracelets on her wrists. The chain was attached to an iron ring jutting from the ceiling and her head was slumped to her chest as if she were sleeping.

As O'Neil stood and began to move to her, his wife lifted her head and looked at him. For a moment her face carried a blank stare, indifferent and unfocused, but then her eyes opened wide and she took in a breath as if she were about to yell.

O'Neil fairly leapt across the room and clamped his hand over her mouth before she could make a sound. The chains made light chinking noises as he crushed her body against his, lifting her from the chair and almost tip-ping it over.

"Oh, Katy!" he breathed into her ear. The familiar smell and feel of his wife were overpowering. O'Neil knew they didn't have time for this but still he held on for twenty seconds before he lowered her to her feet. When he pulled away from her a look of panicked fear snapped onto his wife's face. Tears were streaming down her cheeks as she asked in a hushed voice, "Where is he?"

"I don't know, love. We saw him leave but I don't know where he went."

"There's an outhouse somewhere, I think," she said. "Somewhere close."

"Who is it? Did he hurt you?" O'Neil ran his fingertips across her swollen lower lip, the flecks of dried blood.

"Not too much, no. They're not interested in me for that." She swallowed hard. "Hill's not here, it's the other one."

"We've got to get you out of here."

"The keys!" Katy hissed. "They're over there!"

O'Neil turned to the table in the center of the room. It was a good five feet out of Katy's reach and on it were a small set of keys, a cellular phone, and what looked like the average contents of a man's pockets: billfold, change, a few scraps of paper. The only other thing on it was the kerosene lantern that filled the filthy cabin with light.

He jammed the gun back into his waistband and used the keys to unlock the cuffs from Katy's wrists. "Hurry, Frankie," she pleaded.

Ugly purple and red grooves were inscribed in wicked circles around her wrists. "I'll be all right," she said to O'Neil as he saw the marks. "Let's get out of here."

O'Neil kissed her forehead and pulled the gun free as he moved to the table and the cellular phone. He flipped it upside down and smoothly ejected the battery, sliding it into his back pocket. "Come on, sweets."

Katy reached forward and took his hand while O'Neil extinguished the lantern. They didn't move for several seconds, adjusting to the darkness, be-fore O'Neil gently pulled his wife to the door. He had been inside almost three and a half minutes.

Slowly, he eased the door open, tensing at every rust-hinged creak, until it was wide enough for them to fit through. He squeezed Katy's hand once as a signal then stepped outside, carefully placing a foot onto one of the mud covered planks leading to the river.

The sensation of cold steel appeared at O'Neil's temple while an arm reached across his body toward his gun. A pale hand clamped over O'Neil's with a firm, cold grip while a familiar voice said, "Hold it there, son."

CHAPTER TWENTY FIVE

O'Neil didn't have a choice; he knew without looking what was pressed to the side of his skull, and he knew the voice of the killer that held it.

Fetterman took the gun out of O'Neil's hand and stepped around in front of him. "Back inside, O'Neil," he said. There was not a trace of emotion in his voice. Just another day at the office.

O'Neil backed slowly into the darkened shack, feeling Katy yield and fold into his side as he moved. Fetterman threw O'Neil's gun over his shoulder into the swamp and followed them inside, pulling a disposable cigarette lighter out of his pocket.

"Into the corner," he prodded, motioning with the gun though O'Neil cold barely see it.

O'Neil guided Katy to the chair he had found her in, then stood beside her as Fetterman flicked the lighter and relit the kerosene lantern. As the lamp flared and filled the room with light, Fetterman stepped in front of it, reducing the glare in his own eyes and extended his gun toward O'Neil.

"Don't get any ideas," he said. "I can see you better than you can see me."

O'Neil looked at Katy and felt a surge of anger but choked it back. His wife's eyes were squeezed shut and her shoulders were tense; withdrawing inside herself.

"Pick up the handcuffs, O'Neil. Put them through the big chain and clamp one end on the bitch and the other on you."

O'Neil stooped and picked the handcuffs off the floor and did as he was told.

"Now sit down and throw me the keys."

Fetterman caught them with one hand and dropped them onto the table behind him. Nobody moved or said anything for several minutes. O'Neil covered his wife's hand with his own and tried to will her to relax. Except for the nocturnal background music of the insects he couldn't hear anything from outside of the cabin. Gene was probably halfway back to the other boat by now.

A dry grin cracked across Fetterman's face. "This is an unexpected pleasure, O'Neil. What brings you all the way out here?"

"Shove it, Fetterman. The snappy patter works better for your partner. You don't carry the weight."

The wry smile on the policeman's face disappeared instantly. He clenched his eyes shut then allowed them to open slowly. A different voice, much quieter, said, "Do you wish he was here, O'Neil? Did you hope to see him?"

O'Neil didn't reply. He didn't know what to say.

"Did you wish to see him?" Fetterman roared and stepped forward, sending a vicious kick at O'Neil's head.

O'Neil ducked but not fast enough and not low enough. The light flared and his vision went black as the force of the blow spun him ninety degrees and left his back against the side of Katy's chair.

"Frankie!" Katy screamed and tried to take his head in her hands.

Fetterman stepped back and leaned on the edge of the table, tucking in the front of his shirt, looking down at O'Neil. "He likes you, you know. He's said that."

He placed the gun on the tabletop and reached behind him to get at the rest of his shirt. "He said you were a good cop. He said it back when you were one of us, then he said it again when we brought you in on this." Fetterman seemed calmer now. "Did you know that? Do you give a damn?"

O'Neil was holding the top of his head, waiting for the pain to subside. He didn't say anything.

"He's never said that to me. Not ever. Not one time." Fetterman reached into his pocket and came out with his knife. "I can't kill you, he wouldn't like that." He wrapped his long pale fingers around the knife and caressed it like a baby. "But I can play. He lets me do that sometimes."

Lifting his head from his palms, O'Neil opened his eyes and turned to look at Fetterman as he extended a miniature corkscrew from the body of the knife. O'Neil thought of the marks and wounds he had seen on the breast of MamaLu Bates.

"If you fight me, O'Neil, I'll practice on her first."

Twinges of animal panic flickered around the edges of his nerves as O'Neil watched Fetterman stand and walk toward him. Katy clenched his hand fiercely in hers. "Don't worry, love," he told her. "They need me to get their money."

Fetterman took a determined step forward, eyes locked on O'Neil's. Katy let out a shrill "No!" screaming as loud as she could. Fetterman didn't blink. He took another step.

"He's going to be so proud of me."

The door of the cabin crashed inward, slamming into the interior wall. Fetterman whirled, instinctively looking for the gun he had left on the table while the narrow edge of a canoe paddle cut through the air and collided with his temple.

Fetterman went down in a pile, knife skidding across the floor, with Gene McFarlane standing over him, breathing hard like a prizefighter. Fetterman tried to sit up but Gene brought the butt end of the paddle down on the dazed policeman's forehead, bouncing his skull off the hard wooden floor.

Gene raised the blade of the paddle into the air above the unconscious man's throat, poised for a killing blow. "No!" Katy shouted.

"Don't do it, Gene!"

Gene looked at the man lying at his feet, then at the paddle he held in his hands. Slowly, his features relaxed and he took a step back. "That's the son of a bitch that was going to shoot me," he said.

"He's done now," said O'Neil. "You stopped him."

Gene looked around the cabin, still pumped on adrenaline.

"Thanks for coming back."

"Didn't go far. After you went in, I saw this one come back from around the side of this place, then creep down to the water. I just pushed off and moved behind the trees. I waited for a while after he was gone but when I got back up here, I couldn't see neither one of you."

"You could have left."

"You still got my money."

That was true. The check was still folded in the envelope in O'Neil's back pocket. In fact, O'Neil thought, Gene could take the check from him now and simply leave them chained together next to Fetterman's unconscious body. "So what do we do now?" he asked him, holding his eyes.

"You got a way to get unhitched from there?"

"Keys are on the table behind you."

Gene looked down at Fetterman. "Let's get out of here. We had a deal and I don't need to do these motherfuckers no favors." He sent a light kick into Fetterman's side then swept the keys off the table and tossed them to O'Neil, who caught them with his free hand.

As O'Neil moved to unlock the handcuffs, Katy said to Gene, "Thank you for doing this." He looked at her once, then turned away, mumbling something she couldn't quite make out.

O'Neil freed them both, then leaned on Katy for a moment as he got to his feet. A lightning bolt pulsed through his head where he had been kicked.

"You okay?" Gene asked him.

"Yeah," O'Neil said. "Let's go."

"What about him?"

O'Neil thought about the damage he could do to Fetterman. He knew he could kill him if he'd seriously hurt Katy, but he hadn't. Now she was free. O'Neil wasn't a sadist. He was feeling relief foremost, but anxiety about needing to get out of the swamp. Fetterman could rot in this stinkhole.

"Let him stay until his boyfriend comes. He's not going anywhere."

Gene shrugged. "Guess not." He turned and held the door for O'Neil and Katy as they held onto each other and left the cabin.

The night sounds seemed louder now, yet somehow more peaceful. O'Neil was aware of the sound of the black, unseen water as it flowed past the banks a few yards in front of them. Katy tripped once on the loose boards and O'Neil kept her from falling by squeezing her more tightly around her shoulders. "I feel like I could sleep for a week," she said.

They climbed aboard the canoe with Gene taking the back and O'Neil crawling up to the front as before. Katy sat in the middle, reluctantly letting go of her husband and folding her arms around her knees. Gene pushed off from the bank with a gentle shove of his paddle and they were moving, gliding slowly away from the edge of the river.

"How far do we have to go?" Katy asked. Her voice was quiet with the weight of the swamp, a little more than a whisper.

"Not too far," said O'Neil. "This river flows into another one up ahead, and we have another boat tied up there."

"How did you manage to get out of there that time when you made it into my boat?" Gene asked. "What with the handcuffs and all."

Katy lifted her head from her arms and tried to see him over her shoulder.

Neither man was putting much effort into the paddling. An occasional stroke kept them in the middle of the river as they allowed the soft current to move them along.

"They left me alone after they first brought me here." She closed her eyes and concentrated for a minute. "We came in a small flats boat. When they left, they chained my handcuffs to that ring in the ceiling and said they'd be back. I stood up and turned around and around until the slack went out of the chain. Then I kept turning, using the handcuff chain to take the strain. One of the links finally opened up and I was free." She tried to stop a yawn with her fist but failed. "I'm lucky it was just a kind of dog chain."

"You were lucky, period."

They moved on in silence for a few minutes, the silhouette of the overhanging point that marked the confluence of the rivers becoming visible up ahead.

"Thank you for coming," Katy said to Gene. "Thanks for helping me."

Gene didn't know what to say. He drew his paddle through the water while Katy laid her head back down.

"I'm getting paid," he said finally. His words were quickly swallowed by the night.

CHAPTER TWENTY SIX

Fetterman wasn't out long. The blows to the head had stunned him but the contact with the wooden floor had been what had knocked him unconscious. The realization of what had happened poured over him like a freezing rain and without looking, he knew that they'd gone.

He rolled over to his knees and felt a new pain in his side, a burning feeling in his ribs. He didn't know what that was but he pulled then pushed himself to his feet using the edge of the table. He'd worry about the damage later.

The cell phone was still on the table where he had left it. He snatched it up and began to punch in some numbers when he noticed something was wrong with it. There were no sounds accompanying the numbers and the keypad didn't light up. He turned it over and saw the empty battery compartment.

Damn it, he swore to himself and flung the phone away from him across the room. All their plans, all that money....

Hill was going to kill him. Maybe literally. Fetterman didn't care so much about the money, he was doing this for his partner as much as for anything else. But he knew Hill's motivations were a bit different from his own and he would not be so accepting.

There may be a chance to fix this, he thought. He didn't know a lot about the swamp, only what he had picked up from Hill, but he did know that the shortest way out of where they were was downriver to the south. They were probably headed downstream to the juncture of the two rivers.

There was a path behind the cabin that could take him there. Hill had told him it had been made by Indians years before. Fetterman had no idea if it was even passable but it was his only shot.

He straightened, grimacing with the pain, then saw his gun on the floor where he had been lying. He picked it up, checked the clip, shot it back home. This'll work, he thought as he dropped it into the holster on his belt. If I can get there in time.

He was scratched and bleeding from two dozen superficial wounds caused by the wild branches and serrated edges of the sawgrass that lined the path. He had tripped twice while he ran, going down hard each time, and during the second fall he cut his forehead on a rock or a piece of shell.

The path disappeared behind the mangroves that formed the point of land that obscured the opening of the smaller river. He had to pull up before he got to the end so that he could see around the trees.

The light dripping sound of water on water that marked the unhurried paddling of the man in the back of the canoe drew his eyes to a spot on the river. Against the darkness he could make them out, moving slowly away from him and almost to the opening into the larger river.

He was too late. He couldn't reach them.

He thought about Hill and what he would say, what he would do, when he found out that Fetterman had let them escape. Bad things would happen and Fetterman didn't want that. He didn't want to be the cause of something coming between them. No, Fetterman thought. He didn't want that at all.

These people could not be allowed to simply float away down the river.

He felt for the gun in his holster, never taking his eyes from the pale, irregular shape of what was now his prey. He preferred to be up close, guns and bullets were too impersonal, but this was all he had. It would have to do.

Fetterman brought the gun up and held it with two hands, one supporting the other, and sighted along the pristine line of the barrel.

There.

Slowly, precisely, he began to squeeze the trigger.

Katy had almost fallen asleep sitting upright in the canoe. Her arms were still holding her knees and she was resting her head on top of her forearms, fighting back her fatigue. She still wondered what this whole thing had been about and how it fit in with Tim's death, but she would find out later. O'Neil would hold her, touch her, and tell her everything he knew. In the end it would all come out okay.

A sharp crack sounded behind her, ending the comfortable mental drifting. Before she could focus her thoughts a second and third one ripped through the air. The canoe lurched sideways and she felt a sticky wetness spray across the back of her neck. At the same time there was an awful expulsion of air, of breath, and she twisted around to see the body of Gene Mc-Farlane slumping slowly to the side. An ugly black hole had appeared in his throat.

"Katy, get down!" O'Neil yelled from the front but all she could do was scream. She knew that Gene was dead.

There was another crack and O'Neil suddenly threw his weight to the side, overbalancing the canoe and dumping all of them into the warm black water.

"Frankie! Oh my God! Frankie!" Katy flailed as she slipped under the surface of the water once, trying to touch the bottom and turn toward her husband at the same time.

"It's okay, honey, I'm here," O'Neil said as he slid an arm around her waist. "Are you okay?"

"Yes," she managed after a gulp of air. "He– he's dead."

Gene's body was floating face down on the surface of the water, the air trapped in his clothing yielding grudgingly to the pull of the water. The capsized canoe floated eerily next to him, a temporary marker for the man who had saved their lives.

"We have to swim, honey," O'Neil said, trying to pull her away as the two of them tread water.

There was another crack and O'Neil could see the flash of the gun from shore that marked Fetterman's position.

"Come on." He began to pull his wife downriver, angling toward the shore.

"The canoe!" Katy said, starting to follow.

"The other boat's not far. Let's go!"

Behind them, at the place where Fetterman had been, they heard a shrill scream, a piercing yell carried across the heavy swamp air. Three more gun shots followed and then the sounds of a large weight entering the water hard, splashing and moving toward them.

O'Neil half pulled, half pushed his wife closer to shore where their feet could touch the muddy bottom. It was too soft to stand on, pulling at their shoes. "Keep swimming," O'Neil said. "Follow the shore." The mangroves lining the bank were far too dense to try to crawl through.

O'Neil looked back just once as he began to follow his wife into the larger river. He could hear something moving through the water but it was too dark to be able to see their pursuer. Silently he prayed the canoe had sunk.

Spiked on his own adrenaline, Fetterman howled like a half-crazed animal, jammed the gun into its holster, then threw himself recklessly into the river. He wasn't sure if he had hit anybody but he knew something good had happened when the canoe went over. Their getaway wouldn't be so easy now.

He swam with his head out of the water as fast as he could to the spot he had last seen his prey. The canoe was there, floating upside down with half a foot of its bottom breaking the otherwise smooth plane of the water. In his youth Fetterman had been a Boy Scout and he knew that a capsized canoe didn't sink; it trapped too much air as it turned over.

He held onto it for a moment as he caught his breath, staring at the river ahead for signs of his quarry, when he kicked something under the surface with his shin.

Something soft and heavy.

Warily, he probed beneath the surface with his free hand until he took hold of it. A piece of fabric connected the thing to a point somewhere under the canoe.

As he worked to free it, he felt the object roll over, part of it rising up and breaking the surface of the water. Fetterman found himself looking down into the dead eyes of the man who had hit him with the paddle. The man who was responsible for the others' escape.

The fabric of the man's shirt came free and Fetterman gently shoved the carcass away from him, looking briefly at the two holes, front and back, that marked the pale neck below the beard. Should have known better, you fool, he thought. He watched the body begin its slow glide beneath the surface. Gator food.

There was no sign of the other two. O'Neil and his wife must have swam downriver. Fetterman was familiar enough with this area to know that there was no way they could get through these mangroves onto the shore. There wasn't any solid land through here and the islands themselves were no more than tight stands of mangrove trees rising out of the water.

Holding his breath, he dipped below the surface and came up under the middle of the canoe. Gripping the sides, he pushed himself down until his feet sunk into the river bottom then straightened, extending his legs and arms, lifting the canoe as far as he could out of the water and dropping it to one side. The canoe rocked onto its bottom, mostly empty, and Fetterman grabbed for it as it began to float away from him.

One of his shoes stayed behind, buried in the mud but he couldn't worry about it. He was in a hurry and he needed to find a paddle. At least those damn things float, he thought.

The river bank in front of him was slightly indented, one lip of it marking the end of one river and the continuation of the bank of the larger river it joined. If the paddles made it beyond that strip of land he would never find them but the direction of the current could have carried them into the natural recession.

Fetterman pulled the canoe around until he could grip the point of one of the ends of the fiberglass craft. Trailing down into the water was a length of tie down rope. Perfect, he thought, and let go of the canoe in order to lop the end of the rope around his ankle. He began to swim in a modified breast stroke toward shore.

Katy was struggling. The physical and mental ordeals she had been through had taken their toll. Her leaden arms were screaming for a rest and her mind was alternating between nightmare visions of what she had seen and imagined twelve foot alligators cruising the river looking for food.

She swam closer to the shore and folded her legs underneath her, settling her weight onto her knees. O'Neil came up behind her and took hold of her shoulders.

"What is it, honey?"

Katy couldn't answer. She was trying to both cry and gulp air at the same time. O'Neil wrapped his arms around her and pulled her close, kissing her forehead. When she looked up at him, even in the minimal light he could see the tears on her face. Her voice was shrill and her words were difficult for him to understand.

"I can't do this, Frankie, I can't do it. I don't even know what's going on. They kidnapped me, they hit me, and they were going to hurt you with that knife. I don't want to die, I don't want to see you...." She trailed off, swallowing a mouthful of air. O'Neil gently pushed a strand of her hair off her face.

"And that man, he helped us, didn't he? He was behind me, then he was dead. I saw the hole in his throat and I knew it. Why, Frankie? Why is this happening?"

O'Neil squeezed his wife tightly to his chest. How was he supposed to answer her? All this had happened to her because of him, because of the thing inside him that drove him to find out who had killed his best friend. But what about Gene? What about Lu Bates and James Rooker? What about their best friends?

He thought about Fetterman somewhere behind them, maybe catching up, maybe not. Now was not the time for this. Whatever had come of the choices he'd made had happened and there was no going back. They had to keep moving.

"Katy, honey," he said, stroking her tangled hair. "We can't sit here, we have to keep going. It's not much further."

"How far is it?"

Good, O'Neil thought. A question: her mind is functioning.

"Not far, honey. We're almost there."

In truth, he wasn't sure. Time, distance, and circumstance didn't translate their position well and O'Neil was at least as afraid they'd swim past the boat as he was that they wouldn't make it that far.

"Come on. Let's go."

Katy let herself be pulled gently forward to her knees. She began to swim away from the shore into the river. O'Neil stood for a moment, listening for other sounds of man, but couldn't hear anything above the soft splashes of his wife's simple strokes and the more complicated sounds of the nighttime insects. Not wanting to be too far away, he slipped into the current and followed his wife.

Fetterman paddled hard, leaning into his strokes as he pulled himself through the water. He used long, straight strokes that directed the canoe off line with almost every motion, forcing him to shift the paddle from side to side as he zigzagged down the river.

His back ached and his bruised head throbbed with the beat of his pulse as he concentrated on both banks of the river. Hill would never forgive him if he let the girl get away. He wasn't sure exactly how he would react but he knew things wouldn't be the same between them. That was the worst part of all of this.

He thought that he should have caught up to them by now. He was sure there was no open land around here so they shouldn't have been able to leave the river. It was more likely that he passed by them in the dark. Maybe he should go a little further, turn around and wait for them to come to him. There really wasn't any other place they could go. They were frightened; they were running.

He imagined himself as a dark-winged bird of prey, circling high above his hunting ground, searching out his next kill. Swiveling his head from side to side he swooped down along the surface of the water, intent on finding movement, anticipating his prey.

There was something ahead of him, in the water.

Fetterman pulled the paddle out of the water and into his lap. Whatever was floating in front of him definitely should not be there. He stilled his breath as he stared at the shape, drawing nearer with the current.

It was a boat.

He withdrew his pistol from the holster on his hip, carefully forming his fingers around the grip. The damned thing should be dry enough to fire, he thought. If not, there were other things he could do. He moved his hand over the right front pocket of his trousers and froze. His knife was gone.

It had been in his hand when that hayseed with the paddle hit him in the cabin, he knew. When he came to....

The knife, like the gun, was simply a tool, and Fetterman considered himself a skilled craftsman. What mattered to the artisan was not the wielding of his implements but the results they produced. He weighed the gun in his hand and knew he would do fine.

He laid the pistol in his lap and held it there while he used the paddle to steer closer to the boat. From fifteen yards away he switched the paddle for the gun and waited for the current to carry him the rest of the way.

The bow of the canoe nudged the side of the boat and Fetterman grabbed hold of the craft with his free hand, pulling the canoe alongside it. Even in the dark it was clear the boat was empty.

There was no sign of O'Neil or the girl. A life vest lay on the floor next to a gym bag and a windbreaker was tucked under a seat but that was all.

This wasn't right. He whipped his head from side to side, staring at the banks of the river. Where were they? This boat wouldn't just happen to be floating here, stationary, in the middle of the flaming river waiting for him to drift into it. They had to be here.

Something large erupted from the river behind him. He was half turned, leading with the gun, when a heavy object crashed into the back of his skull, turning the night into something blacker still.

O'Neil gasped for breath as he pushed Fetterman's stunned body the rest of the way to the bottom of the canoe. He swam around it then tossed the large adjustable wrench he was holding into the bass boat and pulled himself in over the side.

"Katy!" he called. "Come on out!"

His wife released the mangrove branch she had been hiding beneath and swam out to meet him. "Is it over?" she asked him as he reached over the side to pull her up. She was still whispering, afraid to relax enough to overcome her fear.

"Almost," O'Neil said. He grabbed onto the canoe before it floated out of reach and brought it in closer. He reached inside and took the paddle, handing it over his shoulder to Katy. "Take this."

As she did, she asked, "Is he dead?"

O'Neil was feeling the swelling at the back of Fetterman's head.

"No, he's not." The gun was wedged between Fetterman's body and the side of the canoe. O'Neil worked it free and sat up in the boat. "I can't tell how badly he's hurt but he won't be needing this again." He flicked on the safety and jammed the gun into his waistband. The canoe began to float past them down the river.

"We're not taking him with us, are we?"

O'Neil turned to his wife and leaned towards her, taking her face in his hands. He wouldn't do that to her. "No, we'll leave him to drift." He kissed her forehead. "If he makes it far enough, somebody might find him. We'll notify the authorities when we get back."

Katy closed her eyes and O'Neil let her go. He moved to the rear of the boat and began to pull in the rope he had attached to Gene McFarlane's heavy tackle box before throwing it over as an anchor. When it cleared the surface, he rested it on the side as he cracked the lid and poured the rest of the water out. Then he stowed it under the seat and started the boat's small motor.

Katy folded herself into the other chair, never letting her eyes leave the canoe as the distance grew between them. She watched as it faded from sight. "God help me," she whispered. "I hope you never come back, you bastard."

CHAPTER TWENTY SEVEN

Hill circled the plane once over the wide, straight section of river he used as a strip before he gently touched down on its surface. There was no sign of anything unusual, no sign of any other people, as he guided the plane downriver along the water's path.

In a bag under his seat were the items he had spent the past few days pursuing: new passports, new driver's licenses, virgin credit cards. All the trimmings of two new, manufactured identities. There was one more piece of business to conclude and after that, there'd be no more worries for the rest of his life. He'd simply be too rich to take notice of any.

The mid-morning sun sparked off the brown water forming piercing shafts of light that shone into Hill's eyes. He squeezed them into a tight squint behind his sunglasses, already looking forward to the hour when he could kiss this snake infested bog of a state goodbye. It would be fine hotels and luxury resorts far away from the heat and high humidity, and these horrid swamps, from now on. When the weather became disagreeable, it would be like nothing to climb aboard his new jet and fly off to a finer, more seasonable place. One that welcomed important self-made men of means like himself. A light tremor shook his body. He was anxious.

He had to look toward the sun to find the point of land that covered the entrance to the other river when he approached from this direction. This was the only challenging part of the flight, successfully navigating the plane around the outcropping and up into the narrower channel that ran past the cabin. Hill accomplished this without a problem, however. He was too close to his goal to be put off by logistical details.

The cabin itself looked as it always did, shit brown, weather beaten, and looking like it could fall into itself at any minute. Ugly piece of crap, Hill thought as he brought the plane close to shore. But it did have its advantages and they'd used it well in the past. He thought about the body that was buried behind it, a foot and a half into the sandy muck, that had belonged to the glorified pusher that had tipped them off to the existence of all this glorious money. He thought of the things they had made him do both before and after he had told them.

Smiling, he thought about what Fetterman could get out of people with that little knife of his.

He killed the engine and pushed open his door as the propeller abruptly stopped spinning. Hill's ears adjusted to the new quiet and he looked to the cabin, expecting to see his partner but no one was there. In fact, there seemed to be a curious lack of any activity at all.

Hill quickly tied the plane to a stump and drew his gun, clicking the safety off with his thumb. Damn it, he thought. Nothing was out of place and everything looked right, but where was Fetterman?

He kept his eyes on the cabin as he ran up to the door. The noise of the plane had certainly announced his arrival so there was no need for subtlety. There wasn't much for cover along the narrow dock anyway.

The lock was loose and hanging in the hasp, the way they always left it when they were there. He nudged the door open with his foot and entered in a crouch, leading with his gun. As soon as he was in, he could feel it. The place was empty.

What the hell is going on here, he thought as he stood and holstered his weapon, his mind reeling with disbelief. Where was the girl?

The length of chain lay in a pile behind her chair, the handcuffs with the key still in the lock on the floor next to it. Did Fetterman take her somewhere? Why would he uncuff her?

He saw the cellular phone on the floor and picked it up. It felt light and when he turned it over he saw the empty compartment where the battery should have been. He recognized his partner's wallet on the table, as well as the other things Fetterman had dumped on the table to dry after the girl had kicked him into the river.

What had made him leave and take the girl?

The one idea that kept running through Hill's mind that made any sense was a double cross. Problem is, he didn't think Fetterman had the balls for that kind of move. But what else could it be?

He slammed his fist into the top of the table, spawning a new crack and upsetting the kerosene lamp. Hill swept it to the floor as it began to leak across the wood.

Did that slimy prick make a deal of his own with O'Neil? When did he have the chance?

The mobile phone.

Damn it, it made sense. Otherwise he wouldn't have left his wallet behind, or the phone, all the things he carried with him everywhere he went. He just didn't need them any more.

He must have talked to O'Neil and told him where to find them. He wouldn't have had any other way to leave.

A murderous rage washed over Hill and he gripped the underside of the table and heaved it to the floor. He moved to the corner where he had last seen the woman, helpless and chained to the ceiling, and kicked the chair into the wall. He picked it up and beat it into the wood planking until it came apart in his hands.

"You son of a bitch!" he yelled as loud as he could. *We were fucking partners, you bastard! I trusted you with everything. Everything! And you did* this!

Hill moved about the cabin, pulling the shelves off the wall, breaking out the painted windows, smashing and breaking until the anger began to simmer. It was when he got to the corner near the generator when he found the thing that made him finally stop.

His chest was heaving and he was dripping with sweat, his hands and forearms bleeding. He picked up the object and held it in front of him. He stared at it and tried to decide what it meant.

This was a new and sudden revelation: wherever Fetterman had gone, he hadn't gone willingly.

He folded the extended implement into the handle of the knife and dropped it into his front pocket. He took long, deep breaths while he tried to decide what to do. He didn't know what happened but the only thing that mattered, he thought, was to find out if there was still a way to get the money.

There was one place to go to find out.

O'Neil shook Katy's shoulder lightly. "Wake up, honey," he told her. "Today's the day."

Katy rolled over in the king-sized bed, uncurling her body into a feline stretch. She opened her eyes, a half dreaming smile gracing her lips, then she sat bolt upright. All the fear and tension of the previous night dropped over her face like a veil.

"Frankie!" she yelled. She grabbed for him as she looked around the motel room, her sleep having made her forget where they were.

"Easy, sweets, easy," he said as he sat down on the bed and held her. "Everything's all right now." He held her until he felt her body begin to relax. She listened to his voice, slowly allowing herself to believe what he was telling her. Her hair smelled like plants as he stroked it, a pleasant shampoo bottle smell left over from the steaming shower they had taken when they had arrived here sometime after midnight. The stink and dirt of their time in the swamp had long since vanished down a sterile drain and he could remember few things as wonderful as the feeling of sliding his clean naked body between these soft cotton sheets next to hers.

"It felt so nice to sleep like that with you." She pushed away from him gently and laid her head against his chest. "Do we have to get up now?"

"You don't, honey, but I do." O'Neil kissed his wife's forehead and took himself off the bed. He went to a pile on the floor and began to pull on the clothes he had discarded the night before.

"Where are you going?"

"Well, first," he answered, fastening his belt. "I'm going to find some new clothes somewhere. Then I have to get to an appointment in Miami." He picked up his shoes and brought them to the bed.

"You don't have to go. I'm safe now."

"This thing isn't quite over, honey. And I have to pick up a friend."

"What about Hill?"

"If he does what I think he will, he'll be there, too."

Katy put her hand on her husband's shoulder as he worked with the stiff laces on his shoes. "I don't want you to go."

O'Neil was sitting with his feet on the floor and his back to his wife. He stopped moving, holding the remaining shoe in his hand. "I know you don't, honey. But you're safe now and I have a friend who has been helping me do this. I need to pick him up, honey. There are a lot of things still going on that you don't know about."

"So tell me."

"I will, but not right now. I promise. I've slept too long as it is. I have to get moving." Getting to Miami from their Naples hotel was nearly a three hour drive.

"What about me? What do I do?"

"Stay here and rest. You'll be safe until I get back."

"The hell I will." Katy tossed the sheets aside and got out of the bed, stepping to her own pile of clothes.

"Katy—"

"Damn it, Frankie. I've had enough of all of this. I didn't think I could deal with you going off and being Dick Tracy again. I've seen too well what it does to you, how it changes you. How I always get pushed to the side." She was dressing as she talked, alternately looking at her husband and paying attention to what she was doing. "I just wanted to be included in your life, Frankie, you know that. I wanted to share it with you, to be 'Katy and Frankie,' not just 'Katherine Collins from Plantation, Florida.' But that can't work when there's this huge part of you I can't touch."

"Honey—"

"Let me finish." Katy moved to the small bathroom area, teasing her hair with her fingers as she spoke. "I know I made you choose before, and I shouldn't have done that."

"It's okay."

She ignored him. "But I left you before and I was miserable. Then when this thing happened with Tim, I knew what would come over you. I could see it coming a million miles away. And I left because I wanted to punish you. I left because I didn't want to be forgotten again."

"I'm sorry."

"And look what happened." She stepped toward him and held out her hands, which he took. "This just makes me think of one thing." She looked into his eyes. "I'm not going to be apart from you again."

O'Neil pulled his wife into his body, wrapping his arms around her and feeling the intensity of his emotions.

"My God, honey, if I had lost you...."

Katy said into his shoulder, "But you didn't. You came and you rescued me and now we have to go find your friend so we can leave all this behind us." She pushed her way backwards out of his embrace. "But after we find a clothing store, I think. We smell bad."

O'Neil laughed out loud. "I love you, Katherine Collins from Plantation, Florida."

"I love you, too, Frankie O'Neil. Let's get moving. You know you have a lot of talking to do between here and Miami."

CHAPTER TWENTY EIGHT

Fetterman woke up slowly, the skin on his face burning in the morning sun. He rocked the canoe as he pulled himself up into a sitting position then made the mistake of pressing his fingers into his head. There were several places that were very soft and very tender.

His mind was shouting questions but he didn't rush to come up with any answers. Instead, he lowered a hand into the river and brought splashes of tea-colored water to his face.

The river.

The canoe.

The details of the night before filtered their way through the thick mental haze as slowly he began to remember what had happened.

He had lost the girl. O'Neil, too, who wasn't even supposed to be there.

Weights were attached to his eyelids and he knew if he allowed them to close he would be asleep again almost immediately. He forced himself to sit hunched over forward so he couldn't lay back.

A tiny smile cracked his dry lips as he recalled one pleasant thought from the night before. Fetterman's eyelids touched and he visualized the black holes in both sides of the dead man's neck.

He dried his hands on the front of his shirt and checked out the canoe. There was no paddle in the bottom of the craft, no paddle floating in the water anywhere that he could see. They had stranded him.

Fetterman studied the land along the banks of both sides of the river. He looked upriver and downriver, trying to recognize the shape of its path, but if he could trust his eyes and memory they told him there was nothing familiar about any of it. There were some breaks between the mangroves, some treeless patches of dirt or grass where he might be able to climb ashore, but there was nothing but sawgrass and palmetto beyond. He knew that he must have drifted a good distance to the south.

He slumped back into the point of the canoe, not caring about the uncomfortable pressure from the fiberglass sides pressing into his back. Unconsciously, he fingered the largest lump on his forehead, wincing when he pressed too hard. What was supposed to happen now?

At some point, Fetterman had no idea exactly when, Hill would show up at the cabin looking for the girl. When he found no one there what would he do? Would he figure out what happened and take off, try to save himself? Would he go on to Miami without either Fetterman or the girl?

Would he come look for me?

A moment's hope but Fetterman let it die. He knew better than to think that he or anybody else would come between Hill and getting that money. Hadn't they proved that with all the bodies they'd left behind? Still, it was a pleasant thought if not a realistic one.

He knew that the river eventually connected to the Gulf of Mexico and that there would be boats there, someone who would come to help him if he waved them down. If he were more himself, he could take their boat from them, he knew that. But then what? With O'Neil and the girl loose he couldn't go back. And he had no money, no credit cards, nothing but the filthy clothes on his back. He'd have a hard time going anywhere.

He had cast his lot in with his partner's schemes and they had come up short. They had lost everything and it was just a matter of time before somebody named the price they'd have to pay.

His eyelids were so, so heavy.

Ahead of him the river bent sharply to the right and the current carried him toward the river bank that was now looming in front of him. He didn't notice until it was too late to try to do anything about it. He let the canoe carry him straight into the overhanging branches of a mangrove tree.

Leaves and branches scraped at his face as he threw his hands up, wresting his momentum from the current. He slowed to a stop, buried in the leafy canopy, then grabbed a branch and pushed hard backwards against the resistance. He moved and something heavy fell into the canoe.

He heard it more than he felt it and as the canoe pulled away from beneath the tree he saw what it was. A large, dark snake twisted its body into a tight compressed S, its head, wider than its neck, facing Fetterman from six inches in front of his feet. The thing opened its mouth, exposing a milky white interior and Fetterman knew what it was.

It seemed that he only thought about moving after the cottonmouth struck him the first time. A pair of needle pricks pierced the inside of his thigh, leaving a tremendous burning feeling, and Fetterman panicked. He kicked at the snake in desperation while he tried to sit up, to leverage himself so he could get out of the damned canoe. The snake bit him again, lightning fast and this time burying its fangs deep into the calf muscle of his other leg.

Fetterman went over the side, rolling the canoe and inhaling water directly into his lungs. He came up coughing, facing the shore as he fiercely began to push himself backwards through the water. His heart felt like it was beating two hundred times a minute as he saw the snake swimming alongside the overturned craft. Its head was well out of the water and it seemed to be looking at him, as if in some way admiring the damage it had done.

Fetterman couldn't stop coughing. He had inhaled so much water he couldn't breathe without gagging. Powerful fits shook his body as he continued to move awkwardly downriver, still panicking over the thought of the snake in the water with him. The wounds on his legs felt as if puddles of molten lava had been injected into his skin.

There was so much adrenaline in his system, Fetterman couldn't have stopped swimming if he had wanted to. He was into the middle of the river, still coughing and gagging when the feeling began to leave his legs.

His brain was telling his legs to kick, to keep him afloat, but no matter how hard he tried each movement became smaller than the last, each kick carried less and less force. Waves of nausea began to ride through him and it was terribly hard for him to swim with only his arms. His face bobbed beneath the surface and again he inhaled part of the river.

Oh my God, Fetterman thought. Oh my God. Never before had he felt so weak, so vulnerable.

He had to get out of the water. He knew that but he didn't know how. His arms were tired, exhausted, and his strength was ebbing from the nausea. His useless, swollen legs hung like burning anchors, dragging him down beneath the surface. With each wracking cough he grew weaker and weaker. If he could just clear his lungs, breathe normally....

Fetterman tried to roll onto his back but it made the coughing worse and again his face went under. For a moment his mind seemed to detach itself from his body. I've failed myself, he thought. My badge, my partner, now me.

He realized he was looking up at the burning Florida sun wondering why he felt so cold.

Overhead the roar of an airplane engine tickled his consciousness, disturbing the peace of the blue sky and the emerging thunderheads. *Randy?* he thought. Was Hill up there?

It didn't matter. A larger part of him simply didn't care. Go away, Fetterman wanted to shout. I don't need you anymore. A coughing spasm shook him and he inhaled even more water as he struggled to hold his head above the surface. I don't need you.

Still he could hear the sound and it was disturbing him.

Fly on, he thought. You bastard.

A thin current of warm brown water slipped past his sunburnt lips and Fetterman thought about the creatures that lived there in the swamp, that surrounded him at that moment. The snakes, the alligators, the insects, the birds. I am the alligator man, now, he thought. I belong to the swamp. I was wet when I was born.

I am wet when I die.

Hill flew his plane to the small airport in Homestead and called a taxi to take him the rest of the way to Miami International. This way he didn't need special permission to land and if things worked out right it would be easier to abandon the Cessna without drawing as much attention.

Once inside the airport, he saw the usual crowds of travelers and Spanish speaking employees that trafficked through the terminal building. Hill checked his watch. There were still three hours before he was supposed to meet with O'Neil.

He walked into one of the numerous food shops that lined one wall of the terminal building and stood in a short line for a hot dog. It took five minutes before a Cuban woman finished servicing the two customers ahead of him and finally asked him what he wanted. Damned refugees. Couldn't work fast enough in this stupid little job, no wonder their own country had gone to hell.

Someone had told him a joke once about how you could drop an atomic bomb on Miami and kill maybe six Americans. Based on his experiences in this town he wasn't going to argue.

He finally got his lunch and looked about for a place to sit. The little restaurant itself was full so he wandered back into the terminal and found a group of chairs that were set facing an otherwise bare wall.

He was impressing himself with how cool and calm he was. He let it go when he was back at the cabin but got himself under control once he got back in the airplane. Once he had a handle on what must have happened and what he needed to do.

Whoever had taken the girl had done something to Fetterman, probably killed him. That was too bad; he had been good for a certain number of things. He wouldn't miss him, exactly, but it would make things different.

The big question was who had taken the girl. Unless Fetterman had tipped him off, O'Neil wouldn't have had a prayer of figuring out where they were keeping her. That was impossible. But if there was some way it could have been O'Neil, about a thousand other cops wold be out hunting for Hill right now, most of them right here. And that just wasn't so. He had called his office from Homestead and everything had been normal. He hadn't been missed.

So who took the girl?

He popped the rest of his lunch into his mouth and wiped his fingers on the fabric of his pants. Probably some renegade band of swamp mutants, out avoiding civilization and poaching for some gator tail. Didn't matter who it was, really. So long as O'Neil didn't have her he had a chance to buffalo him into paying off the money. Failing that, of course, he would have to kill him. Hill stood up, excusing himself for an abrupt belch. Maybe he'd go get himself another one of those hot dogs. That Cuban woman was good for burning some time.

Reed Larson stepped out of the jetway and into one of the concourses that belonged to Miami International Airport. He followed the clear plexiglass enclosed ramp down and into the customs area along with the rest of the passengers that had disembarked with him. None of them, he thought, had checks worth nearly sixty million dollars burning holes in their jacket pockets. None of them had come to Miami to meet a murdering Tampa policeman who was holding his friend's wife as a hostage.

Clearing customs was a formality and Reed immediately exited the concourse and walked out into the main terminal building.

Miami International was an old airport, originally built in the late fifties and added on to in order to keep pace with the exploding growth of the city. The terminal building itself was a long, crooked structure with a multitude of concourses branching out and away from it. As Reed walked along looking for concourse G, he saw a sign advertising rooms for the hotel that was built onto the terminal:

It's all here.... At concourse E, 2nd Level
Miami International Airport Hotel
260 Completely Soundproof Rooms

He came to concourse G, which branched off to his left before heading past a row of metal detectors and x-ray machines before disappearing behind a set of thick glass doors. Across from the security checkpoint, to his right, were the lockers O'Neil had described. There was the wall with the elevator set next to a pair of automatic doors that led outside.

Reed dug a handful of quarters out of his pocket and carefully placed the cashier's check for twenty six million dollars into one of the lockers. Ten feet away, the elevator opened unexpectedly and he jumped as he twisted and removed the small plastic-headed key. A group of chattering teenagers speaking French pushed behind him into the terminal. He hadn't heard the chime announcing the elevator's arrival and it made him nervous to be standing there.

He picked his one bag up by its shoulder strap and slung it over his shoulder, pocketing the locker key. He walked quickly away from the money and the elevator, feeling as though a hundred sets of eyes were watching him. He didn't stop until he was almost out of the terminal, past the first concourse and in an alcove of fast food restaurants.

Despite the heavy air conditioning, Reed was perspiring. He wiped at his forehead with his sleeve and set his bag down on the floor. Staring into the terminal, back the way he had come, he looked to see if anyone was showing any interest in him. He let out his breath when he couldn't see anybody even looking in his direction.

Two things I don't need, Reed thought as he checked his watch, are gangsters and bad cops. This day can't end too soon.

There were almost three hours to go before he was to meet with O'Neil, and Reed made a decision. Pulling more quarters out of his pocket, Reed moved to another set of lockers and gently slid his bag into one of them, dropping the change into the slot. Before he removed the key, he pulled the remaining series of checks out of his pocket and held them out of sight inside the locker.

Thirteen checks of roughly two million dollars apiece. Again the weight of the money nearly staggered him, with flashback visions of Lu Bates's body, sprawled out on her kitchen floor, dead eyes looking for Heaven and assaulting his imagination. He wiped his forehead again and left three of the checks in the locker with his bag.

Before he could give himself time to reconsider, Reed shut the door and twisted the key, pushing away from the lockers and walking back into the heart of the terminal. Three more hours.

Hill had spent most of his time walking end to end through the airport, and the last hour examining every square foot of concourse G. He wanted to know the exact layout, all the nooks, all the crannies, every inch of O'Neil's chosen meeting place.

It really was an inspired choice, thought Hill as he finished counting the actual number of jetway gates. An airport concourse with its security would keep out their weapons, and since the concourses themselves connected directly to the terminal, there were no overhead trams or underground trains that could be used as a bottleneck to trap either party. That would have been the weakness with the Tampa Airport. O'Neil was good, Hill thought, but he would be better.

He felt the weight of Fetterman's pocket knife bouncing heavily against his thigh as he walked. They had let him take it through security. Apparently they didn't classify the small tool as a weapon. He smiled wryly as he thought of some of the things he had seen Fetterman do with it.

He checked his watch again. It was almost time. He began to work his way back down the concourse, to the deli booth O'Neil had specified. Hill's eyes worked every face, saw every motion, led him around each food kiosk and newsstand. There was nothing suspicious going on around him. He stepped over and around waiting passengers and greeters as if they were pieces of jumbled furniture.

Hill was halfway to the deli when his eyes locked on something familiar. The face of someone he knew was walking through a small knot of people in the middle of the concourse.

Without turning his head to give himself away, Hill kept moving at the same speed, angling himself toward a stainless steel drinking fountain that was set into the wall on his left. He bent over, briefly touching his lips to the arcing water, then stood and turned casually toward the person he had seen.

Thirty feet away from him, moving with the crowd in the direction of the deli, was the face of a young man that he definitely recognized.

It was O'Neil's little helper.

Oh, this is too good, he thought as he jammed his hand into his pocket and pulled out Fetterman's knife. He shrugged off his light jacket and draped it over his arm. With the knife out of sight, he extracted one of the blades and locked it in place, slowly moving into the stream of people.

"Larson, isn't it?" Hill said softly as he moved in behind the man, extending his arm underneath Reed's jacket and pressing the knife into his side.

Reed whipped his head around and tried to stop but Hill turned his shoulder and bumped him forward. "Keep walking, kid," Hill said as he pressed the razor edge of the blade into the soft flesh just above Reed's hip. "I mean it."

The two men caused a ripple of annoyance as their stutter step disrupted the rhythm of the people walking around them.

"This is the edge of a very sharp knife you're feeling in your side. Maybe O'Neil told you what we could do with it."

Reed swallowed and nodded once. Hill was pressed against the left side of his body, keeping himself just behind the man. Sweat broke out along his forehead.

Dead bodies on kitchen floors.

"Where is he?"

Reed tried to speak but his throat had gone dry. Hill pulled the knife along his side and Reed could feel the cold steel slice through his shirt and into the surface of his skin. "I haven't seen him yet. I was on my way to the deli up ahead."

"Does he have the girl?"

"What girl?"

"Don't fuck with me, boy!" Hill hissed, again sliding the knife. Reed could imagine himself opened up at the side, spilling blood and pieces of kidney as an anonymous figure stepped away from his body, losing himself in the crowd. He cast his eyes about frantically but there was no one looking back at him. Everyone was busy with their own little activities.

"Settle down, God damn it!" said Hill. "Where's O'Neil's wife?"

"You're supposed to have her." Reed's stomach was in knots and he was feeling sick. What was happening here?

Hill could tell from long experience that the kid was terrified and probably not lying. So someone else had found the shack and had taken the woman. She was probably scrubbing pots and trimming the fat off gator tails for some inbred first cousins like he thought. Hell only knew what would have happened to Fetterman. Life's fucked up.

The deli consisted of a long counter surrounded on each end by stainless steel coolers that held fruits, vegetables and sterile pre-made sandwiches and salads. Twenty or thirty small round tables filled an area bounded by a decorative rope. Hill led Reed to one of the tables toward the rear corner that was furthest from the counter and mostly free of customers.

With his foot he slid one of the green wooden chairs over next to another one and prompted Reed to sit down by altering the pressure and angle of the knife.

"Okay, listen to me, kid," Hill said, sitting next to him. "There is only one thing in this world that is going to make everybody happy and that is me getting out of here with that money. Got it?"

Reed nodded. Their backs were to the wall and they were watching the steady stream of people saunter past the counter.

"Good. Put your hands on the table where I can see them."

Slowly, Reed took his hands out of his lap and folded his arms on the table in front of him.

"The only thing standing between O'Neil and me, Larson, is now you. We had his wife but that arrangement fell through. Do you want to live, kid?"

Reed nodded.

"Say it."

Without looking at Hill, Reed said in a quiet voice, "I want to live." There was no doubt in his mind that Hill would bury that knife halfway to his spine if things didn't go his way. He could feel the sweat dripping on his forehead while at the same time a numbing chill was spreading throughout his arms and legs.

"That's good, boy. Now I want you to tell me everything you know about O'Neil's plans. Start by telling me what it is you're supposed to be doing here." Hill gave the knife a small twitch to get him going.

Reed jumped but didn't say anything. If Hill didn't have Katy, did that mean O'Neil had been successful with his other plans? And if he had been, would he still show up here? He opened his mouth to speak but then shut it.

"I'm not playing, boy. Talk to me." Hill pressed the blade deeper into Reed's side. He could feel a warm stickiness at his hip.

"He's here," Reed said.

"What do you mean? Where?"

Reed nodded with his head and Hill followed the motion. Across the concourse, standing next to a square support column, was O'Neil. He was staring at their table, a hard look on his face, oblivious to the stream of people moving between them.

Hill smiled.

"You say one word about the girl, boy, and I'll make you pay."

O'Neil took a step away from the column and as he moved a figure moved with him. Katy O'Neil was holding her husband's hand as they walked slowly toward the deli.

The smile disappeared from Hill's face and he pressed himself closer to Reed's side. What the fuck was this? How the hell did he get her?

O'Neil and Katy moved to the table directly in front of Hill and Reed. Two of the tables that were between them and the counter were occupied but they were at least ten feet away and the people there involved in their own conversations.

"Have a seat," said Hill. "Looks like we both have us a surprise."

O'Neil sat without taking his eyes off Hill. Katy moved a chair closer to her husband and sat down slightly behind him.

"We meet again," Hill said to her, nodding.

"Don't talk to me, you pig," she breathed. Katy grabbed O'Neil's arm and looked at the table.

"Whatever you say."

"Are you okay?" O'Neil asked Reed.

Hill answered for him. "Do you mean does he have a razor sharp knife pressed into his side at this very moment?" Hill smiled again. "He does, yes."

"I'm bleeding," said Reed.

"Back off him, Hill. You'll get your money."

Hill chuckled. "I know that. First tell me, Frankie. Where's Fetterman?"

"You mean what happened to him after I slugged him with a wrench and left him in a boat floating down a river? I have no idea."

The smile never left Hill's face. "Did you kill him?"

"One can only hope."

A chuckle. "Oh, well. More money for me, then." Still looking at O'Neil, Hill used the knife to make Reed jump again. "Where is it?"

O'Neil didn't answer him. Instead, he looked at Reed.

"It's where I put it," Reed whispered.

"What did you say?"

"Tell him," said O'Neil.

Reed opened his right fist, spilling a red-capped airport locker key onto the table. It bounced and clattered, stopping at a spot near the center of the table.

"Let him go, Hill."

Hill reached out with his free hand and picked up the key. "Where's this at?"

O'Neil told him in a quiet voice. "Walk out of the concourse, cross the terminal, and you'll see a bank of silver lockers near an elevator."

"Just like that, huh?"

"Just like that."

"Well," said Hill as he pocketed the key. "I think someone needs to show me the way. How about you, honey?" he said to Katy. "You know, your wife, Frankie, she cleans up nice."

"You're not taking anybody, Hill. Not if you want all the money."

A noisy group of a dozen or so men wearing yellow tee-shirts emblazoned with the words "Ft. Lauderdale" across the front piled into the deli, forming an unruly line.

"Oh, Frankie," said Hill, all humor gone from his expression. "You don't want to be fucking with me now."

A new wave of sweat broke out on Reed's brow. Some of the yellow-shirted tourists began to sit at the empty tables to his right as others browsed at the coolers.

"Listen to me, you son of a bitch. There is nothing I want more than to see you walk out of this concourse and get that money. All of it, and without taking anybody with you." O'Neil leaned forward, keeping his voice low so he wouldn't be overheard. "But when you took my wife I had to come up with some way to get her away from you before you got what you wanted."

The smile was back on Hill's face. "How'd you do?"

"Okay, I think. In that locker is a cashier's check for one half of the money I cleared out of Lankford's."

"I hope you're not trying to be cute. The other half is...." Hill twisted the knife and Reed squirmed in his chair.

"The other half is in a series of smaller checks." O'Neil looked at his friend. "Reed?"

The younger man reached into his jacket pocket and grabbed the remaining checks. In one motion he pulled them out and flung them into the air high above the deli. The men in the tee-shirts looked up to see what was happening.

"Son of a bitch," growled Hill as he pushed Reed off his chair and jumped to his feet.

Reed rolled away from him as O'Neil and Katy pulled him to his feet.

"I'm okay," he told them as they moved him toward the boundary rope and away from the commotion.

"Let's go." O'Neil lifted the part of the rope that was closest to them and held it while Reed and Katy ducked under to the other side. Hill was snatching checks off the tables and out of the hands of the tourists from Ft. Lauderdale.

"What do we do now?" asked Katy.

"We disappear." O'Neil ushered the two of them into the crowd moving down the concourse and away from the terminal. A few seconds later, Hill and the deli were out of sight behind them, obscured by the weekend travelers and their people.

When they got to the end of the concourse, the trio leaned their backs against a railing and the windows overlooking the runways and watched the thinning tide of people flow toward them.

Katy leaned into her husband's side and asked, "Are we safe?"

O'Neil kissed her on the forehead. "I think so, honey. Hill's got no reason to come after us, he's busy grabbing the money he's been after for so long, and there are too many people here for him to try anything against the three of us."

"He didn't have much trouble with me alone," said Reed. He was examining the narrow slice in his shirt and the thin layer of sticky blood inside it. "I'm okay," he told Katy as she moved to help. "He just cut me a little."

She lifted his shirt and looked at the wounds. "You might need some stitches."

"Later," Reed said. "I can wait."

O'Neil asked him about the other check. "Please tell me you put it in the right bank of lockers."

"I put it in exactly the place you described to Hill."

"Good."

Katy was incredulous. "You mean he's going to find the money and get away, just like he wants?"

"He'll find the money, sweets," said O'Neil. "But I don't think he'll get away."

Hill had to pull out his badge before he could get all those yellow shirted assholes away from his money. It was a good thing he had brought it with him. He had planned on dumping it along with the rest of his old identity.

One dickhead wanted to fight but Hill had all the checks he had seen the kid throw and he had already drawn too much of an audience. Damn that O'Neil, he thought. The man knew what he was doing.

Hill stormed out of the deli and out of the concourse, looking for the lockers O'Neil had described. He crossed the wide hallway of the terminal and there they were, just as O'Neil had said.

He stopped in front of them, looking back the way he had come. No sign of O'Neil or of any pursuit whatsoever. He didn't think there would be. The man would have been figuring a way to get his wife back, not a way of capturing Hill or keeping the money. It would have been much too high a risk for him to do anything else.

Hill was going to win.

There were two Hispanic men standing next to the lockers and another one in a dark suit next to the nearby elevator but after a glance Hill ignored them. He took the key from his pocket and located the corresponding locker. Subconsciously he held his breath as he fitted the key to the lock and turned it to one side, listening for the sharp metallic click.

He pulled back the locker door and it was there. A negotiable cashier's check in the amount of twenty six million dollars.

Strong hands gripped both of his arms and a heavy metal object was jammed into the small of his back. Hill tried to turn but another hand gripped the top of his head. A line of dark-suited Hispanic men screened what was happening from the rest of the terminal.

"There is a gun with a silencer pointed at your spine," a voice spit into his ear. Before Hill could react, he was forced into the elevator next to the lockers. The men spun his back to the wall and a man in a suit, the one that Hill noticed earlier, pressed the barrel of a gun into his forehead.

They had taken him in seconds and nobody had seen a thing.

As the doors of the elevator slid shut, the man with the gun said, "Please do not even blink your eyes."

A pair of hands worked at the sleeve of Hill's right arm. A moment later he felt a sharp prick, then a smooth numbness began to work its way up his arm and into the rest of his body. My money, he thought. *My money....*

Ten seconds later he was out.

"There's something I need to show you."

Reed used the second locker key to open the locker where he had stored his bag. He withdrew the three cashier's checks and handed them to O'Neil.

"I don't know why I did it. Some kind of impulse, I guess. I couldn't stand to think of Hill–"

O'Neil looked at the amounts printed in the boxes on each of the checks. Almost two million dollars each. Jesus fucking Christ. He didn't want to deal with six million dollars of blood money.

"The question is," O'Neil asked Reed slowly. "If they decide they miss it, do you want them coming after you looking for it?"

"Will somebody please tell me what's going on?" Katy asked. "Hill's gone but now you two are frightening me. Who are you talking about?"

O'Neil reached into the locker and pulled out Reed's bag and handed it to him. "Come on," he told them. "Let's get out of this damned airport."

Together they walked out of the building and into the humid afternoon sunshine. Massive cumulus clouds threatened showers as they crossed through the busy traffic and up a small ramp toward the short term parking lot where O'Neil had left the car.

"After these past few weeks, I feel like somebody just rolled a truck off my back," said Reed.

"We all feel that way."

They climbed into O'Neil's car, left the airport, and began the long drive north out of Miami towards home. O'Neil didn't tell Katy what had happened until she insisted, about twenty miles later north on I-95.

"Please, honey," he told her. "I'd rather not talk about it."

"You have to, Frankie. No more secrets, remember?"

Maybe she was right. Perhaps Katy could one day help him look past what had happened, help him forgive himself for the lives he had seen lost since that day he had learned about Tim Clayton and been approached by Hill and Fetterman.

"Okay," he said. "After Hill had taken you, I went to see one of the men who had given that money to Lankford's company."

"Where did you find him?" Katy asked.

"In jail. Up in Starke at the state prison. I told him three things." He took a long breath and blew it out from his cheeks. "I told him that Hill and Fetterman had stolen his money. I told him where they would be, and I told him when they would be there."

"Oh my God, Frankie," Katy said. She closed her eyes and leaned her head into his shoulder. "Those people were here?"

O'Neil shrugged. I hope so, he was thinking.

"What do you think they'll do to him?"

He didn't answer. He was thinking about each of the people that had been hurt or killed since he had agreed to work with Hill. Katy could figure that one out herself.

O'Neil had been after justice, but was it justice that Lu Bates was killed? Or James Rooker? Or Gene Somebody, a man who had made such a difference to them but who hadn't even mentioned his last name?

Would it have brought Tim Clayton back or made any real difference to Marie if Hill and Fetterman had simply gotten the money and quietly slipped out of the country?

So what if in the end Hill pays the ultimate price for what he has done. Is that finally justice, and does it make up for the rest of it? Does it excuse O'Neil for what had happened because he wanted to be the one solving his friend's murder?

He drove on in silence. He was finished talking. Someone can tell it to me later, he thought. I'm through coming up with answers.

CHAPTER TWENTY NINE

Isabella Santorro made a mark on her clipboard then hung it from a hook on her cart. With her key she opened the door to room 512 and kept it ajar by moving the cart halfway into the entrance. I hate Monday mornings, she thought. All the guests party then fly home, leaving what are by far the biggest messes of the week.

The metallic smell of drying blood hit her three feet into the room. Isabella recognized what it was immediately and looked around her curiously, but the bedroom was empty.

She turned down the short hallway to look into the bathroom, crossing herself.

The first time she had seen a dead body in Miami, for that matter the first time she had seen one in this hotel, she had become violently ill. She had thrown up repeatedly and had experienced trouble sleeping for weeks afterward. Eventually the nightmares stopped and she became used to such things. Life in Miami, after all, was the life she had chosen and it would be what it would be.

The body and most of the mess was in the bathroom. Thank God, she thought, at least they put him in the bathtub for a change. She recognized it as a man, coated with so much dried blood that it took her a moment to realize that he was naked.

His hands were bound in front of him and the body was slumped forward onto its knees. She took a step into the small room and saw that a large part of the front of his head was missing. She couldn't tell for sure but he didn't look like anyone she would have known. Disturbing possible evidence didn't bother her. She knew the police would never solve this one. They never did.

Isabella turned to leave. This room wouldn't be cleaned anytime soon. Shortly the police would be here and she would be answering their many questions. She already knew what she would answer. She understood why a hotel attached to an airport would advertise soundproof rooms but the management here needed to realize the kinds of people that such a feature can attract.

The only thing that would shock her, she would find out later, was how badly tortured the man had been before he was executed.

Too many sleepless nights had taken their toll on him. Deep purple grooves sagged underneath his eyes as he carelessly passed an electric razor back and forth over his face. Silver hair, once combed and gelled meticulously into place each morning before he left the house, was merely pushed back away from his forehead and allowed to lie where it fell.

Sheila, his wife for the past thirty two years, knew of course that something was wrong at work, had been wrong for days, but her husband refused to talk to her about it. She had laid an elegant blue Italian suit on the bed for him, along with a freshly pressed shirt, silk tie, and comfortable hand-tooled leather shoes. She knew how good it made her husband feel when he was dressed to kill.

If he noticed the care with which she had selected his outfit he gave her no sign. He was so distracted and so uncoordinated from lack of sleep that Sheila actually had to help him knot his tie properly. When he tried it himself the ends kept coming out wrong.

"I have coffee downstairs, dear," she told him. "And I could make you an omelette."

"I'm not hungry," he answered. Then, noticing the concern on her face as she helped him shrug his way into his jacket, he said, "I'll get something at the office."

"Of course you will." But she knew better. He'd barely eaten in days. She followed him into the living room and then into the kitchen where he had left his briefcase and his car keys late the night before. He gathered these up and turned to the door where Sheila stood, offering the morning paper.

He took it to be polite but he knew he wouldn't look at it. His wife opened the door for him and said, "I love you, dear."

"I know," he said absently and kissed her cheek. "I love you, too."

She watched as he moved down the short sidewalk to the silver BMW parked in their driveway. She waved once as he got in but he didn't see her.

Out of habit, Walter A. Lankford checked his mirrors before slipping the car into reverse. Ten seconds later, after he had backed to the end of his driveway and into the street, he was gone.

The shock wave from the explosion blew out every front window on the block.

Shortly afterwards, Katy O'Neil found a forgotten cashier's check in the pocket of her husband's blue jeans. She put it in a desk drawer and said nothing to anyone about it.

Before the end of that same month, some very large checks arrived anonymously at the homes of three very different people.

One went to Marie Clayton in Sarasota.

Another was delivered to a divorcee named Elizabeth Rooker in Bradenton, Florida.

And in Minneapolis, a man named Carl Pantucket cried out loud when he realized that his dream of a chain of 24-hour sidewalk doughnut stands could finally come true. "If MamaLu could see me now," he thought.

THE END

SHALLOW SECRET'S

. . . .

by Rick Ollerman

For my father

PART ONE:
Spring, 1989

Excerpt from the St. Petersburg Times, April 16, 1989:

A man believed to be responsible for a number of recent killings along the
Sun Coast was arrested last night in Manatee county. William Joseph Donnelly, 33, was pulled over by officers on U.S. 41 north of Bradenton after failing to complete a stop at a red light while driving.

Donnelly did not try to flee from officers but rather "began to cry" when
approached by police. Sgt. Eugene Tully of the Florida Highway Patrol
quoted the suspect as saying "he was sorry and begged us to let him go so
that we could shoot him as he ran."

A search of the automobile led police to the discovery of a young girl's body
in the trunk. Although not yet officially identified, her description matches
that of 13 year old Megan Ann Smith, missing from her Bradenton middle
school since last Friday.

CHAPTER ONE

The telephone rang at three o'clock in the morning, the volume at least ten times louder than it would have been had the sun been shining.

James Robinson sat up, instantly awake. Calls this time of the night were bad news. He had the phone in his hand before the start of the second ring. "Robinson," he said.

"We got him, Jimmy."

He knew what it was about. "Don't play with me, Alex."

"FHP got him down in Bradenton two hours ago. It looks like it's over. Finally."

Robinson was on his feet, pacing the bedroom floor, his knuckles white as he squeezed the handset of the phone. "Are you sure it's him?"

"It is, James. Trust me."

"God." He sat down on the edge of the bed and rubbed his eyes. There was a curling feeling in his stomach but he didn't think about it. "After all this time I'm not sure I know how to believe you. When the phone rang I thought somebody was going to be telling me they found another body."

Alex Kelly didn't reply. Robinson stopped breathing as he got back to his feet. "Tell me."

"In the trunk."

"Motherfucker." He began pacing again. "Who is it?"

"Little girl named Megan Smith."

"The thirteen year old? Jesus Christ." Robinson forced a long exhale. "Okay, I'm on my way. Where they got him?"

"Slow down, partner. It– it's not that simple."

"What do you mean it's not that simple? It's my task force, isn't it? Where is he?"

"Jesus, man, back off, will you? Listen to me." Deep breath. "There's more to this thing than you know."

"What? What else is there? What are you talking about?"

Detective Alex Kelly swallowed on the other end of the line. "This guy, Jimmy," Alex told him. "He says he knows you."

"Of course he does. The press have made me every weirdo's wet dream. Who is he?"

"The name's Donnelly. William Joseph."

Robinson stopped moving. "Oh my God," he breathed. "B. J."

"They won't let you in."

"You're fucking kidding me. My own investigation?" The stomach thing again. He couldn't let it show.

Alex Kelly had met his partner outside the two story brick building that housed the Bradenton Police Headquarters. "I just spoke to the lieut. He wants a low profile until we figure out how to handle this. If the press gets hold of it—"

"Of course the press will get it. They probably had it before we did."

"Take it easy, pal."

"I don't believe this. I need to talk to him, Alex."

"They won't give you access."

Robinson gestured at the front door. It was nearly 4:30 in the morning and the pre-dawn air was slightly chilly and as the temperature fell closer to the dewpoint, springtime fog was beginning to form. "Will they at least let us in the door? I could use a cup of coffee while somebody decides to tell me what the hell is going on." He took a few steps toward the glass doors.

"Jim, wait. That may not be such a good idea."

"These guys are not going to keep me out of my own investigation, Alex. I've been working this case for five years, damn it. Nobody knows it like I do, you know that. If B. J. is the killer I need to get in there."

His hand was on the door handle and Kelly grabbed his other arm. "It's not your case anymore. The task force is done. They're letting Bradenton handle it now." He didn't fight it as his friend shrugged out of his grip. "Harper wants us out of here before the press shows up."

Robinson released the handle of the door and walked toward the parking lot. "What do you mean the task force is done? Who am I? Aren't I the guy who's been working sixty hour weeks for five years trying to catch this guy? Yeah, so I know Donnelly. That's all the more reason why I should talk to him."

"Harper—"

"I don't give a damn about the lieutenant! Do you know what's going on, Alex? You tell me if you do."

Kelly began walking toward his car. "I know a little bit. But not here. Let's go for a ride, get that coffee."

Robinson hadn't moved when Kelly made it to his car. He stood for a moment, looking at the pale building, the disappearing stars, and his friend. "If it were anybody else but you, Alex...."

Kelly nodded. "I know it."

"Shit." Robinson kicked a green unripe fruit across the parking lot as he crossed over to his partner's car. "Get me the fuck out of this orange grove town."

Robinson sat and pulled his door shut too hard. B. J. Donnelly. Childhood friend, petty thief, small time fence. Once a snitch. This was bad, as bad as it could be. Especially if he knew about Rebecca.

"Tell me about Donnelly."

They were sitting in a booth at a 24 hour waffle joint off the interstate. One waitress was doing the serving, cooking, and cashiering for the light early morning trade.

"You sound official, Alex."

"Nothing's official yet. But they're asking me when they should be asking you."

Robinson took a long sip from his coffee and made a face. "They should make this stuff more often than once a week." He wiped his lips with a napkin from the holder on the table and shot a glare at the waitress, who ignored him. Shit, loosen up, he told himself. She didn't do anything. He needed to keep his head. "First tell me this: is it still my case?"

Kelly shrugged and looked into his coffee. "I don't know. Maybe this is the guy, maybe this isn't. Harper's letting it sit with Bradenton until they figure out how to handle it."

"They're going to blow it if they talk to him. They don't know what he is, what he's all about."

"Not like you do, right?"

Robinson waited until his partner looked up from his coffee and held his eyes. "What do you mean by that?"

"Nothing, Jimmy. You don't need to read anything into that."

"Alex, I'm going to tell you this one time. I know what this killer is, I don't know who he is. I grew up with Donnelly, used him as a snitch. But only after I found out he was a punk. He's a clever little bastard and if these hicks from Bradenton talk to him, they'll blow it."

"They've got some pretty experienced guys down here. Hollander—"

"Is an old time asshole who can't keep his emotions out of his cases. Why he washed out of Tampa twelve years ago. Whoever this killer is, he's been raping and doing his thing to these girls for at least nine years. He has a wall built up around him ten feet thick. All that time he hasn't been able to tell anyone, he's had no one to confide in. This man didn't want to be caught. He wasn't writing 'Please catch me before I kill again' on the wall in pink lipstick. If they don't come at him right he's going to dummy up and they won't get a thing."

"So it has to be you."

Robinson ignored the tone. "Damn right." He sat up straighter and looked out the window. "I know this guy. Whether it turns out to be B. J. Donnelly or somebody else, the time to get to him, the time he's going to be the most vulnerable, is right now. If you understand what he needs and how to talk to him, he'll open up. I know he will."

Kelly was making an effort to keep his voice steady and even. "He's already opened a little bit. He told them about you."

After eight years of being his partner, Robinson all at once knew what this was. "You're interrogating me, Alex?"

"Jimmy, for Christ's sake, what do you expect? The lieutenant told me to keep you away and find out what your side is, without letting you go off. That's all. They pick up some scumbag with a body in his trunk who says you know all about him and you think they'll just let that one go? He may be trying to implicate you in these killings, man. They won't let you talk to him until they're sure they know what's up. There's going to be way too much heat."

The bad coffee provided an excuse to delay. Robinson dumped in a sugar packet, stirred it with a spoon, thought about Rebecca and the last time he had seen her. Could Donnelly…?

"Did he confess?"

Kelly pulled a small spiral notebook out of his jacket pocket and flipped it open. "Bradenton's got a perp with a body and he brings the newspaper thing, the Sun Coast Murders, up. He said he knows you, and you know everything, whatever that means. When they got him to the station he said there was more to this than just him and that if they wanted all of it they'd bring you in, too. Before anybody starts looking at him, Harper wants to know what this is about, how you two are connected." He closed the book and left it on the table. "It's about exposure and damage control, Jimmy. Meanwhile, he belongs to the orange boys. That's it. He's not going anywhere."

Robinson pounded his fist into the table. "He wants to talk, Alex. He's telling us he wants to talk."

"Tell me about him."

"Just tell me Bradenton's not interrogating him."

Kelly shook his head. "The lieutenant said he'd ask them to wait. No promises. The Smith girl is from their town. He's not tipping his hand."

What hand, Robinson thought. The walls were closing in. "Assholes." Ordinarily cooperation between jurisdictions wasn't much of a problem but in a case like this where a small timer could grab the chance to be a national hero he didn't rule anything out. But he had to get to Donnelly if he could, before too much got out. But how?

"Okay, I'll tell you what I know about him. Then you call the lieutenant and get this thing straightened out."

"Jimmy, all I can do is what the lieut asked. I don't run things any more than you do."

Robinson nodded his head. Fuck. "I know it, pal. I'm just extremely pissed right now." He tried another sip of coffee. It tasted better when he didn't think about it.

"Okay, here it is. You know I went to high school in Lakeland, right? Back then cars still had hood ornaments and kids used to twist the hell out of them until the cables snapped and the damn things would come off. B. J. used to grab every one he could just to do it. He showed everyone, didn't hide it. No idea what he did with the things.

"It was a small high school class, we played baseball for a few years until he quit. Car stereos got more interesting. He could make money with those. Used to hit the hotels along the interstate and do smash and grabs with the overnight cars. Got busted, went to juvie somewhere, came back a few years later. All of us knew it, no one really cared. Plenty of other crap going down, just not so serious."

"But you knew him later?"

I didn't, he thought, Rebecca did. "A mutual friend introduced us. Turned out we already knew each other. No big reunion stuff."

"Who was the friend?"

This is where it got tricky. "Girlfriend," Robinson answered. "She said he needed a place to stay, my wife was gone, I said sure."

Kelly nodded. "So his girlfriend brought him up to your house, you let him crash. For how long?"

Robinson felt the ice. This was his version. He had no idea what Donnelly was saying. His best advice was always: say less. But what do you do when you have to say something? "A week or two. We drank beers, shot some empties out back, and that was it."

The waitress came by and freshened Kelly's coffee. Robinson kept his palm over his.

"You know what he was up to?"

Robinson shook his head. "Thought he was looking for a job. That was it. Hung around the Hillsborough County Sheriff's Office for a bit, wanted to get a deputy's badge if he could, an office gig if he couldn't. Something. Used to show up at Billy Powell's place on Nebraska and bullshit with the off-duties."

"Who was the girlfriend?"

Time to back off. "I'd have to remember, Alex."

"That it?"

He took a sip of the coffee without thinking, made a face. He was in it now. "He seemed to know the job. Said his uncle was a cop in St. Louis or somewhere, just wanted to catch a break after his wayward youth."

"Why the hell'd you let him stay with you? He that likeable?"

"He kind of was. There was a night back in— would have been 1980, springtime. Julie had left me and I was staying out at the Hole."

Kelly couldn't hold back a chuckle. "You had that place back then?"

"Just got it. The bulldozers would have sunk about a month and a half prior." The Hole was what his friends called the abandoned development project northeast of Tampa in Pasco county where Robinson lived. One model home had been built and the land cleared for the creation of a new subdivision when a sinkhole had formed literally overnight, swallowing a freshly poured foundation and two bulldozers. The developer lost his insurance and had to abandon the project. Robinson had given money down on a lot and taken possession of the model just prior to the developer's going bankrupt. It was that or nothing.

"I had half of one tied on and Donnelly and the girl showed up, upset about something. I can't remember what but something was bothering them. She asked if they could maybe put up with me for a few nights. I was lonely, depressed about Julie, so I told them they could crash."

"You took these guys into your home."

"Yeah, hell, they were somebody to talk to and easier to feed than a dog."

"How long did they stay?"

"Just him." Robinson wrinkled his forehead. Maybe this would work. "The girl lit out after the first night or two. B. J. stayed about six weeks, two months, something like that. It bothered him about the sinkhole, I think. He didn't want to get swallowed up and disappear in the middle of the night. Really freaked him out."

"Where did he go from there?"

"I don't recall. I was drinking back then, I didn't keep in touch."

Kelly made some more notes in his book. "When was the last time you saw him?"

"The Meadows girl's dump site. Saw a familiar face in the crowd on the beach and he waved. I nodded back. Didn't realize it was him until I thought about it later. That was it."

"What do you think he was doing there?"

"What I thought then or what I think now?" Robinson didn't wait for an answer. "Alex, he fits the profile. Same race as the victims, the right age, tried to be a cop, possibly tried to insert himself into the investigation. We have to check the rest of it."

"Have you thought about the timing? When he lived with you?"

Damn you, Alex. "Of course, I have. Yes, if it's him he would have been killing when he was in my house."

The two men sat in silence, Kelly staring into his coffee, Robinson watching the staccato passage of the cars on the freeway through the window. There's more, Alex, and you know it. He'd have to be sure of the date that Donnelly had moved in with him, but it had to have been around the time the third victim, Holly Faith Rivers, had been raped and murdered. Detective Sergeant James Robinson of the Tampa Police Department, leader of the almost thirty five investigators that made up the Sun Coast Murders Task Force, may have supported the multiple murderer with free room and board in his own home.

"When was the last time you saw the girlfriend?"

Robinson coughed. Then swallowed some coffee. Then wiped his mouth with his napkin.

All the way, now. "Oh, geeze, beats me. Maybe it was when they–" He was going to say 'moved in.' "Mabye that first day I put him up. Maybe later. I don't remember."

"Her name?"

"Let's get that from Donnelly. I'd really have to think about that one." And again he turned to watch the cars fly down the interstate.

If that were the only question hanging over him, he'd be lottery-winning lucky.

The sky was a lemon-tinged blue as dawn broke to the east. The odd color annoyed Robinson as he and his partner drove back to the Bradenton Police Headquarters without talking. They'd had enough at the diner. Traffic was picking up but the rush was never as bad as it was in Tampa, or even a closer city like Sarasota. It was a quick and easy drive. Until they got there.

The parking lot was half filled with news vans and cars from all over the Tampa Bay area. There was already a large van from a Miami station and units from the rest of the state couldn't be far behind.

"Jesus Christ," Robinson swore as Kelly pulled over across the street.

The front of the brick building was illuminated by dozens of portable lights. Huge shadows from the throng surrounding the front door swept back and forth across the covered windows.

Kelly said, "We can't go in there. You wouldn't make it past the first microphone."

It was true. Robinson's name and face were too well known to the media. "We need to get to a phone."

"Let's do it a few blocks away from here." He re-started the car and pulled into the street. As they drove past, another van from a Miami station turned into the lot. "How do these guys get all the way up here so fast? The cops down there don't even respond to calls this quick."

Robinson grunted but was more concerned with what had drawn so many of them here so early. Somebody somewhere must be saying something. Damn it! He slapped his palm into the padded dash. This was his case, he should be in there. He needed to be in there.

"Take it easy, bud. I'll talk to Harper and we'll figure this out." Kelly whipped the car into a convenience store parking lot where there was a pay phone mounted outside on the wall.

"I'll call him," Robinson said as he opened his door.

"Hold on, let me do it. He wanted me to talk to you, remember?"

Robinson waved his partner to the phone as they stepped out of the car. He sat on the warm hood with his arms crossed in front of him. Whatever was going on, Alex was right when he said it was happening at the top. No matter how much work you do or how well you do it, you couldn't ignore the politics. Elected officials and appointees were the ones who ran the police department. His own desperation wouldn't change that.

Alex wasn't on the phone long. As he hung up, Robinson checked his watch. Barely eight o'clock. "Well?" he asked.

"Bradenton's keeping him."

Robinson sprang to his feet. "What?"

"They're having a news conference in half an hour. They're going to file charges on the little girl in the trunk while *they*–" Alex emphasized the word "–investigate evidence linking the suspect to the Sun Coast Murders. We've been screwed, partner. Harper wants us back home."

CHAPTER TWO

"Sit down," Harper said as they walked into his office. Kelly stopped and quietly closed the door before taking one of the two seats in front of the desk. Robinson dropped uncomfortably into the other.

"The press conference lasted less than ten minutes. Hollander didn't answer questions but he told them he'd probably have something by the end of the day. James," he said to Robinson. "Alex told you what's going on down there?"

You know he did. "Yes, sir."

Harper's white cotton shirt didn't have a wrinkle in it. With his elbows propped on his desk, he spread his hands wide and asked, "Do you have any input?"

Robinson was going to explode. His mood had gone from bad to worse and he knew that nobody in this room wanted his 'input.' "Alex knows everything I do. Sir," he added through tight lips.

"Look, Jim," the lieutenant folded his hands on the blotter in front of him.

"Let's not start by taking it out on me, okay? There's a lot of work to be done and I don't need the extra crap from you." He turned to Kelly. "Alex? You got anything to say?"

Kelly bailed out his partner and recapped what Robinson had told him about his relationship with B. J. Donnelly. Harper listened without interrupting, nodding his head at different points. The two men carried on as if Robinson weren't present, giving him a chance to calm down.

When Kelly was finished, Harper turned to Robinson. "Alex get it right?"

"He always does."

"Okay, then." He straightened some papers on his desk. "There's something else. Bradenton wants to check your house."

"Let 'em."

"I don't want to. You're one of us and if anybody does this it should be our guys. Any problem with that?"

"None whatsoever. I'll show the team the place myself."

Alex looked down at the pattern of the carpet visible between his shoes.

"Um, no you won't," Harper said. "We all know we have to be above and beyond here. For the time being, I'm going to get this done without you. I don't want you leaving the building."

Robinson shook his head, looking at his partner and his lieutenant. Apparently rank dictated Harper meet his eyes where Alex wouldn't. Oh yeah, he thought. I'm one of you all right. "Help yourselves," he told them. "There's nothing there."

Robinson was sitting at his desk trying to lose himself in the files of the more than twelve known victims that were part of this case. He lingered over one: Rebecca Owens. He couldn't look at the crime scene photos. The one he stared at was what her parents had given them when she disappeared. It was Becky as he remembered her. It always would be.

They'd met while she was waitressing at a deli on Jackson Street downtown. The guys would go in for lunch and Robinson had noticed her the day she started working. He liked her, they made eye contact that was unnecessary but they both knew felt nice. When Robinson started going there alone, when the rest of his group ate at other places, she started comping him his lunch. Things seemed to be inevitable from there, though they'd cost him his wife, a woman he'd thought he'd spend the rest of his life with. Until Becky, when he made the mistake of getting excited.

It was almost three o'clock in the afternoon when Kelly walked in and dropped two plastic evidence bags in front of him. One of them contained a silver bracelet and the other a pair of gold earrings.

"What's this?" Robinson asked. He picked up the bags and studied the jewelry.

"Recognize any of it?"

His partner shook his head. "Should I?" He tossed them back onto the desk and extended his arms over his head in a stretch. He had been sitting there for almost six hours.

Kelly shrugged with one shoulder. "They belonged to Lisa Mitchell and Shawn Long."

Robinson pushed his chair away from the desk. "Victim number one and victim number three. Jesus. Where did these come from? Did Donnelly give them up?"

Alex ran a hand through his thinning blond hair. "Sort of."

"Well?"

"They were at your house, Jim."

Robinson didn't move. He stared at the items in the bags and shook his head slowly. "You have no idea how insane this is."

Alex waited patiently, hands in his pockets.

"Who knows about this?" Robinson asked him.

"Me. Harper. The search team. That's all I know. Maybe the D.A."

They both knew that it would be next to impossible for this not to get out. It didn't matter how hard any of them tried, somebody would talk to somebody else and this would end up as front page news very soon. *Murder Victims' Jewelry Found in Cop's House.* Until now, no personal belongings or clothing belonging to the victims had ever been recovered. "This is nuts. Is Donnelly talking, then? Is he confessing?"

His partner shrugged. "Harper probably knows. He's been in contact with Bradenton. He wants us upstairs."

Robinson didn't move. "Did you go out to the Hole?"

Kelly gave a short laugh. "When are you going to get rid of those god awful curtains in the living room?"

Robinson stood up. "They'd probably look better in your place. Take 'em."

"Don't do me any favors." He grabbed the bagged evidence from the desktop and led the way out of the office that had served as the task force headquarters for the past six months. Robinson stopped him at the door with a touch on his arm.

"Where was this stuff, Alex?"

"In your bedroom. Don't ask me anything more, Jimmy."

With somebody else he might lose his temper but he knew his partner too well to think he'd ever do anything that wasn't by the book. Exactly by the book. Robinson let him go. It would have been like getting upset with the Pope for preaching.

The second floor conference room was a drab concrete block cube with no windows. Two scarred and neglected wood tables stood end to end in the middle of the off-white space, surrounded by rows of faded gray chairs. Harper was in one of them next to his boss, Captain Ron Lucey. Across from them was the district attorney himself, Reginald Baker. The men stopped talking when Robinson and Kelly walked in.

Lucey stood first, with Harper following his lead. Baker merely scowled at the blank yellow legal pad on the table in front of him and scrawled something between two of the lines.

"Detectives," Lucey said. "Come in, have a chair."

Kelly touched Robinson lightly on the back and moved to the chair next to the D.A. Robinson took the chair on the end slowly. He had an idea of what was coming.

The captain sat down, his shirt almost as smooth and clean as Harper's but without the style. "You both know the district attorney?"

Kelly said, "Yes, sir." Robinson remained quiet. Everybody in the room knew that the man himself wouldn't be here if things weren't very, very serious.

"Gentlemen," Baker said curtly.

"Reg wanted to come down here and find out for himself what exactly is happening with the Sun Coast suspect. He asked to sit in on this meeting."

The suspect in Bradenton? Robinson thought. *Or does he mean me?*

"James, we're going to bring you up to speed on what's been going on with Donnelly. We've already covered his background for Reg and now we need to address the issues that have been coming out of his questioning."

Robinson straightened in his chair and Harper shot him a warning look. He got the message. Let the captain play it.

"Sergeant Hollander out of Bradenton has handled the suspect since he was brought in. He has allowed access only to himself. He has followed procedure all the way down the line, obtaining the suspect's signature on the proper consent to interview forms. The suspect has been cooperating and has been somewhat talkative. As we all know, he has come forward with some rather disturbing allegations."

There was a soft tap at the opaque glass on the door and Lucey stood and answered it. "Bring it," he said and stepped back. A uniformed officer wheeled in a cart with a television monitor and a VCR and positioned it in one of the corners near an electrical outlet. He bent to plug in the cords then left, keeping his eyes mostly on the floor. Lucey waited for the door to close again before continuing.

"What I would like to do at this time is obtain Detective Robinson's personal evaluation of what we have so far. After that, the district attorney and myself will determine how we think we should proceed." Lucey was standing next to the cart, handling a videotape in a black plastic case.

Despite Harper's warning, Robinson couldn't help himself. "Has he confessed?"

Lucey and Baker turned to look at him. "Not exactly," said the captain. "What we have here are videotapes of Hollander's meetings with the suspect. Before we decide where we go with this, I wanted the five of us to see for ourselves just what it is that Bradenton is up against."

What *Bradenton* is up against? "So you're just giving them the case? What about—"

Harper spoke up, interrupting Robinson. "Perhaps Detective Kelly could run down the physical evidence that we have to date."

Alex got a nod from Lucey and began to read the details of B. J. Donnelly's apprehension from a page in his notebook. There was nothing more than everyone already knew and Robinson's patience was failing. "As far as trace evidence, they've pulled fibers from Donnelly's car for the FBI to match against evidence found on some of the victims. That's all we have so far." He didn't mention the jewelry.

"That's not much," Robinson said, drawing another look from Harper.

"No, it's not," agreed Lucey as he fed the tape into the machine after pulling the cart closer to the table. He turned on the monitor and carried a remote control back to his seat. "Let's see what this is."

The static pattern disappeared, replaced by a uniform screen of royal blue. A wrinkle passed from the top of the screen to the bottom then a color image of Bradenton's single interrogation room snapped into place. Two men were seated across from each other in orange plastic chairs. A plain wood table was between them.

The light in the conference room seemed to dim while the image on the screen projected its bright light across the faces of the five men in the audience.

Robinson sat forward in his chair. The hair was a little longer, the face a little older, but he could easily recognize the person of B. J. Donnelly. The large, ill fitting form of Hugh Hollander was perched across from him, reciting their names and the details of the meeting into a micro-cassette recorder that he set in front of Donnelly.

"I can't believe this," Robinson said. He looked at his captain who had been watching him from the moment he had pushed the 'play' button. "He's still wearing his own goddamned clothes! How do you let them do this shit?"

Lucey paused the tape, freezing the jagged image on the screen. "Detective," he said evenly.

Robinson took that as a cue to keep talking. "His clothes should be bagged and vouchered as evidence. Alex mentioned fibers; if Donnelly's got any on him they're either gone now or contaminated."

Lucey made a note on the pad in front of him and resumed the tape without speaking. "Fucking dumbshit Hollander," Robinson added.

On the screen, Hollander had finished his introduction and sat back in his chair. The dull hiss of recorded silence filled the Tampa conference room as the men on the screen sat and looked at each other. "Why don't you tell me about it," Hollander prompted.

Donnelly cleared his throat and said, "I thought we already talked about the girl." He was clearly agitated and very nervous. He held his hands in his lap and became preoccupied with his thumbs.

"Not Megan. I want to hear about the others."

Donnelly bit one of his thumb nails.

Hollander watched for a moment, then barked, "Knock that off!"

The mouth closed and the thumb nail dropped back to the lap. Donnelly stared down at his legs.

"You know what you're doing here and you're going to tell me about it."

He'd go, Robinson thought. *He'd fall right now if Hollander did him right.*

Hollander's huge meaty hand slammed down on the table in front of Donnelly, bouncing the tape recorder an inch into the air and making Donnelly blink. Slowly he looked up at the bigger man, narrowing his eyes.

"Don't play those fucking games with me, you little simp. You know damned well what it is I'm talking about. It's not a question of if you did these things, we already know that. What I want from you right now is the story. I want to know the who, I want to know the what, and I want to know the why and when. You may as well talk, boy. You're not ever going to leave this place the way you came in."

Donnelly blinked at him again then placed his hands on the table in front of him. He sat up straighter in his chair as he faced the larger man.

"Let's start with the first one, Donnelly. Does the name Lisa Mitchell mean anything to you?"

"I don't remember anything about that."

"How about Denise Simms?"

"I told you, I don't remember anything about that."

Hollander jumped on him. "Don't remember anything about what? Why not? Do you black out? Do you get high?"

"Maybe. Something." The voice was a little stronger.

"Let me refresh your memory, junior. How about Carole Mannette?"

Donnelly just stared at him. He's getting defensive now, Robinson thought.

"Coquina Beach, July the sixth, nineteen eighty. You strangled her with your hands and left her for the crabs. That was you, wasn't it?"

Robinson felt his blood pressure rise with the stress in his system. *Look at him, you asshole. He wants to talk, damn it. Give him a chance.*

"You don't know anything about it."

"Then why don't you tell me, asshole."

Donnelly sat back in his chair. It was hard to tell on the monitor but it almost looked as if he cracked a slight smile. "You don't know what you've got here."

He's getting it back.

Hollander, being of the old this-is-my-town-and-if-I-want-your-opinion-I'll-give-it-to-you school, was losing his patience. "Boy, you seem to have quite the disrespectful attitude for your position here. We've got you cold for that little girl you had in your trunk. You killed her the same way you did at least a dozen others. I know a lot of people who are going to sleep a hell of a lot easier knowing you're in here and not out driving around in that piece of shit blue Chrysler of yours."

Donnelly shrugged.

Too fucking late.

"You do know what they're going to do to your homicidal little ass, don't you?"

That hung in the air for half a minute. Donnelly creased his forehead as if he were trying to concentrate on something. "Sergeant, I've got something that you might be interested in. But I would need to know that it would be helping me in some way if I were to share it."

"I ain't playing games, boy. You're one step away from being beyond any earthly help. What is it you think you've got to offer?"

He seemed to think about it. "It's a person."

"Another body? We'll get to all of them, anyway."

"No. This is somebody who–" Donnelly paused for a moment, considering. "Somebody who helped me."

"Helped you do what? Tell me."

Donnelly shook his head.

Hollander pushed himself away from the table and stood up. "You know what, jackrabbit? I'm going to throw you back in that puke ass cell of yours for now while we process some more information. I don't have time to play these warped little mind games."

"Sit down, Sergeant," Donnelly told him. His remark drew a short bark of a laugh from the policeman.

"Now you're telling me what to do?" Hollander waggled his sagging chin back and forth and took a step towards the door. "I don't think so. You're making a big mistake by not talking to me, boy."

"It's a cop."

Hollander stopped moving. "What's a cop?"

"The person I can give you."

"Boy–"

"I'm not lying. I told you, you don't know what you've got here."

Hollander bent down and grabbed both sides of the chair Donnelly was sitting in and turned it around to face him, all two hundred pounds of it. "Are you telling me a police officer was involved with what happened to these girls?"

Their faces were inches apart. Donnelly met and held Hollander's gaze. "That is what I'm telling you. Yes."

"Is it Robinson?" Hollander asked. "Detective James Robinson, out of Tampa."

"Oh, I know who he is. He's my friend."

"What did he do for you?"

Donnelly shrugged, fully in control now. "He let me stay in his house."

Hollander stared at him. "That won't buy you breakfast, boy. We know about Robinson. You'd have to give us more than that to make us listen."

"There's more. There's a lot more."

With a wheeze, Hollander slowly pulled away and straightened, then turned toward the lens of the video camera. For a second he looked as though he might pull a comb out of his back pocket and run it through his gelled hair. Moving back to his seat, he pointed to the tape recorder on the table. "Start talking, big guy," he said. "Give me all of it. And so help you God if you ain't telling the truth."

CHAPTER THREE

"Hold it right here," Robinson said, leaving his chair.

Lucey clicked the 'stop' button and all eyes turned to Robinson.

"What is really going on here?"

Nobody answered.

"Because I don't think you have any intention of working this guy. If you blew at him the right way he'd fall over. Instead you're letting him dance you across your own ball room."

He looked at each of the people in the room. Alex was staring at the middle button of his shirt and Baker was scribbling intently on his pad. Robinson's two superior officers were the only ones facing him.

"Perhaps you'd like to give us your interpretation of what we should be doing, Detective," said Lucey. "And may I remind you that the 'we' in this instance is really the Bradenton PD. Until we establish a positive link to our cases it is staying with them."

Robinson felt the urge to move next to the television cart as he spoke. Perhaps it helped him feel on equal ground with the faces from the screen. "I already mentioned the clothes. That's just sloppy and stupid. But there's a lot more to dealing with somebody like this."

"Somebody like what?" asked Harper.

"A serial killer, a multiple murderer, whatever you want to call him. We've got cases going back ten years we can probably tie to this guy. There are likely more. Pay attention to how they got him: on a traffic violation. He didn't walk up to a uniformed cop, grab a young woman, assault her, strangle her—"

"Detective—"

"We got lucky. He wouldn't have been caught otherwise. At least not now. He was too good at it."

"What are you trying to say?"

Robinson couldn't believe how dense these people could be. Were they that focused on covering their own asses? "This guy has been killing people right under our fucking noses for a almost a decade. Ten years and nobody knew that he was the guy. Imagine what it would be like to have a secret that big, that central to who you were, for that amount of time. He's got walls built up around him ten feet thick."

"And you don't think Hollander can get through them?"

"That's the point. You don't get through them. Hollander's busting his head into the brick with a running start. Donnelly's just listening to the thumping. There is only one person in this world that truly knows what happened to those girls."

Nobody said anything so Robinson provided his own answer.

"You have to get Donnelly himself to let you behind the walls. It has to come from him. And look at him now. He doesn't know what we know, how much we've really got. The longer he holds out the more clear that will become to him. The less he'll feel he has to talk. The time to get at him is right now, while he's recovering from the shock of finally being captured."

The district attorney spoke up for the first time, dismissing Robinson and his argument. "Hollander's homicide clearance record is slightly above average. He knows what he's doing."

Robinson thrust his finger at the man. "Not for this kind of case!" He noticed his partner squirming in the chair next to Baker but he didn't stop. Ordinary people just didn't talk to the district attorney like this. "Almost all murders are committed by someone related to or known by the victim, we know that. Investigate the family, investigate the friends, expand the circle and cover the people that the victim came in contact with. We have procedures about how we solve these things. We also have a recipe for a four alarm chili downstairs that will burn the tongue out of your head and it has about as much relevance to this case as Hollander's fricking clearance percentage."

That was enough for Lucey. He stood and approached Robinson, laying a hand on his shoulder. "Take a seat, Detective."

Robinson held Baker's eyes for a moment before moving. He slumped into the seat at the head of the table while Lucey asked him, "So you'd use a different approach to interrogate the suspect?"

"We have to find a way to cooperate with him. Empathize with him, not judge him or condemn him. We have to establish a dialogue with him on his terms, not ours. None of this Dragnet 'where were you on the night of' crap."

"We need those details to prosecute," Baker said. Then he added, "Detective."

Inside Robinson was raging, bristling at his implied lack of willingness to prosecute the suspect. They were close to getting this guy and they were going to let somebody else lose him. "Don't you understand what I'm talking about?" He knew as he said it those were the wrong words to use but he couldn't take them back now. He was questioning the authority of his bosses in front of the district attorney and they couldn't let that go. "You won't get the details if he won't talk to you."

Baker said, "But it's my understanding he is talking." He turned to Lucey. "Captain?"

Lucey's face had taken on an inscrutable expression. He stood, staring at the edge of the table, his neatly groomed and oiled head framed by the blackened television screen. "Let's finish the tape," he said and returned to his seat. His quiet tone was much more ominous than if he had screamed out loud. Robinson kept silent.

There wasn't much more to watch. Clearly Donnelly's confidence grew the longer the interview went on. As long as he was feeding Hollander a line, the sergeant wasn't noticing what was going on. *Christ*, Robinson thought. *He could tell him he took the Lindbergh baby and Hollander's next move would be to swear out a warrant*

"Check Robinson's house," Donnelly said. "I'm not saying for sure, but you might find something."

Hollander was hooked. He was writing things down in his notebook, his breathing audible over the soundtrack. "What are we supposed to find there?"

God awful curtains, you prick.

"There might be some stuff that belonged to some of the–" Donnelly searched for the right word. Robinson knew that any chance to land him had truly passed. "To some of the people you're interested in."

Hollander stopped writing then turned over his shoulder and looked at the camera again, as if making sure it was still working. "I need to have an idea of what we're going after so I can put it on a search warrant." The sergeant stopped, his pen poised above his paper, waiting. It was terribly obvious to Robinson who was in control of the interview now.

"Personal things," Donnelly said.

"Now, look, boy—"

Donnelly started to shake his head.

"What are you doing?" asked Hollander.

"I'm tired." He yawned. To Robinson it looked forced. "Don't make me say the 'L' word, Sergeant. You know I'll be to talking to someone else if I do. If I talk at all."

"Look here, goddamnit," Hollander swore, snapping his notebook shut and pushing to his feet. "You want a lawyer, you'll get a lawyer. You knew that before you sat down there." He glanced at the camera again.

You're still on, fat man.

"Just don't you think for a minute that you're running this show. You and I both know what the best way for you to help yourself is. You've only got one chance here. If you're smart you'll take it."

Gone was the cocksure swagger in Hollander's earlier words and body language. He was posing for the camera now and it made Robinson sick. Hollander was wrong. Donnelly was in command and Hollander was carrying his fricking robe.

On the screen, Hollander walked off camera tracked by his captive's eyes. A moment later, the picture went dark, followed shortly by a smooth pattern of static snow.

"That's it?" Lieutenant Harper asked. The atmosphere in the room dimmed with the picture as the five men turned their attention back to each other.

"That's enough, isn't it?" Robinson challenged. "Hollander turned control of this investigation over to the goddamned murderer and here we sit fifty miles away watching him do it. That was the worst fucking interview I've ever seen in my life."

"And just why is that, Detective?" said Baker. "Because it was your name that came up?"

Lucey spoke next, heading off Robinson. "Reg, please."

"We may as well get to it now, Ron. Before the FBI gets here."

Shit. The FBI. That explains a lot, Robinson thought. *Is it to go after Donnelly so TPD can come after me?* "Get to what?" Robinson asked in a softer voice.

"How do you explain the jewelry?"

Robinson was lost for a moment. What could he tell them? Either they wanted to believe that he could be guilty or not. For the district attorney even to be here he must give some credence to Donnelly's accusations. He grew angrier at all of them the more he thought about it. How could they even think he was capable of being part of this? Everything that he'd accomplished in his career, his whole life, meant absolutely nothing to these assholes. Not on a case like this.

Especially on a case like this, he realized.

"Screw yourself, Baker."

Harper looked deeply distressed as Lucey turned a cold stare toward Robinson. He was about to speak up when Lucey beat him to it. "What did you just say?"

Robinson glanced at Alex then said, "I'm sorry, sir."

"You bet your goddamned little insubordinate ass you are." He stood up letting the chair push backwards with the straightening of his legs. "We have your statement about your relationship with Donnelly. Is there anything else you wish to say?"

Robinson knew he had made a serious mistake. But goddamn it, let them put themselves in his shoes, see how it made them feel. He'd given his whole life to this department and they come at him with this. "No, sir," he said.

Lucey cleared his throat then nodded at Harper. The lieutenant said, "We're placing you on administrative leave, James, while we check this out. Alex will handle the investigation and we—" he checked with Lucey "—are going to do what we can to keep this away from Internal Affairs."

"For now," Baker muttered.

"Excuse me, sir," Robinson said to Harper. "But keep what away? Does somebody here really believe I had something to do with this? Because of what one piece of—" He caught himself. "Because of the statements made by a murderer like B. J. Donnelly?"

"James, there's evidence here. We can't ignore it. You know that."

Robinson shook his head. "No, I don't think so, Lieutenant."

Lucey cleared his throat again. "Gentlemen, this meeting is over."

Nobody moved. The light and sound from the television monitor was a distant memory, a background thought to what everybody in the room was thinking and feeling.

"I want to talk to Alex before I go."

Baker turned to stare at Lucey, who made a point of ignoring him. Instead he looked at Kelly and considered for a moment before he gave a short nod. He wasn't about to be intimidated by the district attorney's office. At this point Robinson went to the door and held it while his partner joined him.

In the hall, Alex asked him, "What's going on, Jimmy? I'm not very comfortable out here."

Robinson waited for a moment, until he was sure there was nobody around to hear them. "You're not comfortable, Alex? How the hell do you think I feel?"

Kelly didn't answer.

"You know what they're going to do to me, don't you?"

"Jimmy–"

"Don't say it, Alex. We've been partners too long. I just need to know where I stand with you."

"What do you mean, Jimmy? I'm just going to do what I always do. I'm going to do my job."

It was a difficult thing for Robinson not to give in to the temptation to shout, to vent his lungs and his anger at the world. "And what about my job, *partner*? What about me? Do you honestly think that I could have had anything to do with this? Anything at all?"

Kelly straightened and his face grew hard. "It doesn't matter what I believe and you know it. An accusation has been made and it has produced evidence. Evidence that was found at your house. Now we have to go through the process."

"That's what this is to you? A process?"

"What do you want from me, man? Huh? You tell me. You're a great cop, Jimmy. One of the best I've ever seen. You have a gut like nobody there is and I have been in awe of some of the things you have done on the job. I do what I do the best I can. And I take orders, too."

He didn't give Robinson a chance to reply. "I'm not like you. I can't do what you do. If I'm any good at all it's because I do it the way it's written. When I see A, I know I'm supposed to do B. Without an intuition like yours, it's the only way I know how to be a cop. I can't do it any other way. You say Donnelly planted that stuff, then Donnelly planted that stuff. It'll turn out."

"Are you so all the time by the book that you're going to help them wash this all over me?"

"You didn't hear me. It's just a process, Jimmy. If there's nothing there everything will be fine."

"What about that 'process,' partner? What about the damage the process itself does to the suckers you grind through it?"

"Jim," Kelly said, putting his hands in his pockets. "The book says this gets played a certain way and that's how I'll play it. Same way I always have. It'll be okay."

"Then just look me in my goddamned eye and tell me you know what you'll be putting me through."

"It's not up to me, Jimmy, don't personalize this," Alex said. "It's what we do."

Robinson's insides were twisted into granite but his voice was soft and even. "You put me through this process of yours and I'm finished as a cop."

"And you're not helping himself with performances like that one you just gave," Kelly told him. He took a breath, released it. "This is the system, James. Mine as well as yours. What choice am I supposed to have?"

"For you, Alex, I guess there isn't one."

Robinson stood eye to eye with his partner. There was no sound coming from anywhere in the building, no movement to distract them. They were alone in their own world, staring each other down. After a long minute, Robinson turned and walked away down the hall. He stopped at his desk and tidied up. At least they gave him the courtesy of letting him leave on his own terms. As he straightened the folders on his blotter, he slid the picture of Rebecca Owens from the case file and palmed it into his pocket as he stood.

I'm sorry, Becky.

Excerpt from the Tampa Tribune, April 18, 1989:

Authorities today charged Oldsmar resident William Joseph Donnelly, 33, with the murder, sexual battery and kidnaping of Megan Ann Smith, 13, from Bradenton. Donnelly, the man police believe to be the killer known as the Sun Coast Murderer, is being held in Bradenton pending further charges.

Excerpt from the Tampa Tribune, April 20, 1989:

TASK FORCE LEADER INVESTIGATED

In a brief news conference held yesterday afternoon in the downtown office of District Attorney Reginald Baker, Captain Ronald P. Lucey of the Tampa Police Department confirmed that Detective James Edward Robinson has been placed on an indefinite leave of absence. This comes on the heels of allegations that surfaced in the interrogation of William Joseph Donnelly, 33, in Bradenton.

Donnelly, suspected in the deaths of as many as twelve young women dating back almost a decade, was arrested two days ago following a routine traffic investigation. He has since reportedly told police that his one time roommate, Robinson, had some knowledge or form of involvement with the crimes. Since the fall of 1984 Robinson had been placed in charge of the on again off again multi-agency task force that had been formed to track the killer. Robinson himself has not been seen since the arrest of Donnelly and could not be reached for comment.

Excerpt from the Tampa Tribune, April 24, 1989:

Sources inside the Tampa Police Department today confirmed the existence of undisclosed evidence against Detective James Edward Robinson, the officer recently placed on leave while authorities investigate the allegations against him made by suspected Sun Coast Murderer William Joseph Donnelly.

Excerpt from the Tampa Tribune, April 30, 1989:

SUSPECT INDICTED

Police yesterday formally charged Sun Coast Murderer suspect William Joseph Donnelly, 33, of Oldsmar, Florida with the deaths of three women. In addition to the charges already filed against him for the murder of 13 year old Megan Ann Smith, Donnelly was charged with three additional counts of murder, sexual battery and kidnapping. Police say more charges are expected to follow. The three women, Karen Elizabeth Moore, 26, from Gainesville, Janice Londen, 22, from New Port Richey, and Elizabeth "Sunny" Dutton, 29, from Ft. Myers, have long been considered three of the dozen or so suspected victims of the so-called Sun Coast Murderer. Bradenton police Sergeant Hugh Hollander, taking over the investigation from Tampa Detective James Robinson, himself the subject of some controversy, indicated that hair and fiber evidence found in Donnelly's car at the time of his arrest have linked him to the bodies of the three women.

CHAPTER FOUR

"He wants to see you."

"Who does?"

"Donnelly. He's telling Hollander he won't talk anymore unless he's allowed to visit with you."

Robinson made a sound through his nose. "Well, we wouldn't want that would we?" He walked to the windows that faced the front of his house and pulled the edge of the curtain away from the wall. Through the sliver of glass he could make out four vans parked outside the metal gate that blocked his driveway from the dirt road that led further into the failed subdivision. He replaced it gently, careful not to cause a motion that would be noticed. He turned back to Kelly. "How'd you get by them, anyway?"

His partner shrugged. "I think they know me by now. They know I won't tell them anything."

"Thanks for that at least. I read enough of their shit in the papers." He gestured toward a stack of old newspapers on a coffee table in front of his TV. "Can I get you anything? You want a cup of coffee or something?" He led Kelly to the kitchen and pulled open a pair of cupboard doors. "As you can see, I'm well stocked."

"No, I'm all right, thanks. Help yourself, though."

Robinson pulled a can of coffee down and set it on the counter. "It's not easy living under siege, Alex." He moved an electric coffee maker away from the wall and shoveled a mound of coffee into a filter. His shirt was untucked and hanging over a pair of ripped blue jeans. On his feet were a pair of plain white socks.

"I've never seen you with a beard before."

He finished adding water to the machine and flicked it on. "Yeah, well. Sometimes things change pretty quickly, don't they? Have a seat." He motioned Kelly to the small kitchen table set just inside the door.

"The case—"

"I've gotten used to it, you know," Robinson said, ignoring Kelly. "I keep my motorcycle at a friend's house about half a mile from here. I get on my ATV and pick my way through the trees until I get there. It took me half a dozen trips to bring in all the food and crap I've got. Check this out." He reached to the counter behind him and grabbed a faded Miami Dolphins cap and a pair of sunglasses. "This is what I wear over at the 24 hour grocery store." He put them on. "What do you think? Goes well with the beard."

"Jimmy—"

"And have you ever seen my house so fucking clean?" He waved an arm through the air in a backhanded sweeping motion. "I've got this place scoured. My hands are raw from so much scrubbing. I've also developed a few insights into the problems of America's housewives, if you're interested." He checked his watch. "Phil's on in a few minutes if you want to watch with me. Today's show is about getting more out of your family life, I think. Some crap like that."

He stood up and opened another cupboard, removing a cup. He pulled the pot out from under the drip of coffee and let his mug fill instead. Replacing the pot he said, "You sure you don't want some, Alex?"

"You want to talk about it?"

"About what? About being trapped in my house watching vapid television programs and having my life picked apart and shredded by the newspapers? What's to talk about? Normal fucking life around here. I'm not sure what there is to talk about." He peeled off the cap and glasses and set them down on the counter. "You've noticed the only thing I've asked you is how you got in here and if you want a cup of coffee or not."

"You're more—" Kelly searched for the word. "Subdued than I expected."

"Yeah, well." Robinson made a motion with his cup. "We all have our days."

"You're not going to ask me anything else?"

Robinson looked at the floor. After a minute he said, "I guess not."

Kelly stood. "They want to know if you'll see him, Jimmy."

"They're still trying to keep that little shit happy, are they?" His tone took on a sharper edge then mellowed again. "Maybe. I don't know. When?"

"As soon as possible. The captain tried to call you but—"

"I know, the phone is off the hook. You can imagine...."

"Yeah." Kelly walked toward the front door. "Take care of yourself, Jimmy." He paused with his hand on the door knob, waiting for something he wasn't sure would come.

Without looking at him Robinson said, "Get the fuck out of my house."

Two o'clock in the morning. All quiet out front. Robinson's doorbell rang. He had fallen asleep on the living room couch about an hour earlier, a book about early discoveries in cosmology steepled on his chest. Robinson wasn't sure what he'd heard until it came again.

What the hell? he thought. *They know better than this....*

He stalked to the front door and wrenched it open. It wasn't the press. A younger man, blond, an inch or two taller than Robinson and stockier, with powerful arms showing through his black t-shirt, stood on the porch, looking tense.

"Drew," Robinson said. "Come in, come in." There were still trailers and a few cars at the end of the driveway but nothing was moving. "How'd you get in here?"

Drew Owens walked in and kept moving down the hallway. He was a big man, six feet four inches and in the range of two hundred twenty pounds. "I left my bike down at the turn off and walked in. Through the trees on the right."

Robinson shut the door and followed him into the kitchen. "I haven't seen you for months." *Not since they found Becky.*

"Is this the guy, Jim?"

"Donnelly?"

"Did this guy kill my sister?"

"Sit down, Drew," Robinson told him, pointing to a chair. He slid one out from the table and sat himself, waiting for his ex-girlfriend's brother to do the same. When Robinson had started seeing Becky, he'd met her brother, Drew, a few times. He had never seemed to warm to the idea of his sister dating a married cop, but who could blame him. Even after Julie walked out, partly because of Becky, Drew still kept his distance. They weren't friends, but Robinson didn't know what they were.

Drew Owens took the seat opposite Robinson, never taking his eyes from his face. "I need to know what happened."

Robinson wasn't sure what to. The hurt, the pain, the rage he had felt when Becky had disappeared and then been found were taking hold of his gut all over again. He'd never reported his relationship with Becky Owens to Lucey or anyone else in the department. Alex probably suspected at one time, but Robinson wasn't sure. He was already in charge of the Sun Coast task force at that point, and didn't want to jeopardize that by exposing himself, or to embarrass Julie any more than he had already.

"You know I'm out, right?"

Drew nodded. "But you must know things...."

"Drew–" Robinson began. "I'd tell you if I knew anything, I would. But I really don't. It looks like Donnelly is the guy. Sometimes, though, not all the circumstances come clear, you know what I mean?"

Robinson waited but Drew just stared at the table in front of him.

"I don't know what you're looking for. A confession? It may come, it may not. Donnelly's a cagey one. It may depend on what happens at his trial. They'll go for the ones they know they can get–" he stared at Drew, carefully watching for a change in expression– "but for the others?" Robinson spread his hands. "They won't keep pushing. The rest may be up to Donnelly."

"So you think there'll be a trial? He won't plea bargain?"

"Not B. J. He was weakest when he was caught, but now? He's in control again, everyone's coming to him. If he pleads guilty, he's over and he loses the glamour."

Drew seemed to spit the words: "That's sick."

"He's a sick man."

"I'd like to–"

"I know."

They sat together in silence, in the dark, the glow from the living room reflecting down the hall providing the only light.

Finally, "Did this guy kill my sister?"

"It looks like it, Drew."

"Because he knew you?"

"What?" Robinson sat back.

"This guy knows you, you know my sister. Did he kill her because of you?"

Robinson noticed Drew didn't use Donnelly's name. He wasn't sure what to say. "I– I hope not, Drew."

The brother of his slain girlfriend nodded his head up and down. "Okay," he said. "Okay. Maybe we find out some day." He put his hand in his back pocket, took out an envelope. "I found this." He slid it across the table.

It was a red envelope, small, like the kind that goes with flowers sent from a florist. Robinson opened it, took out the white card, stared at the blue ink:

Becky,

Please, I'm sorry. Let me make it up to you. You know how much I love you. I can't live without you.

–T

"What the hell is this?" The writing was neat, the words printed but almost run together like cursive. The signature "T" had a particular stylized flourish. Robinson turned the card over, saw it was blank, then slammed it on the table in front of him. "Where did you find it?"

"I don't know what it is. I found it a few weeks back in one of my jacket pockets. It was a leather coat of mine Becky sometimes wore. You know we were close. I hadn't touched it since she–"

He stopped speaking. Robinson waited.

"I could have given it to the, uh, the other cops, I guess. I thought about it. But I decided to give it to you instead."

"Why, Drew?"

"Because," he said. "She really loved you. You know that, don't you?"

Robinson could feel the pain squeeze his insides, his back slump into his chair. "I know," he said. "I loved her, too."

There was an awkward silence with both men alone in their heads for a minute. Then Drew said, "You need to do something for me."

"What can I do, Drew? I told you—"

"Just listen to me." Robinson stopped talking. "If you ever find out the truth, you will tell me. Everything. I don't care if it takes fifty years."

"I—"

"You promise me," Drew said.

"Okay." Robinson nodded. "I promise," he said. "Even if it takes fifty years."

CHAPTER FIVE

He had hoped the beard would be enough of a disguise, but it wasn't. Even wearing his sunglasses and carrying his motorcycle helmet, heads turned as Robinson passed through Bradenton's Police Headquarters. He wasn't going to stop and he didn't return anyone's attention. He knew they'd only look away if he did.

He made his way to the same interrogation room he had seen on the tape. The desk sergeant told him they would get Donnelly ready and bring him in. The man apologized without meeting Robinson's eyes when he said that he had to check him for weapons. He seemed surprised when Robinson extended his arms and waited patiently for the officer to scan him with his wand. Apparently he wasn't living up to his reputation.

One thought ran through Robinson's mind as he passed by each ogling group: how would they feel if they were me?

This was what was wrong with Alex's "process." Every person in this building was asking themselves the same questions: what if he knew? What if he did have something to do with it? Could one of our own really have done those things to those women?

And they would have been kind compared to the press. They had been taking it even further: at least twelve dead women, no good leads, no real suspects. A cop may have been the only one who could pull this off. Especially if he were the lead investigator in charge of the entire task force.

The damage is done at the time the questions are asked, when his friends and fellow officers stop to even consider him in that way. The answers, even the right ones, could never wholly wipe that out.

Robinson entered the room and kicked the chair Hollander had used away from the table. He noticed that particular person was making himself conspicuous by his absence. Suits me, Robinson thought as he set his motorcycle helmet on the floor next to the chair.

The video camera was still set up on a tripod in one corner. He walked over and blinded it by snapping the tethered cap into place over the lens. He couldn't see any microphones but he knew they were there like he knew there were people watching from behind the mirror.

Forty minutes later the door opened and Robinson stood as B. J. Donnelly shuffled into the room, his wrists and ankles manacled. A guard followed him in and shut the door, remaining just inside. Robinson didn't know him. That was probably deliberate, he thought.

Donnelly stood across from him, on the other side of the table, with his head angled down as if drawn in that direction by the weight of his chains. "How you doing, Jimmy?"

Robinson didn't move. He had kept his glasses on and he knew Donnelly couldn't see his eyes. He felt his stomach curl into a ball like a caterpillar and he could almost hear his heart beating in his ears. He was standing across from the man who had likely killed a dozen young women, a man who was also ruining his career, and the man who may have murdered his lover. This was the man who was accusing Robinson of helping him get away with it.

"Look at this," Donnelly said, shaking his wrists. "They're kind of pissed at me since I quit telling them things."

Robinson wasn't sure what he wanted to say. He almost asked if anyone else were coming; an officer should be in the room with them but then he thought they must be trying to see if something slipped while he and Donnelly were alone in the room. He thought again about why he had come and still couldn't come up with a good answer. He swallowed hard, forcing saliva into his mouth, and said, "Why are you doing this, B. J.?"

Donnelly moved his eyes around the room, noting the covered video camera. He looked up at the ceiling and then at the walls. "They can't hear us, can they?"

"Who do you mean by 'they'?"

"You know. Them."

"I'm one of 'them.'"

Donnelly chuckled. "Yeah, yeah, that's right." He jerked his head around and pulled out the chair in front of him with both hands. "I want to sit down."

Robinson hesitated for a moment before joining him. He wanted to at least listen to what Donnelly had to say.

"Been a while, hasn't it?" Donnelly asked him.

"Why are you doing this to me?"

Donnelly studied the table before he answered. "It's not about you, Jimmy."

"It is to me."

Donnelly nodded, conceding the point. "Well, I guess I'm sorry about that. It can't be very easy, going through what they're doing to you."

"Thanks for the sympathy. Now knock it off. What do you want?"

Donnelly looked up into the dark lenses covering Robinson's eyes before turning his gaze to the metal bracelets on his wrists. "I need some help, Jimmy."

"No kidding."

"No, man, I'm serious." He screwed up his face as he talked into his chains. "They've got me on that girl in my trunk, I know that. But those others...."

"You did them, didn't you, B. J." Statement.

Donnelly cracked a half grin and looked into Robinson's face again.

What the fuck does that mean?

"I don't want to die, Jimmy."

Neither did all those women. "So?"

"So I want to give them something else. I want to give them something they want more than me."

"Like the goddamned cop that was chasing your sorry little ass for five fucking years?"

"No, Jimmy, no. I mean, it could have been like that, but it wasn't. I knew they'd never touch you. They couldn't."

"You don't know a whole lot, you son of a bitch. That was a neat trick with that jewelry in my house."

The same half grin appeared on his face but he quickly smothered it.

It wasn't a lot but Robinson had had enough. Maybe it was wrong to have come here. "You've made a mistake. There isn't anything they want more than you, you miserable piece of shit." He grabbed his helmet and stood up. "Make sure they get you a hood that fits good and tight, B. J. I'm told that when they fry you if you pucker too much the first thing that happens is your eyeballs explode."

Robinson started to walk around the table on his way out and Donnelly grabbed one of his arms. "No! I have to tell you!"

"Stop jerking me around, B. J." Robinson snapped his arm out of the prisoner's grip. "I'm gone."

"No! Sit down, Jimmy. Please. I'll talk to you now. I swear it!"

Something in his voice made Robinson think about it. There was a new note there, something that was missing before. *Panic?*

"What is it?"

Donnelly looked over his shoulder at the policeman standing at the door. He hadn't moved. "Sit down, I want to whisper."

Robinson did as he was asked, moving back around the table and taking his seat. Donnelly motioned him closer and without taking his eyes off him

Robinson inclined his head toward Donnelly's. "There is something they want more than me."

"Not unless it's me they don't."

"You're wrong. There is something but none of you know it. You never figured it out."

"Figured what out?"

"I didn't do them all. There was someone else involved."

"Bullshit."

"I'm not lying, man. I need you to prove it for me."

"What for?"

"My life. I need you to show them there's somebody else. I'll confess to everything. Everything I did. I'll tell them about you, Jimmy."

"What about me?"

"That you had nothing to do with this. Whatever you want. Give me life, give me anything, I just don't want them to kill me in the electric chair."

Robinson looked at the guard at the door. He had been watching them but their voices were low and the guard couldn't hear them.

"Look, Jimmy, they're never going to let me out of here because of that little girl. I know that."

"Her name was Megan."

Donnelly blinked and looked surprised. Naming the girl seemed to confuse him. "I'm sorry for that, you know? Of course I am. Is that what you want to hear?"

Robinson didn't say anything.

"It's just– I can't help it, Jimmy. What good is it going to do to kill me, too? I'm in prison now. I can help you guys. I know things. I am more valuable to you guys alive then dead. I can help you understand things like this in ways you'd never know yourself."

Donnelly mistook Robinson's continued silence and went on with enthusiasm. "You never caught me, Jimmy. Think about that. I can show you why."

"I gave you a hand when I thought you needed it. I didn't even know you. And you do this to me?" And lower: "To Becky? Did you kill Becky Owens?"

"Becky? Why would I do that to you, Jimmy? She was–nice."

"Why are you doing this?"

"All I did was tell them a cop was involved. I didn't say who it was."

Robinson slapped the table with his hand and Donnelly shut up. "Where'd the jewelry come from, B. J.? Is there anything else at my house?"

"You see? That's what I'm talking about." Donnelly licked his lips anxiously. "I can answer all those questions. You've just got to give me a little help. I can give you so much more."

"Who's 'T'?"

"What?"

"Who do you know signs their name as a capital 'T'?"

Donnelly sat back in his chair. "I told you, you need my help."

"Go to hell." Robinson stood up, hooking his helmet with a stiff-fingered grip.

"I can't, Jimmy. I've got things to do. God isn't through with me yet."

Robinson went to the door and paused long enough for the guard to twist away from the door and get out of his way. "But I am, you prick."

Hollander burst out of a door to Robinson's right as he left the interrogation room behind, another man in a dark suit following. "Robinson!" Hollander called. "Hold up!" The background noise in the squad room faded to almost nothing. Robinson didn't stop walking until the larger man grabbed his arm and tried to spin him around. He shrugged him off first then turned to face him.

"What do you want?"

Hollander hunched his shoulders, repositioning his oversized jacket. "Let's take this into my office."

"Fuck yourself." Robinson turned and walked toward the stairs.

The second man called out. "Hold on, Detective."

Robinson stopped and turned again. He looked him up and down, noting the cut and quality of the suit and shoes. "Who the hell are you?" But then he recognized him.

"Francine. FBI. We've met several–"

"I'll hold on when you arrest me." And Robinson started walking.

Very aware that every pair of eyes in the room were trained on him, Hollander called, "What were you two doing in there, Robinson? What are the two of you up to?"

The top of Robinson's head disappeared around the first landing.

"If there's something there, I'll find it, you dirty son of a bitch." Hollander's voice chased the echo of Robinson's boots down the thinly carpeted steps. Ignoring the looks of everybody in the room, Hollander pulled at his jacket again then went to the interrogation room where Donnelly still sat at the table, cradling his head in his manacled hands.

Outside the station, a crowd of reporters surged ahead. Robinson was lifting his helmet to his head when a hand grabbed his upper arm. Special Agent Francine.

Robinson looked at him. "You arresting me now? Smile for the cameras."

The roar from the press crescendoed and Francine pulled him back to the front door. Uniformed cops stepped up to keep the reporters back.

"I can if you'd like. Or we can talk." Still not letting go of Robinson's arm.

"Fine. Just to get out of here." He shrugged hard out of Francine's arm and went back into the building. Robinson paused, letting Francine take the lead from the doorway.

"Let's go in here," he said, indicating an empty room down the corridor behind the desk sergeant's station.

It was a small conference room, not an interrogation room, and the chairs had padding and were on casters. Francine went to a coffee machine in the corner. "Want something?"

Robinson shook his head, put his helmet on the table, sat down. "What do you want?"

Francine moved away from the machine without touching the pot, stood across the table looking down at Robinson. "I want the truth, Robinson. Same as everyone else."

"Where you from? These cases didn't cross state lines, we never asked for field help."

Francine shrugged. "Nevertheless, we've been around. FDLE asked for lab help, I got involved."

"Why you, specifically?"

"I have some experience here." Robinson started to say something but Francine cut him off. "But this isn't about me."

"Okay." Robinson sat back. "What is it about?"

"I know how you became lead on the task force. I'm going over your files now."

"Goody."

"What do you know that's not in there?"

"What do you mean?"

"You really think Donnelly was responsible for all twelve of those girls?"

"Special Agent Francine, what exactly do you think I know?"

The FBI man spread his hands wide. "Why don't you tell me."

"I really don't get it. You've got my files. What are you fishing for?"

Francine pulled out a chair and sat down. "Why didn't you see Donnelly for these killings?"

Robinson closed his eyes. "I barely knew the man. Knew him in school. Met him again years later in a bar. Did a bit of drinking those days." He looked at Francine. "Off duty drinking. My wife was gone, we were drinking at the same joint, he needed a place to crash, I let him come to my house for a few days."

"More like two weeks."

"Whatever. I really didn't give much thought to it."

"Did you talk about girls?" Francine asked.

"We probably talked about a lot of things, most of them lost in alcohol. I had no idea he was what he was. That kind of thing didn't come up. What exactly are you after? My statements are all in the record."

Francine took a sheet of paper from his breast pocket, unfolded it and smoothed out the creases. Robinson saw what they were. The list of victims. At least, the ones they knew about.

"You know what this is?" Francine asked.

Robinson swallowed. "Yes."

The list slid to his part of the table. "You have anything to add about any of the names? Anything at all?"

Robinson couldn't help it. He only focused on the one. There she was. Rebecca Sue Owens, 22. Victim number eight. Body discovered October 9th, 1988, Indian Rocks Beach. Raped and strangled, like the others. He choked up inside.

"Robinson?"

He shook his head. "No," he said. "Nothing at all. That all right with you?"

Francine took the list back, held it in front of him.

"What aren't you telling me?"

Does he know about Becky, Robinson wondered. *Was it any of his business at this point? Donnelly was gone. Robinson was disgraced. The girl wasn't coming back. It was over. Everything was over.*

"Well?"

Robinson looked at him. "You know everything you need to know. Whether they mean anything or not, we all have our secrets."

Francine stared at him. "Yes," he said. "Yes, we do."

Robinson started to rise. "You mind if I go now?"

"A couple of these girls waited tables, you know that?"

There was a tightness in Robinson's stomach.

"Wonder if that meant anything to the killer?"

Robinson had tried to remember if he'd ever had lunch at Becky's restaurant when Donnelly was around but he couldn't be sure. He didn't think so. But what was Francine getting at?

"Maybe Donnelly ate out a lot. He certainly didn't cook at my house."

Francine nodded his head, folded the list, returned it to his pocket. "Well, he had to eat lunch somewhere, didn't he?" He stood up, offered his hand across the table. "I appreciate the time, Detective."

Robinson shook automatically. Then he gripped his helmet and left the room, feeling Francine's eyes on his back as he left. *What was that really about?*

CHAPTER SIX

A collapse sinkhole occurs when an underground cavern can no longer support the ground above it. A water deposit in the underlying limestone and interaction with the chemicals in the soil on top of it gradually erode the ground layer until it gives way, sometimes collapsing deeply into the ground. This happens hundreds of times a year in Florida, and most of the holes go unnoticed. In the case of Tampa's planned Palm Shade subdivision, however, the sinkhole that formed was spectacular because of its size.

It was nearly eighty feet across and almost ninety feet deep.

Jimmy Robinson sat within the fenced in border of the hole, the only surviving house from the abandoned project a hundred yards or so behind him. A six pack of malt liquor was planted in the loose sand next to him.

Tonight he was playing the beer game. Start out inside the fence line with a six pack. Sit on the ground, try to avoid the fire ants, and drain the can. When it was empty heave the empty aluminum cylinder as far as you can toward the hole. Then walk or drag yourself to where it lands and start over again. And again and again, until all the beer is gone. He had played this game a lot after his wife had left.

Sometimes Robinson was convinced he could get up and walk directly to the edge, sinkhole and loose sandy edges be damned, but then he always wondered what he'd do next and how much of the inevitable voice in his head was prompted by alcohol. Once he was close enough to throw the beer cans all the way into the hole he never went any further. He didn't trust the ground to stay up.

Today had been a genuinely lousy day. The artificial peace he had been trying to impose on his life, the equilibrium of denial, had all been washed away by the one trip into Bradenton. He had known instantly what had been on the minds of every person that had seen him in that building: was he involved? Could he have done it? He knew what were they saying to each other in there.

His short talk with Donnelly had been a mistake as far as he was concerned. The man was doing everything he could to save his own ass, to manipulate fools like Hollander and the FBI and try to impose a measure of control over his life that he probably hadn't known even when he was free. In a way, Robinson could almost empathise with what was happening.

He drained the last third of the second can, belched, then let it fly. The lightweight aluminum caught a breeze just right and carried on about ten feet further than it should have. Beautiful throw, he thought. Should have been a pitcher.

Made a pun. About beer.

Too many stars dotted the night sky around him and the humid night air felt heavy on his skin. In a few hours three feet of fog would hug the ground all around the fallow land, covering all save the open maw of the sinkhole itself.

You're like my life, he said to the sinkhole as he popped another can. A goddamn black hole that swallows everything that comes near it.

The anger wasn't so bad now. He was doing an adequate job of drowning the fire and he knew it wouldn't do him any good if he weren't. In the past he had thought that his emotions, even the negative ones, helped him get through the job and the life that went with it but now he wasn't so sure. He had the feeling that if he could just forget most of it he'd be a lot happier.

Maybe I can, he thought as he took a long swallow. Maybe that's what I'm learning how to do now. Or maybe it's just too late, I've screwed up too much. First my marriage, then Becky.

He looked ahead to the gap in the earth in front of him and wondered how tempted old Hollander was to find a way to get down in the sinkhole and look for more evidence against him. Let him try. There's a good chance the old hog wouldn't be able to pull his fat ass back out.

Robinson had thought about it himself but he dismissed it for two reasons. Donnelly wouldn't use a place like the sinkhole because he wanted his bodies found. That was obvious from where he dumped them and how he arranged them before he left. Hiding them would reduce the thrill or whatever it was that drove the sick bastard to do what he did.

The other reason was even more simple. It was just too dangerous to drag or carry something like a body close enough to the edge to dump it over. And Donnelly didn't have a death wish. He'd made that very plain this afternoon. They'd get to it at some point, he knew, and soon. They'd lower someone from a crane hanging over the edge and see what they could see. For all Robinson knew, there was still a possibility that something was actually down there. Aside from the two rusting bulldozers.

He finished the third can and threw it toward the hole. It didn't travel nearly as far as the last one but that was all part of the game. Three more cans to go.

At least it's over, he told himself as he pushed his stiffening body to his feet and swiped the sand and insects from his legs. You had to get the fire ants off before they started biting. They'd get on you, crawl to their spots, and when one bit, they all started. Bastards.

Donnelly killed those women and the little prick is behind bars. There would be no more screaming parents, brothers, sisters, friends, neighbors, clergy. No more reporters and photographers, TV cameras, and unending press conferences. Not on account of B. J. Donnelly. What he had thought he could accomplish by dragging Robinson into it he didn't know. His career was probably over. He could maybe fight for something else in some far off piss poor town but it wouldn't be in Florida. Maybe there was an opening for a small town beat cop or deputy in Mooseville, Alaska.

He dropped himself into the sand next to the empty can and reached for number four. No more anything for a while, he thought. Except this. He took a long pull and lay back to look at the moon and the stars, and to listen to the silence that came with them. After a while he thought about his wife, where she would be now. He'd heard she'd remarried and moved to North Carolina. Then, as he always did, he thought of Becky, the young woman he'd used to destroy his marriage. He'd loved Julie, that was always true. But that didn't keep him away from the beguiling new girl from the restaurant.

Maybe it was the attention she gave him, and the drinking he was doing, and the timing and the stress and any other excuse he could come up with. Maybe it was all of it, maybe it was none of it. But one day Becky had gone. Simply disappeared. She showed up twelve days later, near a river.

Rebecca Owens, victim number 8. His lover. He drained number four and let it fly.

Excerpt from the Tampa Tribune, May 5, 1989:

SUSPECTED KILLER SLAIN

Suspected serial killer William Joseph Donnelly, 33, of Oldsmar, Florida was found beaten to death late last night in a room in the Manatee county jailhouse. Donnelly, under indictment for the brutal rape and murder of Megan Ann Smith, 13, as well as three other Florida women, had been moved to the facility earlier in the day after a request was made from his Miami lawyer, Donald J. Blackman.

Officials at the prison say that several inmates are suspected of the beating but no charges have been filed as of this morning. In a brief statement, Sergeant Hugh Hollander of the Bradenton Police Department said that the attack on Donnelly may have been committed as a form of street justice in retribution for his crimes against the 13 year old girl.

FBI Special Agent Timothy Francine, investigating the Sun Coast Murders, is assisting with the prison investigation.

CHAPTER SEVEN

"I can't come back, Alex. Don't you ask me to."

The two men were sitting in Robinson's kitchen, this time without the coffee. "It's over, Jimmy. The whole investigation. Lucey called it off this morning. As far as the department is concerned, you're completely cleared."

"Am I, partner? Because your only 'witness' is dead? You really think this can be over? Do you have any idea what it's like to walk among the people that you work with, not to mention the press and the media, and have them wondering all the time? Just a little doubt about whether or not I'm a murderer, the merest shadow of a question: could I have done it? Could I have been involved with those murders?"

Kelly didn't say anything.

"Will we ever really know for sure? That's what they're asking themselves right now and you know it."

"It doesn't have to be that way."

"Bullshit! Of course it has to be that way. You guaranteed it when you found that damned jewelry here and put me on leave. You guaranteed it when you let Hollander take over the cases."

"You're saying it like it was my responsibility. That's not true."

"I mean 'you' as in 'you guys.' Lucey, Harper, Reg Baker. The Feebs. You're one of them."

"Don't be bitter, James. It's not right. You didn't do anything."

"Doesn't matter, though, does it? That's what your book did to me, Alex. That's what putting me through your sacred process made happen. I couldn't go back now if I wanted to."

Kelly waited, let things cool down. "Are you saying you don't?"

"I'd probably rip some heads off if I did. Including yours. I wouldn't last long." He looked away, to a space beyond the walls of the house, then turned back. "Who got to him?"

Alex shrugged one shoulder. "We don't know. That FBI guy, Francine, took over. Everyone was happy to let him. This took a lot out of all of us, partner."

"He still looking at me?"

"Does it matter?"

Robinson looked out the window. "How did they do it? Get to Donnelly?"

"Something's not right there. Looks like whoever it was got a boost. We don't know yet. Anyway, Megan Smith was only thirteen. You know they'll take care of that inside if they can."

Robinson studied the floor. "I guess there you have it."

"You're a cop, Jimmy. This isn't right."

"Yeah, well." He stood up and moved against the counter. "It would have been nice if you had thought about that before."

Kelly stood and offered his hand to his partner. Robinson, whose arms were folded across his chest, looked at it for a long moment before making the decision to accept it.

"Goodbye, Alex," he said. "I'm sorry."

"No worries."

"I mean, if I insulted you."

Kelly nodded. "Take care of yourself, Jimmy."

PART TWO:
Fall, 1996

CHAPTER ONE

"Gators had nothing to do with that," Frank said. "Not so far anyhow." He spit a yellow-brown stream into the mud at his feet. "This is something different."

The two fishermen were standing on the edge of a small pond half a mile into the Pinhook swamp and about five miles north of the small Florida town of Holton.

"What the hell is it?"

"Don't be an idiot, Willie. You know what it is same as I do." The late fall sun had risen almost half an hour ago and before the men could get a line in the water, they saw the pale white shape floating face down a few yards from the shore.

"I don't think we should do nothing here," Willie said. "In fact, I think we should pack up and get the hell on our way."

"Can't just leave," Frank said, looking back at the lines of trees that covered each side of the small dirt track that led them here. "Wouldn't be right."

Willie followed his friend's eyes and said, "What are you looking for?"

Frank didn't answer. Instead he bent down and began to gather the gear they had unloaded from his truck. "We found her and now we got to deal with it. Come on," he told Willie. "Get your stuff. We can't be out here disturbing no crime scene."

Anything that made Willie feel like they were getting closer to leaving received his full and enthusiastic support. But 'crime scene'? He didn't feel at all comfortable when his friend was talking like that. It made him feel like he had done something wrong, that he was in trouble again.

"So we're leaving, huh, Frank?" he asked hopefully. Frank had a nicer truck than Willie so they usually ended up going fishing in his. It had never been a problem with Willie until now. If he had had the keys that truck would be halfway back to Holton by now.

"Soon enough, Willie. Pick up your gear and come wait back by the truck." Frank had already gathered his own things and began to walk carefully back towards the big Ford dually. Willie scrambled to catch up.

Frank threw his gear into the bed and opened the driver's door. From behind the seat he took out a small padded vinyl bag and unzipped it carefully. "What you gonna do?" said Willie from over his shoulder.

"Take a few pictures is all." Frank withdrew the Japanese made point-and-shoot camera he had gotten from the local Wal-Mart and walked back to the edge of the pond. Willie stayed at the truck.

The body was floating in the same place it had been since they first spotted it, looking whiter now in the brightening sun. She appeared to be nude and Frank couldn't see any wound or injury from where he was on the shore. A fan of stringy blonde hair spread out from her head, tangled with leaves and floating debris.

Frank pushed the button to extend the small telephoto lens that was built into the camera. He tripped the shutter and listened as the camera advanced the film. He started to move to his right for another shot when he noticed the camera was making a sound like an angry bee.

"Damn," he muttered. It was rewinding. He was out of film.

Frank started back toward the truck where Willie was standing by the open door. "You finished down there, Frank? We leaving yet?"

"Not quite, Willie. Just hold on. Hand me that bag on the seat there."

Willie dug out the camera bag and handed it to Frank. There was an unopened package of film in there, 24 exposures. More than enough, he thought as he reloaded. He placed the exposed film in the small plastic canister that came with the new roll and put that in his pocket. "Five more minutes, Willie. Just let me shoot this roll and we'll go call the sheriff."

"Don't he have his own camera?"

"I'm just being careful, Willie. This way we show the area how we found it. Could be a couple of hours before the sheriff gets out here and you never know what might happen, what with the wildlife and all. Besides, it backs up our story, don't it?"

Frank was halfway back to the pond when Willie called out, "You ain't gonna touch her, are you?"

"Going to leave her as she is. Can't help her now anyway." Frank had once applied for a deputy's job with the sheriff but he had been denied due to his lack of a higher education. Or a high school diploma. At least that's what they told him when he asked. In any case, he thought that leaving the crime scene as undisturbed as possible was the smart thing for them to do.

With that in mind, he took all 24 pictures in just a few minutes, not wanting to move around too much and possibly damage any evidence left behind by a killer. When he was through, he turned and left the pond behind.

"Can we go now, Frank?" Willie was already in the truck.

"Slide over, Willie. We can go."

The black and tan colored cruiser pulled up in front of Frank's truck with its lights flashing. The sheriff, a tall man wearing aviator sunglasses and a cocoa brown uniform stepped out of the car pulling on his hat. He looked at the shallow ruts leading into the trees as he passed by but didn't stop as he walked up to Frank's window.

"That's where she's at?"

Frank nodded and said, "Yes, sir."

"What are you boys doing out here, anyway? A little hard to get to just to look for a few damn fish."

"We come back in here once or twice a year."

"Ever catch anything?"

"Get lucky sometimes."

The sheriff looked past Frank into the cab of the truck. They could feel the famous stare from behind the smoked lenses of the glasses as it raked over the interior of the truck, lingering on its passenger.

"How 'bout you, Willie? You ever get lucky?"

Willie worked his throat a little before answering. "I reckon I get my fair share, Sheriff."

"Sure you do, Willie. Y'all take off now. And I don't want to hear no tales of you guys talkin' up what you found out here. This is a police matter now and I'll take care of it. Understand?"

Willie almost fell over himself answering, thankful for the chance to leave again and put this morning behind him. "Yes, sir."

"Sheriff," said Frank, nodding, careful to spit his chaw juice into a cup after he acknowledged the man. Both men knew enough to be respectful of Sheriff Cole Baldridge, especially Frank. He held the container with the exposed film out the window toward the sheriff. "I took these pictures before we left, in case something happened to the scene while we was gone."

Baldridge held out his hand and Frank dropped it into his palm. The sheriff shook it once, feeling the film cartridge inside, and turned his face towards Frank.

"What's on this?"

"Just pictures of what we saw. I had my camera in the truck and thought it might be a good idea."

The sheriff nodded and Frank wasn't sure what he was looking at.

"You done some good work, Frank. Now you boys get. If I need you for anything more I know where to find you." He stepped away from the door and waited while Frank turned the key and shifted the truck into gear.

The name Cole Baldridge was a heavy one in Baker County. He had been sheriff for the past seventeen years, running unopposed in most election years, and the almost nineteen thousand residents knew what the man was about. Half of the county was in the Osceola National Forest, half of the rest was part of the swamp. The biggest problem was the local high school kids running around weekend nights with shotguns and rifles blowing holes in trees from the backs of their pickup trucks as they got drunk. Most of the kids only needed to get caught once by the sheriff before they found a new way to pass their time.

This was Baldridge's kingdom and most of the people who voted for him didn't much care how he ran it so long as they didn't have their houses robbed or their cars stolen or their peace disturbed. As much as any man could, Baldridge delivered what they wanted.

And now these two locals find a body floating in some water that's part of the swamp in his county, miles away from where anybody doing right should be. No matter how he handled it, he knew it was going to be trouble for him.

He waited until Frank Grayton's truck disappeared completely down State Highway 125 before walking back to his car. Then, with the lights still on, he got into his car and slowly picked his way along the ruts leading into the trees, the long tanned fingers of his left hand curled around the canister of film.

Sheriff Baldridge had to call in assistance from the state police since the situation he had in the swamp was beyond what Baker County normally dealt with. The state had the criminalists and the laboratories to process the available evidence from the site but the sheriff told them from the start they wouldn't find much. It turned out he was right.

The body of the nude young women was removed from the water and examined by Dr. Benjamin Haglund, the local practitioner that Baker County contracted with as a medical examiner. Before the body was even placed onto the stainless steel gurney from the ambulance, every person that was there knew what lay ahead.

The victim's right arm ended where the wrist should have been, the white ends of the ulna and radius showing past the tattered edges of waterlogged skin.

Dr. Haglund looked at the arm once before moving back to the woman's face. Mottled swelling and bruises were exaggerated by their exposure to the water. Nobody else moved or made a sound, the usual bustle of a crime scene halting as the men and women crowded into the small clearing listened quietly to the doctor's words as he spoke into a small tape recorder.

The missing hand was enough. They knew what they were dealing with.

CHAPTER TWO

Blinds or curtains covered every window in the tiny one bedroom apartment. Stacks of old newspapers and magazines covered the floor and a layer of grease from too much fried food being cooked there clung to everything, trapping a heavy layer of dust against all surfaces. A few second hand desk lamps with low wattage bulbs shone their hazy cones of light at the yellow and white pages taped to the faded brown walls in each of the two rooms.

Small, pale Albert Duprin sat on the matted shag carpet and ran a skinny hand through his slick black hair and pushed it back, out of his eyes. He was staring at the story he had been waiting for, front page news of the local *Holton Gazette*. They had finally found one of them, he realized. It had taken them a while, but he had known it would only be a matter of time before they did.

It was difficult to tear his eyes away from the grainy black and white picture that was beneath the headline but he needed to find his scissors. He needed to find a special place in his collection for this one. After all, he thought, now it was home.

Perhaps he could make room above the books with the good pictures.

He hummed happily to himself as he slowly clipped the sections of newsprint from the paper. He had been waiting for so long and it had finally happened. A powerful feeling flowed through every limb, all the way down to his fingertips then back up and across his skin. Electrified goose bumps sprouted along his arms and the tops of his thighs as he carefully Scotch taped the clippings to the favored place on the wall.

He'd have to stop at the pharmacy and pick up a Jacksonville newspaper before they ran out this morning. There were probably more articles in there, maybe even another picture. Hopefully it would be a different one.

When he was finished, Albert stepped back as far as he could and sat down on a pile of European porno magazines that had been ordered through the mail. He kicked over a smaller stack of black plastic video tape cases but he didn't bother to pick them up as he backed up to admire his work. The article looked good there on the wall. It was above his precious books and there was still room on either side, which was important. This exhibit had to have the room to grow that he knew it would need. It was perfect there.

There was a clock on the top shelf of a two-tiered end table next to the couch to the left of his new prize. Albert didn't want to look at it but the bright LED display caught him and burned its message into his brain. Damn! That clock was always telling him when it was time to go to work. If only he didn't have to look at the numbers, see them change, he would be all right. But now it was too late.

He was out last night but he wasn't tired. Albert could go a long time without feeling the need to sleep. A new family had moved into a house behind the golf course and they hadn't put curtains up across all the windows yet, perhaps thinking they were sheltered by the reputation of the neighborhood and the emptiness of the wide fairways. There was more he wanted to do there while he still could.

But now this had come up and he knew it was far more important. More important than the pretty country club woman with the long blonde hair and her two teenaged daughters. More important even than his maintenance job at the golf course itself. What Albert Duprin had to do now, and he could feel the pull in every cell of his body, was get out to the place where they found the girl. He had to see what they had done.

The press conference was noisy, crowded, and unlike anything the county had ever seen. It was being held in the gymnasium of the Holton Senior High School and it was more than half full of reporters and cameramen, each it seemed with their own set of cameras, lights and tripods.

Sheriff Baldridge kicked back, pivoting his weight onto the back two legs of his chair, his brawny arms folded across his chest, as he watched the chaos spread itself around him. The governor had called the conference but he himself hadn't bothered to show up, instead sending the lieutenant governor, a woman named Marlene Hoyt. She stood behind the podium to the sheriff's right, waiting for all the different media crews to arrive and set up their equipment. The conference itself wasn't scheduled to begin for another half hour.

When the group from *Time* magazine showed up and immediately forced room for themselves in the front of the crowd, Baldridge felt a spark of nervousness. He lowered the chair down to the floor and considered what the national attention was going to mean. He hadn't expected this.

Most of the people in the small gym were from Florida newspapers and television stations, the rest being from Georgia and one from Alabama. And now *Time* magazine. Baldridge had been prepared to handle the locals, and even what he considered to be the big boys from Miami, but the direct national exposure was something different. This was way beyond his ability to control.

Marlene Hoyt held her arms up and asked for quiet. The crowded gym settled down and intense flood lights flicked on, bathing her with their brightness and wilting heat. A small group of men detached themselves from a gathering near the double wooden doors at the end of the gym and approached the podium. Baldridge watched them step up to the dais, each of the three men shaking hands with the lieutenant governor then taking the chairs next to his. He watched them without expression, the way he did most things, and nodded back when they acknowledged him.

Hoyt began laying the groundwork for the conference, recapping the details of the discovery of yesterday's body in the swamp. She read her words from a series of index cards that had been well prepared for her. Aside from the occasional popping of a flash bulb, she went through her piece quickly and without interruption. When she was through, she introduced each of the four men that shared the stage with her.

Baldridge was offered first and he felt a grim smile crack his lips despite himself as the cameras turned toward him. The man to his left was introduced as Lieutenant Daniel Forsyth out of Jacksonville. Baldridge knew who he was because they had met earlier after already speaking for several hours on the phone. Next to him was the medical examiner for Duval County, a Dr. George Gelman, who was brought along from Jacksonville by Lieutenant Forsyth.

The last gentleman made Baldridge sit up for a second time, the man the sheriff didn't know by either name or reputation. He was an FBI specialist in serial killings, something like that, named Francine.

Damn, Baldridge swore softly. First *Time* magazine shows up and now the FBI. The big guns are coming out now.

The lieutenant governor stood back from the dais with the word "Gentlemen" and a wave of her hand. Sheriff Baldridge stood first. It was his county and this was about his body and as far as he was concerned this was all his show. They could bring in whomever they wanted from the government or the big cities but Baker County belonged to him.

As he took a step toward the podium, Forsyth stood and followed him to the platform, standing off his left elbow as Baldridge addressed the crowd. He was annoyed but he didn't show it as he introduced himself and then, after a quick thought, Lieutenant Forsyth.

"Ladies and gentlemen," Baldridge said. "The lieutenant governor, Ms. Hoyt, has just done a fine job of detailing to you exactly what it is we're here to talk about this afternoon. I'm going to ask Lieutenant Forsyth and Dr. Gelman from Jacksonville to join me now so that we can discuss exactly what it is we do and do not know."

A man from one of the camera crews from a Miami television station was making a motion to Baldridge with his hand, pantomiming the removal of the aviator sunglasses from his face. Baldridge ignored him. Dr. George Gelman got up from his chair and advanced to stand between Baldridge and Forsyth, his white hair shining yellow in the artificial light.

"We do have some more information that we will share with you at this time. Lieutenant Forsyth has come down to see if this case may have any connection to a series of homicides that he has been investigating for the past few months." The sheriff liked the word 'homicide.' 'Murder' was overly dramatic and 'killing' was something you did to livestock.

"The young lady has been positively identified as Lynnette Elizabeth Skokie, aged nineteen, from the town of Sanderson, down near the Interstate. Dr. Gelman will talk more about the condition of the body." Marlene Hoyt gave him an intense look but he didn't return it. One of the reasons for keeping his glasses on was so that he could get away with things like that.

Baldridge cleared his throat and placed his hands on the edges of the podium. He was going to play the rumor that had brought them all here, the one that he had known would be floating around once the body had been found. "After speaking with Lieutenant Forsyth at length about the condition of the body and the manner in which she was killed," he said, "we both agree that this seems to be the work of the same person or persons responsible for a series of similar murders that he has been investigating."

This sent a murmur through the gym and set off a round of flash pictures. This was the confirmation that made a local story a national one. Sheriff Baldridge was going to be front page news across the country by tomorrow. "I'm going to step back now and give Lieutenant Forsyth a chance to tell you what we have so far." He made a motion behind him. "Lieutenant," he said.

Forsyth began by thanking the sheriff and then listing his background and credentials, finishing with a brief discussion of the cases he was currently working on. If he was impressed by the media attention, he didn't show it. When it was time to talk about the body he glanced at Baldridge before continuing, as if seeking his permission to go on. Baldridge didn't look at him. He was too busy studying the reactions of the people that made up the crowd in front of him.

He had expected a small flurry of activity, mostly local, maybe from Jacksonville and even Tallahassee, but this amount of notoriety he hadn't foreseen. He knew he could deal with it, though. That was the important thing, to always be the one in charge.

He listened to Forsyth with only one ear, already knowing what the man was going to say. He imagined himself back at the podium, where his daddy used to be, preaching from his pulpit, inspiring the local masses with his messages of glory and salvation. It was a powerful feeling, controlling people's emotions, one that his daddy hadn't given up until the day he had died and left twelve-year-old Coleman an orphan.

Forsyth finished what he had to say and Dr. Gelman stepped forward, using precise medical terms to discuss the condition of the body. Gelman had officially assisted on the autopsy but in truth had performed it almost entirely by himself. Dr. Haglund was fine for setting bones and prescribing medicines but examining a murder victim's body for evidence was something outside of his regular scope of practice. This type of crime was extremely rare in Baker County.

Gelman read from some notes he had taken out of his jacket pocket and rarely bothered to look up at the people he was addressing. When he was through, he looked to Forsyth as if to ask, Good enough? Baldridge stood and approached the podium, thanking the doctor as he took his place.

"At this time, we will attempt to answer any questions you all might have for us." A dozen hands shot up in the air, half of them calling, "Sheriff!" He pointed to a woman he recognized from a Jacksonville TV station, a tall brunette whose name he couldn't remember.

"Sheriff Baldridge, why do you think the killer or killers struck here, in Baker County, and do you think he or they could still be here?" The woman had a cameraman with her who was shooting from over her shoulder.

"Well, ma'am, I wish I could say, but I have no way of knowing. As you can see, the town of Holton is not a large one and if there is a stranger in town, we should be able to pick him up pretty quick. If it was somebody just passing through in the middle of the night...." He shrugged his shoulders. "There may not be a lot we can do right this minute."

The sheriff took more questions, pointing mostly to the hands of the people from the larger stations and newspapers. It irked him that the crew from *Time* hadn't raised a question of their own. Lieutenant Forsyth responded to a dozen or so queries about his other investigations, referring from time to time to Dr. Gelman.

After nearly forty five minutes of questions, Marlene Hoyt rose and put a light hand on Baldridge's shoulder. Grudgingly, he gave her room as she leaned into the bank of microphones and announced the end of the conference. "We need to get these men back out there doing their jobs as soon as possible," she said and thanked everybody for coming. She promised that new information would be released as soon as it became available.

As the cameras and their lights blinked out one by one, an older man pushed his way toward the front of the crowd, stopping near the brunette from the Jacksonville TV station. "Sheriff Baldridge!" he yelled, loud enough to stop several of the reporters. The brunette's cameraman snapped his camera back on, flooding the man's face with light. Even Marlene Hoyt turned around.

Baldridge exhaled slowly, trying not to show his distaste. The man was a local reporter from right here in Holton, and he had had his hand up for most of the conference. Baldridge had purposely ignored him as a small timer, and one that he didn't much get along with. For years the man and his paper hadn't been overly kind toward the sheriff and his continuing reelection to office. Now he was forced to acknowledge him.

"Go ahead, Ben."

"Thank you, Sheriff," the man said politely. "I just have one quick question for you." The noise in the gym subsided as the reporters stopped moving. *Time* magazine was still set up in front of them all.

"Is this girl, this Lynette Elizabeth Skokie, the same girl that I've seen you with fishing down at the St. Marys River?"

Any movement that had still been going on when the old man began to speak came to a sudden halt. A few more cameras and lights came on and the rest of the people stood where they were, not sure of what they were hearing.

Baldridge's face began to turn red beneath his glasses. From his left he could hear Marlene Hoyt as she inhaled a quick breath and held it.

"Ben Colfax," the sheriff said. "If I didn't know you for what you were I'd be awfully upset with you right now for whatever it is that you might be trying to insinuate. You know as well as everybody else in this county that I spend a lot of my time, my personal time I might add, fishing down by that river. And if I come across other folks that like to do the same, chances are we'll throw a line or two in together. Seems it wasn't terribly long ago I pulled a few catfish out of that river next to your tired old body while you were trying to pump me for some news of some sort or the other. I don't recollect for certain, but if that girl ever fished on weekends in St. Marys, then yes, I probably saw her there a time or two."

For the first time that day, Baldridge peeled off his sunglasses and wiped his sleeve across his suddenly moist forehead. "Goodbye, everybody," he said as he put the glasses back on his face and turned away from the podium.

In the crowd, Ben Colfax stood where he was, a strange expression playing across his face. All around him, the activity of packing and storing cameras and recording gear resumed. Slowly, he folded his spiral bound notebook closed and turned to leave the gym.

On the podium, as he was shaking hands with Forsyth and Gelman, Baldridge was having difficulty putting Colfax out of his mind. Just what did that old man think he was up to, anyway?

CHAPTER THREE

Albert stood in water midway up his thigh as he watched the last of the men stow their gear into two gray and black plastic cases then load them into the back of their four wheel drive truck. It's about time, he thought. He'd been standing in the mud and swamp for several hours now and his legs were tired from fighting the suction of the swamp muck beneath the water.

His camouflage pants looked black where the water had soaked them through and it felt as if he had about a gallon of water in each of his surplus paratrooper boots. The hunting knife with the serrated edge that he usually wore strapped to his thigh was hung around his neck by a strap so it wouldn't get wet.

The men were about finished and Albert couldn't wait to pick his way through the trees that he had been using for cover to the place where the girl had been found. He was used to waiting like this–he did it several times a week, though seldom during the light of day.

When the men spoke he could hear the sounds of the words but he was too far away and there were too many trees between them for him to make out what they were saying. Now they were finally leaving and it would soon be Albert's turn to do what he must.

The two men climbed into their truck, pulling their doors closed with loud thunking sounds that reached Albert just fine through the thick air of the swamp. Go on, he was thinking. Get on out of here so I can come out before a damned moccasin or gator comes out to find me. He was nearly shaking with anticipation.

Just as the truck was about to drive out of the small clearing and down the pair of tire ruts that had become much more worn the past couple of days, the vehicle stopped then backed up a few yards to allow a pair of full sized vans to enter and park far enough from the ruts to allow the truck to pass.

Albert snorted in frustration and pulled his knife from its sheath. He waved it in the air while exhaling evenly through his mouth, furiously pantomiming the motions of a fierce hunter carving up his enemies with his razor sharp blade. He never moved his feet and after half a minute his anger began to fade as a new layer of sweat formed across his face and dripped down his neck, adding to the stains on the collar of his olive drab tee shirt. The truck was gone but the vans weren't, and he held the knife as he watched what was happening.

The large sliding doors at the side of each van opened and out poured a dozen or so gray shirted kids, they looked like teenagers to Albert, with burgundy handkerchiefs tied around their necks. Four men wearing brown shirts got out of the vans as well, and began to point back down the way they had come.

The kids looked like Boy Scouts but Albert was pretty sure those kids didn't wear gray shirts. They wore green or blue or something like that, not gray. In any case, these didn't stay where they were for long. The bunch split up into two groups, each led by one of the men with the brown shirts, and they fanned out along each side of the ruts they had ridden in on. Albert had to move to his left ten yards or so to see what they were doing but he did it with the stealth and silence of a practiced soldier.

The other brown-shirted men got into the vans and slowly drove away, down the ruts and ahead of the boys. As they passed, one of the men called something out and the whole group of them began to move away from Albert, away from the pond, back toward the road and hunkered down low, almost on their hands and knees.

Very clever, Albert thought, as he watched them pick their way across the dry land toward the road. The boys were looking for the small things that may have been missed by the crew of criminalists and crime scene technicians that had covered the area that began with the clearing and ended at the pond itself. They were looking for signs of passage or possibly something that could have been thrown from a vehicle as it followed the only way out of this secluded place. Good luck, Albert wished them. Just hurry on up and get the hell away from here.

With all his frustration, Albert had to force himself to hold his temper a while longer. They boys were slow, which probably meant they were being thorough, but that didn't worry him. What did was the fact that he had been standing out there so long and was so close but still he couldn't move ahead to the clearing and the pond where he wanted to be. Where he needed to be. Albert wasn't very good at dealing with frustration. That was one of the reasons he stayed alone so much of the time.

He noticed he still had the knife in his hand and he slowly and carefully slid it back into the sheath dangling from his neck. There was a certain feel to it when it was drawn and held in his hand, a power he craved but didn't understand, and he didn't draw it often. Sometimes it was very difficult to put away.

It took five minutes before he couldn't see the searchers anymore, even as he moved closer to the clearing, but about fifteen before he wasn't able to hear them, either. Enough of the waiting, he thought. He simply couldn't do it any more. It was his time.

Albert reached the start of the higher ground and dragged his half-soaked body out of the water and up into the clearing. The first thing he noticed was how many tire tracks there were, how flat and crunched down the land looked, and he felt he was still too close to civilization, as if it had followed him out here. He turned toward the pond, the tongue of swamp water that filled the small basin where the girl had been found, and tried to clear all the thoughts out of his head. He inhaled several deep breaths, first through his nose and then his mouth, as he moved closer to the edge and began to strip off his clothes.

He started with the knife, then his shirt, and he undid his pants and pulled them down to his knees before he sat on the ground and began to pick at his wet shoelaces. If there were sounds from behind him he didn't hear them. Albert was entering his own world now, the place he dreamed and fantasized about. The place he knew he could go and be at peace.

Without thoughts of lawmen or Boy Scouts or even snakes and gators, Albert crawled on his hands and knees into the water, feeling the coolness of the water accept his pale body and complete the feeling of exhilaration that had been building up inside him as he stood waiting all those hours for the investigators to finally abandon the scene.

The familiar tug of an erection drew his hand to that part of his body as he worked it while he swam, occasionally touching the muddy bottom with one or both of his feet. At the moment of his climax, Albert shut his eyes and slid completely beneath the surface of the water, all his thoughts concentrating on her, the woman that had been here such a short time before.

When it was over, he floated on his back, exposing himself to the afternoon sky, disappointed that the time had passed by so quickly. He had been more aroused than he had known.

Slowly he kicked his way back to the shore and his pile of soggy clothes, still on his back as he squinted against the loose rays of sun that penetrated the forest around him. When the water was shallow enough to force him to sit, Albert cupped some of the tea colored water into his hands and drank it deep inside himself, feeling it travel downward into his stomach. He touched himself again, under the water, and added more of his own warmth and body to the essence of the swamp.

Content to soak in the juices of himself, nature, and the beautiful blonde-haired girl that had been pulled from this place the day before, he was in no rush to move. Albert didn't leave until the light was failing and he could no longer control the chills that were wracking his skinny body with waves of cold. Only then did he draw himself from the water and fumble into his clothing, an absent but placid expression pasted across his face.

CHAPTER FOUR

For the first time in anyone's memory, every motel room in Holton was booked, snatched up by the horde of state and national press. Sheriff Baldridge and the men from Jacksonville couldn't travel anywhere in town without prompting the formation of a convoy of news vans. Lieutenant Forsyth found it irksome; at least the press had better manners back home. These people here were borderline in the way of the investigation.

Baldridge, not used to the attention, didn't mind it at all. He found himself growing more and more used to it, developing a habit of noting their presence wherever he was. The Skokie girl's body was found barely three weeks after Sharon Smith, aged twenty four, was found decomposing on the banks of the St. John's River. Before that, the interval between the discovery of the bodies had been from eight to fourteen months. The fact that the killer seemed to have increased his pace dramatically accounted for the sudden explosion of media interest. It had also prompted Lieutenant Forsyth to request the help of the FBI.

The night of the press conference found him at dinner with Forsyth, Dr. Gelman, and the FBI Special Agent, Francine. They were seated at a round table in the corner of a steak house across the street from Marge Spoon's Best Western motel. The tables nearest them were empty, a concession by the management in an attempt to lend them a measure of privacy. Most of the other tables were full, surrounded by reporters and cameramen from around the country.

The waitress, a pretty local girl named Bonnie Shue, brought two pitchers of liquid to them, one full of ice water and the other filled with iced tea. She refilled glasses all around the table while the men held their conversation. Baldridge accepted the tea and said thank you, adding a small crinkle to his eyes when he looked at her.

"You're welcome," she responded, redness coloring her face. Forsyth made a point of looking at his nearly finished steak. How the sheriff flirted with the locals was none of his business.

Baldridge was checking out the small glass and plastic containers in the center of the table. There was one with paper salt and pepper packets and another with plastic tubes of ketchup and mustard but nothing sweet for his tea.

"Some of this what you're looking for?"

Baldridge turned and smiled into the pretty face before taking the offered container with both hands. "Well, thank you very much, Miss...."

"Sabrina Wells," she said, though the sheriff knew it after asking about her after the news conference. She was the pretty brunette from the news conference, the Channel Seven Jacksonville reporter he had called on for the first question. She and her cameraman had been seated at a booth along a wall across from the windows that fronted the highway. The sheriff had watched them come in twenty minutes earlier.

"I'm very pleased to meet you." Sabrina had to pull her hands out of his grip. "Can't drink my tea without a little sugar," he said.

He tried the crinkling thing with her but she didn't respond. Her perfect complexion didn't change at all and she calmly folded her hands in front of her. "I'm sure you can't," she told him, then turned suddenly and went back to her table, feeling foolish.

"What was that all about?" Jeff Sturgeon, her cameraman, asked her, his mouth half filled with mashed potatoes when she dropped into her seat.

"I don't know," she whispered, feeling embarrassed but not about to show it. "Silly impulse, that's all." He looked mystified and she picked up her napkin and wiped the food from the corner of his mouth. "Finish chewing, Jeffrey."

"Yes, mother."

She thought about why she had approached the sheriff like that and wondered if she had made a mistake. Sabrina was twenty five years old, barely two years out of college, and this was the first big story she had been sent to cover since being promoted to an on air reporter. She couldn't afford to blow it.

She had known one of the victims slightly, a girl named Monica Brantley, and that was what had gotten her this assignment. They had met briefly at a party back in college at Gainesville and bumped into each other occasionally on and off until graduation. The fact that Sabrina had actually known a girl that had been brutalized in this way both horrified and fascinated her at the same time.

For the past three months she hadn't been able to sleep without at least once thinking about what her casual friend had gone through. She imagined herself being attacked like Monica was, molested, and finally strangled to death. Even now her stomach tightened as she thought about how easily something like this could have happened to her instead. How it could easily be her in those crime scene photos instead of Monica. Sabrina had tremendous difficulty trying to stay detached.

Jeff made a strangling sound as he tried to down the last of his potatoes with a gulp of beer and this time Sabrina threw her napkin at his face. "I'm a pig, alright?" he finally managed. "I thought you knew."

At the round table in the corner, the sheriff was listening to Lieutenant Forsyth as he finished his briefing on his own ongoing investigation. It was a little hard for him to concentrate after finally meeting that reporter face to face. The scent of her faint perfume hung sweetly in the air.

"What about this water thing?" Francine asked. The question brought Baldridge's focus back to the discussion. Three of the bodies had been found on Atlantic Ocean beaches and two near the St. John's River.

Forsyth shrugged his shoulders. His jacket was hung behind his chair and his white sleeves were rolled up to his elbows, which were resting on the table. "This is Florida. I stub my toe and I spring a well."

"So it may or may not mean anything, then," the FBI man said. "What about the men who found the body?"

The wisdom of the feds, Baldridge thought. "Known them for years and years, those boys. They were just in the right place at the wrong time." He talked a bit about Frank Grayton and Willie Meisner but it didn't take long. Francine made some notes in his book but didn't ask anything else.

"The bodies were left at the sites, not posed for discovery. Like yours," Forsyth said to Baldridge, "they were dumped. They may have been killed there, or not." He looked to the doctor.

"We can't tell for sure," said Gelman. "All of them could be either way. We haven't found a fresh enough site to be able to tell." Gelman had already briefed them on the kind of tool used to remove the hands: a smooth blade, at least six to eight inches long, maybe longer. The hands had been sliced off, carefully cut through the cartilage. They hadn't been chopped, he had told them, say, with a hatchet or an axe.

"Anything distinctive about the blade?" Baldridge asked him. "Every cowboy in this town has a hunting knife could do that."

Gelman rubbed his eyes. "Not that I could see. We're sending the arms up to the FBI lab in Virginia, thanks to Special Agent Francine." In fact, most of the evidence they had found in Holton was on its way to the FBI.

"I'll let you know as soon as I hear anything, Sheriff," Francine said. "I'm going to put together a profile of the killer tomorrow. I'll get that to you, too."

Goody, thought Baldridge. He didn't put much stock in the idea of profiling a roving murderer. Nothing Francine was likely to come up with would identify the actual person. More likely he would tell them what kind of car he thought the killer would drive, and that he was a male within a certain age range, crap any fool good guess blind. Baldridge nodded politely and sipped his tea.

Francine held back his next comment. He was a big man, shorter than Baldridge but bigger around in the chest and stomach. He was used to his badge as well as his stature commanding a higher degree of respect from the locals. He didn't care for the sheriff.

Baldridge looked around the room to be sure they were still isolated from the other diners. His eyes stopped briefly on Sabrina Wells. "Were all of the girls handled sexually, Doctor?" he asked Gelman.

"That's an odd way of phrasing it," Gelman said. "In as much as these crimes are undoubtedly sexual in nature, of course they all were. The act of killing itself is most likely the source of the killer's gratification."

"Definitely," Francine said.

"Obviously I'm not a psychiatrist, but the fact that all of the girls were strangled strikes me as being particularly intimate in a way," Gelman continued.

Tell me something I don't know, Baldridge thought. "I mean intercourse, Doctor. Were the girls raped or not?"

"That isn't something we could tell for certain for any of the victims. None of them were found soon enough to say with certainty. Is that what you're after, Sheriff?"

"I was just wondering if you came up with any clues in that area."

"We did not. There is some bruising present on two of the girls which may or may not imply a forced encounter. Beyond that, the killer could have had intercourse with them, he possibly used a condom or did not ejaculate inside the bodies. We haven't found any fluid evidence that would help with an identification."

Forsyth had finished his steak and was picking his teeth with a toothpick from a metal holder in the center of the table. "Gentlemen," he announced. "I'm about ready to head on home." The three of them had planned on driving back to Jacksonville after dinner. Holton's motel owners and restaurant staff had all been questioned but so far no one had turned up as a possible suspect.

Baldridge rose and arched his back in a stretch, then turned to look at the other tables. The girl was gone. Damn it all, he thought.

He shook hands with the other men before following them outside to their car. Forsyth promised to send help should Baldridge find any more evidence. The sheriff thanked him and said that he would continue canvassing the area for signs of strangers that had been through town but there really wasn't much more he could do in that area. They had to track the movements of Lynnette Skokie, and the FBI was taking charge of that. She had been living in Jacksonville, working at a hardware store until she returned to Holton three months ago.

He stood in the gravel parking lot and watched the dark sedan pull out and head south down 125, tail lights disappearing behind the line of trees. Then he headed toward his own vehicle.

"Get ready," Sabrina nudged Jeff. Both of them were slunk almost below the level of the dashboard of their station's white van, watching the green and white police car, the words "Baker County Sheriff" stencilled on the side, as it slowly left the parking lot.

"You're not going to get us in trouble, are you, Bree?" Jeff had nightmares of being locked up in a small town jail, like Paul Newman in an old black and white movie.

"Just be careful," she told him as they waited half a minute. "Okay, let's go." Jeff let out an audible breath and started the van.

"I thought you liked hard-boiled eggs," Sabrina said.

CHAPTER FIVE

The glow from the television screen cast the only light in the room, creating flickering shadows against the faded carpeting. Albert checked his watch against the dim light and knew that outside the sun had nearly fallen behind the trees of the forest. He was growing impatient because he knew he couldn't stay at home long.

He had been drinking cans of beer steadily since he finished work. He had driven one of the tractors into the maintenance shed and clocked out without saying goodbye to anybody. This wasn't unusual; most days Albert didn't speak to the other workers. Most days he didn't notice they were there.

Surrounded by the clippings and photographs he had meticulously arranged on the walls of his apartment, Albert couldn't get the picture of the blonde girl out of his mind. He let his eyes drift across the series of papers that documented the deeds of the men he was drawn to, imagining what they had seen and done. What they had felt. When he came to his newest additions his mind snapped back to how he had felt during his visits to the small pond where the blonde had died.

He knew what he felt was intense but he also knew how great a part his fantasies played in all of it. On the television was one of his special tapes from Thailand. The good part was coming up in a few minutes, and that contributed to his feelings. So did the alcohol he was consuming. But on a deeper level, somewhere inside, he knew that it could still be so much more. Albert was eager to bring himself to the next level. All he had to do was find a way to make his fantasies part of the reality. The afternoon had been spent planning how.

On the flickering screen across the room, the young Asian boy was tied to a chair, his naked body shining with a yellow-tinged glow on the tape. A large knife appeared above him, then a hand, and his blindfold was cut away. Albert drew his own knife from its sheath at his thigh and ran his finger lightly along its edge.

The camera pulled back and a woman, totally nude, walked into the frame and straddled the frightened boy's lap. The knife that had cut the blindfold now danced around his throat as the woman moved her hands from between the boy's legs and followed the contours of her body upwards, finally cupping her own breasts.

Albert stared at the boy's eyes and studied the changing emotions and feelings playing across the child's face. The woman had her eyes closed as she moved and all he could see of the person with the knife were two hands, one holding the knife and the other stroking the black sweat-soaked hair of the boy.

The sound was turned off, the way Albert watched all of his tapes. He didn't need the distraction. This wasn't just entertainment for him. He was trying to understand. His whole life he had felt so out of control, so unable to manage his own life, he couldn't help but be drawn to what he was seeing on the television. Here there were people altering a destiny, forming the development of a child.

As the woman continued her movement against the boy, her hands playing across both their bodies, Albert thought of his mother and the things he had seen her do. He had grown up poor with no idea of who his father had been and they had lived in a small single-wide trailer on a field adjacent to the phosphate plant. The trailer burned once when he was three or four and from then until the time his mother died he had been made to share her bed.

Men would come over and if it was after dark he wouldn't be allowed to go outside. Instead, he was told to sleep on the couch, his face pressed to the back cushions, away from his mother. That didn't stop him from hearing the sounds, though, and the first time he had been afraid but he had peeked anyway. It was after he saw what those men were doing to his mother, and what she did back to them, that Albert grew sick. He stopped eating, except for when she made him, and to most of the world became a practicing mute. When his mother finally noticed it, she gave up trying to make him speak and after a few days said that his silence had been her blessing.

The last words he ever spoke to his mother were to ask her why she let those men do what they did. "It's because of you," she answered him, cigarette ash falling from between her fingers. "If I didn't do it I wouldn't be able to take care of you."

Albert could still talk of course, he just didn't know what to say much of the time. Most nights of the week men would come over and take his place in his mother's bed. This is how he remembers growing up.

Most of the money went to alcohol and the days before the nights were spent drinking herself into a stupor. She could get mean then, but Albert was seldom afraid of her. His mother would speak harshly to him but almost never got out of bed once she started to drink.

One night, one of her regular men came over with a bottle of his own. For a long time they sat in the bed just drinking it, with Albert's back facing them from the couch. But after a while the same sounds of clothing being removed, followed by the moaning and then the wet noises, came to Albert's ears. In all of the years since the fire he had never slept when company had been over. Never once.

But then there came a different sound, a rasping, breathy noise that came from his mother and went on for several minutes. At first Albert wasn't alarmed, especially once it had stopped, but then he noticed all of the other sounds had, too. Slowly and carefully, he turned his head around and tried to peek under his arm.

The man lay there on his side, watching Albert's back. His mother was there beside him, her face turned away. Albert froze, not sure if the man could see him peeking and afraid to turn away in case the man noticed the movement. They stayed that way until Albert's neck hurt, and then the man got out of the bed and left, pulling his clothes on and taking his bottle with him.

Something was different in the trailer, the air was not the same, and Albert stayed frightened even after the man was long gone. He lay there until morning, unwilling and unable to leave his couch until his mother called for him to start making breakfast. But she never moved, she never called.

It was a long time until Albert was able to stand up on his own and move to look at his mother up close. Her eyes were wide open and Albert watched her for a long time, waiting for her to blink. Just blink once, he was thinking. Please. When she didn't, he knew what he had to do. He dressed himself in the same clothes he had worn the day before and went outside to the broken down Chevrolet his mother drove to limp into town and buy her booze, cigarettes and the rest of the groceries.

He sat behind the steering wheel and tried to cry but his eyes wouldn't tear, his heart not feeling the pain he thought it should. He wanted to feel bad for his mother, to miss her, but he was empty inside. All he could think about was what it was like to lie in bed next to his mother, before and after the men came, and feel her heat as she snored lightly next to him, and what it was to smell her sour breath.

Albert left the car and went back inside the trailer. He stood at the edge of the bed for minutes before he finally reached out and touched his mother. Her leg was cool and it felt wrong, like the bottom of a fish that had been out of the water and dried in the sun. He grabbed both legs and tried to pull them straight put they didn't want to move. So Albert kicked off his shoes and climbed into the bed, running his hands over all the parts of his mother's body, doing some of the things he had seen her men do. She never made a sound.

When he was through, he climbed down, put his shoes back on, then grabbed the cigarette lighter from the little shelf above the bed. Albert pulled the stack of old yellowed newspapers out from the kitchen area and knocked them over in front of the bed, kicking them into place all around it. After he started the fire, he didn't look back until the trucks and sirens had come. Then he sat down in the long grass, watching them work, peering through the tiny flame of the lighter he held before his eyes. It was too late for the men to do much.

Now he focused again on the tape on the television and imagined himself in the chair, helpless to prevent anything from happening to him. His mother was the woman in his lap. The person with the knife was the last man she had been with. As he watched, the woman reached her climax, her hands furiously working across her breasts. The boy's head was pulled back and the hand with the knife made a silver streak across the screen.

Albert's pants were bursting with the power of his excitement but he left it alone. He still held the knife in one hand and the other was squeezing his own thigh so tightly that it hurt. Thoughts of the past began to fade, replaced by images of the woman in the house on the golf course. She had blonde hair, too, he thought. And so did her daughters.

Albert didn't think of it just then, but his mother had been blonde, too. At the end, at least.

CHAPTER SIX

By Wednesday, most of the media had either moved on to Jacksonville or else simply gone back to where they had originally come from. Baldridge still received calls daily asking for telephone interviews, virtually all of which he granted, but the intense media presence had faded quickly. No one thought the killer was likely to still be in the area.

The discovery of fresh tracks at the crime scene caused a stir Wednesday afternoon but the sheriff discounted their usefulness after speaking with technicians from the Florida Department of Law Enforcement. The FDLE said the footprints were definitely human but by the time they were found they were much too indistinct to cast. Baldridge publicly attributed them to a prankster or somebody who just wanted to see where the body had been found. Nonetheless, this prompted a spontaneous surveillance by several reporters for a night or two.

Time magazine went home on Wednesday night but not before spending several hours with Baldridge and shooting several rolls of film. The crowning jewel in his otherwise quiet public life, he thought, will be that magazine issue. He had soaked up the attention like a dry sponge and now he was sorry to see it go. From a personal standpoint, this murder had been the best thing that could have happened to his career. For the first time in his life people outside of Baker County knew who he was. He only wished he could keep it going longer.

Throughout the week he had his six deputies working their way through the county questioning motel and restaurant owners, gas station attendants, and anybody else they could think of about any strangers they may have seen passing through. They're all strangers, was the most common response. Everyone's just passing through. No new leads had been uncovered.

Now it was Friday and Sheriff Baldridge took his breakfast at a small diner in Holton as he toyed with the idea of hiring a publicist. A man from Miami had called him and said that the sheriff should consider turning all this publicity into a positive, upward career move. He specifically mentioned politics. The people are always looking for grassroots representation and the sheriff's rock steady image would appeal to the always popular hardline anti-crime sentiment.

Baldridge had never really considered running for an office beyond that of sheriff but now that he did, he kind of liked the idea. The more he thought about it, the more it seemed to be a natural extension of his life's work. He sopped up the remainder of his eggs with a piece of toast and decided that he would call that fellow next week.

"I'll say it again, Bree. They're gonna run our rear ends up a flag pole if you don't pull something off."

Sabrina sighed and ran a hand through her straight brown hair, tucking one side behind her ear. She watched Jeff hold half a powdered doughnut in his left hand while he licked sugar off the fingers of his right. "You've been hanging around cops too long," she told him. But she was worried about it, too. They had been scheduled to be back in the office two days ago but Jeff had allowed her to talk him into staying.

The station's news producer, the famous and tyrannical George Decatur Lyle, had gone into the hospital for a quick check up two weeks ago and ended up staying for a double bypass. Otherwise they both know what they would have had to do and there would have been no decision for them to make. As it was, the assistant producer was a man named Marty O'Reilly who, because of an enormous and unrequited crush on Sabrina, was granting her room to amend her own schedule, a power even a ten-year veteran would have trouble getting. There were no illusions on either side, though. If Sabrina didn't bring back something that warranted the extra time she could easily lose her job. Jeff, too, although they both thought that less likely. He was, after all, just following orders.

"This is it," she told Jeff. "If nothing happens after today we'll just have to try to make something out of what we've already got." Which isn't enough, she could have added, but they both already knew it. They had a promising start but nothing to justify the extra three days stay.

The approach Sabrina had wanted to take from the beginning of the story was to focus on how a shocking and brutal crime like this was treated by the local law enforcement. Not on the people of the town so much, but on the authorities that ran it. Her idea was to contrast the small town investigation in Baker County with the massive effort being put forth in Jacksonville. She wasn't sure what she hoped to find, or what insights might arise from her investigation, but her instincts told her there was a story there. One she hadn't seen told before.

With that in mind, she and Jeff had kept a close eye on Sheriff Baldridge. It got in the way that the sheriff seemed to want to repay the attention multiple times over. She wanted to remain impartial and not be influenced by the man, and his obvious interest made their own activities harder to keep in the background.

All week they had followed the sheriff through the county, usually as part of the media train that he commanded. Often, though, it was just her and Jeff, especially at night when the other reporters had gone back to their rooms to work on their stories, play cards or just watch TV.

Jeff was an excellent driver and had a talent for following Baldridge's car without being noticed. It was difficult because often there wasn't much traffic, especially at night, but Jeff knew when to turn off and when to get back on the tail. Occasionally they lost the sheriff but they'd always been able to pick him up again after a few minutes. In that respect it helped that there weren't many thoroughfares through that part of the state. The swamp and the forest helped keep the road builders at bay.

Guilt was tugging at the edges of Sabrina's thoughts. There was no way she could be doing this without Jeff and the last thing she wanted was to get him or his job into trouble. Still, she didn't want to head home without the story she wanted. Intellectually she knew she had let herself get too close to it, perhaps becoming unable to see that the story she was after may not be here to tell. If there were clues here that pointed back to the Jacksonville crimes, including Monica Brantley's murder, she didn't want to miss the opportunity to find them.

Emotionally, though, she knew something wasn't right with the sheriff of Baker County. The man was like a rooster strutting through the yard making a lot of noise and bullying the other birds. He was clearly soaking up the publicity while, in Sabrina's eyes, avoiding any visible signs of police work. Perhaps he saw himself as too much the figurehead.

He had had his deputies out for the first half of the week but they hadn't come up with anything material. Baldridge himself hadn't bothered to join them. His only role, once he was called in when the body was found, seemed to be to read the test results from the FBI lab as they were faxed to him. He called a press conference each time, milking the spotlight for every photon of attention he could get.

And most of her colleagues ate it up, which was something she couldn't understand. The man was a phony, clearly puffing himself up into something he wasn't. Couldn't they see that? Or didn't it matter as long as it played to the cameras and audiences back home? Sabrina thought being around the sheriff provided the same kind of meaningless excitement people display when they drive past a movie star's house. Something special felt like it happened there and maybe they could reach out just a little and feel close to it. Something like that.

Whoopee. Tell that to Monica Brantley and the others like her.

"Which one's that again?" Jeff asked.

Sabrina looked at her cameraman first, saw what he was focused on, and turned to see the FBI guy climb into a sedan in the parking lot in front of the sheriff's office.

"Francine," she said. "FBI."

"Want to follow him?"

Sabrina thought about it for a second. "He must have come back for a reason." She checked her watch. "Baldridge isn't likely to do anything. We may as well."

Jeff drank the last of his coffee, wiped his fingers on his jeans, and started the van. "If we're lucky he'll lead us back to J-ville."

"Stop it."

Francine had no idea where Greystoke Street was so the first place he went was to a convenience store on the main strip. The clerk there said she'd heard of it but wasn't sure where it was. Wasn't sure? Francine thought. Can't just say you don't know anymore.

He got back in his car and drove over to a car dealership half a block down the way. Between the receptionist and the sales manager he came up with a set of directions, thanked them both, and left. Looking for a small road in a strange town took his attention, and without any reason to be suspicious, he didn't notice the white van trailing him several blocks back.

After driving north and west of main street, he took two more turns and then a third onto a dirt road. Running on that for a half mile, he came upon the junction with Greystoke Street, turned right and started looking at mail boxes. He found the right one a few minutes later.

There was a dusty pick up truck in the gravel drive next to the mobile home parked in the shade of a pair of grapefruit trees, the surrounding ground littered with fallen and split fruit. It occurred to Francine what a waste that was, but he supposed not everyone liked grapefruit. Still, he thought, there ought to be something to do with it other than feeding ants.

Grayton himself stepped out of the front door as Francine walked across the sandy yard, wondering if he'd be picking sand spurs from his trouser cuffs when he left.

"Frank Grayton?" Francine called.

"I am. You don't look like a reporter. What you looking for?"

Francine stopped in front of him. "I'm not a reporter, sir. I'm with the FBI. I have a couple of questions I'd like to ask you."

Grayton stood back from the door. "Best do it in here, then. Air conditioning's on."

"Thank you." As Francine stepped past the man, a white van passed the front of the house just as the door was shut.

"What do you want me to do now, boss?"

"Oh, cripes, I don't know. We're on a dirt road in the middle of nowhere," Sabrina said.

"Which is in its own little middle of nowhere."

"Can we just keep driving?"

"Probably better than pulling over. Someone's going to come out and look at us if we do."

Sabrina looked at the address of the mobile home that she'd written down after they'd passed. "I wonder who lives there."

"And how that FBI guy knows him."

He had to get that from Sheriff Baldridge, right?"

"Bree, right now I'm a chauffeur. You're Miss Marple. What we do?"

Sabrina snapped her notebook shut. "We go back, after Special Agent Francine is gone. Then we find out who lives there."

"And how do we know when Francine is gone?"

She gave Jeff a smile. "Like you said, you're the chauffeur. Drive, James, drive. At some point circle back and we'll do another drive by if we have to."

"Should have said I was Hercule Poirot."

"You'd still have to drive."

Jeff made a gesture with his right hand.

An hour later they pulled into the driveway behind the same dually pickup that was there before. Francine had been gone for at least fifteen minutes.

"You ready?" Sabrina asked.

"Me? What you need me for?"

"Look, Jeff, we don't know who lives here, right? And we don't know why Francine was here, either. So we have to go up to some person we don't know and find out what he told the FBI. Whoever it is might need encouragement."

Jeff looked uncomfortable, reached for his wallet. "How much you got? And you are paying me back."

Sabrina stopped his arm with a touch. "Let's try buying him with something else."

"I didn't bring my lingerie."

"Me either. Get your camera. Maybe he wants to be famous."

Jeff shook his head. "Sure he does. Lana Turner in a drug store." He got up, worked back through the seats, grabbed the camera off the shelf, snapped on the battery belt. "I'm good."

"Let's go."

"At least walk sexy."

Like he did with Francine, Frank Grayton met them outside his front door. "This time it is the press, isn't it?"

Sabrina held out her hand. "Hello, sir. My name is Sabrina Wells, KTAC News out of Jacksonville."

As a gentleman, Grayton shook with her and said, "Frank Grayton. But then I suppose you know that."

Sabrina wanted to look at Jeff, but didn't. "Actually, Mr. Grayton, we didn't. We know you had a visit from the FBI earlier and we're kind of following up on the Skokie investigation, looking for more background to the story." She held her breath, waiting for him to ask, "What background?" but he didn't.

"Call me Frank," he said. "And step on inside. Got the a/c on and it's better in there." He looked at Jeff. "You really gonna film this?"

"It's up to you two," Jeff said, nodding toward Sabrina. "I just take pictures when I'm told."

"Hm. Me, too. Bit of a camera buff myself, though nothing fancy. I s'pose you want to see the picture I gave to that FBI guy." He stood aside, holding the door and letting Sabrina and Jeff pass.

"That would be great, Frank," Sabrina said quickly. "You want to show it to us, then we can talk about what we can do on camera, and take a quick shot."

"I'll be on the news?"

"I'll file the story. It's up to my producer if he runs it. It really depends on what you have to say."

Grayton walked over to a small table in front of a cloth covered couch. "It's not what I have to say, I guess. Willie and me just found her, is all. We didn't touch nothing, just called the sheriff."

"You didn't want any credit for this?"

"Well," Grayton said, scratching a cheek. "Sheriff Baldridge took the film I gave him and told us to git. So we did. I guess the pictures gave him all he wanted 'cause I ain't heard from him since."

That's odd, Sabrina thought. She would have thought the sheriff would have crowed more about actual pictures of the scene. Maybe the FBI didn't want him to.

"So you kept a picture?" she asked.

"Not on purpose, you know," Grayton said. "My camera was in my truck, I took a picture when we saw the body floating in the water, and it was the last exposure. I had a new roll I put in and shot that whole thing."

"And the new roll is what you gave Sheriff Baldridge?"

"Yes, ma'am."

"How did Francine find you?"

Grayton said, "The FBI man? I assume the sheriff must have sent him."

"Can we see the picture?"

"Nope." Grayton pointed to the table. "He took it."

Sabrina felt her excitement ebb. She had been hoping this could have turned into something that would justify their stay. "What's that?" She was looking at where Grayton had pointed.

"I made that fella make me out a receipt on that picture. It was my only copy."

Sabrina picked it up, hoping Grayton wouldn't object. He didn't.

In a quick handwritten scrawl, it merely said, "To Frank Grayton, receipt for one developed print of crime scene." Then there was the date, followed by a stylized signature.

"Mr. Grayton—"

"Frank."

"Frank," Sabrina said, giving him the full on smile. "What was in the picture?"

"Just the body, floating on the water. Same as all the rest I gave to the sheriff."

Sabrina thought for a moment, couldn't think of anything more to ask. She was wondering what they were going to do now in order to come up with a bigger story. "Do you mind, Frank, if we do a quick interview on tape, maybe get something my station can use?"

"It would be my pleasure."

Jeff hoisted the big video camera to his shoulder and flicked on the mounted light. He could tell Sabrina's hope had mostly gone away and assumed this was just a formality to allow them to leave gracefully.

The interview lasted about three minutes. Frank Grayton told about the morning he and Willie had gone fishing, what time they had arrived there, what kind of fish they were going for, and how he first noticed the body. He talked about taking some pictures and handing the film to the sheriff. "Was kind of spooky, finding her like that, just floating there in the middle of the swamp."

"That must have been terrible for you, Frank." Sabrina turned to Jeff who cut off the camera. When the light blinked off, Sabrina held her hand out to Frank again.

"Did I do all right?" he asked.

"You did fine. Would have been nice to see that picture, though." Sabrina followed Jeff to the door.

Frank seemed surprised. "Sheriff didn't give you a peek at his?"

"Not a one."

"Doesn't seem like him," said Grayton. "You could make yourself another one."

Sabrina and Jeff both froze.

"I still got the negative of that first shot, you want to borrow it. Hell, you can probably just take it. It's kind of disturbing keeping it around here."

Sabrina said, "Wow, Frank, that would be really helpful. We need to document as much of the story as we can. If the sheriff isn't sharing everything with us...."

"Well, he probably has his reasons. Never know with that one." He went to an end table propped next to the couch and opened a small sliding drawer. He took out a paper envelope and stood up, extracting a glassine pouch with the copper-colored strips in it. "Here you go."

Jeff had begun filming again, just in case. Sabrina picked the receipt from Francine off the table, showed it to the camera. "This is where the picture came from, the one you gave the FBI?"

"It is."

"Well," she said. "Thank you again, Frank. You've been really great to talk to."

"Did I help y'all out?"

Sabrina flashed him one more smile. "You didn't hurt, Frank. We're just looking for the story. Take care."

"'Bye, y'all."

As Jeff slowly backed the van onto the hard-packed dirt and gravel of Greystoke Street, neither he nor Sabrina saw the dark sedan pull out of a driveway fifty yards further west and follow them at a distance into town.

CHAPTER SEVEN

The call came when Baldridge was just three miles out of Holton on 125, heading for Macclenny and a good night's sleep at home. He lifted the radio from its cradle in the dashboard and said, "What's going on, Arch?"

Archie Baxter, Baker county's night dispatcher in the sheriff's office, answered back, his hurried speech making his cracker drawl even more difficult to understand.

"Damn it, Arch, slow down," Baldridge said. "I don't know what you're saying."

He heard Arch exhaling hard before he spoke again. This time he was better and the sheriff could interpret every word.

An older couple in a house just outside of Holton, out near the golf course, had called in. They saw a man with makeup on, they said, walk into their new neighbor's house. He didn't belong there, they were sure. They watched him in the light from the outside bulb on the porch. After he went inside, the bulb went out. Then so did the rest of the lights, one by one.

"Where's Dougie? Did you call him?" But Baldridge was already slowing down. Dougie Roe was one of his deputies. The man lived in a trailer with his wife and about six bird dogs a couple of miles south from where Baldridge was right now. Dougie often spent his off time at his brother-in-law's hole in the wall bar in Holton.

"Can't find him," Arch said. "Already tried."

"Alright, Arch. I got it." But Dougie would hear about this. If he wasn't doing something for the job, Baldridge had every intention of crawling down that man's windpipe. There was only one sheriff in Baker County and he didn't take well to handling what he considered his deputies' work.

"But you keep trying that boy," he told Arch. "Tell him I'll meet him there." Baldridge had no intention of waiting for Dougie Roe. That was another thing the sheriff didn't have to do. But it should put a little fear of God in his lazy-assed deputy.

The tiny sparks of dancing red tail lights led Jeff and Sabrina down a dark highway and past country neither one of them cared to see again. "I have seen more beat up broken down trailers and mobile homes...."

"Depressing, ain't it," Jeff answered. In the dark with the half moon there was just light to occasionally see a flapping of someone's wash draped across a line at the side of a trailer home. "You know my parents live in something like that. A double wide with an aluminum porch. They love the hell out of it, though. They throw me out when I call them tornado bait." He said it like he couldn't believe they'd take offense at something like that.

"Yeah, Jeff, parents love it when their kids make fun of their lives' dreams. Swells their chests with pride."

Jeff didn't answer right away. He was tired and they were both discouraged with the way Sabrina's story idea was panning out. Sure there was something there, maybe even something halfway decent. The interview with Frank Grayton raised some questions, especially with the FBI showing interest, but all they had was the negative for a picture that hadn't meant a whole lot to law enforcement. The trouble was, they both knew it wasn't going to be good enough. The price for their extra days spent following Sheriff Baldridge was going to be a steep one.

After they'd made it back to town, they stopped for lunch, then went back to the motel to view the footage they'd shot earlier. Grayton was good for local color, but they weren't sure if there was anything more than that.

"Something still bothers me," Sabrina said as Jeff ejected the cassette from the video player he'd brought in from the van.

Jeff didn't bother looking at her. "Go on," he said.

"If Baldridge has all of Frank Grayton's photos, wouldn't Francine have access? Why would he take one from Grayton?"

With the cassette back in its plastic case, Jeff was writing something on the label along its spine. "I don't know, Bree. Maybe he was just being thorough. That would have been the only picture Baldridge didn't have, remember."

"I guess," she said. "But still... I wish we could ask Baldridge to see those prints."

"Why can't we?"

Sabrina shook her head. "What if he says no? We'd have a story there, maybe, the sheriff not willing to show us the pictures, but...."

"It's weak. Cops hold stuff back all the time, Bree. You know that."

"All we know is that Baldridge has kept those pictures to himself. And that doesn't fit his personality as a publicity hound."

"But if he wants to keep some part of the crime scene secret—"

Sabrina gave him the sort of look that froze men who came up to her in bars. "Why would he do that, Jeff? He's got no chance of catching this killer. If he's the same one from Jacksonville, like they say, the chances of his staying around this little town are zero. The sheriff knows that. Everyone knows that. So his only goal, especially given what we know of Coleman Baldridge, is to make himself as famous as he can."

Jeff sat down on the chair by the window, stuck out his legs, and looked at Sabrina. "Unless," he said, grinning.

"What?"

"Unless this is a different killer."

"Then why would they say something different?"

"Why is the FBI still around?"

Sabrina shook her head. "Hell, I don't know. Let's go eat something and see if we shouldn't be going home tomorrow."

Jeff patted his stomach. "Now you're talking," he said. "I'll drive."

"You really want to do more of this?" Jeff asked Sabrina. They were back in the van, after picking up Sheriff Baldridge at his office soon after dark. The cab of the van was beginning to smell like a permanent habitation.

"We don't have anything else. The food in town isn't any good, and DisneyWorld's two hours away."

Before Jeff decided on a snappy comeback, something else happened. "Whoah, look at this."

Ahead of them, sparks flared brightly into tiny beacons, carving a wide and broken arc against the black night. Sabrina said, "What's he doing?"

Now a pair of headlights were coming up in the opposite lane, the white light hurting the reporters' eyes. "It's not us," Jeff said hopefully. And it wasn't. Blue lights spun into existence on the roof of the car as it sped past them.

"Turn around!" Sabrina said, slightly breathless and louder than she meant to.

"Not yet," Jeff said. "He'll know we're following him."

"Well, do something. This could be our story."

"You da boss, lady." He pushed the button that switched off the lights and reached down to the left of the steering wheel. He put his left foot on the parking brake then pulled on the release lever.

"Jeff, you lunatic, it's pitch black out here!"

Jeff slowed the van with pressure on the parking brake, gradually pulling onto the soft shoulder of the highway. "Don't want to show him any brake lights." Now he was accelerating as he pulled the van around and headed north, once again following the sheriff.

"What about the lights?"

"It's your call, babe. We can cut them on but he'll see us. If you want I can slow down until he's out of sight first."

Sabrina chewed on her lower lip, tasting lipstick. They were hurtling down a ribbon of smooth asphalt highway in the middle of the night. In the dark. Jeff was hunched forward in his seat, his face close to the steering wheel, concentrating hard. "If you think you can do it this way, do it," she said, knowing what his answer would be. She reached across her lap and checked her seat belt. "I don't want to risk losing him while we catch up." And what the hell, she thought. There was always room on her resume for wrecking a company vehicle. It could go right next to the part about how she makes up her own assignments and ignores her boss's orders. Maybe she'd even get to explain it to George Lyle from the next hospital bed as she recovered from her own surgery. And she could watch Jeff try to suck a doughnut into his body through a feeding tube.

Baldridge hated this kind of call and much preferred to send one of his six deputies when he could. Invariably these things, rare as they were in Baker County, turned out to be a stumbling drunk high school kid trying to sneak home without being caught by Mom and Pop. These were just a waste of the sheriff's time.

The calls that were worse were the odd ones where a husband, boyfriend, or ex-something or other was up to something wrong, whether sneaking in for a quickie or maybe checking out his competition. The problem with these is that somebody always got emotional, usually somebody of majority age, and Baldridge never liked to alienate a potential voter. Though he hadn't faced a serious challenge for office in years, Baldridge felt it was just good politics to let the dirty work fall to the hired peons.

In fact, he almost made a quick detour to see if Dougie Roe's car actually was at the River Rat Bar but changed his mind just before the turn. With some of the press still around, there was always the possibility that some of them could be there. After all, there weren't many watering holes in Holton to choose from. It wouldn't look good if the sheriff was found ragging out a deputy while a call was going unanswered. And while his star, however dim or insignificant, still shone over the world outside of Holton, he wanted to keep it there as long as he could.

He passed what was generally thought of as the center of town, a three block stretch of old brick buildings that housed the barber shop, the laundromat, and a number of business offices, many vacant with boards covering their doors or windows. The night grew brighter with a bluish glow as the whirling strobes atop his car reflected their light off the remaining plate glass windows lining both sides of the street. Then it was gone as he shot past, ahead into the damp darkness that flowed over the north part of town.

He drummed his fingers along the top of the steering wheel as he drove past the large white painted sign that featured an orange arrow that pointed to his left toward the municipal golf course, one of only two in the county. There was a small subdivision back there, Milk Run, or something like that. A small-time developer creating a slice of the good life in the middle of the trees and the swamp muck. The guy probably lived in a mobile home in Jacksonville or somewhere.

Baldridge drove into the small deed-restricted community, his lights still flashing, and followed the curve of the asphalt around the edge of the development. The addresses of the houses were painted on the sloping cement curbs next to each driveway which made it easy for Baldridge to find 10004 Milky Gate Road, the address Arch Baxter had given him over the radio.

He pulled into the driveway, stopping for a moment to read the name off the mailbox. He liked to know who he was going to be dealing with. The name read 'Putnam.'

Never one to shy away from a crowd, Baldridge stepped out of the car leaving the lights flashing. If it bothered the neighbors and brought a few out to look, so much the better. They could see the law in action and maybe be a little more careful about keeping their own dirty laundry tucked behind their quiet country club doors.

He carried his flashlight with him up to the front door, though it wasn't turned on. The nosy neighbor had been right about one thing, he thought. There weren't any lights on. The single story ranch-style house was as dark as a tomb.

He pressed the door bell button twice and waited for a second, stepping back to look over at the windows on either side of the door. Nothing. Through the door window he could only see down a short hallway and except for the nighttime noises, everything was quiet inside.

He flicked the flashlight on with his thumb and walked around to the side of the house away from the garage. His instincts were telling him maybe there was something wrong here. If someone was home they should have at least responded to the door bell.

There was nothing to see around that side of the house. There were no doors, only uncovered windows that looked into empty living room, dining room, and kitchen areas in the same standardized floor plan of every third house in this subdivision.

On the other side of the kitchen, in the back of the house, was another entrance. Baldridge checked the aluminum screen door and it was unlocked. With the butt of his flashlight, he pounded heavily on the locked inside door. Still nothing. No sound, no movement.

One more bank of windows to check. These must be the bedrooms. Behind him was the smooth rolling openness of the golf course, cresting unnaturally under the pale half-moon light. Real land around here was flat as a pancake, interrupted only by the vegetation that grew out of it. This was nature by bulldozer.

He let the spring pull the aluminum door closed out of his hand and moved to check the remaining windows. He was beginning to wonder now if the dumbass that called this in had seen someone leaving the house, not entering. Jesus, if you're going to be nosy, at least get your facts straight.

There were three windows between the door he had just left and the corner of the house. The sheriff's mood, not good to begin with, was souring rapidly as the cold dew soaked through the tops and sides of his leather shoes. Dougie Roe had better come up with some damned good reasons for not answering that call from Arch.

He brought the flashlight to the first window and pointed it inside. Small stacks of brown cardboard boxes were stacked along the opposite wall. A bed jutted out from the wall to his right, pink unmade sheets with a cartoon character print in a pile on one end. Nothing unusual, Baldridge thought. Kid didn't make her bed this morning. Call 911.

He passed by the next window since it looked in on the same bedroom. The next one took his breath away.

The white yellow beam from his halogen flashlight brushed over a web of white ropes strung from the ceiling above the king size bed. *What the hell is this*, Baldridge thought. He moved the light onto the bed and stopped it dead in the screaming eyes of a woman, her face wide with terror. On either side of her were two little girls. All three of them had gags stuffed into their mouths and the only parts of them that moved were their heads.

A sudden noise, heard from half outside the house and half through the room in front of him made him jump. Baldridge pushed away from the window and ran back to his left, through the slippery grass and toward the door with the screen. He transferred the flashlight to his left hand as he closed on the door, fingers on his right hand groping at the leather strap that held his pistol in the holster at his side.

"Where did he go?"

"I don't know," Jeff said. "I didn't see him turn."

"He must have." Both of them were staring down the long dark stretch of road in front of them. The flickering blue off the sheriff's strobes weren't visible anywhere.

"Turn on the lights, Jeff."

"What if he's trying to catch *us*?"

"Then he already knows we're here."

Jeff turned the switch that controlled the headlights and the landscape in front of them burned to life, making both of them squint against the glare. They had just passed by a three block stretch of red brick buildings and Jeff slowed the van as they approached a series of residential streets, all of them leading into half a dozen new or established subdivisions.

"There!" Sabrina yelled and pointed across Jeff's chin down a side street. A blinking blue glow was barely visible, pulsing off the houses in the dark.

"Got it," Jeff said, braking hard to make the turn.

The road curved to the north after about four houses and then they saw the county car parked in a driveway, its lights trained on an otherwise blackened house.

"What do I do?" Jeff asked.

"Drive past slowly," she told him. "Let's see what's going on."

Nobody was in the car and they couldn't see any lights on in the house. "Turn around and drive by again," Sabrina said.

Jeff turned off his lights again as he pulled into another driveway so he wouldn't disturb the residents. He turned the van around and approached the driveway with the sheriff's car from the other direction. "What now?"

"I don't know." Sabrina chewed her lip again. She didn't necessarily want to tip off the sheriff that they were following him but on the other hand they were about to go home and they didn't have much to show for their stay. "Pull over," she said. "Here." She pointed to the curb next to the driveway. The name 'Putnam' glowed in blue letters with each turn of the strobe. "Get your camera."

Jeff didn't say anything. He turned the key in the ignition, released his seat belt, then ducked through the seats and into the back to get his gear. Sabrina stepped out of the van on the passenger side and waited for Jeff to emerge. Unconsciously, she teased her hair into place with her fingernails.

Together they walked up the driveway behind the car. They still didn't see or hear anything. The spotlight on Jeff's camera came on as he began taping footage of the car and the front of the house. Sabrina didn't speak. Jeff was one of the best she'd ever seen and he didn't need her direction.

Still filming, she led him to the front door. Tentatively she raised her hand to push the doorbell button when the door flew open in front of her. Sabrina screamed as a small dark figure rushed past her and barreled into Jeff and his camera.

The video equipment made a loud smashing sound and the light blinked off as the bodies fell hard to the sidewalk. In the sudden darkness the two men rolled on the cement, each of them wrapped in the cables from the video equipment and each other. A gleaming knife winked at Sabrina from the sidewalk next to the men and without thinking Sabrina stepped in and kicked it into the grass. After that, she couldn't make herself move as she watched Jeff and the other figure grapple.

"Police! Hold it!" she heard from behind her. She backed out of the way as Sheriff Baldridge ran out of the house with his gun drawn, pointing it at the sprawling men.

"That's my cameraman!" Sabrina shouted.

Baldridge ignored her. "Both of you, stop moving! Now!"

"Jeff!" Sabrina yelled.

The sheriff stepped in and with one hand pulled the collar of the smaller of the two men away from the other. Jeff pushed himself away on his side, unable to get all the way up because of his smashed equipment. Still entangled in the cables, the smaller man was forced face down into the sidewalk by the sheriff's knee. Baldridge worked his handcuffs free and secured the man's wrists behind him. Sabrina could see the makeup or shoe polish that covered the man's face.

"Help your friend get up, miss," Baldridge said to her, still keeping his weight on the man.

Sabrina blinked and felt herself start to move, almost involuntarily. She knelt next to Jeff and helped him shrug out of his camera harness. Her heart felt like it was beating a hundred times a minute and she was amazed to see Jeff's white teeth smiling at her out of the dark as he scrambled free. "Looks like we got our story, eh, Bree?"

Baldridge rolled the struggling form over and aimed his light at the man's face. He was fighting to compose his own breathing, to make it look as though apprehending people like this was something he did all the time in Baker County. His only regret was that the video camera was obviously not working.

He recognized the face squinting up at him. Dupin or Duprin, he thought. Something like that. The kid had lived around here all his life, grew up in a foster home or something, had an apartment somewhere now. The sheriff had been aware of him but there had never been any trouble before.

Baldridge jerked him to his feet and pushed him toward the cruiser. Albert was his first name, the sheriff remembered. He was dressed head to toe in black, with shoe polish or something like it blackening his face and the backs of his hands. He hadn't said a word and in the dark his pupils were dilated as wide as they could be.

Behind him Sabrina Wells was scribbling notes furiously on a pad while Jeff was gathering up his broken equipment. Baldridge opened the door and with a huge hand on the top of his head guided Albert into a position in the back seat. He still hadn't said anything.

Baldridge slammed the door and turned around. Sabrina stopped writing as she met the sheriff's eyes, remembering something important.

"He dropped this," she said, pointing at the gleaming knife lying still in the moist grass.

Baldridge walked over to it and knelt down, then looked at Sabrina. Both of them were thinking the same thing.

Lynnette Elizabeth Skokie.

CHAPTER EIGHT

Albert Duprin's small apartment was located above the town of Holton's only hardware store. Sheriff Coleman Baldridge entered it alone, an unusual practice, using the set of keys he had taken from his prisoner. It was just past four in the morning and there had been no traffic on the street outside.

After he had taken Duprin down to Macclenny, he had spoken briefly with that woman reporter, the babe from Jacksonville. He had asked her how her and her cameraman had happened to find their way to the Putnam house at the particular time but she hadn't given him a satisfactory answer. He didn't want to push it, though; he would probably need her later on. He had sent them away and then driven back here, with Albert's keys.

What he saw when he turned the lights on was appalling, even to him. Stacks of porno magazines, many of them hard core and with titles in languages other than English, dotted the floor. A large collection of hard plastic video cases stood in piles next to the TV and VCR stand. But it was what was on the walls that grabbed his attention most.

When he found the section devoted to the Skokie girl, the whiter newsprint standing out among the yellow, he thought he had a plan that just could work for him. And in the process, if he did it right, could get all those press and media folk back here and make him a genuine headline-making national hero instead of the bit player in someone else's larger story.

He would give them their serial killer. And they would love him for it.

There was a knock at the door and Baldridge moved to open it, hand on his sidearm. It was Francine. "You still in town?" Baldridge asked.

"Just packing to leave, got the call. FDLE will be here in the morning."

"Tell me something I don't know."

Francine stepped past the sheriff, surveying the room. "Mind if I look around, Sheriff?"

Baldridge didn't like it; there was more here than he'd seen already. He was thinking that with another person here there'd be no opportunity for deeper study, or possibly an enhancement or two.

"Going to take a while to go through all this video, isn't it?" Francine asked.

"Not my job. Thank God."

Francine passed over the various piles of magazines and focused on the displays taped to the walls. It was a virtual tribute to a who's who of violent crime in Florida. And there was a lot of it in the Sunshine State. As he moved along the walls he got to a section that stopped him in his tracks. The biggest pieces were from Tampa, dating from the late eighties and on into the nineties. He had an idea.

"What you got?" Baldridge said from behind him.

"Oh," said Francine. "I'm sure there's nothing here you haven't seen for yourself." He stepped back and said, "Well, I think I'll go and see if I can get my room back at the hotel. Might get crowded again tomorrow."

Baldridge moved away, gave the FBI man a clear path to the door, forced a smile. "Well, if there's anything I can do…."

"I'm sure you'll do it," Francine said. "Good night, Sheriff."

PART THREE

CHAPTER ONE

James Robinson hung up the phone and pushed it across his desk so hard it almost went over the edge. Damn it, he thought. It's been more than seven years and they're still calling. It had taken him all of half a second to hang up on the reporter after she'd told him who she was.

He hadn't meant to be rude but an immediate and unbidden spike of anger, the old frustration that had grown to become a constant part of his life, took command and fired the muscles in his arm. He couldn't help it. If he thought he saw a snake he jumped back.

In one of his desk drawers was a slightly less than half full bottle of Johnny Walker Red and he fought the urge to take it out. He reached for the drawer in spite of himself then pulled back without opening it. It was getting to the point where any excuse was enough and he didn't want that. As it was he gave in much more often than not but the idea of needing the alcohol, of being psychologically addicted to it, was something he'd been fighting for years. He knew he'd give in soon enough, anyway. He just didn't want to give the reporter the credit for it. They'd taken enough from him already.

When he stood up to leave hours later, the day's work being finished and the blood red sun hanging low, just two inches above the horizon, one thought kept surfacing in his mind: why now? What was making them interested in him now?

He climbed into the front seat of his truck and put the key in the ignition. A minute later he turned out of the small parking lot that fronted the garage where he did his motorcycle work and was on his way home. There was beer there. Maybe he'd toss a few more empty cans down the sinkhole when he got there. Making them empty was the fun part. The sinkhole was just the furniture.

While it was true that the press tried to look him up from time to time, this woman had said she was from Jacksonville. Long way from Tampa. He wasn't sure what that meant.

Robinson unrolled his window and stuck his head outside as he drove. He didn't want to think about it. Sand pebbles and insects collided with his face, some of them sticking to his beard as he accelerated down the county road toward home. Whatever it was she wanted, he kept telling himself, it wasn't his problem. This is what they'd created seven years before.

When she walked in on him the next morning, Robinson didn't move. He had never seen her before but as soon as she stopped in front of his desk he knew who she had to be. Casual but too well dressed. Perfect hair and make up. His eyes focused on his desk drawer.

"Hello," the woman said.

Robinson didn't answer right away. For a long minute neither of them moved. Then he said, "I don't want you here."

The woman looked puzzled and Robinson didn't try to help. After a minute she asked, "Do you know me?"

"I don't need to."

"I see." A flash of anger or something like it passed over her face then disappeared. She looked around for a chair and pulled one over from against the wall. She sat down in front of his desk, waiting patiently.

"I'm sorry," Robinson said. "I didn't offer you a chair."

"No, you didn't."

"That was because one of us was leaving. It can just as well be me." Robinson stood up to go but before he could walk around his desk, the woman tossed a stack of blown up color photographs on his desk.

"Do you know about these?"

This woman was not behaving like most of the other reporters that had come after him. Something in the way she threw the pictures made him look at what she had. Right away he knew that these were not what he thought they would be.

"They're from Jacksonville," she said. "And one from a town called Holton. Are you familiar with them?"

He flipped through the pile. "Just what I read in the papers." But he knew everything about them in every paper.

"Then you know the sheriff in Baker County arrested a man in connection with the murders."

Robinson nodded. What did any of this have to do with him? Was she trying to connect him somehow, put him together with these killings the way B. J. Donnelly had all those years ago? A noise like rushing water filled his ears and again he thought of the bottle in his drawer. He wished she would leave but he stood there, unable to say anything.

"My name is Sabrina Wells," she said, apparently deciding she was staying.

Robinson swallowed and forced saliva around the insides of his mouth before he spoke. "Why did you come here?"

"Please sit down, Mr. Robinson. I only want to talk to you."

"If you know enough about me to find me you ought to know that I don't talk to reporters."

"Or just about anyone else, it seems. But this isn't about you."

"Oh, really?" he said. Something inside of him relaxed anyway and he pulled out his chair and picked up the stack of pictures. He flipped through them more slowly the second time.

"By any chance do you know Sheriff Coleman Baldridge of Baker County?"

"After all this–" he gestured with the photographs. "Who doesn't? But not personally, no." The sheriff's face had been all over the newspapers, magazines and television for the past week. Ever since he had caught the person that had been responsible for what was in these pictures. "I have no idea why you'd expect me to."

"I think he's doing something wrong up there."

"So one bad cop deserves another?" He got to his feet again. "This has nothing to do with me. Please go. Please go now." He wasn't angry, he just wanted this reporter out of his office.

Sabrina Wells stared him down, with a cool but stubborn look on her face. If she were riled or impressed by his outburst she didn't show it. "You don't have to be so paranoid. I know this has nothing to do with you."

The repetition was deliberate and it helped calm Robinson a bit. He slowly sat back down.

"I really do appreciate your time, Mr. Robinson."

"I can't help you." Robinson kept his eyes on the stack of photos. Despite himself, the woman made him curious.

"Eight days ago Sheriff Baldridge arrested a man named Albert Duprin and charged him with the murder of Lynette Elizabeth Skokie, a local girl whose body was found in Holton. She was the only victim from outside of the city of Jacksonville and Duval County. The only one in the sheriff's jurisdiction. You must have read about that?" Her raised eyebrows asked Robinson the question but he didn't answer.

"Since then, Duprin wont talk to anybody but Baldridge. He doesn't want a lawyer and refuses all visits from anyone else. He has no family anybody can find and when they sit him in front of a shrink he curls up into the mental equivalent of a frightened caterpillar."

"So what's the problem?" Robinson asked. He still didn't understand why she was here. "Is he going for insanity? Showing he won't participate in his own defense, or what? These things go on all the time."

"The problem is that everything we know about Albert Duprin and what he has or has not done comes directly through the mouth of Coleman Baldridge."

"And you have something against him doing his job?"

The spark of anger flared through her eyes again but she kept her temper out of her voice as she spoke. "You still sound like you're a cop. I was told you were a difficult man to talk to."

"Meaning...?" His tone matched hers perfectly.

This time she did go off. "Meaning that eight years ago, since you stuck your head in the sand, the world decided to keep spinning and while it did people like B. J. Donnelly kept on killing and molesting people you never heard of. Just because you got out of it, Mr. Robinson, doesn't mean it stopped happening and doesn't mean the rest of us stopped giving a damn."

He felt the familiar twinge in his stomach when he heard her say Donnelly's name. He was growing angry though he wasn't sure why. It was a reflective thing. "I didn't ask you to come here," he said.

Sabrina Wells took a visible breath and folded her hands on top of the portfolio in her lap. She is a beautiful woman, though, Robinson thought. Shoulder length brown hair matched the gold-brown of her large round eyes and the perfect skin of her face was accented by the bright red lipstick expertly applied to her mouth. She looks like an anchorwoman, he thought.

"No," she said at last. "And I have no right to speak to you like that. I thought that after all this time you would have gotten over some of what happened to you." She turned her eyes away from his so he wouldn't respond. "This is why I came." She opened the portfolio and removed another set of photographs. Instead of tossing them on his desk like she did the last time, Sabrina held them out to him with one hand. If Robinson wanted to see them he'd have to get up and take them.

They sat like that, each one staring at the other, until Sabrina's arm began to bob and tremble with fatigue.

"You must want something awfully bad." Robinson stood up and leaned across his desk, accepting the pictures. Sabrina dropped her arm to her side.

Some of the pictures were easier to read than others and it took Robinson some time to sort them out. "Where did you get these?"

"They're from the walls of Albert Duprin's apartment."

Robinson flipped back to one of the pictures. It was a close up of a longer shot showing dozens of newspaper clippings papering an entire wall. His own face, seven years younger and without a beard, was reflected back at him many times from the collection of laminated articles and pictures. There were more stories about him than could be shown in just one photo and still be readable in the picture he held.

"What does the sheriff think this means?"

"Isn't it obvious?" Sabrina asked. "It's a shrine. To the crimes you were… associated with. Look at the rest of the pictures."

Robinson bent his head forward and examined the rest of the collection. The walls of this Duprin's apartment made up a good history of Florida homicide. He recognized several cases that he had worked in his previous career. He finished with the photos of himself and the Sun Coast case on the top. These particular articles appeared to be the only ones encased in plastic. A lamp with a spotlight attachment was visible in one of the pictures.

"Forgive me, Miss...."

"Wells," Sabrina said.

"Let me ask you again: why exactly are you here?"

"Call me Sabrina, please. I want you to come up to Baker County with me and talk to Albert Duprin."

Robinson couldn't stop the laugh. "You've got to be kidding."

"Why should I be?"

Robinson was astounded. "First of all, if you haven't noticed, I'm not a cop anymore. I restore junk motorcycles and sell them. It was a job I could do when the rest of the world kicked me out on the street on my face. I have nothing to do with any of this. Why would this Duprin or anyone else want to talk to me now? Secondly, what do you hope to gain from this? Publicity? What kind of story is a television reporter from Jacksonville going to get out of me talking to this guy that would possibly do anyone any good?"

Sabrina took a deep breath, let things in the room settle down. "My cameraman and I have followed Sheriff Baldridge like a dog through that county for two weeks. In all that time, if he's done any investigating of anything other than the physical attributes of the female reporters that came to town, we haven't seen it. Suddenly this man rushes out of a darkened house in the middle of the night and presto, the sheriff has himself a notorious sociopathic killer."

"You telling me you think Duprin's innocent?"

"No. I don't know. Not really. But that's not the point. It's more the sheriff I'm concerned about. I think he's up to something and he's using his office to hide it."

"You're basing this on, what? General incompetence?"

Sabrina didn't answer.

"Assuming you're correct, what do you think the sheriff is hiding?"

"I have no idea."

"So based on this hunch or intuition, you're asking me to take time off from my work to go talk to a man who is probably responsible for murdering—what is it seven?—women and cutting off their hands for whatever reason God or grandma tells him. And you want me to find out whether or not this sheriff is up to something that is not good."

"When you were a policeman you had a homicide clearance rate of over ninety four percent. I checked. Nobody does that. You don't solve that many cases unless you give that much of yourself to each one. At least that's what everybody tells me. You were successful because you cared. Somewhere in there you must still. You can't just turn something like that off."

Robinson was silent for a minute, his fingers passing over both sets of photographs. "And why do you care so much?" he asked at last.

Sabrina stood up and reached for the photos, pushing the first two off one of the piles and leaving a shot of a pale white body propped naked in a sitting position against the scaly trunk of an Australian pine. "Her," Sabrina said. "Monica was my friend. I knew her when I was in college."

CHAPTER TWO

"What about the Jacksonville cops? I'd imagine your people would have some pull with them."

Sabrina shrugged. "I've asked. That's all I can do. Right now they're happy with Duprin."

Robinson drummed the oily desktop with his fingers, then grabbed a rag from his pocket and wiped it down. "How about the FBI?"

"I spoke with Special Agent Francine—"

Robinson froze. "Timothy Francine?"

"I—I don't know. Hang on." Sabrina went back to her portfolio and drew out a notebook, flipped to a page. "That's him," she said. "Why?"

"He was here when…." Robinson trailed off. Once B. J. Donnelly had confessed, Francine's FBI took over and kept the locals away from Donnelly just long enough for him to kill himself in his cell. Two of the cases had been closed, all the others made inactive; for all intents and purposes everything was over. Once there was no more Donnelly, there were no more answers.

"If I did go with you, how do you know they'd let me see him?"

"Obviously Duprin feels a connection to you," Sabrina said. "Yours are the only clippings he had laminated and spotlighted."

"I'm probably the only one alive."

"At least the only one not in prison."

Robinson looked at her, not sure of what to say. "Listen, Ms. Wells—"

"Sabrina. Please."

"No. You people took my life away. I lost everything I had for doing my job." He swallowed hard, thinking of Becky Owens. "Things—maybe could have been done differently, but they weren't. Look at me now, what do you see?"

Sabrina didn't answer.

Robinson almost laughed. "I'll tell you what you see. Nothing. A bum. I work alone in a garage wrenching on motorcycles. I get a small pension and earn spending money from selling salvaged bikes." He stood up, wiped his hands on his pant legs. "I'm sorry, Miss Wells or Sabrina. I don't have anything left to offer."

Sabrina kept her seat. "How about this," she said. "Only two of the Sun

Coast cases were officially closed. The rest were never officially solved, right?"

"They had Donnelly. And most importantly, there were no more killings."

"But what if Duprin knew something about those others?"

"I thought he was just a kid. How old is this guy?"

"Twenty two."

"Then he was what, fourteen or fifteen when Donnelly was caught, and a toddler when those killings began. What could he know?"

Sabrina shrugged. "I have no idea. But why did he have this?" Sabrina pulled another envelope out of the portfolio in her lap. Inside was a smaller envelope, greeting card sized. She took it out and handed it to Robinson.

He accepted it with a tremor in his hand. He didn't know why. The flap wasn't sealed and he slid the card out of the envelope. A picture of a pelican painted in watercolor was on the front. The texture was rough, the way some paper gets as it ages. Slowly he opened it, looked for the preprinted message he hoped was on the inside. There wasn't one. It was a note card, one he now knew he recognized. Inside, in faded blue ink, was the inscription:

Becky,

I knew you wouldn't regret meeting me at the beach. What a perfect day. When are we having the next one?

He knew how it was signed without having to look. He ran his finger over the neat and tidy "J" that started out the name "Jimmy," an optimistic scrawl against a blank background that should never have been there.

"How did you get this?"

"Truthfully? Someone left it under the wiper of our van. It was wrapped in this." She handed him a single, folded sheet of paper. In an almost childlike scribble was the name "Albert Duprin" in blue ink.

"But how—" Robinson held his head in his hands. This wasn't possible. "How could he— How could you—"

Sabrina took a manila envelope from her case and handed it over. "It was all in this." On the outside of the envelope, in block letters written with a permanent marker, was his own name: James Robinson.

This was too much for Robinson to grasp. "Why didn't you give it to Baldridge?"

Sabrina reddened. "I– I don't know, except that we really just didn't trust the sheriff. We thought if it were important we could always turn it in anonymously. But then, when we saw what was inside Duprin's apartment—"

"Pictures of me."

"Your shrine. We knew we had something, we just didn't know what. We still don't. For some reason you're important to Albert Duprin, Mr. Robinson. Why is that?"

Now he really was looking at that desk drawer. He reached down, pulled it open, took the bottle into his lap. All he could think about was the name he had written on that card: Becky.

"I'll go."

"Pardon me?" Sabrina asked.

"What makes you think this sheriff will let me see Duprin?"

Sabrina couldn't help but smile. "He's already agreed. I told Sheriff Baldridge that we were producing a documentary about him. Since you seem to mean something special to Albert Duprin, I told him we want you part of it to help develop the story."

"And that's okay with him?"

"Let's just say the sheriff likes to chase more than criminals in Baker County."

Robinson stroked his beard. "When do we leave?"

It had rained that afternoon and irregular brown puddles filled the ruts and potholes of the dirt road leading to Robinson's home. Large drops of water fell from the overhanging canopy of trees, exploding against the windshield and roof of the truck. Sounds like tiny tin cans being crushed filled the cab as they jolted along the track.

"Where do you live, the jungle?" Sabrina asked. Robinson wrinkled the corner of his mouth in something that could have been a polite smile.

He had taken her to the airport where they had returned her rented compact car. They had made plans to stop here and pack a few of his things before driving the three hours up to Baker County. Their short time in the truck so far had been spent mostly in silence, listening to the thwack of the windshield wipers across the glass.

Robinson stopped the truck in front of the iron gate leading to his house and got out to unlock it. Sabrina felt the heavy moistness of the air push its way into the cab as soon as his door was opened. Ahead of them she could see an asphalt road but the area they had just been through looked more like a place to pasture cows or put in a landfill.

"Nobody bothers me out here," Robinson said. He got back in the truck and drove them through the gate.

"I guess not." *He speaks*, Sabrina thought.

They parked the car in the driveway and both of them climbed out, Sabrina not waiting to see if Robinson would open her door. "What's that over there?" she asked.

Robinson followed her gaze. "That's where I keep the bulldozers," he told her.

"No, really," she said. "What is it?"

Robinson started walking to the front door. "A collapse sinkhole. Formed overnight years ago and swallowed two bulldozers and the start of the house they were building. This one here," he nodded toward his house as he fit his key in the lock. "Was the model home. It was all they had finished when the developer went belly up."

"But you're so close to it. What if the hole gets bigger?"

"It does, all the time. Come in and take a seat. I won't be long." Suddenly he was tired of talking.

Sabrina took the hint and followed him inside, taking a seat on the sofa. The living room was immaculately clean. There was no dust on the television screen, no magazines or old mail stacked on the coffee table. This isn't normal, she thought. A single man, living alone. Doesn't he have anything better to do with his time?

Twenty minutes later Robinson emerged from his bedroom carrying a suitcase and a garment bag. "You set?"

Sabrina nodded and stood up. They went outside and Robinson threw his bags in the back of the truck next to hers. They drove past the gate and into the city, the silence picking up where it had left off.

Sabrina finally broke it with, "Why did you agree to help me?" It was half curiosity and half an attempt to start a conversation but once she asked, she found she really wanted to know the answer.

"I didn't. I agreed to talk to Albert Duprin. I have no idea what you want."

"Then why are you going with me?"

Robinson was silent for a minute. Of course he had known that she would ask him this but he wasn't sure what he would tell her. "Most people, including law enforcement officers, don't know what kind of people do the things that Duprin is accused of. Why he is what he is. I want to get to know him a little."

"That sounds a bit cute. And this is because of what happened to you before?"

The temptation was to look at her, to give her a good view of the ugly look on his face, maybe discourage her. But he didn't. "I suppose so," he managed. "In some way." Then, "Jesus, you're direct."

Sabrina knew she was on delicate ground but she asked anyway; her reporter instincts were too strong. "Are you hoping to meet B. J. Donnelly up there?"

Robinson didn't answer.

"You do know he's dead, don't you? For quite a few years now."

They approached the on ramp for Interstate 275 heading north. Robinson put on his left turn signal and made the light, accelerating to just over sixty miles per hour. Off to their right a rainbow shone against two blue-gray clouds.

"You do know where you're going, right?"

"If I make a wrong turn you'll tell me," he said. Both of his hands were on the steering wheel as he merged into the far left lane.

Sabrina sighed and ran her fingers through her hair, her long legs chilled by the blast from the air conditioner. "There's no one up there for you to pay back, you know."

Maybe there's not. He thought of Becky's brother Drew and the promise he'd made. He'd always dreaded having to actually fulfill it, and give Drew actual news of what really happened to Becky. Maybe it was Donnelly. Maybe they'd never know for sure. The not-knowing was what kept Drew Owens and Robinson tied together, no matter how much time went by.

The tires of the truck went clump-clump, clump-clump over the seams in the cement highway.

What about Monica, Sabrina thought. What if it's me that's looking for a payback? After a few minutes of nothing she lay her head back against her seat and turned to look out the window.

The sounds and rhythms of the truck on the highway made her sleepy and she covered a yawn with the back of her hand. When she looked for the rainbow again it was gone, blown away with the bundle of clouds.

A little while later, she slept.

Robinson drove on, wondering how he would have responded had the reporter stayed awake.

CHAPTER THREE

Albert Duprin was a pale man with dark hair, twenty seven years old, approximately five feet eight inches in height and weighing a hundred and fifty five pounds. Sitting by himself, chained to a wooden chair, he appeared much smaller.

Overhead fluorescent lights were the only source of light in the windowless room and a three by five section of one wall held a panel of mirrored glass. Robinson thought of the last time he had been in an interview room. It had been a lifetime away in Bradenton. He looked at the mirror and knew that people were behind it, watching them.

Duprin hadn't moved when Robinson entered the room. His eyes had flicked to the door once than settled back to the table in front of him. Robinson guided the door shut quietly and stood waiting for several minutes. Watching Albert, he suddenly felt very unprepared. He had an idea that he didn't know if he could do this because he wasn't sure what *this* was.

He took the few steps across the room and stood behind the chair opposite Albert. "Do you mind if I sit down?" he asked.

No response. It was as if Albert hadn't heard him. Robinson waited a moment then pulled the chair out from the table and sat down slowly.

Sheriff Baldridge hadn't been there when they'd arrived, which was annoying. No one had briefed him on what he could expect out of the prisoner, what his state of mind was. The deputy that was on duty had been instructed to set up the interview but Robinson hadn't even been allowed to see the case files. He was flying blind and had no idea how to proceed.

Sabrina Wells had met him at the coffee shop of the motel this morning with her cameraman, somebody named Jeff something or other. Neither one of them had been very happy when he told them they couldn't be present in the interview room. "Why the hell not?" Sabrina asked.

"Because of what this guy thinks women are," Robinson had told her. "He wouldn't be the same person with you in the room. Literally."

"Then take Jeff and the camera. I'll wait outside."

"I don't want Duprin posing. Assuming he talks at all. Listen," he said and led her by the elbow down the hall. "You withheld evidence from the sheriff. I want to know about that damned note on your windshield but I can't ask him without exposing you, can I?"

Sabrina looked pale under her make up as she realized her situation. "I don't know what to do. What do you want from me? Should I apologize?" She looked like she could cry. "Should I give the card to the sheriff now?"

Robinson thought about it. "That would probably be the best thing," he said.

Eyes glistening, Sabrina said, "Okay. I'll go find him now."

"No," he said, grabbing her arm. "Don't do it." He tried a smile. "We'll figure it out." They both knew that going to Baldridge now could mean she would be throwing away her career.

"Thank you," she said.

"You know, you shouldn't have kept the card."

Sabrina just nodded, blotting at her eyes with her cuffs. Robinson was embarrassed.

In the end she was happy to settle for filming through the one way mirror. Robinson didn't really care what she did with her camera just as long as Duprin didn't see it. He was here now facing the man and he had to figure out what to say. As a cop he'd be trying to get information. As–whoever he was now—he wasn't sure what he was after.

"Hello, Albert."

Nothing. A slight hum from the overhead lights and Duprin's light breathing were the only sounds.

B. J. hadn't been like this. B. J. had been only too happy to talk.

"Do you know who I am?"

More nothing. Still life with humans.

"Look at me, Albert."

Albert didn't move, his eyes directed toward the surface of the table.

Robinson reached out and took Albert's chin with his fingers, careful to keep them out of the way of the man's mouth. He lifted Duprin's head until the small black pupils of his eyes were level with his own. He held it there. Albert didn't resist.

"I said, look at me, Albert. Do you know who I am?"

Albert blinked twice and the muscles in his face began to work. He creased his forehead and Robinson pulled his hand away from Albert's chin. Duprin's head didn't move.

"You have a beard." He tried to lift a hand to his face but was stopped a few inches short by his chains. "I could never grow one like that." His voice was thin and reedy, almost feminine, and the sound of it danced around the corners of the room.

"So you know me?"

Albert nodded once, slowly. "I was hoping that I'd get to meet you."

"Oh? Why is that?"

An ugly grin spread across Albert's mouth, showing rows of uneven, yellowed teeth. He didn't speak.

"Tell me, Albert."

"You already know."

"I'm not sure I do."

Albert's grin grew even wider. Robinson wondered if Sabrina and Jeff could see it from where they were behind the glass.

"Do you want to talk to me, Albert?"

Thin lips worked over yellow teeth. "I want to know you."

"Why do you say that?"

"Because you've done so much more than me."

Whatever Robinson had been expecting, this hadn't been it. His pulse quickened and he looked away briefly, giving himself a chance to maintain the neutral expression on his face. He didn't want to give up control this early.

"Did you kill those women, Albert?"

Duprin shrugged with one shoulder, making echoes of the clinking chains bounce around the room. "Haven't you spoken to the sheriff? I already told him that I did."

Sabrina hadn't mentioned that the man had confessed. Maybe she hadn't known herself. What more was he supposed to get?

"What else have you two talked about?"

Albert ignored him. "Are you still in Tampa? I'm surprised they let you come up here."

"Why?"

"Because of who you are." Albert was staring at him, his small dark eyes boring into Robinson's own.

"Tell me who exactly you think I am, Albert."

Duprin placed his forearms on the surface of the table, dragging his chains along the scarred wooden edge. He leaned forward, getting as close to Robinson as he could. Robinson imagined he could smell the prisoner's breath like sour milk from across the table. "I understand how you may not want to talk." He turned his head toward the one way mirror then back to Robinson. "But I hope that you can find a way."

"What is it you want me to tell you, Albert?"

The light in his eyes flared as he said, "What it feels like to you."

"What is it you want to tell me?"

Nothing.

"Have you ever been to Tampa, Albert?"

No response.

Robinson pushed back in his chair. It was repulsive to be this close to someone like Duprin. It had been different with B. J., he realized. He had known B. J. as a normal person once and during the brief visit he'd had with him after his arrest he hadn't been able to fully reject that persona.

He entertained no such illusions about Albert. Duprin was a classic manipulator, trying to impose his will on the circumstances he couldn't control in real life. He had been governing the interview since it started and Robinson had been too caught up in his own problems to keep it from happening.

He was not going to get anything out of Albert this way. In fact, it was Albert doing all of the taking. Robinson had been in the room less than fifteen minutes and he felt his head begin to ache. And the thirst—

He was angry at himself but he didn't let it show.

"I don't know if I want to tell you anything."

The smile on Albert's face broke. "Don't say that."

Robinson stood up and pushed the edge of his chair under the table. He felt it touch Albert's knees. "You wouldn't understand it."

He stood like that for a moment, fingertips resting on the chair back, then he turned and took a step toward the door.

"Wait!"

Robinson turned around slowly. "What is it, Albert?" he asked.

"I thought you wanted to talk to me." His voice was higher and softer than it had been before. "You came from Tampa."

Robinson glanced at the mirror and then moved back to the table, inclining his head to an almost intimate distance to Duprin. "I don't think you can understand," he said again, softly.

"Of course I can! Of course I can! Look at me! Look where I am!" He tried to hold up his chains as if they were evidence of his sincerity.

Robinson pulled his chair out from under the table but didn't sit. He waited until the quiet hum of the lights dominated the room again before he said, "Tell me about the women, Albert."

Their eyes locked again and neither man moved. In a few minutes, or a few seconds, Robinson's legs began to cramp with tension as he stood there, meeting Albert's stare. He matched whatever was in those eyes, unknowable thought for unknowable thought. Black emotion for black emotion. Mental whirlwinds of fear and self doubt whipping through his mind. His whole career had been taken from him, his whole way of life, and it was unfair and it was unjust and it was because of people like Albert Duprin. Him, and the weaker people that were worse in many ways, the men he had worked for. He flung all this into the black pits of Albert's pupils, touching whatever dark stuff lived there and adding his own. Images of innocent women brutalized and murdered lived there. All of the things, the madness and the hate, that Albert was trying to send to him.

"Then you'll stay, right?"

"Tell me and we'll see."

Duprin swallowed. It looked painful. Then he nodded. "Okay," he said. "I just need a few minutes."

But Albert had cracked too much and Robinson needed to trust what he said, not be told what Albert thought he was supposed to say. And he needed to get off his feet and he wanted to look at those case files before Albert got into it. Mostly he wanted to keep the power and to do that he needed to know facts. He made a point to look at his watch. It was almost ten thirty.

"I'm a little hungry right now, Albert. I'll see you again after lunch." He turned and walked to the door without looking back.

From over his shoulder, he heard Albert call, "I'll be here."

Robinson was exhausted. He pulled the door shut behind him and leaned against the wall next to it. He closed his eyes, trying to block out the light.

To his left he heard a door open and close, followed by a set of sharp foot-steps on the tile floor.

His senses were hyperactive and he smelled the fruity scent of her perfume before she touched his arm. "Are you okay?" Sabrina asked him. He felt the surface of his skin tremble at the contact.

"Did you get all that?"

Sabrina nodded. A look of concern was on her face. "I'm not sure if we could pick up all the audio but I think so. Jeff's still in there filming for a few minutes. It was–frightening somehow, but–"

"What?"

She shook her head. "I don't know. So *real*, I think. Something."

"Sheriff Baldridge show up?"

"No. The deputy said he should be back this afternoon." She glanced at the door she had come from. "There's someone else in there."

Robinson rubbed his fingers into his eyes. "Who's that?"

"FBI. Special Agent Francine."

"Shit."

"What's wrong? Do you know him?"

"We've met. The FBI's the FBI."

She didn't know how to take that but she let it pass. "Well, there's some-thing I should tell you about him."

"Go on."

"I don't think he's a fan. Of yours, I mean."

Robinson looked at her and wondered at the concern on her face. "That's okay. That's how it's been since.... For a while now." He was aware that Sab-rina was still touching his arm.

The door to the observation room opened and Jeff came out, looking for them. He walked rapidly to where they were standing, stopping a little out of breath. "That's one of the damndest things I've ever seen," he said.

"Stick around. It'll get better." Then to Sabrina, "Did you know he had con-fessed?"

She shook her head. "What? No, I didn't. The sheriff must be keeping it quiet."

"What's your friend from the FBI doing, Jeff?"

Jeff looked back over his shoulder. "He's on the phone. Or was, when I left. I'm hungry. You guys hungry?"

"We meet again, James Robinson." Francine nodded his head and applied a little extra pressure to his handshake. "I haven't heard much about you for a while."

Robinson could see into the interrogation room where Albert had turned his head to look at the mirror. The effect was eerie, as if he knew they were there and he could see through the glass. "How you guys doing on this case?"

If Francine was offended by Robinson's slight he didn't show it. "Well, we got the cocksucker that killed those women. You heard him admit to that. That was a nice show you put on in there."

Robinson found it hard to look away from Albert. When he did, Francine was smiling at him.

"I need to see the case files before I talk to him again."

Francine shrugged. "There they are," he said, gesturing to a stack of manila folders on a table. "Already pulled them. Help yourself. Looking a bit rough, aren't you?"

"Thank you." Robinson went to the table and dragged over one of the chairs set in front of the glass. He settled in and examined the headings written on the tabs of the folders before pulling one toward him and opening it. A set of gruesome color photos was on top of the papers inside.

"What do you hope to hear in there this afternoon?"

Without looking up, Robinson said, "I want him to tell me what he did to those girls."

"This the voyeur in you talking?" he said.

I'm not the one putting nose prints on a spit-stained glass window, thought Robinson. He didn't say anything. Suddenly he wished he hadn't asked Sabrina and Jeff to go pick up some lunch.

"Why do you want to listen to that?" the agent asked.

From a law enforcement point of view the answer would be obvious but Francine was trying to dig for something. Something to do with why he was allowing Robinson to be there, see the case work. Listening to him made it difficult for Robinson to concentrate. It took tremendous effort to keep his emotions out of his voice as he said, "We need to know if it makes any sense."

"Uh huh. 'We' do." He made a sucking noise with his teeth then leaned one hand against the wall and studied Albert. "Look at him, the poor fuck. He just sits there staring at himself in the goddamn mirror."

Robinson was tired of the talk but he said, "I don't think that's what he's doing."

"What are you talking about? Look at him, for chrissake."

"I think he wants us to think he can see through the glass."

Robinson could almost hear the answering smirk across the dimly lit narrow room. He didn't look up but after a few minutes Francine turned another one of the chairs away from the glass and sat down to watch him work.

CHAPTER FOUR

Sabrina and Jeff showed up nearly an hour later with a bag containing half a dozen sandwiches. Robinson's mind had been absorbed with the files and he had managed to avoid any further conversation with Francine.

He didn't want to break his concentration but he heard Jeff ask, "Why is he still in there?"

Robinson turned around and looked past Francine and the glass into the tiny dark pits of Albert Duprin's eyes. No one had asked the deputy to take him back to his cell and apparently Francine had been content to keep him where he was.

"Doesn't blink a lot, does he?" Jeff asked.

Robinson put down what he had been reading and took the bag of sandwiches from Sabrina and asked, "What did you get?"

"I didn't know what you liked, so I grabbed an assortment." She watched as he pulled the sandwiches out one at a time and read the labels stuck to their outside wrappers. He kept the last one in his hand.

"Anybody care for egg salad?"

Sabrina and Jeff shook their heads no and Francine didn't bother to answer.

"Me either," Robinson said and left the room.

A few seconds later, they watched as he entered the interrogation room and placed the sandwich on the table in front of Albert. "Lunch," Robinson told him. "I'm going to eat mine and then I'll be back."

Albert didn't say anything and Robinson turned and left the room. When he had gone, Albert began to carefully unwrap the food, his vigil at the one way mirror finally ended.

"What the hell did you do that for?" Francine asked Robinson when he got back.

He walked past him and took his seat. "If you wanted the egg salad you should have said something sooner."

Baldridge still hadn't shown by the time Robinson was ready to continue with Albert. Sabrina followed him out of the observation room and asked him to wait in the hall.

"You know," she began. "I don't even know what to call you."

"Jim's fine. Or James. It doesn't matter," he said. He was impatient to get back to Albert.

She seemed to sense his mood and she grew more serious. "I want to apologize for bringing you up here. Since he's confessed I guess there's not much point in questioning him further."

"What about your story? Hell, what about your problems with the sheriff?"

"I'm not sure they matter any more."

"It always matters," Robinson told her. He studied her face. "Is this about me?"

"What do you mean?"

Robinson looked both ways up and down the quiet hallway. They were somewhere up on the second floor of the county courthouse building and except for two appearances by the sheriff's deputy they hadn't seen or heard anyone conducting any business. Even now the hallway was clear and silent. Still, though, he wasn't sure if he should tell her anything.

"Look, Sabrina," he said. It was the first time he had called her by her first name and they both noticed it. "I'll tell you what I'm thinking but it's not something you can report. It's off the record only. I'm not your story here."

"I understand," she said. "You never were." As she said the words she knew they weren't true. Of course he had been part of her story, she just wasn't sure how big a part it would turn out to be.

"The sheriff knew I was coming today, but where is he? If he's been guarding Albert as closely as you say, why would he just give him up to me now?" He held his arms out from his sides to indicate the hallway. "Where is everybody? Does this look like any courthouse you've ever been in? It's like a federal holiday in here."

She looked down the hallway then nodded as if she were agreeing with his point but the truth was she hadn't been in enough courthouses to notice anything amiss. "What are you getting at?"

"Why am I here? Who left that card on your van? They did it to get *me* up here. What for?"

Sabrina just shook her head.

"I need more time with the files but as far as I can see, all the sheriff has against this guy are his confessions, assuming they're real. Say all of the sudden Albert decides to ask for a lawyer and for some reason they get his confession thrown out. There's nothing left to get him on."

"What about the knife?"

"It *could* have been the weapon used in all seven killings, but the files say it's forensically impossible to prove that it is the actual knife that was used. It's circumstantial at best and by itself doesn't prove a damned thing."

Sabrina was quiet for a minute. "You think the sheriff may try to tank his own case?"

Robinson almost chuckled. "I suppose it's possible but I'm not saying that.

I know nothing about the man. But if I were you, I think I may want to find out where he's been today. It's probably nothing but I think it's damned strange for him not to be here."

"What are you going to do with Albert?"

"As long as the sheriff's not here and Francine isn't trying to interfere, I want to see how much Albert is willing to say. We have seven dead women and a man who professes to be the killer. He is the only witness we have. All we know about him comes from HRS files, the stuff that was in his apartment, and the fact that he's willing to eat an egg salad sandwich. I want to hear what the man has to tell us." He left her with that, unwilling to spend more time sharing his theories with her. He liked the woman, but she was the press, and seven years hadn't been long enough to be able to forget all he had been put through at their hands.

He paused at the door to the interrogation room and took a deep breath. With a glance back toward Sabrina, he said, "You can do me a favor if you'd like."

"Of course. What is it?"

"Keep Francine offline for a few minutes. Put the camera on him and ask him some questions so he'll have to pay attention to you. Can you do that?"

She nodded. "I can do that. Give me a minute to set it up. How much time do you need?"

"The question is how much time will he give me. I owe you for this." He knocked twice before going in.

"I think I owe you," Sabrina said to the door.

"So you want me to talk to you, is that it, Albert?"

Duprin installed the same grin he had had before lunch across his face. Small bits of egg salad and a smear of mayonaise stuck between his gums, making the yellow teeth appear dingier against the contrast of the white food.

"What is it you want me to say?" asked Robinson.

"I told you before."

Robinson nodded and stroked his beard. "Yes. You did." He nodded to himself as if he were carrying on a conversation inside his own head. "You know I'm not a cop any more."

"Of course."

"Do you know why?"

"Of course."

"Why?"

"You had already done it all."

"Done what, Albert?"

The voice that answered him was lower than Duprin's normal speaking voice and although he was only two feet away Robinson couldn't make out what he said. Robinson looked into Duprin's face and the eyes brightened when they met his.

Resisting the urge to look at the mirror, he leaned in close to Duprin. "What about the card, Albert? Where did you get it?"

"Card?"

"With the pelican. To Becky."

"I– I don't know–"

"It was wrapped in a sheet of paper with your name written on it. Your name, as in your signature."

There came a muted bump from the mirror. Damn, Robinson thought and slowly pulled back.

"Why have you only spoken to the sheriff, Albert?" He had to change direction.

"Because he's a great man."

"How do you know that?"

Albert looked puzzled. "Because he told me so. He understands."

Robinson leaned back in his chair, away from Albert. He didn't say anything for a few moments and Albert seemed content to work his Mona Lisa smile back onto his face.

"There was a girl from Tarpon Springs, Albert. Pretty girl, long blonde hair, straight, parted in the middle. Long legs, too, and she liked to show them. In fact, the only times I ever saw her she was showing off those long, thin legs. But never to me. She never even looked at me. You ever know any girls like that, Albert?"

Albert worked his head up and down in a long, slow nod. His chair could have been on fire but Robinson would have had his complete attention.

"She used to go down to the beach a lot. Her and a bunch of other girls. There was something about *her*, though. Something that made me watch *her*." Robinson stared into Albert's eyes, concentrating, imagining that his pupils were becoming like Albert's, that his face was taking on the same focused concentration. "I used to think about her all the time, I used to see her face in my dreams and whenever I closed my eyes. She lived in a one story house near a high school and at night I could fit my body between the hedge along the house and her bedroom window. The things I saw her do, Albert....

"She made me mad. You know what I mean, don't you? The way she used her body to get what she wanted. It wasn't right because I wanted to do to her what she was doing to everybody else. I wanted to have her, Albert, I

wanted to take her and I wanted her to know that I knew what she was doing. How evil and cruel she really was. And you know what that's like. I
know you do. I finally took her at the beach one night, near the water. And
before she was gone I made sure she knew what I was."

Albert's pupils were as small and sharp as they could be. The air in the
room seemed warmer, as if it were absorbing the heat coming off the two
men's bodies and forming a cloud that enveloped the table. Robinson and
Duprin were staring at each other, eye to eye, a breath by one matched by
a breath from the other. Their bodies were in the same rhythm, the same
tempo, and their minds were some place that one of them truly did not want
to be.

"Tell me, Albert," Robinson said, the words painful in his throat. "Tell me
what it was like for you."

Albert closed his eyes slowly and Robinson became aware of the sound of
the young man's breathing. Where was he right now? Where had he sent
him?

Several minutes passed. Robinson didn't move. Finally, he reached out and
touched one of Albert's hands. It was hot, like from fever, but there wasn't
any perspiration. Robinson pulled his own hand back. "Tell me, Albert," he
repeated.

The dark eyes flicked open, catching Robinson off guard. "I need to leave
here." The voice was the same low one that Albert had used earlier, only
slightly louder, more intelligible.

"You have to tell me something first."

Albert threw his head back and opened his mouth wide as if to scream but
instead accepted massive swallows of air into his lungs. His body had begun to shake and Robinson thought he might be having a seizure of some
kind. The shaking of his chains against the chair sounded like change being run through a counting machine at the bank. Between breaths a thin
wail escaped from Albert's pale throat. Robinson glanced at the mirror.

"I don't understand what you're saying, Albert," Robinson said.

"I can't," Duprin said, louder. "I can't...."

"Try for me, Albert."

Duprin's head came forward and his mouth closed. While Robinson
waited, the shaking gradually eased, the clinking of Albert's chains replaced
by the insect hum of the overhead lights.

"Tell me how you feel, Albert. Tell me about any one of them: Dorfman,
Brown, Stearns, Brantley, Mulcahy, Smith. Tell me about Skokie." Robinson
recited the names from memory. "Tell me about the first one, Albert."

Duprin licked his lips and shook his head. "No," he said. "I can't. Not her."

"Then tell me about the last one, Albert. Tell me about Lynnette Skokie.

How did you feel about her?"

Albert's breathing evened out and Robinson waited for him to say something. The grin had not reappeared and his eyelids drooped slowly and stopped halfway over his pupils. Robinson wasn't sure that Albert could still see him.

"The swamp," Albert began suddenly. "I left her in the swamp."

"How did you know her, Albert?"

"She was the same as all the others. I used to watch her while she was fishing."

"Is that how you chose her?"

"No."

"Tell me about Lynnette."

"You know about her. You know all about her."

"I want to know what made her different to you, Albert. Why did you choose her?"

"She spoke to me once while she was fishing. I was behind her, in the trees. She must have heard me because she called me out and asked who I was. After that I knew what I wanted to do with her."

"Because she spoke to you?"

"Because she spoke to me *that way*."

Robinson fought the temptation to ask him when this had happened, what day and what time, but he didn't want to break Albert's concentration, such as it was. "What else can you tell me about her? How many times did you see her?"

"Some. A lot. I don't know."

"Did you have sex with her, Albert?"

His eyelids drooped lower, almost closing but not completely. A tiny crack was left below the pupils. Robinson sensed panic. "Many times."

Robinson knew from the file that the forensic evidence here was sparse. He took a chance and asked, "Did you wear condoms?"

"Um, I always wear condoms."

That could explain something about all of the victims, though not much. "How did you kill her, Albert?"

Duprin's adam's apple worked up and down in his throat. His small, pointed tongue flicked out and ran across his dry lips. The chains clinked again as he began to move his hands back and forth against his leg. "I choked her."

"With what?"

The muscles in Albert's forehead began to contract and relax, contract and relax, matching a tempo inside his head. "Red scarf. I used my red scarf."

That's it, Robinson thought. The police had never released a critical piece of information, something they could use to separate the dozens of crack-pots that invariably tried to confess to crimes like this. A red silk scarf had been used to strangle at least four of the victims. Fibers had been found on the bodies of Dorfman, Stearns, Mulcahy and Wright. Brown and Brantley had been found while it was raining and Skokie had been in the swamp which could explain the absence of the material. With the exception of Brown and Brantley, Albert had just tied himself to five killings.

"What did you do with the hands, Albert?"

"The hands?"

"The right hands, Albert, that you took with you."

The forehead made a crease between his eyebrows and the motion of his hands stopped, silencing the chains and making the room seem quieter than before. "I took them with me," he repeated.

"Where? Where did you take them?"

The tongue made another dry appearance and Albert cleared his throat. "I buried her hand. I buried it with the scarf."

We're still on Skokie, Robinson thought. "In the swamp, Albert? Did you leave it in the swamp?"

Duprin's head slowly nodded up and down. His breathing became deep and regular and Robinson wondered if he could have fallen asleep. "Albert?" he asked gently. "Albert? I would like you to tell me why you took their hands."

Nothing.

It was difficult to ask, but Robinson didn't want to give it up now. "I never did something like that, Albert. I want to know why you did."

But Albert didn't answer.

He tried again with, "Could you show me where you buried the scarf, Albert? Could you draw me a map?"

"I'm tired. I want to sleep."

"Why did you bury the scarf, Albert? Why bury it now?"

"No," Albert worked his eyebrows furiously. "I strangled all of them with the scarf and I buried it." He opened his eyes all the way. "I want to sleep now."

After several minutes Robinson stood and left the room.

Back in the observation area, Sabrina and Jeff were quiet as Robinson seated himself at the table and began to dig through several of the case files. Francine stood up from his chair and couldn't seem to decide who he wanted to look at: Robinson or Duprin, who was seated at his table with his head in his hands.

Finally, he said to Robinson, "I'm not sure I feel very comfortable with you going back in there, cowboy."

"Why's that?" Robinson slowly closed the file he was looking at and turned his head to look at the FBI agent.

"The man has confessed to a half dozen capital crimes and all I see you do is go in there and swap war stories with him. Was I mistaken, sir, or did you actually share with him the fact that you are a murderer?"

"I never said that."

"Well, it sounded a hell of a lot like it to me."

Robinson ignored the implication of Francine's words. "Agent Francine, did Duprin have a way of getting back and forth from Jacksonville by himself?"

Francine hesitated, then pointed at the table. "It's in there somewhere. He's got a car, an old Ford T-bird. He could be there and back in an hour and a half, two hours."

"But was he? Is there anything actually tying Duprin's presence to Jacksonville?"

"How about five dead bodies?"

"What's wrong, James?" Sabrina asked. Jeff moved to the camera and began to swivel it on its tripod toward Robinson.

"Don't, Jeff," he said.

The cameraman hesitated and Sabrina shook her head. "Leave it off." Inside her, though, she knew Jeff would keep it running, at least pick up the audio.

"I'm not sure. I need him to tell me something about the girls in Jacksonville."

Francine looked even more uncomfortable. "I think you should be waiting for the sheriff to get here before you talk to him again."

"Oh?" Robinson asked. "As far as I know, he's the one who gave me permission to be here."

Sabrina stepped closer to the table, inserting herself between Robinson and Francine. "He told you he—" She thought about her friend Monica Brantley and the pictures she had seen of her, naked and bruised, large flakes of tree bark tangled in her hair.

Robinson stood, took her arm, and guided her to his chair. She resisted for a moment and then let him lead her. Damn it, she swore to herself fiercely.

Softly, he said, "Albert told me how he killed Lynnette Skokie but when I asked him about the others he wouldn't say anything."

"That's not unusual," came Francine's voice from behind him.

"No. No, it's not," Robinson continued in his same quiet tone. "But he said something else that doesn't add up."

"Why is it you want to know?" Sabrina asked him. She looked into his eyes and he held her gaze.

"I've studied a lot of men who do these things, Sabrina. Committing murder is not an immoral act to most of them. They don't show remorse because in their own minds they've done nothing wrong."

"I don't understand."

"If an animal like that picks up a girl, a total stranger, clubs her over the head and stuffs her into his car, he will do what he wants with her because she's nothing to him. Something about her flips his switch and the woman is nothing more than a thing, an object. She was never a person to him."

Sabrina shuddered but he kept going. "But if he knows her somehow, if he thinks of her as a real person, a personality, then he's done something wrong if he hurts her. He could even be ashamed of what he's done, probably the closest he can come to feeling bad about it."

"And you want him to feel bad about what he's done to those women," Sabrina stated. She missed the point but Robinson let it go.

"Something like that," he said. He didn't want to get into it further with Francine watching over his shoulder.

"Albert, you told me that you want to get to know me. Isn't that right?"

Duprin's eyes were wide open and the gleam was back in them, a reflection of the overhead lights. He nodded sagely.

"Then you have to help me a little bit more, partner. I have to ask you one more question."

A slow smile formed across Albert's lips, his eyes not blinking, staring at Robinson.

"Why did you say you killed those girls in Jacksonville when you didn't?"

Albert's eyes bulged from his sockets and his face froze, locked in an expression of shock.

"Tell me, Albert."

Slowly, Duprin worked his tongue in his mouth then swallowed. "But I did. I was with them all. I strangled them with the scarf."

"Which one didn't you strangle, Albert?"

Duprin's eyes dropped to the chains on his wrists. His head began to shake back and forth like a small child in denial.

"Did the sheriff put you up to this, Albert?" Robinson asked him quietly.

Albert looked up. "The sheriff's a great man, too," he said.

"You mentioned that before, Albert. What else did he tell you?"

In response Albert dropped his head again. It seemed as if he might begin to cry.

"Goodbye, Albert." Robinson pushed his chair back from the table and stood to leave.

Without looking up, Albert said, "Don't leave." The voice was thin and pitiful.

Robinson walked to the door. As it was closing behind him, he heard, "But you came all this way to see me." Francine was already in the hall with the deputy. He glared at Robinson.

"I'm leaving, Agent."

Sabrina met him in the hallway but Robinson spoke first. "I think we need to find the sheriff." His breathing was rapid and he felt like he wanted to do something with his hands. He had never smoked a cigarette in his life but he knew that if someone were to offer him one just then he would accept it.

"He's on TV," Sabrina said. "The deputy just told us. Baldridge is holding a press conference."

"Don't tell me. He's announcing the very grave confessions of Mr. Albert Duprin."

She nodded and said, "James, what's going on?"

Francine blurted, "What the hell was that all about?"

Robinson let the man walk all the way to them before he answered. "I think maybe the man you have in there didn't kill those women."

Francine snorted in disbelief. "Are you kidding me? I don't know why Baldridge let you in here." He looked at Sabrina, then back to Robinson. "That's not a man in there. Let me tell you what that is. Are you ready?"

Robinson stood mute.

"What you have in there is a hollow, empty monster. A flesh and blood clothes dummy tailor-made to model the latest in Death Row orange. And that's it. No former city detective with his own skeletons to hide is going to come in here and convince me otherwise. Jesus Christ." He swiped a set of fleshy fingers through his hair then squared his shoulders to Robinson. "I want to know what kind of reason you have for saying this crap. You two related, maybe? Or do you just like the way he listens to your shit?"

Sabrina grabbed Robinson's arm but he shrugged it off as he took a step toward the taller FBI agent. Jeff walked out of the observation room just then, his camera slung over his shoulder. Francine saw him and backed away from Robinson.

"Don't forget, Robinson. I heard what you said in there. You might be the next one through that door."

Sabrina took hold of Robinson's hand and tension ebbed away as he let her lead him down the hall toward the staircase. His face was empty as he turned away from Francine and that frightened Sabrina. Jeff edged past Francine and hurried to catch up with them.

CHAPTER FIVE

Jeff was driving the van with Sabrina sitting sideways on the passenger seat, half turned so she could see Robinson. He was sitting on the floor between the custom storage racks filled with audio/video equipment.

"Francine made me promise to send him a copy of the tape," Jeff said over the highway noise.

"What do you mean, 'made you'?"

"You had to be there, Bree."

"It's okay," Robinson said. "It doesn't matter." These were the first words he had spoken since the three of them had left the courthouse building.

They lapsed into an uneasy silence, each of them lost in their own thoughts. For his part, Jeff couldn't wait to drop Sabrina and Robinson off somewhere and get the footage he had taken onto the editing console. It was raw stuff but it was hard and Jeff thought he could put together something with tension, something with an edge.

Before he could ask, Sabrina said, "I guess we should head back to the motel."

Jeff nodded and estimated how long it would take to get there. They had already been headed in that direction anyway. Robinson didn't comment.

"Would you really have fought him?"

Robinson shook his head. His thoughts were far from Special Agent Timothy Francine of the FBI. "When I was younger, perhaps," he said.

"What stopped you now?"

Robinson looked at her, the pretty face blurred against the backdrop of the sun glare through the windshield behind her and wondered: is she always a reporter?

"There wouldn't be any point."

At the motel, Sabrina followed Robinson to his room with Jeff reluctantly in tow. He didn't want to leave her until she told him it was okay to go.

Inside, she sat on one of the two double beds while Jeff took the faded chair near the single round table just inside the door. Robinson walked to the sink and turned on the faucet, waiting for the water to get cold. After a moment, he splashed the coolness on his face and wiped it off with a towel as it dribbled through his beard and down his neck. He turned around. Sabrina was looking at him and Jeff was examining his own fingernails.

"What do you want me to do?" he asked.

Sabrina shrugged. "I don't know. Tell me why you said Duprin might be innocent."

"Because I don't think he killed those girls."

Again the gruesome, familiar images of Monica Brantley flashed across Sabrina's mind. She began to realize that in her own thoughts she had already been using the face and name of Albert Duprin as a means to a closure she hadn't known she'd needed. It was difficult to think of giving that up. "But why do you say that? He confessed, damn it."

"I just had the strong feeling that Albert wanted to talk." To *me*, he thought, which was spooky.

"And he did, didn't he?"

Robinson shook his head. "Not really. Other than the fact that he was eager to take the credit, did he really indicate that he knew anything about the crimes?"

Sabrina looked confused. Jeff was beginning to forget about rushing down to the editing equipment in the van. "What about the red scarf thing? Was that true?"

"Yes. That information was not released to the public. It is in the files, though."

"Doesn't that prove something?"

"The question is, what? Albert said he strangled each one of the girls." He stopped talking and waited.

"Rachel Stearns," Sabrina said. "She wasn't strangled."

"That's right," Robinson said.

"What if he was guilty," Jeff said. "But was just trying to tell you what you wanted to hear anyway? I mean, that's happened before, right? This guy obviously has some kind of hard-on for you. Maybe he was just trying to please you somehow."

"Who knows?" Robinson lay back on the bed with his arms folded behind his head. "But I look at those crime scene photos and read the reports and I don't see a killer who wants to be caught. Except for Skokie, all of the other girls were purposefully placed where they would be found. That's done by a person who thinks he can pull something over on the cops and the rest of the world." Just like B. J. Donnelly, he wanted to add. *You may have heard of him.* "Albert doesn't strike me as that person."

"So what are you really saying?" Sabrina asked. "That Albert isn't guilty? That he didn't kill anybody? What the hell do you think he was trying to do at Connie Putnam's house? Tie them up and tell them bedtime stories?"

Robinson sat up. Sabrina was close to breaking down; he could hear it in her voice.

Jeff stood and put his hands on her shoulders but she shrugged him off. "Damn," she swore. "I keep seeing the pictures of Monica's face against that tree. Behind her all I can see is a giant balloon in the shape of Albert Duprin and I want to take a long needle and burst it into a million goddamn little pieces."

A loud knock came at the door. Sabrina and Jeff both looked at Robinson who was studying Sabrina. Then he nodded at the door to Jeff. He seemed uncertain, as if something bad was about to happen, but he turned and opened it.

Sheriff Coleman Baldridge was standing at the threshold, his beefy frame outlined by the late afternoon sunlight that poured in behind him. "Well," he said. "Looks like this is where the party's at."

Jeff stepped aside as Baldridge walked into the room. Robinson stood and offered the larger man his hand. "You must be the famous Sheriff Baldridge." He kept his face serious but there was a light tone to his voice that was out of place. Baldridge's eyes twitched behind his sunglasses as they shook. He wasn't sure if he was being mocked.

"And you're the infamous James Robinson." He squeezed hard enough to make a point. In his left hand was a video tape case that he tossed back to Jeff. "Here's what you missed today, sport." He looked at Sabrina. "Don't worry, it wasn't much. Just shootin' the breeze with some of your colleagues and it kind of grew into a little something more." He turned back to Robinson. "Heard you had a little fun, though."

"I just talked to your prisoner, Sheriff."

"And created a bit of a commotion, I understand."

"I don't know, I thought it was pretty routine."

Baldridge lifted the wrinkles in his forehead with his eyebrows. "Is that so? That damned feeb seemed to have a different idea."

"Oh?"

"Hm hmm. He seemed to think you were trying to stir something up. Said you swapped some war stories. Then he said you thought our young Mr. Duprin may not have done the crimes."

"Did he really?"

"How about that." The sheriff took his hat off his head and drew a uniformed forearm across his hairline, then pushed the hat back down on his head. "Any truth to that?"

"To what? That Duprin is innocent? You tell me. I understand that you're the only one he talks to."

"Until today, that was true. Listen," he said and took a step closer to Robinson. "The man did it and he said so." He pointed to Jeff. "Watch the tape I gave the young buck there. Duprin had the knife, he's an honest to God psychopath, and we caught him red-handed going after a family of women, or didn't your friends here tell you about that? You want to start singing about this nutcase's innocence you go right ahead. But I'd remember something more if I were you."

"What would that be, Sheriff?"

"Nothing much," he said. "But with your history I don't think you're going to find a whole lot of people willing to listen to what it is you've got to say."

He turned and touched the brim of his hat with his thumb and forefinger as he nodded to Sabrina. "Ms. Wells," he said, then, "Jeff." A moment later the door closed behind him and he was gone.

Robinson sat down again on the bed and stared at the wall. After a minute, he heard Sabrina say, "Why didn't you ask him anything about Albert?" She was confused and her voice sounded tired.

"Because," he said. "If Albert didn't do it, someone who knew about it had to tell him about the red scarf."

Sabrina thought about this for a moment. She looked at Jeff and had no idea what he was thinking. He was bouncing the tape Baldridge had tossed him up and down in his left hand as if he were trying to guess its weight. She turned back to Robinson. "At least you didn't want to fight him."

"Give me time."

He was joking, she knew, but she still felt irritated at his answer. "So what now?"

Robinson knew what she meant but said, "I'll stay the night and in the morning I'm heading back to Tampa."

"What about Baldridge?"

"What about the situation in the Middle East? What about higher taxes, missing school children and puppy farms? What about baby seals? You're the one that thinks Baldridge is being shady—here's more conspiracy theory stuff for you."

"None of that's the point and you know it. This is a thing that you can actually do something about."

Robinson turned to face her, annoyance showing on his face and in his voice. "Who really left the card on your van?"

"What?"

Robinson studied her face. "You tried to talk me into coming up here. I didn't want to. At the last minute you pull out that card, and it worked. I came. I appeared in your film, you can add me to your story. But now I'm done."

Sabrina took a deep breath, and sat back on the bed. "You think I lied to you?"

"Tell me where you got the card."

"I already did." Defiant.

Robinson looked at Jeff.

"It was left on the van, dude. Swear to God."

He felt like punching the wall. All the old frustrations, the injustices, were seething through him again. All the baggage he'd left behind.

"You don't need me for your story."

Sabrina got up and moved to stand in front of him. Her voice was shaky and he could see lines of moisture at the bottom of her eyes for the second time today. "Is that all you think this is to me? A story?"

In spite of himself, Robinson was shaken. "I don't know," he said.

"You have no idea what I want, goddamn it. This has nothing to do with the news or my job or anything at all with me. It's those women, it's Monica Brantley propped against a tree naked and waiting for the sun to rise, something she'd never see again. It's about what happened to those other girls and what's going to go on happening as long as we let it. What could just as easily happen to any one of us."

From the corner of the room by the door, Jeff said, "Bree–" but didn't go further.

A part of Robinson, the part of him that had swelled and filled most of him since he had left the police force years ago, wanted to tell her that it didn't matter. Nothing they did would protect the Monica Brantleys of the world and there wasn't anything they could do to make the world safe from people like Albert Duprin or Coleman Baldridge. Or B. J. Donnelly. But he didn't.

"Other than you, Sabrina, who would have wanted me up here?"

She shook her head. "I don't know. I really don't."

He reached back to a part of himself that he hadn't been in touch with for a very long time and he said gently, "Tell me what you want me to do."

They started with the tape that Baldridge had left them. It was a one inch tape, the kind used in professional cameras, so they knew the sheriff was on more than casual terms with another reporter. That should have bothered Sabrina but it didn't. The documentary for Baldridge's benefit had been something of a ruse from the start anyway.

Jeff showed them the tape on the equipment installed in the back of the van and afterwards they returned to Robinson's room. The tape hadn't been anything more than Baldridge showing himself off to a few selected members of the press. His presentation of the confession was offhanded, almost conversational, as he came across as a local, caring law enforcement official whose job occasionally called for him to deal with such monumental tragedies. It didn't tell any of them what they didn't already know.

"You two have been up here longer than me," Robinson said. "Do you have any idea what's going on?"

Jeff shrugged and dragged a package of beef jerky out of his shirt pocket. Sabrina ignored him and stood up, not wanting to think about food just then. "If Albert is innocent, than the sheriff must be getting something out of it, right?"

"You're here. Your colleagues and competitors are here. Along with a couple thousand of your closest friends."

"A lot more people than that have been watching this story. Baldridge is becoming more well known every day."

"And that can turn into a lot of clout for a man like him."

Sabrina shook her head. Something was bothering her. "But it's not enough," she said. "It couldn't last."

"Why?" Robinson asked, leading her.

"Because if Albert didn't do it, the real killer is still out there."

"And eventually he'll kill again."

Sabrina sat down on the bed next to Robinson. The breeze from the air conditioner carried the greasy meat smell of Jeff's snack food across the room.

"So the sheriff's run of popularity will last exactly until the next body turns up. What is he going to do then?"

When Robinson didn't answer, she said, "I can't imagine he's just going through all this to say, whoops, maybe ol' Albert didn't do it after all."

"Never underestimate what some people will do for fame," Jeff tossed in.

The two of them were looking at Robinson, waiting for his opinion. "There is another possibility."

Sabrina said: "And that is...."

"That the good sheriff knows something more about these crimes than we do, and that with the production of Albert Duprin as the guilty party, whatever it is might not come to light."

"What do you think it could be?"

"I have no idea," he said carefully.

Sabrina thought for a few moments. Then she turned around and asked Jeff, "Do you still have the stuff we shot at the first press conference here?"

"You mean in Holton? Yeah, I've got copies of that in my room."

Sabrina turned to Robinson and grabbed his knee. "We need to look at that tape. There may be something on it that will help."

"Such as?"

"I'm not sure. But there was something that seemed a little strange at the time. Let's go."

"Who is he?" Robinson asked after they had watched the tape.

Sabrina flipped through the pages of a small notebook she had pulled from her purse. "His name is Ben Colfax. He's a stringer for the local paper."

"I didn't know they had one."

"It's mostly things like shopping news and video store coupons. What's on special at the liquor store this week, that kind of thing."

"Is he still covering this story?"

Sabrina looked at Jeff. "I haven't seen him since that first week. Have you?" Jeff shook his head, the tail of a beef jerky stick wagging back and forth in his mouth.

"Run it again, please," Robinson said.

They watched twice more as the old reporter put the sheriff on the spot with a question that clearly seemed to make Baldridge uncomfortable: had there been some kind of connection between the sheriff and Lynnette Skokie?

"We need to find this guy."

CHAPTER SIX

He was alone in his room but he couldn't sleep. He alternated between flicking through the cable TV channels and rolling back and forth on the bed trying to find a position that was comfortable enough to bring him sleep. Nothing he did seemed to help.

The analog clock on the bedside table told him it was just after two o'clock in the morning. He could feel the fatigue behind his eyes but every time he tried to coax it forward it ran out of the dark and hid behind something light and distracting. Again he flicked on the TV with the remote control and scanned through the channels. Trying like hell to find something interesting enough to put him out.

On one of the movie channels was a film that had a man sitting in a prison cell recounting the sins of his life to a priest. If he had just made a few different choices, he cried, his life would have been totally changed. He wasn't a bad guy, not really. Things just kind of turned out that way, you know? Life's a little funny like that. A quarter turn the other way and *he* could have been the one sitting there with the round white collar around his neck, listening to some piece of shit talk his last fifteen minutes of life away.

Even in the movies, Robinson thought. Even in the movies it's not their fault.

Robinson turned off the TV and imagined B. J. Donnelly giving that same speech the actor had just made. It wouldn't have worked. Where the actor elicited sympathy as a basically good man who'd made a mistake or two, B. J. would have been working the priest, trying to get an extra novena or rosary or something. The audience would despise him.

And what about Albert? Robinson stuffed a pillow under his head and stared at the ceiling in the dark. How would he come across in the big repentance scene?

The last thing Robinson could recall thinking that night was of an image of Albert sitting calmly on a chair in front of a priest. His shirt would be neat and nearly wrinkle free. On his face would be an ear to ear grin and a gleam in his eye as he told the world, "I killed those girls. I killed everybody. Then I used their hands to touch me."

Sabrina woke him the next morning. It took more than one round of her knocking, then some pounding on the door before he woke up enough to know what was happening. He pulled on a pair of pants and unlocked the door. "Come on in," he said.

She entered holding a styrofoam cup of coffee that was obviously for him. He took it, said thank you, then set it on the bureau as he made his way to the bathroom sink. "You look like hell," she told him.

"Oh, I'm sorry," he said. "Good morning to you, too."

"Didn't sleep well?"

He turned the water on in the sink and splashed several handfuls onto his face. "Just not much. What time is it?"

"Not too early to be going after Ben Colfax. I already talked to the paper. Should I tell you what they said now or do you want me to wait until you regain full consciousness?"

"No, go ahead."

"It seems Mr. Colfax is no longer employed by the *Holton Examiner*. He was let go a week and a half ago."

"Did they say why?"

"Nope."

"How long had he worked there?"

"Twenty seven years," she said. "I asked that, too. I don't think the person I was speaking to was very pleased to see Colfax go. She sounded upset when I brought it up but she wouldn't say any more than that."

"We really need to find this guy."

"Well, clean yourself up." Sabrina pushed off the wall she had been leaning against. "Take a shower and meet me downstairs when you're through.

According to the woman at the paper, old Ben is probably out fishing the river this morning. She said that was all he ever talked about doing when he left the paper."

A man behind the counter of a roadside bait and tackle shop told them about a gravel turnoff near the river where they could find a number of trails that lined both sides of the river. He suggested that if they worked their way north they should have a pretty good chance of finding somebody doing a little fishing. And for fifty bucks, he told them, he'd guide them himself. Robinson told him no thank you and they left. "You still didn't buy anything," the man called after them.

Jeff hadn't been with Sabrina when Robinson had gone downstairs after his shower. He wanted to begin work on editing the footage they already had and Sabrina thought they could get away without filming anything that day. If they found Colfax and he had something to say, they could always come back. Regardless, they had to have something to send back to the station to justify their stay.

Sabrina and Robinson locked the doors of his truck and together walked along the edge of the sandy gravel until they found an opening into the trees. With Sabrina leading, they pushed their way through weeds and branches on a blanket of reddish brown needles. As they entered the shade, swirling clouds of dust and gnats formed about their faces.

"What do we do if we can't find him?" Sabrina asked from the front as she waved a hand in front of her face.

Robinson's body was strong but he could still feel the lack of sleep behind his eyes. He was doing his best to ignore the bugs and he hoped that Sabrina wasn't in the mood to begin any long conversations. "We'll go back to his house and wait for him there. Let's give this a good try first, though."

The trees thinned out after about a hundred yards and the sunlight was enough to keep most of the insects in the shade. Almost all of the time the river was in view to their left, often just a few yards away. "This is pretty, isn't it?" Sabrina said. "Makes you forget the rest of the world is even out there."

Until you find the body of a strangled young woman lying on the bank beneath you, parts of her eaten by ants, maggots and raccoons. The rest of the world may be forgotten but there's another one in here, too. "Yeah, it's beautiful," he said.

Several boats passed by in both directions but none of them carried anybody that looked like the man in the video tape. When they did find him a little over an hour after they had started, they almost walked right on by. If they hadn't heard a muffled "Damn!" followed by a loud splash in the water, they would have.

Sabrina almost slipped down the steep riverbank as she left the path to investigate the sound. Robinson tried to catch her but almost fell himself. Sabrina grabbed hold of a handful of weeds and was able to keep from sliding the rest of the way down. "Hello?" she called.

"Who's there?" The voice was startled and had a rough edge to it. "I don't need any company down here."

Sabrina made her way down to where the voice was coming from. When Robinson caught up to her, she was standing in six inches of moving water looking at a man who was six feet from shore. He was wearing a pair of black rubber hip waders, an old hat, and a pair of Ray-Ban sunglasses. As Robinson came the rest of the way down the bank he had no choice but to step in the water next to Sabrina.

"You're Ben Colfax, aren't you?" she asked.

"Who wants to know?" In his hands was a fly casting rod but he wasn't moving. His eyes flickered back and forth from Sabrina to Robinson.

"Relax, Mr. Colfax," Robinson said. "This is Sabrina Wells from Channel Seven over in Jacksonville. I think you may have met her at a news conference you both were at a few weeks ago." Sabrina smiled her on-camera smile and Robinson was pleased he had decided to introduce her first. The old man seemed to relax a little.

"I knew this was coming," he said and shook his head slowly. "I never should have opened my big mouth. Huge mistake." To Robinson: "Who might you be?"

"James Robinson, sir. I'm a friend of Ms. Wells."

The old man's eyes squinted behind his sunglasses as he took them both in. "You're more than that and we both know it. Tell me what you want from me."

"Do we have to stand here in the water, Mr. Colfax?" Sabrina asked. "My feet are getting wet."

"Looks like they already are," he said. "I came here to fish and that's what I'm going to do. If a couple of strangers stop to make conversation, there's nothing I can do to help any of that." He turned and worked his reel, then cast his fly across the river and beneath the shade of a tree several yards from the other bank.

Sabrina looked at Robinson and he nodded at her to speak. "Mr. Colfax, I was there at the news conference when Sheriff Baldridge talked about the body that was found in the swamp. Acutally, I stood right next to you."

"Damn fish don't know good action when the hook bounces off their snouts. Look at this." He was gathering up the spent line in his reel as he prepared for another cast.

"You said something kind of interesting back there. Something about a relationship between the sheriff and the murdered girl. Was there any truth to what you said, sir?"

Colfax gave a chuckle then sent his hook whizzing through the air to land an inch or so from his previous cast. "Old Coleman, he didn't like that one, did he? The little bastard. I thought his old daddy was an ass but he didn't skimp when he handed things down to his little boy."

"So it was true? There was something going on between Sheriff Baldridge and Lynnette Skokie?"

The old man looked down at the water as he spoke. The humor was gone from his voice and he sounded genuinely sad. "People told me Lynnette was a good girl. She didn't deserve treatment like she got. I didn't know her well but I saw her down here often enough."

"With the sheriff?" Robinson asked.

Colfax nodded. "Usually. At least for the past three months or so."

"What were they doing?"

The old fisherman turned around and looked at Sabrina first, then back to Robinson. "Now what do you think two people would be doing down here, alone, with neither one of them anything to catch a fish with?"

"Did anybody else know about the two of them?"

"Didn't seem like it. You hear anybody else bring it up? You see anybody else lose their job over it?"

Robinson said, "Mr. Colfax, are you saying your knowledge of Sheriff Baldridge's relationship with Lynnette Skokie was the reason you were let go at the *Examiner*?"

He chuckled again then readied himself for another cast. "William Reelfs owns that paper. Didn't used to spend too much time worrying about what I put in it, either. Until that news conference, that is. Did I mention that he and Cole Baldridge play cards every Thursday night at Baldridge's home in Macclenny? Hear he makes a hell of a bean dip, that one. And he's not too good at poker, either." Again he hit the same spot as before with his hook, slowly taking in the line with smooth turns of the reel as he jerked the rod up and down, side to side.

"Do you know of any reason that Sheriff Baldridge might want to see something happen to Lynnette Skokie?"

"Those are harsh words, miss," Colfax said without turning around. "You just ask yourself: a seventeen year old high school girl like that messing around with a forty two year elected officer of the law, that wouldn't look too good if that got around the county, would it? And they didn't seem to get on famously all the times I saw them down here, if you know what I mean."

"Do you realize what you're implying, sir?"

"Yup," he said, drawing in more line. "But I'm just a fisherman now, boys and girls. And you're just two hikers who need to get back up on that trail there before the next boat comes by and somebody starts talking. Something might come out that could interfere with my fishing."

"One more thing, Mr. Colfax, and we'll leave you," Robinson said. The low rumblings of a small motor could be heard coming downstream from their right. "What do you know about Albert Duprin?"

"Never met the boy," Colfax said. "But I'd say he's in for a world of hurt being on the wrong side of Coleman Baldridge. Now get the hell up that bank and out of my face. Hurry on now."

Back at Robinson's truck, Sabrina manipulated the controls of the air conditioning and sent cool streams of dusty air into both of their faces. Robinson watched her as she pulled the sun visor down on the passenger side and used the mirror to guide her as she worked her chestnut brown hair into place. "I should have put it in a pony tail," she said.

Robinson didn't answer. She was gorgeous and anyone could see how this woman belonged in front of a camera, no matter what her hair looked like. She seemed to do all right climbing through the trees above the river, too.

Sabrina saw him watching her and was polite enough to ignore it. It seemed that she could never get a handle on what was going through that man's mind. "What do we do next?" she asked him.

"Do you have it in your notebook about how the body was found?"

Sabrina reached for her bag on the floor and pulled out the small loose leaf binder. "Two locals found her on their way into the swamp." She found the right page. "Frank Grayton and Willie Meisner."

"Did you talk to them?"

"One of them. Grayton. He and his friend found Lynnette's body. He took some pictures, called the sheriff. Baldridge sent them home."

"How close to the body did they get?"

"Grayton had a camera with him. He said he took pictures of the scene while they waited for the sheriff."

Robinson sat back in his seat. "Anything in the pictures?"

"We haven't seen them. Grayton said he gave the undeveloped roll to Baldridge and that was that."

Thinking of the case files he'd seen, Robinson said, "I don't remember any pictures of the Skokie girl that weren't taken by the police." He thought some more. "Would Baldridge be keeping them to himself for some reason?"

"What?"

Robinson shook his head. "Just thinking out loud. But it's something."

"What do you mean?"

"Well," he started, feeling his old instincts again. "It just doesn't seem kosher. I don't know the sheriff or how he does things but this has a feel to it."

"So you're a cop again." Sabrina smiled. "What kind of feeling?"

"Well, he's either incredibly careless or he's hiding something. And I'm not a cop."

"What could he be hiding?"

Robinson looked at her. "Really?"

Sabrina blushed. "Sorry. If he's hiding something, we wouldn't know what it is, would we?"

"And it could be for a perfectly valid reason," he said, liking the color in her face. "Maybe the film didn't turn out, something like that."

"The first one did."

"What?"

Sabrina told him what Frank Grayton had said about taking the last picture on his roll before changing the film which he later gave to the sheriff.

"So you have this negative?"

"Right here." She patted her brief case.

Robinson was quiet as he drove, noting the height of the huge pines lining the road.

"What do you want to do next?" Sabrina asked as Robinson headed toward the motel. She had the air conditioning going full bore again, trying to dry the layer of perspiration and dust that had been glued to her skin most of the day. Her shoes and jeans up to her knees were soaked through.

"The same as you, I suspect. A good strong shower and some clean clothes." And perhaps a Budweiser or two.

Sabrina slapped the tops of her legs lightly and watched a small cloud of dust push upwards from each denim covered thigh, then drift into her cotton tee shirt. "What about the pictures? Do you want to see if we can find the sheriff tonight?"

"I'd just as soon see what's on that negative, first. It's only one picture taken by a fork lift driver with a drug store camera. Chances are the reason we haven't seen any of the pictures is because they're of various aspects of Frank Grayton's thumb."

"There's a same day photo processing shop in Macclenny near the courthouse."

Robinson could tell that Sabrina didn't want to be through for the day. It was almost six o'clock in the evening and he wanted a chance to relax and think about what they had learned the past few hours. If the sheriff could be romantically linked to Lynnette Skokie, a young woman little more than a girl, then perhaps there was a motive there for the sheriff not wanting to see a full scale investigation into her death. Someone like Ben Colfax might put the two of them together officially and that could be disastrous for Baldridge's career. It would be the end of a bubba like him.

But does that make Albert just a patsy? Then what was he doing at the Putnam's house with a large knife and three bound and gagged women? Could Baldridge have set him up?

"We'll stop there first," he said, meaning the photo shop. "Tomorrow maybe we can talk to that lieutenant over in Jacksonville about how well they can place Albert Duprin at the scenes of the crimes."

"Great," Sabrina said. She was relieved and he could hear it in her voice. He knew she had been afraid that at any moment he'd drop her off and head back to Tampa, a thought that had been in his mind dozens of times since the day before. The problem was, he thought, he was becoming fascinated again, not so much by the case itself, but by being on the scent; trying to solve a puzzle that was thrown at them from a maniac who was attacking and butchering young women. For the first time in years he felt like he might be doing something substantial or significant. He wasn't sure he wanted to let it go so easily. And he liked the company.

"Your enthusiasm is contagious. You're quite good at this, you know."

She felt complimented and a little heat rose to her face. She turned toward the window so he wouldn't see. "I'll buy you dinner after we clean up," Sabrina said and held her breath. Oh my God, she thought. Where did that come from? I can't believe I said that out loud.

But Robinson only chuckled. "You've got a deal," was all he said, and she was glad.

Dinner was short mostly because Jeff did most of the talking and Robinson didn't want to listen to a lot of it. It was helpful, though, to hear him talk about the events at the Putnam house and his collision with Albert Duprin. When it was over, they went back to the motel and Robinson asked if he could see the tape of the interview with Frank Grayton.

Jeff looked at Sabrina and hoped she'd say tomorrow would do. She didn't. As he hauled his equipment from the van, Robinson unlocked his room door and stood aside for Sabrina. They cleared the table for Jeff and sat on the edge of the bed, next to each other, waiting.

"Okay, here it is," Jeff told them.

On screen, Sabrina did a quick introduction and asked Frank Grayton to talk about the morning when Lynnette Skokie had been found.

"I ain't never seen anything like that before," Grayton said to the camera. "Never in my whole life. She looked like she was just floating there with her head down, peaceful as could be."

"We were wondering if you could tell us anything more about that day."

"What is it you want to know?"

"Just talk about everything as it happened."

"Okay." Grayton paused for a moment and then began his story.

"My boy Willie and me, we was going out fishing that morning. We hit that same spot in the swamp once or twice a year, no big deal. My daddy used to take me back there when I was a kid."

"That's Willie Meisner?" Sabrina asked.

"Yep. He's my ex-wife's cousin. Scared hell out of him what we saw that morning."

"Why was that, exactly?"

"We don't see too much of that sort of thing up here. This ain't your big city. If it were up to Willie, he'd have been out of there as soon as he understood what it was he was looking at. I had my camera in the truck, though, and I thought it would be smart of me to use it before we left. I made Willie wait by the truck while I shot the whole roll of it. Twenty four exposures, it was, something like that."

"What happened to that film, Mr. Grayton?"

"Gave it to the sheriff when he showed up."

"What exactly did you take pictures of?"

"That whole place. I didn't touch the body, you know. I got as close to the water as I could without going in and I got a couple of her that way but she was about six or eight feet out. The rest I took of the trees and the ground all around the water's edge. Then I took a couple of the way we drove in."

"Did Willie take any pictures?"

"Nope. It was just me with the camera."

"What did the sheriff say after you gave him the film?"

"Nothing. He just told us to get the hell out of there and we did. Willie about jumped out of his skin when the man said we could go."

"Can you remember anything new about the scene since the time you last saw the sheriff?"

This time Frank Grayton's face flushed a bright red beneath his beard as he stared at the beautiful celebrity across from him. "I got to be honest with you," he told her. "I took most of those pictures to cover our butts. I didn't want nothing coming back on me and Willie just 'cause we were the ones who found her. I took pictures of every damn thing. I don't remember nothing else."

"It's okay, Mr. Grayton." Sabrina gave him an encouraging smile. "By the way, did you know her, Mr. Grayton? Lynnette Skokie?"

"Naw, not to speak to, anyways. I may have seen her around here and there. You know."

"Yes, Mr. Grayton, I know." Sabrina nodded at Jeff and the camera cut out.

"Well," Robinson said. "That's not very helpful. Other than the negative."

An image popped back onto the screen. It was Sabrina holding the receipt Grayton had got from Francine for the one print of the crime scene.

"Hold it there," Robinson said, his voice tight.

"What is it?" Sabrina asked as Jeff paused the display.

Clearly legible was every word that Francine had written.

"What's wrong, Jim? Tell me."

Robinson's fingers were clutched tightly into the bed covers. "I– I have to think about this," he said.

CHAPTER SEVEN

The little photo shop didn't open until nine o'clock and Robinson waited impatiently until a clerk showed up at three minutes to and opened the door. The clerk, a young man with his hair pulled back into a pony tail, kept him waiting another five minutes while he put on a work apron and turned on the machinery. Eventually he came back to the counter and asked Robinson how he could help him.

Robinson dropped the packet of film negatives on the counter between them. "I need these developed as soon as possible."

The man pulled an envelope off of a stack and began writing on it. "Name?" he asked.

"You don't need it," Robinson said. "I'll wait for the pictures."

The man looked up at him and grinned. "That's okay. I know who you are anyway." He bent back to the task of filling out the header on the envelope and Robinson watched as the man printed something that looked like his name in an almost indecipherable scrawl. He knew how things were in a small town; he didn't need to ask how the man knew who he was.

"My name's Darryl," the clerk offered as he tore the numbered strip off the flap and handed it to Robinson. "It'll gonna take me about an hour or so to do these."

"Thanks, Darryl," Robinson said. "I'll be around here somewhere."

He walked outside into the already humid morning air. There was still fog surrounding the outlying trees and the sky could only be seen through a layer of white haze. It probably wouldn't burn off until Robinson's pictures had been developed. There was a set of white plastic lawn chairs on the sidewalk outside a frozen yogurt shop and Robinson sat in one of those and closed his eyes.

The first thing he thought about was the note that had been left on Sabrina Wells' van. There were only a few people that could have left it there and the only one he knew who couldn't have was Albert Duprin, already in jail at the time. He wondered, not for the first time, if Sabrina herself could have somehow been behind it. There would be a story there but it didn't make sense. She was too naive, too young–she couldn't have any connection back to Becky Owens, at least none that he could make out. Jeff was just her cameraman. And clearly that was all.

He couldn't help but think good things of Sabrina. Her physicality was part of it; she was attractive and driven and hungry for a story. Not just any story, but this story. Whether she'd been close with the victim she'd known or not, it didn't matter to her. Her instincts told her something was wrong here, and she was doing her best to find out what it was.

The sun broke through and shone brightly on his face. He turned his chair to keep it from his eyes. When he had stopped drinking in bars he'd stopped going anywhere and he'd stopped meeting women. They were never the right ones, anyway. Being with Sabrina felt good because they were there for a different purpose altogether. He could like her without maneuvering. It made things easier.

The rest of his misgivings about being involved with this thing had filled his mind as soon as he'd stepped out of the shower the night before. Sheriff Baldridge was on the television, proudly conveying nuggets of information from Albert Duprin's purported confession. He knew Sabrina was in the crowd of reporters but couldn't see her.

Nothing new came out of the session, at least to him, and Baldridge came off as he always did, as the kind but stern big brother that wouldn't let anything truly bad happen to his constituents. At least not on television. All of his personal PR and schemings seemed to keep paying off for the man; he was being treated as a true hero and celebrity.

Robinson had uncapped a lukewarm bottle of beer and taken a long pull. When he was through, he toasted the screen and said, "Here's to you, Hollander, wherever you are." Sergeant Hugh Hollander of the Bradenton PD had passed away two years earlier following a massive stroke. Another cop who had sought recognition with a murderer the same way Baldridge was doing, although that time it had been at Robinson's expense.

Fat old bastard, Robinson thought. He had access to Duprin, could surely find Sabrina's van, but how would he have gotten the card? Again he wondered if it could have somehow come from Albert's apartment but that just pushed the question further down the line: how would Albert have come to possess it?

The next morning at breakfast Sabrina announced that she and Jeff would try to find the sheriff. She wanted the camera rolling when she asked Baldridge about the missing pictures taken by Frank Grayton. "What do you expect him to say?" Robinson had asked her.

"I don't know," she'd replied. "But it beats waiting around for a roll of pictures of some guy's jon boat to be developed. Besides, I want to keep a camera in his face, keep the documentary thing going as long as we can."

Now he stretched into a yawn and checked his watch. Quarter past the hour. He folded his arms across his chest and closed his eyes again, thought it wouldn't be a bad thing to take a nap. The best times for him to relax were always the ones where he was forced to do nothing, like now, so he didn't mind.

Forty five minutes to wait.

The sleep never really came: too many random thoughts, too few passersby walking in front of him arrhythmically. After a while he gave up trying and thought about Sabrina and how her hair would look this morning. Long for the camera, he thought. He got up to stretch his legs, then walked around the block. Finally he headed back to the store.

Darryl was waiting for him at the counter when he returned shortly after ten. His stupid smile was gone and he couldn't seem to decide where he wanted to look. "Hey, man," he said. "I got your pictures done."

Robinson held out his hand and Darryl pushed a yellow envelope across the counter while looking down and to his left. Robinson ignored him and pulled out a set of prints, flipping through the shots of a camo painted flat-bottomed boat with a Bondo plug the size of a bowling ball in the hull. He stopped when he got to the very last picture.

It was clearly a body, unnaturally light against the dark black and green background of the swamp. Robinson recognized the same pattern of long blonde hair floating on the water that he had seen in the official crime scene photos. Grayton must have taken the picture with his camera's built in zoom because the foreground was all water. The forest was visible but out of focus to either side and the area behind the floating girl was another ten feet or so of swamp water.

He was about to put it down so he could pay the pony-tailed man and leave when he noticed something that shouldn't be there. Darryl, who had suddenly focused on Robinson's face, asked, "What's wrong?"

"Do you have a magnifying glass that I could use, please? Or a loop? Anything like that?"

Darryl licked his lips but nodded his head. "Sure, man," he said. "Come around back here." He pulled aside a swinging gate and Robinson walked through, leaving the boat pictures behind on the counter. Mounted on a telescoping arm bolted to the edge of a small table next to the developing machine was a large magnifying glass about six inches across. "Help yourself."

Robinson sat down in the chair and pulled the lens toward him. He could feel Darryl hovering over his shoulder but he didn't care. The details of Lynnette Elizabeth Skokie's body leapt out at him and he moved the photo away for better focus.

She was floating face down with her body pointed toward the lower left hand corner of the photo. Her legs were slightly spreadeagled and from her knees down her legs were below the surface. But it was the end of the right arm that had caught Robinson's eye.

When Frank Grayton and his friend Willie had come across the body of Lynnette Skokie and taken this picture, something was different from when the police had pulled her body out of the swamp several hours later. Very different. When Lynnette Skokie had been found the first time, she had been in definite and unquestionable possession of both of her hands.

Robinson pushed himself away from the table and stepped to the counter, not bothering to go out the gate. "What do I owe you?" he asked as he put the photo on top of the others and tucked them all away in their envelope. Darryl told him and Robinson dropped a bill on the counter and said, "Keep it." Then he left, not looking back.

Darryl worked the cash register, gladly pocketing the change, and wondered what it was that had so captivated the former cop from Tampa. Yeah, he had looked at the body but he hadn't seen anything unusual about it. Not that he had looked at a lot of pictures of dead bodies before but after a few minutes it didn't seem all that exciting. It was kind of ugly actually, and it made him feel sort of funny for staring at it so much. Unfortunately, the man had come back before he had had a chance to make an extra copy for himself. He would have done it just in case. You never knew what the value of a souvenir like that might turn out to be.

Still though, it had been exciting being so close to that guy and to see the picture of the girl who had been such a big part of the news lately. Most things like that just stay on TV and in the newspaper, they don't walk into your workplace at nine o'clock on a weekday morning. That was something special. He had never heard of Lynnette Skokie before, but that might have made everything feel worse. This way it was just an anonymous thrill.

Darryl was buzzing and he didn't want to sit still, didn't want to start on the rest of his work. He reached for the phone and pulled it across the counter, lifting the receiver from the hook. At least he could talk this over with his cousin, Hank, tell him what had happened. After all, Hank worked for the sheriff, didn't he? There had to be some advantage to being related to a real Baker County sheriff's deputy. Lord knows he hadn't ever fixed a ticket for him or anything like that. Well, Darryl thought, we'll see what he thinks of his little cousin now.

He couldn't miss the bright white van with the red number seven painted on the door, parked half a block away from the Baker County courthouse. Robinson pulled into a handicapped space directly in front of the main entrance and vaulted up the steps, then moved in a half run inside to the sheriff's office.

"Is the crew from Channel Seven in here?" he asked the startled secretary.

"No," the woman answered. "I haven't seen them but I just got here myself."

"Where's the sheriff?"

The woman didn't answer right away. She looked around the room slowly, trying to regain her control. "He isn't here," she said. "Guess he must be upstairs. Is there an emergency?"

Robinson pounded the woman's desk knowing it would make her jump but not waiting to see. He ran down the hall to a set of wide stone steps and took them three at a time. He was assuming that 'upstairs' meant the area where he had met with Albert Duprin.

A deputy intercepted him as he moved down the second floor hallway but Robinson sidestepped him, asking, "Where's Baldridge?" on his way past. The deputy hesitated, then pointed to the door he had just come out of, five feet to the other side of Robinson. It had the words "Baker County Sheriff's Department" in gold and black letters painted in two lines across the glass. He grabbed the handle and began to turn it as he heard the footsteps of the deputy coming up behind him. The sound of a single gun shot exploded through the air from the other side of the door.

"Sabrina!" he yelled and rushed in.

An intense cone of white light was focused on the floor behind an oak desk, wavering slightly as Jeff moved behind it, aiming his camera at the floor. Sabrina stood in the middle of the room, her eyes wide open, face pale, tears beginning to stream down both cheeks. No sound was coming from her mouth. Robinson grabbed her by the shoulders and pulled her into him, feeling her resist at first and then melt into his body, wrapping her own arms around his chest.

The deputy blew by them, gun drawn, and had it aimed at the floor behind the desk. When he saw what was there he sank to his knees and said, "Oh my God." His boss, and lately his hero, had just shot his brains all over the office floor. "Get out of here!" he yelled at Jeff. "Now, God damn it! Get back! Turn that camera off!"

The spotlight blinked out and Jeff stepped out from behind the desk, slowly taking the camera down from his shoulder. His face was pale and he was swallowing deep breaths through his mouth as he met Robinson's eyes. His lips formed the words "Holy shit" as Robinson asked him what had happened.

"Baldridge, man," Jeff said. "He just offed himself right in front of us."

A small crowd of uniformed shirts was filling the room and Robinson guided Sabrina to a back corner of the room. Nobody was paying any attention to them but Robinson knew that wouldn't last for long. He pushed Sabrina away from him gently and asked, "Are you okay, Sabrina?"

She nodded as she blinked her eyes then began to dab at them with the sleeve of her cotton jacket. "I'm okay," she told him. "I've never seen something like that happen before." She looked up at him with an illogical question in her eyes.

"I know it."

"We came in and he was talking on the phone. He didn't even look at us. There was a deputy here but he left. Then all of the sudden the sheriff slammed the phone down on the desk and told us to get out. He looked so...." She groped for a word. "Panicked, I guess. Then Jeff...." More tears filled her eyes and she held her sleeves up to her cheeks to stop the moisture.

"I didn't know what to do, you know?" Jeff said. He was still breathing through his mouth and his voice came out an octave higher than normal. "So I turned on my camera, just to kind of push his buttons and next thing you know, the dude pulled his gun and started waving it at us. I didn't know he'd get that pissed. I started to back away when he just all of the sudden sticks the gun in his mouth and pulls the trigger. It was freaky, man, he didn't even hesitate. He just put it in there and did it. Bam, he's gone, just like that. It's all on the tape."

Sabrina was still looking at Robinson. "What's going on?" she asked. "Why would he have done something like that right in front of us? Do you know?"

A white-faced deputy with a sweaty forehead walked up to them and in a quiet and stressed voice told them that they needed to go with him.

"I think we do," Robinson said to Sabrina as they were led through the jostling crowd that had begun massing at the doorway.

CHAPTER EIGHT

"What do you mean you're still going after Albert Duprin?"

"Well, we're at least not letting him go just yet. Sit down, Robinson." Francine indicated the chair on the other side of the table. They were in the twin of the room where Robinson had met with Albert Duprin. "I have a few questions to ask you, as well."

Robinson studied the FBI man carefully, then went to take the seat. Francine had a "professional" smile on his face, one that didn't reach his eyes, and a tone of voice to match. Interesting, Robinson thought.

Still standing himself, Francine slid a sheet of paper out of a file folder and passed it across the table. Robinson took the list, looked at the list of dates, slid it back. "So?"

"No, no, you keep that," Francine said. "Those don't mean anything to you?"

Without looking at the paper, Robinson said, "Nope."

"I'm going to need you to provide me with details of your whereabouts on each of those days."

Robinson laughed. "I'm not sure I can do that. I'm sure most of those nights I was at my garage working on bikes."

"And the others?"

"Probably at home, I'd guess."

"Probably? You 'guess'?"

"I don't go out much."

Francine tapped the paper with his index finger. "Anybody see you at your garage? While you were working on the bikes?"

"Nope."

"You know what these dates are, don't you?"

"No," said Robinson, "but I can make another guess. Let's see. I'll bet you can't put Albert Duprin in Jacksonville at the times all those girls disappeared. That means either he didn't do it, or he didn't do it alone. If he didn't do it alone, you better find who he was working with pretty quick. And here I am, an out of towner at the scene of a similar crime, likely with no alibis for at least some of the dates you can't pin on Albert. How's that?"

Francine pursed his lips and held Robinson's eyes. "We don't have to be quick, as you put it, Robinson. We have all the time we need."

"Really?" Robinson said, as he stood up, pushing the chair back with his legs. "When you can't pin this on Albert and nothing sticks to me, where are you going to be?"

"Sit back down."

"What are you going to do when he starts talking about Tampa?"

Francine cooled down. "What about Tampa?"

"Beats me." Robinson shrugged. "Albert said he knew some things about what happened. In Tampa."

"What things?"

"You'd have to ask him. Though he says he'll never talk to you."

"Why would he say that?"

"Huh. I got the feeling he thought you'd know."

Color returned to Francine's face but before he could say anything else, Robinson started walking toward the door.

"I'm leaving now. You know where to find me, Francine. I just hope Albert stays okay. At least long enough to find the truth."

"And that's supposed to mean what, exactly?"

Robinson gave him a nod. "We never got the whole truth from B. J. Donnelly, did we, Agent? Those files were closed when he died."

"We had the right man."

"You know what?" Robinson ran his fingers through his beard, thinking how much he was starting to hate the thing. And he knew he should leave now, before he kept speaking, but he didn't.

"Of course you did. Let me tell you something, partner. I'm from this place. Maybe not this town but one like it. I'm not some dipshit Yankee from up north like you and everyone else buying postcards from Miami Beach. Baldridge was sheriff a long time and I know what that means around here. Before you settle too far deep in your Old Spice after shave and your favorite television interview suit, ask yourself just what the hell you're going to do if you're wrong about Duprin. When the real killer lays another body on your doorstep, laughing at the idiots who made Albert Duprin's name a household word, where are you going to be?"

But Robinson already knew. Francine kept silent.

"So yes, Francine, of course you did. To you, they're all the right guy. The rest of us just look alike."

"Fuck you, Robinson."

"No problem, Tim. Hey, you seeing anybody right now?" Then he turned and walked out the door. He didn't look back. There was a tight, crooked smile on his face. This was going to be over one way or the other soon enough.

Sabrina caught up with him as he was climbing into his truck. "James!" she called and held onto his door as he rolled down the window.

"I was just on my way out."

A puzzled look came across her face. "Way out? Are you leaving?"

"This isn't right, Bree." That was the first time he had called her that and it sounded funny coming from his mouth. It was a lot different when Jeff said it. She reached through the window and grabbed his shoulder.

"What do you mean?"

"I just left our Special Agent Francine. They're still going after Albert. They don't care if Baldridge cut off Skokie's hand himself. They don't give a damn that he killed that girl. They have no interest in what Ben Colfax told us."

"Where were you going?"

"Back to the motel, get my things. Then back to Tampa."

She still held his shoulder. "What aren't you telling me?"

He patted her hand and she slowly withdrew it. "He's going after me now."

"What? Who is?"

"Francine. Says I'm not alibied on some of the nights of your Jacksonville murders. And with my past...."

Sabrina shook her head. "That's a crock. Wait right here." She turned and ran into the courthouse parking lot where Robinson could see the white Channel Seven van parked among a crowd of other media related vehicles. He looked away and concentrated on a group of white ibises that were busy plucking unseen morsels out of the empty grass field across the street. As they bobbed their long, curved beaks forward their dark rumps flashed up at the sky, in contrast with their otherwise white bodies. Take a step, spear something. Take two steps, spear more. Eat hardy, boys. He looked toward the van and wondered how Sabrina could be so convinced that he was truly innocent.

She came around the front of the truck, this time with her purse on her shoulder, and waited while Robinson reached across the passenger seat and unlocked the door. "Thanks," she said breathlessly and settled into the seat.

Robinson didn't say anything. He waited for her to attach her seat belt and then he turned the key in the ignition, pulled into the street and headed toward the motel. After a few blocks, he thought to ask her about Jeff.

"I left him behind for some more filming. He's really getting into this documentary thing. We're really going through with it now, just the way we told the sheriff."

"I don't think he'd have cared much for the ending."

"Do we have one yet?"

"The sheriff does."

They drove past a fast food place and suddenly Robinson didn't want to go back to the motel. "You hungry?" he asked, stroking his beard again.

"Yeah, sure. That's fine."

There was a place that served Italian food in a building that looked like it could have served burgers or chicken or any other sort of cuisine. The interior decor wasn't any better but the food was good. Sabrina stayed within her own head until they took a table in the corner of the restaurant. There were only two other occupied tables.

"So," Sabrina said brightly. "We're off the hook for staying so long. We do this feature or documentary or whatever they end up calling it, and Jeff and I look good for staying here like we did." She smiled and tried to look pleased.

"I'm happy for you," Robinson said.

It was a bit early but they both ordered dinner and didn't talk again until after the waitress had gone back and forth bringing bread and oil for dipping and red wine for Sabrina and a Coke for Robinson.

"I don't suppose you'll want to be in the doc?" Sabrina asked.

Robinson looked at her, washed down some bread with a sip of the Coke. "Um, no."

"Well, you already are, in some ways. Does that bother you?"

He gave a backhanded wave of his hand. "That's fine. Whatever helps you. I'm just background. I don't want to be in front."

She sipped her wine and looked at him. He kept his eyes down. "Why is that, James?"

"Just the way it is." He wasn't sure what to tell her yet. And he wasn't sure if whatever he did tell her was something she'd want to put into her film.

"But you have so much to offer. I've read about your–your career. It shouldn't have ended like it did."

Now he looked up. "No," he said. "It probably did."

"I can't believe that. And even if that were true for some reason, it doesn't have to stay the ending, does it? Endings change all the time. Every new beginning will have a new ending."

Robinson shook his head. "That may not be true. Many beginnings have the same ending. Look at life."

"What do you mean?"

"Doesn't matter what we do, how many fresh starts or changes of direction we make. How many careers we have, how many times we get married. Ultimately it all ends in the same place."

Sabrina shook her head, confused. "Not all things have to end, James. Not if you truly don't want them to."

He wanted to laugh but he didn't. She was so young in some ways. "Well, we all die, don't we?"

"Oh, don't go all nihilist on me."

"Is that the right word? I haven't been to college for a while."

She took another sip of wine as the waitress brought their food. Robinson said thank you and the waiter left. Steam wafted upwards from both plates and neither Robinson or Sabrina made a move to eat.

"You're not that much older than me," Sabrina said.

This time Robinson did laugh. "Compared to what? I'm forty five years old. You're what? Twenty something?"

"You're only forty two and I'm twenty six."

"You're twenty five."

They picked up their silverware, played with their food.

"You knew how old I am."

"So did you."

They began eating in silence, each in their own thoughts. Outside the sun moved lower in the sky.

Robinson drove them back to the motel. Despite the awkwardness of the early part of their meal, they tacitly agreed to leave the documentary, Sheriff Baldridge and Albert Duprin aside for the time being. They ended up spending a very comfortable and surprisingly relaxing evening together.

"Why do you keep doing that? It's new," Sabrina said.

It took Robinson a second to realize what she meant. He let his hand fall from his beard. "Oh, this damned thing. It's about time it came off."

"Oh, really? Why?"

Robinson looked at her. "Don't tell me you like it?"

"Oh god no. It's awful." And she laughed.

He joined her. "It is, isn't it."

They pulled into the parking lot of the motel and Robinson drove in front of the door to his room. Sabrina climbed out of the truck on her own and walked around and joined him on the mat. He looked at her in mild surprise. "Coming in?"

"For a while," she said. "If that's okay."

"It's fine with me. We should probably talk a little more, anyway."

She nodded and followed him inside. "What are we talking about?" She moved to the bed and sat on the edge.

"I think I need to leave," he told her.

Sabrina nodded, though not in agreement. "I know you do. Why?"

Robinson had already moved further into the room, and stood at the foot of the bed, looking back at Sabrina's profile. She is pretty, he thought. Again.

"You wanted me up here to see if Duprin would open up to me, to get you a story. Your instincts about Baldridge being bad were right on. You've still got a lot of work to do up here, and not just on your doc or your feature or whatever it is. There's still a lot of truth that has to be revealed up here and you're in the best position to do it."

Again she nodded but she didn't turn her head. "So your work is done."

"Such as it was, yes," he said, and thought of Special Agent Francine.

Sabrina noted the past tense and didn't say anything. He's probably right, she thought. *Oh, of course he's right.*

Robinson moved into the sink alcove and dug into his shaving kit. He came out with an electric razor and a set of attachments. The buzzing of the razor and the nature of the activity precluded a continuation of the conversation and after a while it was forgotten as he focused on what he was doing. It had been so long he grew annoyed at how much time it was taking to remove the entire beard.

It was over in about a half an hour. It felt like he'd been through a minor war. When he was finished, he was raw, red, and bare-faced. He looked over at Sabrina on the bed. She was laying on her side, her back still to him. Again he thought how beautiful she looked, even in silhouette. *Been too long for me,* he thought.

Through the gaps around the curtains he could tell that it was finally dark outside. He went into the bathroom, closed the door, and took a shower, feeling his face for the spots he'd inevitably missed. When he was finished, he saw that Sabrina still hadn't moved. He touched up with a disposable razor and quietly slid into some clean clothes.

When he finally walked around the bed to look at Sabrina's face, he confirmed that she had in fact fallen asleep. She'd been working so hard on this story, both her and Jeff, it was no wonder she was in for a physical letdown. He took the opposite edge of the bedspread and gently eased it over her, stopping just at her shoulders.

Then he took off his shirt, kept his sweat pants on, and laid on top of the bed. He thought for a long time but after a while, his breathing matched Sabrina's and they slept.

CHAPTER NINE

A car horn and loud voices awoke Robinson. Standard motel patron courtesy. The light around the curtains told him it was morning. His left arm was extended, resting just below the pillow where Sabrina's head would have been. He was trying to figure out what that meant when he heard movement behind him and rolled over to face the bathroom alcove.

"Good morning," Sabrina said.

"'Morning."

"I like it."

Robinson yawned into his fist. "Like what?"

"The new face." She turned back to the mirror and teased out her hair with her fingertips.

Not knowing whether he was intruding or not, Robinson watched her and finally said, "Should I have awakened you?"

Sabrina turned around and sat next to him on the bed. Closer than she would have yesterday, thought Robinson.

"No."

"Well, good–" and he froze. "What the hell...." He reached up, pushing Sabrina's hair back from her ear.

"They were in your suitcase."

Sabrina was wearing Becky Owens' earrings.

"Wha– I–" Robinson stood up, reaching for the beard that was no longer there. He wasn't able to make sense of anything for a minute. Sabrina stood up, touched his elbow.

"I'm sorry. I'll take them off."

He grabbed her hand and turned her toward him, and stared at the earrings. Becky Owens, dead eight years. By a killer the cops thought was B. J. Donnelly but who Robinson knew wasn't. "Take them off. Quickly."

"O-okay," Sabrina said, pulling her hand away, hurt coloring her eyes.

"No, honey, no," Robinson told her. "It's not safe. We have to get them out of here."

"I don't understand."

She reached up to remove them but he grabbed her hands again.

"Wait," he said. "Keep them on." He let her go, started looking for her purse.

"James, what are you doing? What is going on?"

He found the purse between the bed and the end table and brought it to her in quick strides. "They were in my suitcase?"

She nodded.

He went to the dresser, took the suitcase and dumped it out onto the bed. There wasn't much in it so he could see pretty quickly there wasn't anything else that didn't belong. Unzipping the pockets, he looked first and then ran his hands inside along the interior liner. There was nothing else.

"Okay, Sabrina. Out. Now." He tried to usher her toward the door but she stood firm.

"No."

"No?" Robinson was puzzled.

"What's going on? Take them off, leave them on? James?"

It was coming to him now. "Becky Owens. Do you know the name? One of the Tampa victims?"

"Yes, I know it."

"Those are hers."

"What? How do you know?"

"I gave them to her."

"James–"

"She– I knew her when I was married."

Sabrina pulled her hands away. "The card on the truck...."

"Was from me."

"Oh my God." She turned around where Robinson couldn't see her face. "Why do you have her earrings?"

Robinson felt both the crush of not enough time and the need to explain things to this woman. "There's no time, Sabrina. Bree. You have to go."

"I'll go," she said woodenly.

Anger began to flare. "Listen to me, damn it." He spun her around. "This isn't me. I did not take her earrings. I did not pack them in my bag." He tried to stare into her eyes but she wouldn't look at him. "Believe me, Bree."

"Why didn't you tell me...."

"I will," he said. "I will if you'll promise to leave here *right now*." This time she let him start her toward the door. "Get Jeff and get into town, get some breakfast."

The girl was shaken. "Okay," she said.

Something popped into Robinson's mind. "Wait," he said. "Where are your earrings?"

"Oh. I left them on the sink."

"Hold on."

Robinson ran to the alcove, scooped up the earrings and dropped them into the small garbage can under the sink. He took the motel-provided soap and tossed that in, too, then knotted the bag. Then he went into the bathroom and unlocked the small window. It was too small for an adult or even a large child to get through. He could barely get it open. He heard Sabrina behind him as he finally managed to slide the frame up enough to fit his arm through.

He plucked the bag from the top of the closed toilet lid and swung it back and forth, the bar of soap giving it enough wait, he hoped, to counter the wind resistance of the floppy plastic bag. When he let go of the package it sailed eight or ten feet deep into the palmetto scrub that was out the back side of the motel.

The window went down easier than it went up. He re-locked it and bumped into Sabrina as he turned around. "You have to leave. Right now. Drive off, make sure you're not followed. If you are, keep going, I'll figure something out. If you're clear, if you're sure, you can park somewhere else and get back through those trees and get that bag. Can you do that?"

Sabrina's mind was reeling. "But what about Jeff? Where would we park?

How would we get back there?"

Robinson put his hands on her shoulders and looked down into her eyes. "Sabrina, there's no time. I don't know. They could be here any second. You have to leave. If you can get that bag, so much the better, but we should be okay if you're gone when Francine arrives."

"But what if they find the bag?"

"Who knows? Unless they can tie them to you. The point is they can't frame me for Becky." He spun her toward the door. "At least for now," Robinson said. "We're still playing catch up. Now go. Quickly."

The color was back in Sabrina's face. "Okay. Jeff and I will handle it. But you will find me? And you will tell me–"

"Everything," he said. "But you have to go right now."

"But these–"

"Will probably go unnoticed if you pass them on your way out. They'll be here soon. Trust me. Please."

She still held her purse and she turned and walked out of the bathroom and to the motel room door. Robinson tried to open it for her but she didn't wait. She pulled the knob, went out without turning around or saying another word.

Robinson shut the door, locked it, took the unused garbage can by the room's only table and put it in the top of the one in the bathroom. He wadded up some dampened tissue and threw it on top, along with the wrapper from the bar of soap that was in the last garbage can, the one in the bathroom.

He quickly refilled his suitcase, replaced it on the dresser, and threw himself on the bed. Then he waited.

He was surprised it took nearly three minutes. He willed himself to stay in bed until after the sounds of squealing tires and car doors stopped and the pounding on the door began.

There were four of them and the search took all of about forty minutes. There just wasn't that much to look through. One officer did take the back cover of the nineteen inch television off but was good enough to put it back on after he'd looked inside.

Deputy Dougie Roe stood with Robinson outside the room until the search was finished. Robinson hadn't spoken and Roe was uneasy, constantly glancing at Robinson. He hadn't asked any questions, he hadn't made any fuss, and he looked as calm as if he was rousted by the sheriff's department every other Thursday. When his men finished the search, they came outside and waited for Roe.

"Wait here," he told Robinson, who just nodded.

Always keeping him in sight, Roe walked along the walkway closer to the door. He had moved Robinson away from the room so he couldn't interfere with the search, or hear any of the conversation between the searchers.

"Nothing there," said one of the men. "Not even a wrist watch."

"Doesn't wear one," said Roe, looking at Robinson's wrists. "No tan lines." He scratched his chin. "How about his vehicle?"

"Same thing."

Roe jerked his head. "Okay, you boys head on back. I'll be along."

The searchers peeled off their latex gloves as they walked back to their waiting cars. Roe went back to Robinson, still standing casually on the sidewalk. "Well, we didn't find anything, Mr. Robinson."

"There was nothing to find, Deputy."

"Just the same, sir, if you don't mind, I was wondering if it wouldn't bother you coming back to the station with me."

Robinson straightened. "Under arrest?"

"No, no," said Roe quickly. "Just to answer a few questions."

"About what? Specifically."

Roe was uneasy. "That's, uh, that's not up to me, Mr. Robinson. But if you wouldn't mind, I'm sure it won't take too long."

Roe was acting sheriff. Clearly being here wasn't his own idea and any questions for Robinson weren't his. "All right," Robinson said. "I'll follow you in."

"That's not necessary, sir. I can have one–"

"You want me at your headquarters, I'll follow you in. When we're done there I will be on my own. Does that work for you or not?" He almost felt bad putting Roe on the spot but he was going to learn sooner or later what was going on.

"Yes, sir, I suppose it does."

When they got to the sheriff's headquarters, Roe led Robinson up a flight of stairs to the second floor and into a room with a few desks and some chairs. There was no one way mirror on the wall. Behind one of the desks was Special Agent Timothy Francine.

"Agent Francine," Robinson said.

"Robinson," Francine said. "Take a seat."

"Thank you." Robinson pulled out a chair across the desk from Francine, still affecting a casual and laid back air.

Francine stared at him, a few extra lines cutting into his cheeks and forehead.

"You going to tell me why I'm here?" Robinson asked.

"We had a tip." Francine picked up a pencil, slid a legal pad in front of him but didn't write anything down. "We got a warrant to search your room and your truck."

Robinson said offhandedly, "Couldn't find a judge until this morning, huh?"

"What do you mean?"

Since Robinson had been in the room with Sabrina since last evening, the only time for the earrings to appear in his suitcase would have been while they had been out to dinner. They sure as hell hadn't been there earlier. "Search warrant said you were looking for personal items belonging to or related to the victims from the Jacksonville killings, as well as from the local girl."

"We didn't find anything."

"Nothing to find."

At this point Robinson knew Francine was confused. Had Robinson discovered the earrings first? Had one of these hick deputies pocketed the jewelry for his girlfriend? Were the earrings still in the suitcase and had they somehow missed them?

"So what did you want to ask me?"

Here Francine cracked a crooked smile. He started asking Robinson about his whereabouts and alibis for specific days and times. They both knew what he was doing. Robinson repeated what he told Francine before and the other made scrawling notes on the pad. After the last one, Robinson said, "So, we done here?"

"Almost," Francine said. "We had one other tip, strangely enough."

"Sure," Robinson said. "Strange."

"Someone seems to think they may have seen you the night Rebecca Owens was murdered ten years ago."

Robinson didn't expect this. He covered his reaction by replying immediately. "Rebecca Owens? From ten years ago?"

Francine sat back in his chair, wiggling his pencil back and forth from the middle. "Seems strange, waiting this long. Probably nothing to it. Thought I'd ask." He tossed the pencil ahead onto the legal pad. "Still, this is how cold cases are cracked. New evidence comes forth. Maybe something jogged somebody's memory. You've been in the news again, you know."

"I know."

"And after all this time hiding out in your little motorcycle garage."

Robinson wouldn't let Francine bait him. He kept silent. After a while Francine said, "Well, we'll track it down, get to the bottom of it." He paused. "Probably nothing to it."

"Probably. Maybe someone trying to play a joke on the ex-cop."

"You understand how it goes, I have to check into everything." Francine was still wondering about the earrings and they both knew it.

"People see you on TV and think they know you."

"Big star, aren't you?"

"Albert Duprin thinks so, doesn't he?" Robinson shook his head, let out a small laugh. "Said he knew me in Tampa."

Francine straightened in his char and leaned in. "You mean you knew Duprin and you didn't say anything?"

"No," Robinson said. "Of course not. He said he knew *me* in Tampa. I'd never seen him before I came up here."

"So he was full of crap, huh?" Francine slumped back again, his eyes never leaving Robinson's face.

"Who knows? Guy's batshit, isn't he?" Robinson pulled up the heel of his shoe. "He did seem to know where I live, though. Mentioned the sinkhole by my house."

A sort of smile appeared across Francine's face. "Did he now? What did he say?"

"You'd have to ask him."

"I might just do that." Francine checked his watch. "You planning on sticking around?"

"Not much longer, no," Robinson answered. "I've got work waiting for me."

"Well," Francine said as he stood up. "I know where to find you."

"You certainly do."

Robinson got to his feet, held out his hand. "Good luck with the case." Francine reached forward and shook.

"Thanks," he said.

Francine told Robinson he'd walk him out. Robinson shrugged and led the way out of the room, down the hallway and stairs, and out into the glare of the cloudless morning. The Channel Seven van was parked in the first spot by the door. As the two men exited the building, the passenger door opened and Sabrina Wells climbed out.

Robinson saw her and thought, *Shit*. He tried to will her back into the van. Sabrina said, "James."

"Good morning, Bree." He walked toward her, a heavy frown on his face.

Behind him he was listening to Francine's steps as he walked away along the sidewalk. Then they stopped.

Robinson grabbed Sabrina by the elbow and spun her back toward the van. He saw Jeff looking dumbly at him through the windshield. START THE

VAN, mouthed Robinson slowly but with force. Jeff's hand moved to the key.

Sabrina stopped fighting him when she saw his face. She reached out and pulled open the door. "Go," he told her fiercely. "Right now." He knew Jeff was watching and knew he understood. He had the van backing up as soon as Sabrina was in but before the door was shut.

Robinson stumbled backwards and into the body of Special Agent Francine, who tried to shove him aside but Robinson reached back and grabbed one of his arms.

"Whew," he said. "Thanks for the assist. I almost fell on my ass."

He turned, looking straight into the paralyzed face of the FBI man. "You think of more questions, Agent?"

Francine stared back at him, features still frozen. The van was out of the parking lot and disappearing down the street heading east. Francine whirled around and went back inside the headquarters building.

Robinson stood there a moment, then began walking toward his truck. He realized he was still taking only shallow breaths, and he forced himself to breathe normally. *Too damn close*, he thought. *If he didn't know before, he does now.*

Sabrina Wells had still been wearing Becky Owens' earrings.

CHAPTER TEN

Robinson drove back to the motel, cleaned up the room a bit, and packed his suitcase. He went to check out and found that "the woman from Channel Seven" had already covered it.

"Did she leave anything for me?" he asked.

The clerk shook her head. "No, sir."

He patted the counter. "Okay, thank you very much."

Neither Sabrina nor Jeff had been in their rooms. The large white van, impossible to miss, was not in the parking lot. He wasn't sure what to do. Sabrina had seemed determine they talk after the expected search this morning, and had even waited outside the sheriff's department headquarters. Had she changed her mind, gone back to Jacksonville?

No, he thought. She was too much of a reporter on a story. More likely she was spooked about what had happened and was staying out of sight somewhere.

He headed over to his truck, tossed his suitcase into the back, and climbed in. He waited just a minute, started it up, then slowly drove out of the parking lot. Heading left would take him back toward the sheriff's department. Turning right would take him past some of the outlying businesses, away from downtown. He made the right, still driving slowly. A block up the road was a large Ford dealership on the left. As he passed it, the familiar white van pulled in behind him. Jeff flashed his lights and Robinson pulled over at the next driveway, a boarded up laundromat. The van followed him in.

As soon as they stopped, Sabrina jumped out of the passenger side and held her closed hand out to Robinson. "Oh my God, I am so sorry. I was thinking so hard about what was going on, I—"

"It's okay, it's okay," he said, holding out his hand and letting her put Becky's earring in his palm.

"Do you want them? Should I keep them? Now that he knows—"

"Now that he knows we can finally end this thing."

"But is it safe for you to have them?"

Robinson had no idea. "Hot potato," he said. "Right now, Francine thinks you have them. If he finds you and looks, he'll go back to thinking I have them."

"Or that I've stashed them."

Robinson nodded. "Maybe. But we're all so far from home that might be harder than you think. Francine knows that."

Jeff came out of the van and walked around the front to where Robinson and Sabrina were standing. He was eating more of his beef jerky and looked at Robinson with an expression Robinson hadn't seen before. "She was with you last night?"

"Jeff—" Sabrina said.

"No, no, it's cool," he said. Then, looking at Robinson, "Isn't it?"

"Jeff, she fell asleep and I didn't see the point in waking her. Nothing happened."

"That's what she said." He took another bite of the jerky. "How's the new face?"

"White as a seagull's bottom."

"So maybe we shouldn't stand around in the sun, waiting for that asshole from the FBI to find us." He pointed back over his shoulder with his thumb. "We're a tad on the conspicuous side."

Sabrina said, "He's right, James. I'm a little freaked out."

Robinson nodded. "We need to get off the street."

Jeff said, "We need to get out of town, man."

"You're right. You guys up for a drive?"

"How far?" Jeff asked.

"I've got a spare room and some blankets, soft couch."

"Down to Tampa, eh? Well, like the story says, anywhere but here with anyone but you."

"You're stuck with me."

"Still a better deal than sticking in this burg. Let's hit it, Bree. The sooner we're out of here the better I'll feel." He was chewing his jerky like a rabbit.

"I'm riding with James," she said.

"What?"

"He owes me some talking." She walked around both of them and went to the passenger side of the truck and let herself in.

Robinson looked at Jeff. "We good?"

Jeff swallowed everything in his mouth. "You hurt her—"

"Jeff," Robinson said. "I never touched her. Really. That's the truth." He turned and climbed into the driver's side of the truck. Jeff looked puzzled, went back to the door of the van.

"Dude," he said out loud, thinking of Robinson. "What the hell's wrong with you?"

They headed out of town north on the state road fifteen miles out of the way. Robinson wanted to stay as far away from Francine for the moment as he could. They cut onto another road that led them, after another seven miles, to an onramp for the interstate, Jeff following all the way.

"You okay?" Robinson asked Sabrina.

She looked tense. "Not yet," she said. "I need to get out of Holton, get out of this county, for a while."

Robinson tried to reassure her with a smile. "Don't worry," he said. "We will." She didn't even look at him.

Since their overdue conversation wasn't possible right now, Robinson settled down for the three hour drive. Once past the borders of Baker County, Sabrina seemed to relax into the contours of her seat. After a while she closed her eyes.

They drove along in silence for a long while, Robinson's thoughts on hold while waiting for Sabrina to start questioning him. At some point he was going to turn on the radio but then reconsidered. Coming into Ocala, Jeff flashed his lights then pulled around Robinson with his turn signal on for the next ramp. Robinson followed and Sabrina opened her eyes when she felt it.

"What's going on?" she asked.

"Gas stop or something," he said. "Jerky refill?"

She gave him a tired smile as they drove into a large travel plaza and each vehicle pulled up to a pump. Sabrina took her purse and went inside the store. Jeff and Robinson started filling their vehicles.

"You getting things figured out in there?" Jeff called.

"Haven't tried yet."

Jeff looked frustrated but didn't say anything. Just knowing what Sabrina must have told him, he probably felt more up in the air than any of them.

They finished fueling and Sabrina came out and stood next to Robinson. "What now? Back in the car?"

He looked at the van. He knew she was ready to start asking things. "You've got the tape of that guy that found the Skokie girl's body?"

"The interview we did with Frank Grayton?" Robinson nodded. "Yes, of course. In the van."

"Can you show me?"

"Now?"

"Sure. We can pull in back there, watch it in the van, can't we?"

Sabrina called Jeff over, told him the plan. He didn't question it. "Let me make a pit stop inside and I'll be right back."

"I better run in, too," Robinson said. "Wait inside?"

"Nervous?"

"Right now? Yes, and for the next few days."

"Then what?"

"Yes," he said.

The dark in the back of the van was a stark contrast to the bright of the day outside. Jeff left it running so the air conditioning could stay on, as well as power the videotape machine from the engine and not the batteries. Robinson and Sabrina sat back on a narrow bench while Jeff crouched on his knees in front of them, facing away at the monitor on the rack mounted against the panel behind the front seats.

Robinson resisted the urge to touch Sabrina or hold her hand. She seemed intent on what Jeff was doing, and when her cameraman hit play, the van was suddenly lit by the glow from the screen. "Let me know if you want me to pause it anywhere," Jeff said.

"Why is this important?" Sabrina asked.

"I don't know. Maybe it's not. But Francine went there, got that picture, and hasn't said boo about it."

On screen Sabrina was interviewing Grayton and they watched it silently for the next three minutes before the screen went black.

"Okay," Robinson said. "That was—"

"Hang on, man," Jeff said.

A new image blinked into being on the screen. Robinson recognized Sabrina's carefully tended nails along the top edge of a piece of paper as the camera slowly zoomed in on the writing it contained, maintaining focus all the way.

"Hold it there," Robinson said, and Jeff paused the image. Robinson leaned forward, getting a closer look, but he already knew what he was looking at. "Is there more?"

Jeff said, "Nope. That's all, folks."

"Okay, I'm done."

Sabrina spoke up as Jeff ejected the tape from the console and inserted it back into its plastic case. "What did you see?"

"Francine," Robinson said. "It's always been Francine."

CHAPTER ELEVEN

Albert Duprin sat across the table from Special Agent Francine. No one would tell him what had happened to the sheriff. He hadn't been to see Albert in days. He stared calmly and silently at Francine. If he waited long enough, the sheriff would come back.

"I asked you about Tampa," Francine said.

Albert was thinking about swimming naked in the pond on the new golf course at night. First, he had to watch during the day to make sure there weren't any gators in there. Even then, there was no way to be positive about it, but unless they'd been used to humans, they were more likely to leave him alone than not. They always had.

"What did Robinson tell you?"

Robinson. James Robinson. Reluctantly Albert pulled back from his daydream. He wished they'd let him have his magazines in here. At least some of them. It wasn't just the pictures, it was the smell of the ink and the paper, the *ideas* they represented. They showed parts of the world he belonged to, or the world he would like to belong to.

"What do you know about Tampa?"

Tampa. James Robinson. All those girls. He thought he knew Robinson but he didn't. He was wrong about Robinson. He thought he'd know him, feel him like he felt the world of his magazines or how he felt the presence or the aura of the sheriff, but Robinson hadn't had any of that. But he was a good talker. Albert liked his voice.

In a harsher tone, Francine asked, "What do you know about me?"

This was something. Francine was giving off something, almost an odor. For the first time Albert really focused on the man. No, he was wrong, Albert decided. He wasn't part of anything great. He was just starting to smell.

Francine asked his question again.

Albert went back to his apartment in his mind, pictured himself taking down the clips of Robinson but leaving the other ones there. He'd put up some of the sheriff. There had to be some somewhere. He would find them.

Across the table, Francine pounded the surface with an open hand. Albert jumped, became aware of him again. Maybe there could be a clip of him on his wall after all. The more Albert looked at him, and the more Francine stared back, he could imagine it more and more.

"You belong with the sheriff," Albert said, then went back to swimming naked in ponds still warmed by the heat of the day.

"What did Robinson tell you, damn it?" Francine asked. He looked at the mirror nervously, though he knew the room behind it was empty. "What?"

But Albert was gone and there was no reason for him to come back. He wished he was holding a magazine.

PART FOUR

CHAPTER ONE

Robinson was riding alone in his truck, following Sabrina and Jeff in the van. Sabrina had wanted answers but he needed time to think. And he wanted them in front of him in case they changed their mind about going to Tampa. He knew what Francine had done already but he didn't know what Francine was going to do now. Until he was sure he wasn't about to let Sabrina and Jeff go off on their own.

But what was he going to do? During his years on the force he'd drawn his gun numerous times but he'd never fired it at another human being. He had no doubt he could–that was what the training was for. But that was on the job, and a long time ago. As a civilian could he do it? For revenge, vengeance, protection, what?

He had no idea.

Something had to happen. Whether he was doing the right thing or not, he'd wound up Francine and let him loose to see what happened. He couldn't see how he'd had much choice. After all these years, Francine had finally upped the stakes and made moves against him. Was it a question of opportunity? Was it a reaction to seeing Robinson at another murder site? Could it be something else?

Almost to Tampa now, then home. He needed rest. He needed time to think. Mostly he felt he needed to feel safe but he didn't know how to do that.

Visor down, sunglasses on, he followed the mundane and familiar rear end of the Channel Seven van down Interstate 75 with the feeling that something bad was going to happen soon. He really hoped this was just a mood and not a prediction. They'd all find out soon enough.

"Francine left the note on our van? Why?"

The three of them were seated in Robinson's living room. Bottles of water were on the table in front of each of them but only Jeff was drinking.

"To make sure I'd go with you to Baker County."

Sabrina shook her head. "I don't understand. What does Francine want with you?"

Robinson stared at the floor. Jeff stood up, said he wanted to get something from the van. Should he bring the camera?

"Absolutely not," Robinson said. "Go get your jerky. We'll wait."

Jeff went out of the house and while he was gone, Sabrina looked at Robinson and said, "I want you to tell me. You owe it to me."

He didn't want to hear her say it that way. It hurt him some place he didn't know how to define. "I'm going to, Bree. I always was."

They waited another minute for Jeff to come back, a wad of processed meat stuffed in his cheek like a squirrel. "I'm back." He settled deep into an arm chair, Sabrina to his right in the matching one, and Robinson alone on the couch, facing them.

"It's about Rebecca Owens," he said.

Sabrina nodded, already knowing. "Go on," she told him.

Robinson looked at the big windows facing the front yard. The bright late afternoon sun was painting the landscape in clear but washed out colors, a day for beaches and amusement parks, not dark confessions. The Florida weather could be beautiful, terrible in a storm, almost something you could touch, but sometimes it played like the wrong set for the wrong movie. Robinson wished it were raining, with huge, dark clouds twisting and funneling and dropping fat, wet drops onto the house, the cars, everything, damping the atmosphere both inside and outside the house.

"I was married. I was a bad husband. I met Becky and she– Well, she was young, she was new, she was bright and shiny."

"Did you love her?"

"I loved my wife," Robinson said. "That doesn't mean you don't–"

Jeff said, "It's a guy thing."

"No," Robinson said quickly. "But yes."

He reached forward, twisted the top off his water bottle, took a long drink. "Sometimes people do things more for the thrill than for anything else."

"Like be with other women?" Sabrina asked.

"Or jump out of airplanes or stick needles in their arms or drive fast cars. Yes," Robinson said. "Sometimes like be with other women."

"Did your wife know?"

"Not specifically. It didn't matter by then. We were still married but we'd been apart for so long.... We were dead but no one had buried us yet and we hadn't taken the time to do it ourselves. It wasn't a secret, we knew it was coming."

"How did you meet Becky?"

"Waitress at a cop joint. We'd go in there a lot for late breakfasts, lunch. She was cute, blonde, had a way of lighting up the room just by being in it. She was an 'instant like' kind of person, if you know what I mean."

Sabrina just nodded.

"She made everyone feel like she liked them, and in some way I think she did. Not necessarily in the way we were all thinking, but that's just who she was. She was pretty but she wasn't the best looking girl you've ever seen. You'd never put her face on a makeup commercial, or trot her down a fashion runway. But she was *attractive*. She made you want to be noticed by her. After a while you wanted to know it wasn't just the job, you know? She was a waitress, she had to be nice. But she made you want it to be more."

"Bet she cleaned up on tips," Jeff said.

Sabrina glared. "Shut up, Jeff." He put his hands up and took another bite off his jerky stick.

Robinson's reminiscence had broken. He was back in the present. "Anyway, I started going in there on my own, at odd times so it wasn't likely there'd be other cops around. When it wasn't busy she'd talk to me, more than with other customers."

"How did you know?"

He shook his head. "I didn't, not really. But I was looking for it, and that's what I thought I saw."

Sabrina picked up her water bottle and held it in her lap. "Did she know you were married?"

Robinson nodded. "When I met her I was wearing a ring. I couldn't just take it off. But I told her about my wife, our marriage, and that it was over. Maybe a bit more over than it actually was but not a lot." He took another sip from his bottle. "Anyway, I tried to get her to go out somewhere, meet me out of the restaurant. She'd let me meet her after work and buy her a cup of coffee at another place."

Jeff asked, "So she was into you?"

"I thought so, but it wasn't until Karen moved out that she'd actually go out on a date date with me. It was hard with my schedule, and the Sun Coast killings were my case and it seemed all I ever did was work and when I could, think about seeing Becky." He stared out the window again, resenting the sunshine. "Anyway, we started something. I may have loved her. I don't know anymore."

Sabrina opened her bottle, didn't drink. "Did she love you?"

Robinson spread his hands wide, not looking up.

"Guilt, man," Jeff said. "Men are motivated by guilt, we just don't admit it. I bet you felt bad about your wife, so you couldn't feel good about the new girl. Then, when she died–"

"Jeff," Sabrina said. "Please shut up."

"I met her brother," Robinson said. "Becky wanted him to meet me. I think she wanted his approval. He was tough. I was a broken guy in a destroyed marriage, consumed by my work and obsessed with his sister. But Drew tried, he really did. For his sister. We rode bikes together when I could get away. The motion helped when I was thinking about the case, getting out on the state roads, heading into the old cattle country. The focus is on not getting hit by some asshole kid and the back of the mind sort of helps straighten things out. Sometimes anyway."

Jeff was nodding, seemed about to say something, then looked at Sabrina and kept still.

"After– after she died, Drew gave me this." Robinson got up, went out of the room and down a short hall, came back a minute later with an envelope. He handed it to Sabrina and Jeff hunched over to see it, too.

Sabrina removed the card, read the message:

Becky,

Please, I'm sorry. Let me make it up to you. You know how much I love you. I can't live without you.

–T

"I know this–" she said, pointing at the initial used for the signature. Jeff settled back into his chair, mouth frozen in mid-chew.

"Yup," Robinson said. "Same as in the signature–"

"From the tape," Jeff said. "From that dude's trailer."

Sabrina said, "The receipt. Francine gave it to Frank Grayton. That's the way he wrote the 'T' in his name. 'Timothy Francine.'"

She tossed the card onto the table in front of her. Robinson didn't reach for it.

"Did you know?" she asked.

"About Francine and Becky?" he asked. Sabrina didn't answer, so he said no, he hadn't. "All of us from the task force knew her. When the FBI was around, sometimes they ate where we did. It–it isn't surprising."

"What isn't, exactly?" Sabrina asked.

"I don't know. That he met her. That he was attracted to her. That he pursued her."

Sabrina tried to be gentle, and Robinson appreciated her for it. "Was she seeing him, too?"

Again, the window. Still nothing but sunshine, a few growing shadows. Somewhere out there the giant sinkhole gradually filling up with his beer can empties, a place where he would dearly like to be right now. Playing the beer game.

"I hope not," he answered. "I really fucking hope not."

Silence fell into the room. Sabrina and Robinson didn't look at each other. Eventually Jeff said, "But he killed her?"

Robinson closed his eyes. "The killer took her earrings. The same ones I'd given her. The same ones planted in my suitcase up in Holton. Someone connected to the case up there left that card, the one I'd given to Becky, on your van."

"How did he get that?" Jeff again.

"Same way as the earrings," Robinson said. "She probably had it with her when he....."

Jeff wrinkled his forehead. "So he's had a hard-on for you all this time?"

Robinson didn't answer. Sabrina finally took a drink from her bottle, dabbed at her lips, then took another. She screwed the cap back on and leaned forward, placing the bottle on the table. Then she sat back. "He was jealous. He did it."

Both men looked at her.

"My friend Monica was a little like Becky Owens. Men met her and wanted to know her. Women seemed to keep their distance."

"But how–" Jeff started.

"He did it. And he hated James for–for getting to Becky himself. The hate just never went away."

"So now what?" Jeff asked.

Sabrina looked at Robinson. He was thinking about what Sabrina had just said. He knew she was right. He finally had the answers to what happened to Becky. Not the details, but he didn't think he even wanted those. He thought of the promise he'd made to Becky's brother and how he had to get hold of Drew and finally tell him what had happened to his sister. If Robinson didn't get through this, Drew would know the truth, would know that it was never B. J. Donnelly. But Robinson still had to worry about Francine.

"He knows," Robinson said. "His trap didn't work, he doesn't give a damn about Coleman Baldridge or Albert Duprin or Lynnette Skokie or any of those girls in Jacksonville."

"He just wants you," Sabrina said.

"It's worse than that." Jeff stood up, started pacing. "It's way worse than that now."

Robinson said, "He's right. He knows we know. The three of us."

Sabrina shook her head, as though she were physically clearing her thoughts. "What does that mean?" she asked.

Jeff stopped moving, looked at Robinson.

"I think he's coming," said Robinson.

"He could always run," said Jeff. "Light off to Mexico, wherever guys like that go. He's FBI, man. He must know how to do that shit."

"No," Sabrina said. "He'd still have his hate."

"But running would be so much easier," argued Jeff. To Robinson: "He could do it, couldn't he?"

"There's no evidence he killed Becky. He was part of the Sun Coast investigation, he was here when we–" The window. The damned sunshine. "When we found the body. He knew what he was doing."

"But the earrings–"

"He gave those back."

"And the note–"

"Doesn't say he killed her. There's nothing to get him on." Robinson looked at Jeff. "Unless he runs."

"Shit." There was another long silence in the room. Sabrina had found the window, too. "So he's coming here?"

"I think so."

CHAPTER TWO

Jeff went outside to move the van behind the house while Robinson walked down the driveway and thirty yards of road to close and lock the gate. He wasn't sure exactly why he wanted to do that but it felt like it gave them a psychological buffer to be a least sealed off from the roadway.

He saw Jeff come around the house with an armload of video gear. Let him work, Robinson thought. Just no filming.

When he got back to the house Jeff was organizing his stuff on the floor in a corner of the living room. Sabrina was on the phone, clearly talking to the station back in Jacksonville.

"You'll have it, Jack, I promise." She looked a Jeff untangling cables from a pile on the floor, listening. "Jeff is working on it now." Listening again, not looking at Robinson. He felt she had disconnected from him back in Holton and he wasn't sure how he should handle that.

"No, I can see him. What more do you want me to say?" Jeff had stopped working and was watching Sabrina. "Okay. Tomorrow. 'Bye, Jack." And she hung up.

"I know that look," Jeff said. "What's going on?"

Sabrina ran a hand through her hair and let out a breath. "Jack wants footage tomorrow."

Jeff nodded as if he understood. "Of what, exactly? Did he say?"

"Of the reason why we haven't been to the station for a week."

Jeff reassured her with a smile. "We can do that, Bree. I can set up the editing bay right here and we can rough out the story."

Which story, Robinson wanted to ask. The one he was in had no ending. Sabrina turned to him, all business, and asked, "How do we include Francine?"

Grateful that she had finally established contact again, Robinson shook his head slowly. "How can you? We know he left the card on your van, that he planted the earrings in my suitcase. But we can't prove anything."

"We can tie him to Becky Owens with the card. The one he signed."

"We can tie him to *someone* named 'Becky,' but can you assert in your piece that it was–" he almost said 'my Becky.' He stopped speaking, stared at Sabrina, unable to come up with the right words.

"Becky Owens," she said. "You can say her name, James."

"No, I– I know," he said. "It's–"

"Awkward."

"It's difficult."

Now she stepped toward him, touched his arm.

"We'll make it all right, James. We will."

He reached across his body with his other hand to touch hers but she withdrew it and he just brushed the spot where her fingers had been. They stood there, physically closer than they'd been in hours, and he was at least grateful for that.

"How well do you know Francine?" Sabrina asked. Jeff had gone outside for more gear from the van.

Robinson shrugged. "It was a long time ago. When I was on the Sun Coast task force he was one of the FBI group that was around. I worked more with his boss, the Special Agent in Charge." He thought for a moment. "Harkness was his name. Sam Harkness. I heard he died a few years ago. Heart attack."

"So Francine was what part of the investigation?"

"He did what Harkness wanted him to do. We gave the Feds access to the evidence through Harkness. He directed his own guys. Other than Harkness, my contact with the rest of them was more or less as a group."

Sabrina thought about this. "And the money question," she said. "What's he going to do next?"

Robinson just looked at her.

"Yeah," she said, "I thought so, too."

Jeff had come back in and was setting equipment into a small wheeled rack that he'd disconnected from the inside wall of the van. "You about ready, Bree?"

"Um, yeah. I'm coming." She looked back at Robinson. "What are you going to do?"

"Pick up the phone," he said. "Keep a promise." He left her there, went down the hallway to his bedroom, closed the door. He sat on the edge of his bed, only cursorily made days ago when he had first met Sabrina Wells. There was a phone on the small table next to the side of the bed where he usually slept. After a while he picked it up.

Still later, he dialed.

When the call was answered he said, "It's James Robinson."

"Oh," said Drew Owens, nonplussed. "I wasn't sure this was ever going to happen." He paused, waiting for a contradiction. "This is what I think it is?"

"Becky."

Owens' sigh was audible over the line. "Tell me," he said.

Robinson did.

There was a bag of pasta and some marinara sauce in the kitchen cupboards. Robinson made the spaghetti while Sabrina chopped browning lettuce for a salad. They didn't speak much.

Sabrina and Jeff had worked for three hours on a tape to get to their station manager. They decided to stay in for dinner, such as it was, and talk about what they should do. Robinson and Sabrina brought the food to the living room where Jeff had the television on. "Beautiful," he said. "I'm starving." He began eating while Robinson went back to the kitchen and returned with three cans of beer.

They ate out of their laps in silence except for the sounds of the show Jeff had turned on. They all knew they had to talk about Francine but none of them quite knew what to say so no one was in a hurry to start. Dinner was a welcome distraction. It gave them distance, especially after Sabrina and Jeff had done more taping and editing on the story in Baker County. From what Robinson had seen, they had come up with a compelling piece on Coleman Baldridge. Whoever Jack was, he thought, he should have no reason to complain.

The program cut away and a local news anchor appeared on screen. The three of them stopped eating. A young woman's face appeared next, with the word 'abducted' along the top of the screen.

"Crap," Jeff said, his mouth red with marinara sauce.

Elizabeth Randell, a student at the University of Florida in Gainesville, had failed to return home after going for an evening run. When she didn't get back, her roommate began calling their friends. The entire state was aware of what had been happening to young women just a short distance away in Jacksonville. Two of her friends had actually seen her while she had been out running. The first said she had seen Elizabeth heading west, toward the interstate, along a busy road. The other thought she had seen Elizabeth stopped alongside that same road, talking with an older man in a suit. He may have led her to a black sedan but the friend hadn't seen Elizabeth actually get in as she herself was driving by.

The newscaster came back on and asked for anyone who may have any information about the whereabouts of Elizabeth Randell or the black sedan to please call the toll free number listed at the bottom of the screen.

Jeff's show returned to the screen and Sabrina picked up the remote control and turned the volume down. Jeff said, "We passed through there on the way down here."

"Oh my God," Sabrina said. "It just isn't stopping."

Robinson sat back into the cushions of the couch, saying nothing.

CHAPTER THREE

At midnight they were awakened by the first shot.

Robinson, on the couch in the living room sat up, looked around in the dark. The second shot had him rolling off the couch and colliding with Jeff, bundled in some blankets on the floor.

"What the hell, man...."

"Quiet," Robinson told him. "Get up. Now."

Crouching low, he started down the hallway toward his bedroom and Sabrina. Before he was halfway there the door opened and Sabrina came out, pulling on her shoes.

"What is it?" she asked.

"I think we can guess."

He turned around and made his way back to the living room. He looked out along the bottom edge of the window and off to his right, near the edge of the sinkhole, was a lantern. Two figures were framed in the glow, one of them waving his arms at the house, the other slumping against him.

Robinson stood up. Jeff and Sabrina were standing just behind him.

"Francine?" Sabrina asked.

"I can't make him out from here, but who else?"

"Who's the other one?" Jeff asked.

The man by the sinkhole started waving again and Robinson said, "I guess we need to go find out."

"Are you crazy, man?" Jeff said. "Dude's got a gun."

"And a hostage," Robinson answered. "I'm going out."

Sabrina said, "Me, too."

"Jesus Christ, are you two both nuts?" Jeff said. He walked a crazy pattern into the carpet. "He's got a gun! What do we have?"

Robinson went to the desk in the corner, pulled open one of the drawers. "Here," he said, pulling out a pistol. He held it out to Jeff. "Knock yourself out."

"What? You're the damned cop! You take it!"

"He'll just take it away," said Robinson. "Then he'll have two guns."

Sabrina asked, "Do you even know how to handle a gun?"

"How hard can it be?" shrieked Jeff. "If he's just going to take it away from Robinson here—"

"Then he'll probably just shoot you."

Jeff looked down at the gun, backed away. "Goddamnit," he said.

A third shot went off and this time they could hear the muffled scream from the second visitor. "We going?" Robinson asked.

"Hang on," Sabrina said, and quickly went to the phone. She picked up the handset, pressed a button. "It's dead."

"He probably cut the connector off at the box outside the garage. Simple thing to do." He walked to the front door, opened it, and began walking the eighty yards toward the sinkhole, hands held out to his sides. Behind him came Sabrina, and then Jeff, still muttering to himself.

They marched in almost single file and stopped when Francine told them to. They were about ten feet away. The other person was a young woman, duct tape wound around her mouth, her hands, and her ankles.

"That's good right there," Francine said. He pointed his gun at Robinson. "You two, don't stand behind him." He waited while Sabrina and Jeff spread out to the sides, keeping Robinson in the middle.

"Lift up your shirt," Francine said.

Robinson pulled up his t-shirt, then turned slowly around in a circle.

"Good. Now the pant legs."

Robinson lifted the legs of his sweat pants one at a time, showing his ankles to Francine.

"Okay," said Francine. "So far, so good." He thrust the quivering body of his hostage to the ground in front of him. Her shirt and running bra had been cut open and the halves flopped to each side of her body as she struggled to breathe and cry at the same time.

"Now you, Ms. Wells. Come here."

Sabrina didn't move. She couldn't.

"Ms. Wells," Francine said.

Robinson turned to look at her. Their eyes met and he nodded. Slowly, she nodded back. She moved ahead on the balls of her feet but she kept her head back and met Francine's eyes. With one hand he patted her down, told her to turn around, then motioned her back with his gun.

"And Mr. Sturgeon."

Jeff shook his head as though he couldn't believe this was happening to him and stepped forward. Francine stopped him. "Your shirt," he said. Jeff lifted his shirt up to his arm pits and turned around like he had seen Robinson do. He was still wearing shorts so there was no need to check for an ankle rig.

For a minute no one spoke. The kerosene lantern on the ground beside Francine cast a powerful light, making it difficult for anyone to look directly at Francine. It was perched about three feet from the edge of the sinkhole, with Francine just in front of it. He could see them better than they could see him.

"So, Robinson," Francine said. He pointed at the girl on the ground with the toe of his foot. "She about your type?"

"She hurt?" Robinson asked.

Francine shook his head. "Not yet. Scared, though."

Robinson bent down but didn't move any closer. "Elizabeth," he said quietly. "Elizabeth." It took six or seven times for her to calm herself enough to look at him. "You're going to be okay," he told her. The wild snuffling sounds stopped but her eyes were still wide with fear.

"Sure she is," Francine said. "You know her?"

"We know about the girl from Gainesville who disappeared with an older man into a black sedan," Robinson answered.

"Hunh," Francine said. "You just came through that part of the state, didn't you, James?"

Robinson didn't answer.

With his left hand, Francine tossed something to Robinson, who caught it out of the air. It sparkled in the harsh light from the lantern. Robinson didn't look at it. He knew what it was. He saw that Francine was wearing latex gloves.

"That's just her watch," Francine said, "and a ring she had on her index finger. Nothing in her ears, though." He held out his hand, gesturing with his fingers.

Robinson arced them high over Francine's head where they disappeared somewhere into the abyss behind him. Francine's eyes never left Robinson's, nor did his gun waver. He gave a laugh. "That's fine," he said. "They were probably going to end up there anyway."

Sabrina said, "Why are you here?"

"Lookin' for you, darlin'," he said. "Your boss, Jack Lowington, is it? He works well with the FBI. Said you and your friend here haven't filed anything for a few days and that he was looking for something from you tomorrow. That right?"

"He wouldn't talk to you," Jeff said.

The gun never wavered from Robinson's belly. "Well, you're wrong, son. You can't forget he was talking to the FBI and the FBI is officially worried about the well being of two of Channel Seven's finest journalists."

"Get to it, Francine," Robinson said. "What do you want?"

The false humor disappeared from his voice. Francine's eyes narrowed a bit as he said, "What did you tell Albert Duprin about me?"

Robinson shook his head. "Absolutely nothing."

"That's not what you said in Holton–"

"You saw Sabrina wearing Becky Owens' earrings. I needed to buy time for her to get away from you."

"The earrings."

"Good try," Robinson said. "Didn't work, and you gave yourself away, but it was a good try."

"You already had it figured," Francine said. "It was worth the risk."

"Why did you do it?"

"I just told you–"

"Why did you kill Becky Owens?"

Francine didn't answer. To Sabrina and Jeff, he said, "Listen to me, very, very carefully. You two have one way out of this and one way only. I want you to bring me every bit of video tape you have in that house, in your van, and in your cameras. Ms. Wells, come here please."

Jeff said, "Sabrina–"

"Shut up," said Francine. "Ms. Wells?"

Sabrina stepped forward.

"Please get down on your knees and clasp your hands behind your head."

She looked at Robinson quickly and then lowered herself to the sandy ground and locked her fingers together at the back of her neck.

"Slide on over here to my left, please."

Sabrina started shuffling her knees back and forth, her jeans sliding across the dirt. She winced as she went over bits of rock and clumps of grass.

"All the way to the edge of the sinkhole, darling."

"It's not safe," Robinson said.

Sabrina paused.

"Keep moving," Francine barked. "The point is that none of this is safe."

Sabrina moved closer to the edge of the sinkhole than the lantern, which stood upright on the other side of Francine.

"Damn it, Francine–"

"If I were Mr. Sturgeon," he said, "I'd be moving just as fast as I could to get those video tapes."

"Go, Jeff. Do what he says. Hurry up."

Jeff took off running without a word.

The three of them listened to Jeff's flopping footsteps disappear toward the house. Robinson said, "You didn't answer my question."

"I didn't kill Becky Owens," Francine said.

"What?"

"You did."

Sabrina started and Francine shot her a freezing glance.

Robinson just shook his head. "What the hell are you talking about?"

"She loved you, you son of a bitch. She loved you, but I loved her more. You were married. You had a wife, a house–"

"I didn't kill her."

"And you didn't need her. I did. I needed her. I loved her. But she wanted you. She was waiting for you."

"I didn't kill her."

Francine laughed. "You just didn't know it. If it weren't for you, do you think she'd be dead now? Do you?"

Behind him, Robinson could hear the door of his house open.

"If it weren't for you she'd be with me. She'd be with me now, here, today. Alive. If it weren't for you she'd be my wife, we'd have a family, but instead–"

"You killed her."

"Because of you, you bastard. Because of you. It was your fault."

No one spoke for a few minutes. Each of them were locked in their own thoughts. Still, though, the gun never moved from Robinson's belly.

"I didn't mean to do it," Francine said. "I was just trying to show her–"

Sabrina said gently, "Show her what?"

"I was just trying to show her what it could be like, what it would be like. But then she ran, she started to fight. Something happened."

"And later you killed Donnelly."

Francine's head snapped up. "What did you say?"

"You killed B. J. Donnelly. Why?"

"You know why. I couldn't let him prove he didn't kill–any of those girls."

"You mean Rebecca."

Francine raised the gun, aimed it at Robinson's face. "Don't you say her name to me again. Ever. Donnelly got himself killed. I just arranged for the company."

There was more noise from behind Robinson and Francine squinted at the void between the house. There was no moon and the night was dark but for thousands of brilliant stars casting negligible light upon the earth. Robinson's abandoned subdivision was so far from any other development he knew that Francine's gunshots, if they were even heard, would never be recognized as such.

Soon Jeff came trotting up with an armload of plastic cases. "Here," he said, and dropped them to the ground.

"How many are there?" Francine asked him.

"I don't know, man. Twenty or thirty."

"Ms. Wells?"

"I don't know. Really, I have no idea."

Francine nodded his head and sidled over toward the lantern. He reached down and picked up a carton of kerosene from behind the lantern. He held it out toward Jeff. "Take it," he said. "Pour it over the tapes. All of them. Use plenty."

Jeff worked the screw top off the container and started pouring.

"While you're doing that, I'm going to tell you something. I don't care about you. I don't care about your reporter friend. I'm here for those tapes, and Robinson. Do you understand?"

Jeff looked at Robinson. He knew it was worse than that. Or was Francine telling the truth? How was he supposed to know?

"But here's the thing. You have one chance out of this, and that is to give me exactly what I want. I will ask you one time, and I want an honest answer. If you don't give it to me, if I don't think you're giving it to me, I'm going to put a bullet in Ms. Wells' perfect little face. Do you understand?"

This time Jeff said, "Yes."

"Good. Are there any other tapes?"

The hesitation gave Francine his answer.

"Say goodbye to Ms.–"

"Wait!" shouted Jeff. "Wait! Behind the cushion on the couch, left side. There's one tape."

"I gave you your chance–"

"No, man, stop it! That's it! Just the one more!"

"Okay," Francine said. He moved the gun from Robinson and shot Jeff in the leg. Robinson stepped forward but the gun snapped back to his belly. With the sound of the shot the girl on the ground began screaming into her gag again. Francine kicked her in her low back. "Hush," he told her. She writhed from the pain and saw Francine, his foot poised for another kick, and the screams subsided into a hysterical breathing.

Jeff was rolling on the ground, his palms pressed to the hole in his leg, murmuring, "Oh man, oh man, oh man..." over and over.

Sabrina yelled, "Jeff!" but Francine stopped her with a sound. Robinson never moved.

"How about the card I left on their van, James? It wasn't in your motel room when I looked."

Robinson said, "In the living room. Desk, top drawer, right."

"Okay," Francine said. "I'll get it when I get the tape." He used his left hand to take a cigarette lighter out of his pants pocket. "Use this to burn the tapes."

Robinson caught the lighter, took a step to his right and bent down to ignite the kerosene. The flame started with an explosive whoosh. Francine's eyes never left Robinson; Robinson's never left the gun.

Elizabeth Randell's eyes were clutched tightly shut as she lay whimpering on the ground. Jeff was moving less and growing quieter. Shock, Robinson though, or bleeding out.

Sabrina's arms were heavy as she struggled to keep her fingers locked and her elbows up. She was slipping into shock, too, thought Robinson.

"What's next, Francine?"

CHAPTER FOUR

The man with the gun said, "We're going to wait a few more minutes for these tapes to burn. Then we'll see." He picked up the kerosene container from where Jeff had set it down and using one hand tossed more around the pile of burning plastic cases.

"Finally," Francine said. "I'm going to see you pay."

"I loved her, too."

"No!" shouted Francine. "No!" The gun came up again. "You do not get to have her, too. You had a wife. You had Becky. Now–" He gestured at Sabrina. "You've got this one, too."

Sabrina said, "What–"

"Stop it!" said Francine. "I know you spent the night in his hotel room. You don't think I was watching him the whole time?"

"Frank Grayton knows," Sabrina said. "He's got your receipt. The picture you got from him–"

"Is already gone, darling. So is the negative I got from the kid at the photo shop who developed it for you."

Sabrina started crying. Robinson said softly, "It's all right, Bree."

"It's all gone," said Francine. "It ends here. You're going to be famous all over again, James. You killed Becky. Who knows, you may have killed some of those girls in Jacksonville, too. And after a while, Albert Duprin's going to say anything I tell him to, I think."

"You're insane."

"No," Francine said. "I'm not. But when you're gone, I can start again. No more looking over my shoulder. When were you going to make your move?"

"About Becky?"

"Of course about Becky! You knew, didn't you? You had to know! Donnelly couldn't have taken a girl like her! It had to be me! If it weren't for you she'd have been with me. When were you coming for me?"

Robinson shook his head from side to side. "I wasn't, Francine. I never got over her death, either. But I tried, every day. I wasn't looking for you. I was looking for me."

"Liar!" Francine shouted. "Liar!" He put a bullet into the ground between Robinson's feet. Robinson didn't move.

Elizabeth Randell whimpered more but didn't scream, her eyes wide and staring at Francine. Jeff had gone quiet. Sabrina seemed frozen at the edge of the sinkhole. Another noise, like metal striking metal, sounded back by the house but it was barely audible with the echo of the gunfire and the crackling of the flames.

"What was that?" Francine asked.

"Going to start killing raccoons, Francine?" Robinson said.

Francine waved the gun toward Sabrina. "Get over there. On your knees, next to the reporter."

Robinson raised his hands, moved over to Sabrina, and lowered himself down, next to her. He kept wondering how strong the lip of the sinkhole was this near the edge. It could stay this way for years or it could give way any second. He'd only been this close to the edge once or twice, always lying face down on his stomach, so he could look over the edge. The sinkhole wall tended to erode from the inside, leaving an overhanging lip along the edge. He had no idea how solid the ground was here.

"Now this one," Francine said, giving Elizabeth Randell a light kick, "looks a bit like Becky, don't you think?"

Robinson said nothing.

"Don't you think?" shouted Francine.

"No," said Robinson.

Francine looked down. "Well, it was kind of short notice. A victim of opportunity." He raised the gun again, pointed it at Sabrina. "You move and a bullet goes through your girlfriend's head. Understand?"

"James–" Sabrina said.

"I understand," said Robinson.

"Good." He knelt down and grabbed Elizabeth by her duct-taped wrists and pulled upwards. "Stand up, dear, that's a good girl." She tried but she was weak and shaky. "Stand up!" Francine yanked her arms violently upwards and she clambered to her knees and then to her feet. She fell against Francine but again, the gun never moved away from Sabrina and Robinson.

"What's really down in that hole, Robinson?" Francine asked. "You sure there's nothing worth finding? Other than Ms. Randell's jewelry?"

"Why don't you find out yourself?"

"Ladies first," said Francine, and shoved Elizabeth closer to the edge of the sinkhole. Robinson had a wild flash of himself playing the beer game, chugging a beer and launching the can as close as he could to the edge. Once he got close enough for the cans to go over, he'd stop playing.

"Beer cans!" he said. "Just beer cans."

Francine stopped. "What?"

"You asked what's down there. I said beer cans."

"Go to hell, Robinson."

"For not recycling?"

A new sound reached them from the house. The glare from the fire was dying down but it was still difficult to see outside the cone of light. Francine stepped further from the sinkhole, leaving Elizabeth, as he moved in front of the lantern light so he could see.

In the time it took for his eyes to adjust, he could plainly hear the sound of an engine and of a vehicle bouncing over the uneven ground between the house and the sinkhole.

"Who's there?" shouted Francine. "Who's there?" He was waving the gun back and forth between Robinson and the oncoming vehicle. It was moving fast and Francine could make it out now, even in the dark. It was big and it was white.

"Damn it, Robinson!" He aimed and took a shot at the Channel Seven van as it barreled toward them at the edge of the sinkhole. They heard a metallic thwack as the bullet hit home. He shot again, then brought the gun around to keep Robinson still.

They could all here it as the van slowed down. It was still moving and moving fast, but there was no more acceleration. It was less than twenty yards away. The cracked windshield reflected the lantern light and they could see there was no one behind the wheel.

Francine turned toward Robinson and Sabrina. "Things just got uglier for you two," he said.

A streak of fire and sparks flew through the air and hit Francine in his side, the same one where he was holding the gun. Like a pro he switched the weapon to his other hand as Jeff howled in new pain from the burning plastic and ashes covering his foot and ankle.

The van was coming close. Jeff saw it at the last minute and rolled away from Francine, who moved closer to his left. Robinson dove forward and grabbed Elizabeth Randell, dragging her toward Sabrina. Francine let it happen. They were between the sinkhole and himself, the cameraman was out of the way, and the van had an open path right between them. Still slowing it hit the edge of the sinkhole and as it pitched over the side, the edge started giving away. Francine backed away further as the lantern fell over. The ground beneath Sabrina's right leg, the one nearest the sinkhole, gave way and she started to fall over, toward the growing opening. Robinson grabbed her and pulled her across his body—all he could do since he was on the ground, too. He held onto Sabrina with one hand and Elizabeth with the other and they were all lying down now on the ground.

In the sinkhole they could hear the wrenching of metal, the shattering of glass, and then, before the echoes died down, the sound of a whoosh a hundred times louder than that of the kerosene and a wildly flickering light was casting hellish shadows upwards from the wreckage.

Francine stepped forward, still ten feet from Robinson and the two women. He seemed uncertain whether it was safe to come closer. The edge of the sinkhole had moved almost the entire distance to the lantern.

"Stand up," he said to Robinson. "Slowly."

Robinson stood in a way that moved Sabrina two feet further from the hole. She lay next to Elizabeth, wrapping her arms around the other woman.

"All of you!" Francine yelled. "Now!"

"They're not going in there," said Robinson.

Francine laughed hard, with genuine humor. "What else did you ever expect them to do?" He aimed the gun at the bodies still on the ground. "They can go with or without holes in them. It's up to you."

Robinson held Francine's eyes, knew he was serious and that the final moment had come. "It's me you came for, Francine. Leave them be."

Francine shook his head slowly. "It's you I came for but I need them, too. They're going to destroy you."

"What are you talking about?"

"They're the evidence. Against you. For what you did to Becky."

He aimed the gun and Sabrina, her body still wrapped around Elizabeth Randell, screamed. So did Robinson.

Footsteps came pounding out of the dark, from the direction the van had come, from the direction of the house. Francine whirled but a two hundred twenty pound mass of black leather took him just under the shoulder, propelling his body to the very edge of the sinkhole. Drew Olson rolled to his feet, his momentum carrying him into Francine's rising body. He wasn't quite to his feet but he still held the gun and he brought it down with as much force as he could on Drew's skull. Drew's body pushed up against Francine, shoving him back still further.

Drew was stunned and had rolled to a stop on his back. Francine looked down at his face in the dancing light and a look of shock spread across his features. "What the– Becky...." and he took one step further back. "Oh my God," he said, aiming the gun.

The ground lurched beneath his feet and the gun jerked up, the bullet cutting a path through the night to the stars. The sand poured faster and faster over the diminishing ledge and Francine went over backwards, yelling "NO!" and trying to level the gun in Robinson's direction. He dove for Drew, his body laying out away from the edge of the sinkhole and held on to the sleeves of Drew's black leather jacket with all of his strength.

When the sound of sliding dirt finally stopped, when Sabrina had dragged Elizabeth Randell as far from the sinkhole as she could, darkness had descended upon them, the lantern having disappeared into the sinkhole and the burning tapes reduced to a pile of dying embers.

Francine was gone.

CHAPTER FIVE

It was funny, he kept thinking. This is the safest he's ever been since he began taking the girls. They've got that mess over in that Cracker town he'd never even heard of, and some jackass sheriff copying his crimes, and it's possible that no one's been looking for him for several weeks. At least not around Moncrief Park, where he lived.

The need was building though, and he'd been trolling. Window shopping. There had been three girls he could have had, three he could have taken, but he wanted to see what happened in that other town before he exposed his work again. Clearly he was famous but that may not be a good thing. Should he use this situation somehow, take advantage of it, maybe do something new? Is there a way he could throw them off track for a long time? Would forever be possible?

Moving would be the best thing, change his town, get far away from the Jacksonville area. But where would he go? He'd tried going south once before, gone to Ft. Lauderdale during spring break week. The girls were amazing and he still got excited when he thought of all the opportunity....

But he was never comfortable. He always felt like he stood out, like everyone who saw him instantly knew he wasn't from there, that he didn't belong. It didn't matter that most of those people were from out of town, too; he had felt too much like an alien. And he didn't know the police force, except to see that they were everywhere. He didn't know the roads, he didn't know where to hide, where to do the work. In the end he'd only lasted three days and then he'd had to leave. It was far too difficult.

So he'd come home. For him to change now, he thought, he'd have to go somewhere and stop everything for a while. Find a place to live, a new job, places for his other work–everything would have to start over. And he couldn't imagine doing that now. What would happen to the work he'd already done?

He buried the last one in a pitcher's mound at a Little League field southeast of here in Bowden. The palm was down, the fingers reaching toward home plate, as if they'd just thrown a ball. He despised all sports and he thought this was especially funny. The last place anyone would expect him to be was at a baseball diamond.

The feeling was strong right now. That business in that other town made him more excited than usual and every time he thought about it he wanted to go out hunting. So far, he'd been able to move around and around, visiting places, looking for girls, like going through one of those game parks in Nairobi or somewhere where you'd drive through the wild plains and veldts looking for the animals.

That's what he was doing now. He'd taken a different car from the lot that night, one that had just come in as a trade against a new convertible, and it still smelled of old cigarette smoke. He'd head over toward the ocean, park somewhere near the beach, then go for a walk. He looked at the bag on the seat next to him. He'd probably leave that here again. Just like last night. He really should, see how everything shakes out in that backwoods swamp town wherever the hell it was, before he made another move.

Yeah, that's what he'd do.

Probably.

CHAPTER SIX

Robinson had gone to Drew Olson and checked to see that he was okay. Olson was awake but groggy. Concussion, Robinson thought. He took the small lockback knife from Olson's belt and turned toward Elizabeth Randell. Sabrina was with Jeff, trying to look at the wound in his leg.

"James," she said. "We have to get Jeff to the hospital."

"Here," he said, opening the knife and handing it to Sabrina. "Cut her loose. The tape on her face is going to hurt. Keep an eye on Jeff's leg. If it bleeds a lot, keep pressure on it."

"But James—"

"He's in shock, Drew looks like he has a concussion, the girl is probably in shock, too, and if she throws up she could suffocate with that tape on her face. Do it, Bree."

She scrambled toward him and reached for the knife. "Okay. I can handle it."

"Good," he said. "I'm going to get my truck and drive it out here. If the girl and Drew can move, try to get them closer to the house. I don't want to drive the truck this close to the hole."

He was gone running before she could answer. Things had been happening too fast, but they couldn't stop yet. He got to the house, tore through the front door and snatched his keys from the kitchen table. There was a flashlight plugged into a wall outlet over the counter and he took that, too, as he ran outside the kitchen door. He made a quick stop at the back corner of the house where the power and phone lines ran down from their mountings on the roof. He ripped the cover off the green plastic box that served as the junction for the phone lines and saw that the connector had been cut from the end of the wire. No help there. If Francine had just unplugged it, he could call for an ambulance. They'd have to drive.

He sprinted to the truck, started it and drove across his front yard and over the sandy scrub toward the others. A few sparks were still rising from the sinkhole and he could see the flickering light against the sloping sand and dirt. When he threw open his door, he could smell the burning van.

Sabrina had moved Olson and Elizabeth Randell about twenty yards further from the edge. Robinson stopped there, shouted for the two of them to get in the front, hoping they'd understand. Jeff was not moving, but he was breathing, and Sabrina was bending over his leg.

"I can't tell if he's still bleeding," she said.

Robinson scooped up Jeff in his arms and started carrying him back to the truck. "The shock should slow the bleeding," he said to make her feel better. The real problem may be that Jeff had already lost too much blood. "Open the gate of the truck."

Sabrina ran ahead and fumbled with the latch until the tailgate dropped. "Get in," Robinson told her. "You'll have to ride in back with him. Cover him with those blankets. If his leg starts bleeding, try to elevate it."

"But—"

"Doesn't matter. We have to hurry."

He lifted the tailgate, leaving Jeff's care to Sabrina. He jumped into the truck and took off toward the gate. After he'd unlocked it and pushed it open, he saw the black sedan pulled next to the dark and deserted road. He continued down the sandy lane until he got to the blacktop and made a right onto the roadway. He'd need close to fifteen minutes to get to the hospital, and that was probably quicker than an ambulance could have gotten to them.

Next to him Elizabeth Randell was wearing Drew Olson's leather jacket and was resting in Drew's arms.

"You okay, Drew?" he asked.

"My head is killing me and my eyes keep watering. You'll have to tell me."

"How are you, Elizabeth?" Robinson asked.

In a quavering voice she said, "All right, I think. Who are you, anyway?"

"Nobody, Elizabeth. Don't worry about it. We'll be at the hospital soon."

Drew reached over and clasped Robinson's forearm. "Thanks, man."

"For what?" Robinson asked. "You're the one that saved our asses back there."

Olson shut his eyes and tried to rest his head against the back of the seat. Every bump and vibration caused him pain and he didn't keep it there long. "You kept your promise, James. You found out about Becky."

"Take it easy, Drew. We're almost there."

"You took care of my sister. I never thought you would."

Robinson didn't answer. In the rear view mirror he could see Sabrina's back bent over Jeff's body in the bed of the truck. He wondered if Drew Olson's answers had been worth any of this.

CHAPTER SEVEN

He started at the ocean and drove slowly back inland, following busy streets, taking random turns, feeling comfortable in the knowledge of his whereabouts in the area. Here and there people were out, some walking dogs, some strolling along their sidewalks. Still others sat on porches or in the open doors of their garages, just looking out at the streets in front of them.

No one was alone.

He drove for another forty minutes, feeling the urge, the thrill, knowing what he was looking for but not knowing what he was going to do about it. Not yet.

A mile or so to the north was a park tucked in the middle of a subdivision. It had a paved path that ran along the edge of a rather large drainage pond, with older live oak trees—the kind you don't see anymore in cities south of Tampa, he thought—and took a right. He knew the park well, had worked in one of the corners, in an empty house that was a long-neglected cinderblock one-story that had been for sale for months and months. He could work there again, he thought.

Four blocks from the park was a strip mall with three quarters of its parking spaces empty. One of Florida's grocery store chains, the cheap one, the kind usually found in the run down areas, had a market there. It was still open and he pulled into the parking lot. There were a dozen or so cars parked in front of the store. He pulled in to one of the aisles, two spots down from the last car.

There was no activity in the parking lot and he just sat and waited. A few minutes later a man came out of the store carrying a six pack of beer in each hand. He got into a truck with a bad muffler and drove off in a cloud of noise and stink.

A woman and her small daughter came out next, and two teen-age girls went in together. He was looking for someone to be alone in the parking lot. Just... looking.

The mother and daughter drove away. Still he sat, his right hand idly fidgeting with the tools in his bag. He rubbed the red scarf that had belonged to his aunt, the one she used to tie him to his bed with when she was angry. Not when he'd misbehaved, that would just call for a spanking or something fleeting like that. She used this when she was mad, really mad, and she had to work out her frustration on someone weaker than she. Once she had him immobilized she could draw out her rage and make it last much longer.

Cars came and went in a desultory fashion, one here, one there, no flurry or sustained activity. He was thinking about leaving when a woman came out of the store, a purse over one shoulder and two plastic grocery bags hanging from each hand. Al-

most without thinking he got out of his car, and quietly closed his door. Nice to be out of that cigarette smell, he though. He realized he still had the hammer in his hand.

The women was walking down the same aisle where he was parked.

Good, he thought.

As she came closer, he stayed by his door, pretending to look down and move his hands as if fluttering through his wallet. When the woman stopped by a small light blue hatchback, he began to walk to the store, as if he were on his way to shop.

The woman was dropping her bags into the hatch as he passed. She glanced at him and then shut the door as he passed. Then she moved toward the driver's door.

"Is this yours?"

She turned around. He was standing behind the car next to hers, holding out something shiny in the dim light.

"It looks expensive."

"I don't think so," she said. It looked like a watch or a bracelet, something like that. He held it out to her and took a step. She felt her wrist and looked into her purse, in case she had dropped something. Those bags were heavy, she might not have noticed....

"Nope," she said, looking up. The flat side of the hammer hit her square on the crown of her head and she sagged instantly. He stepped up and held her to him, working her arm around his shoulders and half dragging, half carrying her to his own vehicle, three spots away. There'd been no sound. The lot was quiet.

He thrust her into the front seat, then pushed her across to the passenger side and got behind the wheel. He looked over at her as he started the car. She'd make noise when she woke up, he thought. That's what they do. On the other hand, they didn't always wake up. There was a little blood, not much, but he wasn't worried about that. This car would be scoured, detailed, then tagged and put on the lot the next day.

The parking lot was quiet as he slowly pulled forward and headed toward the exit.

There were five of them crowded into Andy's mother's Buick, two in front, three in the back, a glowing cigarette being passed among them, the smell of marijuana filling the car.

Andy ran up to the car and pulled the driver's side door open and jumped into the seat, startling everybody. "Holy shit!" he said.

"The hell's wrong with you?" Art asked.

"I was taking a leak in those trees over there, where that 'for sale' house is. This car pulled into the driveway and this guy got out and pulled a– a body from the passenger side."

"What are you talking about, a body?"

Andy reached for the beer he'd left in the car and took a healthy swig. "I saw it. He took her out and dragged her around the side of the house."

Art said, "You didn't see anything."

"Screw you, Art. It may not have been a woman but the body had long hair." They'd had a football practice that afternoon and they were finishing a twelve pack of beer that Chuck, their starting fullback, had bought at a convenience store. His sister was the cashier and never carded him. Flip had fired up a joint as they sat in the Buick in the small parking area of Bretzfeld Green. Ahead of them was a large drainage pond and a paved jogging path that encircled it.

From the back seat, Hardy asked, "Should we go look for them?"

"And do what?" Art asked. "Guy probably clocked his wife. Who cares?"

"Bullshit," Andy said, finishing his beer. "She was out cold. If she was alive."

Chuck said, "Maybe they live there. Maybe he's an asshole and she told him how much of an asshole he was." The three in the backseat erupted in laughter.

"No," Andy said. "That house has been vacant for months. They can't sell that wreck."

Hardy, their nose tackle, sat forward in his seat. "Let's go get him, then."

Andy looked at all of his friends in his car. "Shit," he said.

"What the hell do you expect us to do?" Art asked, getting nervous. Art was a cornerback but he wasn't terribly fast. He didn't play as much as the rest of them.

"We're going to help that chick," Chuck said.

"Damn right," said Hardy.

Art sat back, thinking about guns and knives and blood and bodies. "You guys are crazy," he said.

"We're all doing this, right?" asked Andy the quarterback.

"Hell, yeah," said Hardy. "That were your mother in there, what would you want someone to do?"

Flip carefully put the joint out on the top of an empty beer can. "Let's just sneak up on them, man."

CHAPTER EIGHT

Jeff had been taken off to surgery and Drew was put in a darkened room while waiting for the results of his x-ray. Elizabeth Randell was also on an emergency room bed, blankets wrapped around her while a nurse asked her questions.

Robinson and Sabrina sat in the reception area, waiting for more police. They weren't long in showing up. "Call Alex Kelly," was all Robinson would say after giving the officers their names. The patrolmen tried to get tough but Robinson held firm. "Call Alex Kelly," he repeated.

It took Kelly almost an hour to walk in. The hospital let them into an office that opened off the reception area and they all took seats. Robinson started talking. Kelly took notes, occasionally asking Sabrina questions. After a long while, Kelly sat back and read over what he'd written.

"I'll be right back," he said, and left the room.

Robinson reached over to Sabrina and took her hand. They were seated side by side in chairs facing a desk. "How are you doing?" Robinson asked.

"Not well." Sabrina shook her head. "I feel like I'm about to pass out."

Robinson squeezed her hand and she looked at his face. "You'll be fine," he said.

"I just want it to be over."

He almost laughed. "You're a reporter. This is just starting for you."

Sabrina offered a weak smile then hung her head down, exhausted.

Kelly opened the door and walked back into the room.

"We've got cars going out to your place, James. The girl will be fine, her parents are on their way up from Naples to get her. She just finished her statement." He tapped another officer's notebook.

"How about Drew Owens?"

"Doc says concussion, no skull fracture. He'll be fine."

"And Jeff?" Sabrina asked. "My cameraman?"

"He's still in surgery. I don't know anything yet."

Robinson looked at his former partner, who looked away. He knew more than he was telling.

"I'm going to need to get you two into the station," Kelly told them. "You want to make any phone calls, take a few minutes?"

Sabrina nodded and said, "I'd like to, if that's okay."

Robinson stood, asked Kelly: "Mind if we leave her alone?"

Kelly shook his head. He led the way to the door and held it open. Outside the office he asked, "She doing okay?"

"She's a tough lady. How is Jeff Sturgeon, really?"

"Not so good."

"Damn it," said Robinson.

Kelly clapped him on his back and said, "Why the hell didn't you call me sooner?"

Robinson didn't respond. There hadn't been anything to arrest Francine with until a few hours ago. At least that's what he was telling himself.

"Instead you called Drew Owens." Kelly was looking for a connection now, Robinson thought, to what ultimately happened tonight.

A promise is a promise.

"You're a good cop, Alex."

"Go to hell, Jimmy."

"Thanks for coming down."

CHAPTER NINE

The five of them held up at the stand of trees where Andy had been when he'd seen the man get out of the car.

"Why you stopping?" asked Art.

"Just checking things out."

Art wondered if Andy were as spooked as he was but he didn't say anything. They could all see the house now. There was a car in the driveway but no sign of lights or anything else inside. Hardy said, "C'mon, guys, if we're going to do this, let's go."

"We'll get him," said Andy. He crouched low and ran along the edge of the trees nearest the house and parallel to the driveway, his four teammates following. The house was a tiny dwelling with a small, one car attached garage.

"Let's go around," Chuck whispered. "Check all the windows."

The five of them stretched out and, still crouched, made it to the windows on the side of the garage. Art stopped there to look while the rest of them moved on. There were two windows in the garage and an outside door and all of them looked in as they passed. The garage was empty. No one tried the door.

They rounded the corner to the back of the house; there were no windows for the garage here. The next one looked into the deserted kitchen. No one suggested going to the front of the house first or splitting up. Behind them was a small yard bordered by more of the trees from the park.

They moved on to a small window of frosted glass they couldn't see through. Bathroom. They kept going.

Here was a bedroom and it was the first window that was covered. A bed sheet looked like it had been attached to the top of the window from the inside. There were gaps in the corners and for the first time they could see something inside. It was the beam from a small flashlight.

"That must be the girl," Art whispered.

"Let me see," said Andy quietly while Art gave way. "She's not moving."

Hardy was at the other corner and he moved aside for Chuck to see. The man came into view and the boys stiffened. He bent over the woman's body and looked to be doing something to the front of her shirt.

Chuck and Hardy moved off to their right and Flip stepped up to peek. Art stood with his back to the wall, happy to let the other boys watch. Andy still couldn't see exactly what the man was doing. He ducked down and stepped back, tugging on the leg of Flip's jeans to get his attention. Flip pulled away from the window and that's when Andy noticed Chuck and Hardy were gone.

"Shit!" he said in Flip's ear. "Where did those two go?"

Flip didn't have an answer. Like Andy he'd been caught up in watching what was going on inside the house. The night around them was unusually still.

Two booming thuds echoed through the nearly empty house. They sprang up to their corners in time to see the man picking something up from the floor and running out the bedroom door.

"The garage!" Flip said, and took off running, with Andy following. After a second Art took up the rear.

The outside garage door opened just as they rounded the corner and the man sprinted out.

"Hey!" Andy yelled, mostly because he couldn't help it. The man froze, turned his head toward them, then took off for the trees. Chuck and Hardy came thundering through the garage and out the same door.

"Get him!" yelled Hardy.

"Stay with the girl!" Andy shouted to Art, who said, "Right!" only too grateful to go back.

Ahead, Andy heard Hardy call, "There he goes! Toward the lake!"

Andy couldn't see clearly but he heard Chuck and Flip just ahead of him, the noise diminishing as each of them left the stand of trees and came into the grassy area around the drainage pond. Then came the unmistakable sound of one person crunching into another, and then, as he cleared the trees himself, saw the pile of writhing bodies on the ground four yards ahead.

"Shit!" Hardy screamed. "Fucker's got a knife!"

The man they'd been chasing was on his back, Hardy rolling off him clutching his left arm. Flip was in next, diving on the man's arm that was holding the knife.

Hardy felt the blood on his arm, felt it still move, said "Motherfucker." Chuck climbed over Flip to grab the man's other arm. He was pinned to the ground, growling and spitting like a trapped raccoon when Andy got there, having clearly heard Hardy say the guy had a knife. Without really thinking about it, he jumped into the air and came down with both his knees on the mans abdomen.

They heard ribs crack as the air whooshed out of the man's lungs. He dropped the knife and Flip let go of the arm he was holding and pushed the blade further away in the grass. Hardy moved over and started punching the man's face.

"Fucker cut me, man!" he was saying.

Andy got to his feet and stood next to Flip while Hardy swung again and again. Chuck was holding the man's arms back and over his head.

"Dude," he said a few seconds later. "Maybe that's enough."

Hardy hit him again. The guy wasn't moving. Then pushed off him. As he did, a burbling scream came from his bloodied lips. Now that Hardy wasn't hitting him, they could hear his breathing didn't sound very good.

There was an overhead lamp on a pole about twenty yards away and Flip stepped out of the way of the light, freeing the man from his shadow. It was dim but they could see what looked like a bloody froth coming from the guy's mouth.

Andy said, "I think we messed him up pretty good."

"Fine with me," said Hardy. "Motherfucker tried to stab me." He walked toward the light, trying to get a better look at the damage done to his arm.

"We need to get the cops, check on Art," said Flip.

"I'll go for the cops," said Andy. "I'll drive to the convenience store." He looked toward the house but all he could see were the trees.

"He doesn't sound so good," said Flip. "What do we do?"

Andy was coming down from his adrenaline rush. He could feel the jitters in his shaking hands. "Just watch him. And don't touch that knife." Hardy was pulling his shirt over his head and Andy called, "You all right, Hardy?"

"Yeah, man, fucker gashed me. Probably need stitches."

"Chuck, stay with Hardy. Flip, you should check Art and the girl," Andy called as he started jogging along the grass toward his mother's car. He was beginning to wonder what kind of trouble they'd be in.

Flip was cautious but after he made his way into the house, he found Art leaning over the woman's body. "How is she?" he asked.

"Man, I don't know," said Art. "She's breathing. I don't know what to do for her."

She doesn't look much older than we do, thought Flip. "Just stay with her. Hardy and Chuck got the guy on the ground by the lake," he said.

"Everyone all right?"

"He cut Hardy with a knife," said Flip. "In the arm. Doesn't look bad. Andy went for the cops."

"Should we try the neighbors?"

None of the houses had had lights on inside, which is why they sometimes came here. This was a poor, half-empty neighborhood. "By the time I talked someone into letting me use their phone, it'd probably be quicker to get to that convenience store back on Wilston."

"Andy better hurry," said Art.

By the time the police arrived, the woman was sitting up, holding her hands to her face. Art was next to her, his arm awkwardly around her shoulders, a panicked look on his face. The first officer in the house stayed with them, moving Art aside and talking to the woman. Andy led the other around the trees and up the path to find the others. As they left the yard, three more police cruisers pulled up, with an ambulance just behind. Andy had left the car on the street so that the police cars could pass him and get closer. He also wanted to leave himself a chance to get rid of the beer cans and the remains of the joint, if he could find it; at least get everything moved into the trunk.

The night was lit up with flashing red and blue lights and the sounds of radios crackled through the night air as one of the police cars drove onto the grass behind them. Chuck and Hardy were standing together, a few feet away from the unmoving figure of the man on the grass.

Another cop came through the trees and jogged over to them. He saw Hardy holding his shirt over his arm and called for someone to get one of the guys from the ambulance over here.

The cop that Andy had brought to the scene was leaning over the body of the man on the ground. Andy could hear him call for another ambulance over his radio. He heard the word "body."

"Shit," he thought. He didn't think they called ambulances for injured "bodies" unless they were....

"How is that guy?" he asked the officer after he stood up.

The cop looked at him, walked over. "He's dead," he said.

"What?" Andy felt his bowels loosen.

"May have choked on his own blood. Suffocated. They'll let us know."

Art's voice was shaky as he asked, "What happens now?"

"We need to get your friend's arm sewn up, and we need to get your stories."

Hardy was driven off to a hospital in one of the police cars. The first ambulance left with the woman as two more cruisers and a second ambulance arrived. Flip, Chuck and Art were taken to two of the cruisers, the three of them quiet and somber. Andy was allowed to drive his own car down to the police station, flanked by yet another cop.

Later they found out that the man's ribs had been broken and both lungs had been punctured. He had indeed suffocated from choking on his own blood. The woman, 22-year old Stephanie Glass, was treated for a concussion and released by the hospital. Hardy had taken twenty five stitches in his left upper arm. The parents of all five boys spent a great deal of time in the police station, listening to their sons tell their stories again and again and again.

It wasn't long, though, before the authorities had identified the man and begun to look into his background. From the knife as well as the collection of implements in the small duffel bag that had been in his car, it was clear from the start that the man hadn't been up to any good.

It wasn't until a detective recognized the significance of the red scarf they had found on the seat of the car that they finally realized the so-called "Jacksonville murders" would stop. That nightmare was now over. The five boys were never charged.

EPILOGUE

"Don't grow it back," Sabrina said.

"The beard?" Robinson laughed. They were holding hands, walking along the beach in Pass-A-Grille. Sabrina was used to the harder, rockier sand on the Atlantic coast near Jacksonville; she'd wanted to see the Gulf of Mexico and walk along the smoother beach. Robinson had driven them here over a bridge to the tip of this barrier island near St. Petersburg because of the smaller crowds. He didn't like the crowds. "Don't worry," he answered. "I don't miss it."

Laughing gulls hovered and landed and took off and waddled, all around a small boy who was busy tossing his popcorn into the ocean breeze by the handful. They stopped and watched the black-headed seagulls chase each other away from the tumbling kernels. Sabrina pointed to one of the birds. "That guy's getting more than anybody else."

Robinson tugged her hand and they kept walking, staying close to the water and leaving fresh tracks that washed away after a dozen or so seconds.

"Have you decided what you're going to do now?" he asked Sabrina. He felt her stiffen just a little bit and when he looked into her face he saw that her mood had changed.

"I'm sorry," he said. "If you don't want to talk about it...."

"No, no, it's fine," she said. "It's just now that it's all over, it seems like it's really not all over, you know?"

Not really, Robinson thought, but he didn't say anything.

"Once the phone started ringing, it never seemed to stop. There was the Baldridge piece, and then the Francine piece, and my God, Monica's killer.... I could stay at Channel Seven, of course, and I hate to be greedy, but the money some of these big market stations are offering is just out of their league." She stopped and she let go of Robinson's hand to pick up a sea shell with a twisted cone shape. When she turned it over she could see that the back half of it was gone.

"What is this, do you know?"

"Some kind of mollusk," Robinson said.

Sabrina tossed it into the water and took Robinson's hand again.

"Well," she continued. "I don't want to go to Miami, I know that."

Robinson thought, *I don't blame you,* but didn't say anything.

"Atlanta's probably the best job, though. And CNN is there, too."

They were approaching a jetty at the end of the beach. On the other side of it was a channel of water, and another island a little ways off, with dozens of boats anchored just offshore. They'd have to turn around soon.

"What about the networks?"

She shrugged. "They want me to travel. I don't know if I'm ready for life out of a suitcase."

They reached the jetty, watched a twenty-foot boat rock in the cross-currents of the channel, two bikini-clad women sunning themselves in the back, a pot-bellied man behind the steering console. Turning around, they headed back up the beach, Sabrina switching sides with Robinson to stay closer to the water.

"This is nice," she said. "Thanks for taking me here."

"You're welcome," Robinson said. "It's nice to see you again after all these weeks."

"I didn't know if you'd want to," she said. "See me again, I mean. I was– I got a little rattled there for a while."

Robinson gave her hand another squeeze. "You were fine."

A pair of pelicans swooped by them, twenty yards offshore, the tips of their wings an inch above the tops of the waves.

"How about you?" Sabrina asked. "Still plan on being a hermit?"

He laughed. "For now. It's hard to sell your house when you have a gaping hole next to your front yard."

"That's not what I mean."

"I know," he said.

They walked along slowly, occasionally passed by a runner or a faster pair of walkers. "I could work here in Tampa," Sabrina said.

"Hey," Robinson said. "You'd be close to me!"

She punched him in the arm with her free hand. "It's a good job. Good offer. Wouldn't have to travel."

"It's not Miami," Robinson said.

"It's not Miami," Sabrina repeated, laughing. "We'll have to compare notes on why we don't like it down there."

"Land of excess," Robinson said. "Too much traffic. Not enough quiet."

"No place like here."

"Nope. No place like here."

"What's Jeff going to do?"

"I just spoke to him. When he gets better, he'll be back at Channel Seven."

"Homebody."

"Doesn't seem fair somehow," Sabrina said. "Both of us were involved. He took the bullet–"

"No survivor guilt," Robinson told her. "Look at me. My reputation was in ruins before all this. Now…."

"Still in ruins?"

"Oh hell, yeah," he said. "Disgraced cop sort of forgiven but a married man who was fooling around with another woman–"

"Your wife had already left you."

"But I was still married," he said. "That's what people hear. Now I'm a famous motorcycle mechanic."

"You mean infamous."

"Shut up," he said.

They walked along in silence, feeling the heat from the sun, smelling the faux tropical scents of an abundance of suntan lotion, listening to the gulls laughing their laughs.

"When are you going to decide?" Robinson asked.

"Soon," Sabrina said. "Soon."

THE END

Other Stark House books you may enjoy...

Clifton Adams Death's Sweet Song /
Whom Gods Destroy $19.95
Benjamin Appel Brain Guy / Plunder $19.95
Benjamin Appel Sweet Money Girl /
Life and Death of a Tough Guy $21.95
Malcolm Braly Shake Him Till He Rattles /
It's Cold Out There $19.95
Gil Brewer A Devil for O'Shaugnessy /
The Three-Way Split $14.95
Gil Brewer Nude on Thin Ice /
Memory of Passion $19.95
W. R. Burnett It's Always Four O'Clock /
Iron Man $19.95
W. R. Burnett Little Men, Big World /
Vanity Row $19.95
Catherine Butzen Thief of Midnight $15.95
James Hadley Chase Come Easy—Go Easy /
In a Vain Shadow $19.95
Andrew Coburn Spouses & Other Crimes $15.95
Jada M. Davis One for Hell $19.95
Jada M. Davis Midnight Road $19.95
Bruce Elliott One is a Lonely Number /
Elliott Chaze Black Wings Has My Angel $19.95
Don Elliott/Robert Silverberg
Gang Girl / Sex Bum $19.95
Don Elliott/Robert Silverberg
Lust Queen / Lust Victim $19.95
Feldman & Gartenberg (ed)
The Beat Generation & the Angry Young Men $19.95
A. S. Fleischman Look Behind You Lady /
The Venetian Blonde $19.95
A. S. Fleischman Danger in Paradise /
Malay Woman $19.95
A. S. Fleischman The Sun Worshippers /
Yellowleg $19.95
Ed Gorman The Autumn Dead /
The Night Remembers $19.95
Arnold Hano So I'm a Heel / Flint /
The Big Out $23.95
Orrie Hitt The Cheaters / Dial "M" for Man $19.95
Elisabeth Sanxay Holding Lady Killer /
Miasma $19.95
Elisabeth Sanxay Holding The Death Wish /
Net of Cobwebs $19.95
Elisabeth Sanxay Holding Strange Crime in Bermuda /
Too Many Bottles $19.95
Elisabeth Sanxay Holding The Old Battle-Ax /
Dark Power $19.95
Elisabeth Sanxay Holding The Unfinished Crime /
The Girl Who Had to Die $19.95
Elisabeth Sanxay Holding Speak of the Devil /
The Obstinate Murderer $19.95
Russell James Underground / Collected Stories $14.95
Day Keene Framed in Guilt / My Flesh is Sweet $19.95
Day Keene Dead Men Don't Talk / Hunt the Killer /
Too Hot to Hold $23.95

Mercedes Lambert Dogtown / Soultown $14.95
Dan J. Marlowe/Fletcher Flora/Charles Runyon
Trio of Gold Medals $15.95
Dan J. Marlowe The Name of the Game is Death /
One Endless Hour $19.95
Stephen Marlowe Violence is My Business /
Turn Left for Murder $19.95
McCarthy & Gorman (ed) Invasion of the
Body Snatchers: A Tribute $19.95
Wade Miller The Killer / Devil on Two Sticks $19.95
Wade Miller Kitten With a Whip /
Kiss Her Goodbye $19.95
Rick Ollerman Turnabout / Shallow Secrets $19.95
Vin Packer Something in the Shadows /
Intimate Victims $19.95
Vin Packer The Damnation of Adam Blessing /
Alone at Night $19.95
Vin Packer Whisper His Sin /
The Evil Friendship $19.95
Richard Powell A Shot in the Dark /
Shell Game $14.95
Bill Pronzini Snowbound / Games $14.95
Peter Rabe The Box / Journey Into Terror $19.95
Peter Rabe Murder Me for Nickels /
Benny Muscles In $19.95
Peter Rabe Blood on the Desert /
A House in Naples $19.95
Peter Rabe My Lovely Executioner /
Agreement to Kill $19.95
Peter Rabe Anatomy of a Killer /
A Shroud for Jesso $14.95
Peter Rabe The Silent Wall /
The Return of Marvin Palaver $19.95
Peter Rabe Kill the Boss Good-By /
Mission for Vengeance $19.95
Peter Rabe Dig My Grave Deep / The Out is Death /
It's My Funeral $21.95
Brian Ritt Paperback Confidential:
Crime Writers $19.95
Sax Rohmer Bat Wing / Fire-Tongue $19.95
Douglas Sanderson Pure Sweet Hell /
Catch a Fallen Starlet $19.95
Douglas Sanderson The Deadly Dames /
A Dum-Dum for the President $19.95
Charlie Stella Johnny Porno $15.95
Charlie Stella Rough Riders $15.95
John Trinian North Beach Girl /
Scandal on the Sand $19.95
Harry Whittington A Night for Screaming /
Any Woman He Wanted $19.95
Harry Whittington To Find Cora /
Like Mink Like Murder / Body and Passion $23.95
Harry Whittington Rapture Alley / Winter Girl /
Strictly for the Boys $23.95
Charles Williams Nothing in Her Way /
River Girl $19.95

Stark House Press, 1315 H Street, Eureka, CA 95501
707-498-3135 www.StarkHousePress.com

Retail customers: freight-free, payment accepted by check or paypal via website. Wholesale: 40%, freight-free on
10 mixed copies or more, returns accepted. All books available direct from publisher or Baker & Taylor Books.